Issued to the Bride: One Soldier

Cora Seton

Print Edition
Published by One Acre Press

Author's Note

Issued to the Bride One Soldier is the fifth volume of the Brides of Chance Creek series, set in the fictional town of Chance Creek, Montana. To find out more about Logan, Lena, Cass, Brian, Sadie, Connor, Jo, Hunter, Jack and Alice, look for the rest of the books in the series, including:

Issued to the Bride One Navy SEAL
Issued to the Bride One Airman
Issued to the Bride One Sniper
Issued to the Bride One Marine

Also, don't miss Cora Seton's other Chance Creek series, the Cowboys of Chance Creek, the Heroes of Chance Creek, and the SEALs of Chance Creek

The Cowboys of Chance Creek Series:

The Cowboy Inherits a Bride (Volume 0)
The Cowboy's E-Mail Order Bride (Volume 1)
The Cowboy Wins a Bride (Volume 2)
The Cowboy Imports a Bride (Volume 3)
The Cowgirl Ropes a Billionaire (Volume 4)
The Sheriff Catches a Bride (Volume 5)
The Cowboy Lassos a Bride (Volume 6)

The Cowboy Rescues a Bride (Volume 7)

The Cowboy Earns a Bride (Volume 8)

The Cowboy's Christmas Bride (Volume 9)

The Heroes of Chance Creek Series:

The Navy SEAL's E-Mail Order Bride (Volume 1)

The Soldier's E-Mail Order Bride (Volume 2)

The Marine's E-Mail Order Bride (Volume 3)

The Navy SEAL's Christmas Bride (Volume 4)

The Airman's E-Mail Order Bride (Volume 5)

The SEALs of Chance Creek Series:

A SEAL's Oath

A SEAL's Vow

A SEAL's Pledge

A SEAL's Consent

A SEAL's Purpose

A SEAL's Resolve

A SEAL's Devotion

A SEAL's Desire

A SEAL's Struggle

A SEAL's Triumph

Visit Cora's website at www.coraseton.com

Find Cora on Facebook at facebook.com/CoraSeton

Sign up for my newsletter HERE.

www.coraseton.com/sign-up-for-my-newsletter

Prologue

"GENERAL? PHONE CALL for you."

General Augustus Reed waved Corporal Myers inside the temporary office where he sat at a flimsy metal desk. This forward base was thousands of miles away from USSOCOM in Tampa, Florida, where he'd been stationed for years. It wasn't often he found himself in the field these days, and much as he hated to admit it, he was feeling his age this morning. The desert heat left his mouth dry, his skin itchy and his temper quick.

"I'll be glad to get out of here tomorrow," Corporal Myers said in a low tone, handing him his phone and setting a black briefcase on the desk. The General grunted. Myers was a godsend in many ways, always anticipating what he would need next, and doing his best to keep everyone else at a distance, but the young man talked too much. "What about you, General? Ready to go home?" Myers pressed.

About to answer the call, the General's gaze snapped up, and he took in the flush that spread over the corporal's throat and face.

"I mean—to USSOCOM, sir."

"I know what you mean." He hadn't been home to Chance Creek, Montana, in years. Eleven years, to be exact.

"I… I'll let you answer that." Myers backtracked quickly out of the room and shut the door firmly behind him. When the latch caught with a click, the General rubbed a hand over his jaw and sighed.

"General Reed here," he said into the phone.

"General? It's Cab. I've got some bad news."

"Tell me." Cab Johnson was the sheriff in Chance Creek, where the General's five daughters still lived on the family ranch. Over the years they'd become estranged from him. He'd been sending them husbands these past few months with the hopes of keeping them safe and getting them back in line.

"Your girls are fine," Cab assured him quickly.

The General let out the breath he'd held.

"What's the news?" he made himself ask, hoping Cab didn't hear the tremor in his voice. He was getting too old for all this worry. Getting soft.

Last spring, a passel of unscrupulous men had tried to take over Two Willows and turn it into an outpost for their drug operation, wooing his daughters to get control of the spread. In response, the General had assembled a team of hardened warriors, honorable men who'd each gotten into the kind of trouble the military frowned upon, and had made them a deal. Go to Chance Creek, run the infiltrators off Two Willows, marry his daughters—or else.

He couldn't believe how well things had gone. He'd sent four men home to Montana so far, and each of them had made a good match with one of his girls. Only Alice was left. Time to stay the course and get the job done.

"Ron Cooper went missing three weeks ago," Cab said.

"And you're just telling me now?" The General surged to his feet. Ron Cooper had taken part in one of the attacks on his daughters, but he'd been caught and sent back to Tennessee where he had prior felony charges. Neither the General nor Cab had been able to figure out the connection between Tennessee and Two Willows yet, but they hoped they would with Ron's help.

Four times trouble had arrived from the east. Four times the men the General had sent had fought them off—with help from his daughters, he admitted reluctantly. Some of the interlopers were dead. Some had escaped. Others were in jail.

When Ron was extradited, Cab's counterparts in Tennessee had begun to work on him, trying to get him to finger the man at the head of the organization who was causing them so much grief.

Ron had finally started to cooperate. He'd agreed to wear a wire.

Now he was gone? The General paced around the room.

"I held off telling you because I hoped we could find him in time," Cab explained.

"What happened?"

"He turned up dead last week. Another man was with him. Also deceased. Apparently shot by Ron."

"Last week?"

"Calm down, General. We were trying to find answers before we let word get out. And we did."

The General forced himself to be patient. Cab wouldn't keep him in the dark without a good reason. "What did you find?"

"The other man was the head of the organization. Remember Beau Ellis?"

"Of course I remember him," the General snapped. Beau Ellis and his twin nephews had gone to Chance Creek ostensibly to start a horse-breeding business. Instead, Ray and Harley had tried to kill his daughter, Lena, steal her prize stallion and burn down his family's home. Ray and Harley were dead now. Beau had skipped town too fast to be apprehended.

"Beau's father-in-law is the one behind all this mess. His name is Duke Manson."

"Duke Manson?" The General stopped in his tracks. "Did you say Duke Manson?"

"That's right. You know the man?"

"Could be. It was a long time ago. A real long time." Somehow he knew it was the same man, though, which meant that all this fuss and bother—all this danger unleashed on his daughters—might be his fault.

The muscles in his neck, already tight, got tighter.

"What's the connection?"

The General appreciated the way Cab got right

down to brass tacks. "We were at boot camp together. He was one of those jokers you wondered why they even bothered to enlist. Hated the Army. Hated everything it stood for. Hated the discipline and the drills. He was bringing in drugs—all kinds. Passing them out like candy. Getting people hooked, then taking their money. I turned him in." He'd do it again in a heartbeat. The Army didn't need men like that.

"You think he held a grudge?"

"For thirty years?" The General thought it over. "I don't know. Maybe. You think this is the end of it? Manson's dead, so it's over?"

Cab was quiet a long moment. "My gut says no. Sorry—wish I could say otherwise."

The General's gut was saying the same thing. "What's your thought process?"

"From what we can gather, Manson's organization has been half-assed for a long time. He was squeezed between two other major crime families with no room to expand. So… he looks around. Where else can he go?"

"Chance Creek, Montana," the General answered for him. He started pacing again.

"That's right. Maybe Manson's been tracking your career—the way we track down our high school nemesis on the internet, hoping he's having a lousy life. Instead, you've risen to a general's rank. You have five daughters. A beautiful ranch. Maybe Manson thinks he can kill two birds with one stone—expand to Montana and cause you some grief at the same time. I don't think he was the sharpest tool in the shed."

"You're right on that." Sharp enough to cause trouble, but not sharp enough to make it to the big time.

"He sends Bob Finchley, who almost pulls off marrying Cass—and getting his friends to marry your other daughters—before your girls catch on to what they're doing. He sends Ron Cooper and Grant Kimball, who try to kidnap Jo. Bob, Ron and Grant are young men, probably only been with Manson a few years. They can't get the job done, and Bob and Grant both end up dead, so Manson goes up the ladder to one of his lieutenants."

"Ramsey." The General had gone through this same litany dozens of times in his head, sorting through all the men who'd attacked his home, trying to figure out the connection between them.

"That's right. Ramsey burns down your stable, but not before Jo gets all your horses out. He's failed at his job, but at least he gets away. Manson sends his son-in-law next. But Beau and his nephews fail, too."

"And then Ron Cooper murders Manson."

"But not before Manson gets a shot off that takes him to his grave."

"Ron Cooper doesn't strike me as the kind of man who'd kill his boss."

"I'd bet just about anything it was Manson who drew first," Cab countered. "He must have sensed Ron was snitching. Ron must have known he was in danger and came armed."

"Now they're both dead. Who's heading up the organization? Beau or Ramsey?"

"That's the million-dollar question. We don't know the answer to that."

"At least we know who to look for." The General stopped his pacing in front of a photograph of his late wife. Amelia's kind gaze held his. God, he missed her.

"They can always hire new soldiers," Cab cautioned him. "Whichever of them steps into Manson's shoes will have Manson's people, Manson's structure, his war chest—and, we have to assume, his plans. Better tell your girls to be careful."

"I will." He'd send a message to Brian Lake, the first man he'd sent to his ranch. Brian would tell everyone else. The General returned to his desk, sat down and pulled his laptop from the briefcase Myers had left.

"I will, too, when I go to Lena's wedding. Wish I'd see you there."

The General didn't rise to the bait. He wouldn't be at his daughter's wedding. He opened the laptop, turned it on and began to compose the email. "You know I'm overseas."

"Yeah, well, come home soon. I'll let you know what else I learn."

"You do that."

Cab cut the call, leaving the General to think over what he'd just learned. Duke Manson had tracked him down after all these years. And now the idiot was dead, leaving someone new to contend with.

He finished up his note, sent it off and sat lost in thought until his gaze touched on the black briefcase again. Inside it was a letter from his wife—one of the last two left from the box of letters Cass had forwarded to him after Amelia died eleven years ago.

Amelia had been an uncommon woman with an uncommon gift for seeing the future, and the letters she'd left him had helped him through the years since her death. In them, she pointed out upcoming problems, gave him advice. Told him what to do. It had taken several years for him to learn to accept she'd known what she was talking about when she wrote them. Now he knew he ignored her wishes to his peril.

Swallowing hard, he reached for the letter. He had to read it, no matter how hard it was to move that much closer to the time when there would be no letters left. He hoped her calm words would help untangle the thoughts swirling in his mind.

Dear Augustus,

It will be Lena's turn to walk down the aisle soon, and I'm so happy she's found a worthy man to share her life with.

I know better than to think you'll be walking down the aisle with her, helping our daughter bridge the gap from single to married life. Augustus, you can't run anymore. You have to go home—before the choice isn't yours anymore.

A chill traveled down the General's spine. Not his choice? What did she mean by that?

You're overdue, and our girls need you.

I need you to mend things between you and them. I

need to know my family is intact.

Augustus, if you won't do it for them—or for yourself—do it for me.

I'm fooling myself, thinking you will. I love you so much, I can't bear to see what comes next. Oh, Augustus—why are you such a stubborn man?

My only consolation is that I see you with our daughters. With our grandchildren—

Hang on, Augustus. This next bit is going to hurt!

Love,
Amelia

A familiar ache squeezed his heart. It killed him to know how he kept letting his wife down. A real man would have faced his pain and gone home to Two Willows years ago. Would have raised his girls himself, keeping them close.

Keeping them safe.

Instead he'd stayed away. Sent overseers to run the ranch. Sent guardians to raise them when his daughters were younger. Dedicated his life to the Army—

Faced his own death rather than facing his wife's.

If she said hard times were coming, then they were coming. If she said it was going to hurt, then it was going to hurt. Did she foresee a widening of the gap between him and their girls? If so, then all he'd done by sending husbands was waste everyone's time.

He needed to do better.

Maybe Amelia was right. Maybe it was time to think about going—

"General?" Myers opened the door and stuck his head in. "Your next appointment—"

The room exploded in a burst of sound and light. Pain sliced through the General's side.

All went dark.

Chapter One

LIEUTENANT JACK SANDERS walked into the empty conference room at USSOCOM in Tampa, Florida, crossed to his desk and set a breakfast sandwich and a bottle of orange juice from a fast-food restaurant down by his computer monitor. He took a quick look around to make sure he was alone, kissed the palm of his hand and touched it to the photograph that hung close by.

"Hello, baby girl," he said softly to the image of Alice Reed, with a silent nod to Logan Hughes, the cocky man who'd started this silly tradition. He'd been surprised how much he'd missed Logan since General Reed had sent him to Montana. He'd missed all the men who'd been in the General's bogus Joint Task Force for Inter-branch Communication Clarity. One by one, the General had sent them to Chance Creek. He'd sent Brian Lake, a Navy SEAL, to marry his oldest daughter, Cass; Connor O'Riley, a Pararescueman, to marry Sadie; Hunter Powell, a Navy SEAL sniper, to marry his youngest, Jo; and Logan, who was a Marine, to marry Lena.

Now it was Jack's turn to go to Montana. Soon he'd

be with the other men again, and he knew he could work with them. That wasn't the problem.

Could he marry Alice Reed? Spend a lifetime with a woman he didn't even know yet?

More to the point—could he love her?

Could she love him?

If the answer was no, was he willing to give up his chance at future happiness to clear his name?

Jack knew he had unrealistic expectations when it came to marriage. His birth parents had set the bar so high—at least in his memory—their example was impossible to meet. He'd never doubted their love for each other, or for him. His impression of his early years was all unrelenting blue skies and happiness. A huge ranch to roam, a father to show him how to ride and rope, a mother who gave him plenty of hugs and kisses. Ranch hands and hired help equally disposed to shower him with attention and praise.

It wasn't that he'd been spoiled. Jack had worked hard alongside his parents at their tasks. Both of them had demanded that he pay attention and learn when it was time for such things. Still, they had plenty of energy left over for laughter, games… fun.

His parents' love for each other was equally clear. He remembered them holding hands. Kissing. Their faces brightening when they caught sight of each other—the same way their faces had brightened when they caught sight of him.

He'd learned early such happiness couldn't last—

And that most families, while loving, weren't anything like the one he'd known when he was young.

He'd been lucky to know such a life at all, he told himself. Lucky, too, with the home he'd found once his parents were gone. His adopted parents, Richard and Janet Drake, cared deeply for each other, and for him, even if they didn't extend the kind of boisterous love that made you utterly certain of your place in the world.

Jack didn't blame them for that. He'd watched other couples through the years and realized few of them possessed what his parents had. When he was younger, he'd told himself he'd hold out for it. Search the world for the woman who'd spark the kind of understanding, respect and mutual passion that could coalesce into a joyful commitment like his folks'.

Now that he was older, he realized it wasn't likely he'd find such a woman—especially not now he was being forced into an arranged marriage.

Better to focus on his other goals. Clearing his name. Making sure he didn't humiliate the good people who'd raised him. He'd already let Richard down in his choice of career. If he left the military a failure, it would render useless all the time and effort he and Janet had expended bringing him up.

He had to succeed at this one last mission. Had to trust he could be a good husband no matter what. He'd learned everything he could about Alice Reed—

Which had only made things worse. Alice was lovely and talented, and like Janet, ambitious. Jack knew what that meant. There was nothing wrong with talent and ambition, but you had to understand the trade-offs.

Long hours at work meant fewer hours for the people who loved you. Janet's career was crucial to the security of the United States. Richard was busy with his own career and didn't mind Janet's absences—he was hardly around himself.

Jack wanted something different. The kind of marriage his birth parents had. They'd worked the ranch together. Saw each other all the time. Spent long evenings on the back porch together. Walked through life side by side.

He wanted his wife's face to light up like his mom's had whenever his dad came into the room, and he couldn't fool himself into believing a woman like Alice would ever light up like that for him.

It was time for him to grow up and face facts. Live in the present, rather than in some glorified past.

He'd been grateful he was the last of the men the General was sending to Two Willows, but now the day had come, he wondered if it would have been better to be the first. If he failed now, it would affect all the others. Brian was happily married to Cass, and Cass was already almost five months pregnant. Connor loved Sadie, and Hunter thought the sun rose and set over Jo. Now Logan was marrying Lena.

If Jack didn't marry Alice, the whole house of cards would come tumbling down.

Marrying the Reed women was the mission. The prize for successful completion was part ownership in Two Willows. Jack didn't think any of the other men had needed that extra inducement by the time they married their brides. All of them had truly been in love by then, by their own admission. Still, the Reed women loved their ranch. If Jack failed to marry Alice—

And the General stuck to his ultimatum—

None of them would have a home.

What would that do to his friends' happy marriages?

He had to succeed—for everyone's sake. It was as simple as that. It didn't matter that Alice was so beautiful she could have her pick of men, or that she'd been recently hurt by a boyfriend who had dated her to get access to her ranch, or that she was ambitious enough to be going after a position as lead costume designer for a Hollywood movie—and therefore probably had little time or energy to create the kind of life he'd hoped for with a woman.

Jack was a realist, and he was willing to give up his childish ideas about marriage in order to clear his name, but one thing about Alice tripped him up and made him wonder if they could be compatible at all.

Alice thought she could see the future—and she'd convinced just about everyone around her to believe it, too.

Jack was a stickler for facts and truth. Could he marry a woman who lived a lie?

When his phone buzzed in his pocket, Jack grabbed it with relief, although he sighed when he saw the name on the screen. It was Richard Drake. The man who'd rescued him, raised him—and would be mighty pissed if he knew how badly Jack had messed things up.

Jack accepted the call, and Richard's voice boomed

in his ear. "What's this about a trip to Montana? You're not due for leave. And I can't find any record of a Joint Special Task Force for Inter-Branch Communication Clarity, either. I smell a rat, Jack."

Nothing got by him. Jack didn't know why he'd even tried to pass this assignment off as something normal. "It's an unusual situation."

"How did you get involved?"

"How do you think? I was ordered here." Jack wasn't going to get into particulars. He hoped like hell Richard hadn't been able to uncover the "task force's" true purpose. "It's not leave. The General has had some trouble at his ranch." Maybe that would satisfy him.

"Two Willows. Read all about it. Looks like some bad characters have been trying to move into Chance Creek lately. Strange, though, the pattern of attacks on the ranch. They're not very rational."

"I don't think we're dealing with a rational enemy," Jack said, falling easily into the kind of shop-talk in which he and Richard spent most of their time communicating.

Richard hadn't been the first on the scene at the murder of Jack's parents in New Mexico—he worked in Washington, DC, but was in town on an unrelated case at the time. He'd been invited by one of the local departments to come along because the murders had been so unusual, and he'd arrived at a moment when Jack's life hung in the balance between helplessness and action. Richard had given him the tools he needed to survive, thrive and be a force for good. Without his influence, Jack wasn't sure where he'd have ended up.

When Richard and Janet offered to adopt him, Jack had joined their family willingly. His new parents had loved him and done their best to raise him right, even if their careers often kept them on the run. It had taken years for Jack to put together what it was they actually did. Over time, he realized that the bland job titles they'd repeated so many times covered up their true positions. Richard worked for the FBI as an intelligence analyst. Janet, though a warm and loving mother at home, filled a far more shadowy position with the Bureau that kept her away sometimes for weeks. He respected them for what they gave to their country. Wished he measured up.

"You can save people with a mind like that," Richard had told Jack early on. "You notice everything. Remember everything. That's a gift."

Jack had wanted to save people. He'd gratefully learned every lesson Richard had to share, and when his new father ran out of things to teach him, he'd joined the Army and the Special Forces, looking to take that purpose further. Richard would have preferred for Jack to follow in his own footsteps—or Janet's—and reminded him of that often. Janet, when she was around to hear the conversations, told Richard to let Jack have his own way. "We don't choose our passions, or our abilities, Richard," she'd say.

Somehow that made Jack feel worse.

Now the Army was kicking him out. What would his parents think of that?

"I think you're right," Richard said. "Whoever is behind all this isn't rational. There's something more going on here."

"Desperation," Jack said. He'd sensed it for months as the attacks on Two Willows escalated. "They're not getting more organized; they're getting more desperate." He wasn't surprised Richard knew all about Two Willows and the trouble there. As soon as Jack got reassigned to the General's command, his pop would have looked into every aspect of the man. Richard dealt in information, and he was constantly collecting facts.

"A desperate man is a dangerous man," Richard said. "But I didn't think generals got to send men on personal missions."

"I don't think anyone other than Reed would get away with it." Jack had no idea how the General was managing it. Didn't want to think about it too much, either. All he wanted was an honorable way out. A chance to start over. A chance to go back to his roots. Richard wouldn't think much of his desire to start ranching, but ranching was all Jack could think about these days.

"Are you in trouble?"

Richard's question knocked the wind out of Jack's sails, although it shouldn't have, since this was his pop to a T. He put clues together until he had a picture he could understand.

"I can't talk about it." Jack prayed that would put an end to this line of questioning. Knew it wouldn't, though.

"Jack, if there's something I can do—"

"It's just an assignment. I've got it under control." A lie. A desperate lie, even. Jack glanced at Alice's photograph. Was she mocking him? She looked like she was mocking him. Maybe he'd studied the ranch and its surroundings, the men who'd attacked it and the men the General had sent to defend his daughters. Maybe he'd done every bit of research and reconnaissance he could.

That didn't mean he could win the enigmatic woman staring back at him.

Did she know he was coming for her?

Probably. After watching the General send men home to marry her sisters, she'd know what to expect.

Jack had no doubt she was smart. She'd fooled everyone into believing she could see the future, after all. He'd bet his life Alice's *premonitions* were based on the same kind of fact-finding, minutiae-noting, pattern-matching brain he had. He was looking forward to comparing notes.

"Jack—"

"Gotta go." Jack hung up. What else could he do? If he didn't manage to marry Alice—and solve the mystery of who was coming after Two Willows once and for all—he'd let down the Army, the General, himself—and his family.

He couldn't do that.

Which meant he needed to get on that plane. Now.

Shoving his phone in his pocket, he walked the perimeter of the room, closing the blinds, running his eye once more over the charts and maps—and photographs—that lined the walls. This was goodbye to USSOCOM, to his career as he'd known it—to his past.

He stopped in front of Alice's photograph one last time. "Hello, baby girl. I'm coming to see you today."

She didn't answer, and Jack felt foolish. He marched toward the door and flipped off the lights but hesitated, his hand on the doorknob. He didn't want to leave Alice's photograph behind. One way or another, she was his future.

He was going to keep an eye on her.

He turned again, crossed the room and grabbed the framed picture. As he shut the office door behind him, a man flagged him down. "Sanders? Hold up a minute."

There was a tightness in his voice. A pen tucked behind his ear. A phone in one hand, a folder in the other. Jack would bet he'd been carrying that folder when he answered the call that had put him in such a panic.

Bad news. Jack could read it in his eyes. Bad news that concerned someone the man counted on.

"What happened to the General?" Jack snapped.

"How did you know—?" The man shook his head. "It was a missile. It hit the compound. The General's alive," he said to forestall Jack's question. "But he's hurt. He's been transported to the Landstuhl Regional Medical Center with the rest of the injured. He's heading into surgery."

"I'm on my way to the airport—to Chance Creek."

"Understood. We'll keep relaying you information as soon as we get it."

"How much danger is he in?" Jack couldn't believe it. The General taken down by a missile strike? He understood the corporal's shakiness. The General was the sun around which they all orbited. They depended on him to remain fixed in the firmament.

"Unknown, sir."

Jack's stomach sank. How would he face the General's daughters with this news?

"HOW DID IT happen?"

Alice Reed stood in the freezing darkness knee-deep in the snow, shining a flashlight on the water streaming from one of the spigots outside the old farmhouse she and her sisters had lived in all their lives. Two Willows was over a hundred years old, and so was the house, which meant sometimes emergencies like this one happened. Still, she had no idea what would make a spigot break at four in the morning.

"I don't know," Connor O'Riley said. Connor was married to her sister, Sadie, but apparently Sadie had slept through the excitement. He bent down nearby to get a better look, gently pushing his dog, Max, out of the way. "It must have just broken. We need to get the water turned off."

"Shouldn't it already have been shut off for the winter?" Alice asked. Usually Cass was the one who took care of things like that. She couldn't imagine her careful sister wouldn't have shut it down at the end of fall, but then things had been pretty unsettled around Two Willows for months. Maybe she'd simply forgotten.

"Is there a shut-off in the basement?" Logan Hughes asked. He was marrying Lena today. Alice could understand the worry in his voice.

"I think so."

"I'll go find it." He hurried around the corner toward the back door. Alice had woken to hear him and Connor talking in low tones in the hall a few minutes ago and had followed them outside to see what was the matter.

"Sounded like an explosion when it happened," Connor told her, keeping the dog back from the gushing water.

"I've never heard of something like this."

"Pipes freeze now and then."

"But taps don't just fall off. Besides, if the water was frozen, it wouldn't gush out like this." Alice hugged her arms to her chest. It was one of the coldest nights they'd had this year. "I hope we can get a plumber out."

"We'll call first thing in the morning. I'm sure we'll get it fixed."

Alice wasn't as confident. A few months back, when Cass had been renovating the first-floor bathroom, she'd complained about how Walter Eddings, their usual plumber, was booked for weeks, and had ended up doing the work herself. Alice could only hope things had slowed down for the man since then. She didn't think Cass could replace a spigot—not while preparing for Lena's wedding.

"The water's stopping." Connor pointed as the gush turned into a trickle and died away. "Good ol' Logan."

Logan reappeared a few moments later. "I got the water shut off, but the valve's leaking inside. We'd better get a plumber out as soon as we can. I'm afraid it's going to get worse."

"Today of all days for this to happen," Alice said. "The house will be full of guests later."

Connor patted her arm. "Leave it to me. You make sure Lena's ready for her wedding. I'll keep an eye on the leak until the plumber comes—and an eye on Logan here. Make sure he doesn't get cold feet."

"My feet are freezing already." Logan indicated their snowy surroundings with a sweep of his hands. "But I fully intend to marry Lena today. No worries there. Go get some sleep now," he said to Alice.

"I'll try." Alice wasn't at all sure she'd be able to go back to sleep, though. The sense of dread that had plagued her for weeks was even stronger this morning. Something bad was going to happen. She just hoped they made it through the wedding before it did.

She'd always gotten flashes and hunches about the future. Unfortunately, her visions were rarely clear. This was one of the murky ones. Just a feeling, nothing concrete.

"Any news from the General?" Logan asked as they headed toward the house.

"No." None of them had heard from him since he'd gone abroad a few weeks ago. The General had traveled all over the world during his career, and she'd never worried about him like this before. Years ago, when he'd entered the service, her mother had made a kind of deal with the land. She'd never set foot off Two Willows while he was gone, and the General would come home unharmed.

When she'd died, Alice and her sisters had worked together to honor their mother's superstition. They made it a practice to check in with one another when they left the ranch, always making sure one of them stayed put.

Until Alice had ruined everything. A few weeks ago, she'd assumed Jo was still in the barn and hadn't checked before she'd gone to run some errands. Only when she met up with all her sisters in town—including Jo—did she realize her mistake.

They'd rushed home, but it was too late. The damage was done—

Except they didn't know what that damage was yet. They'd gotten no word from the General himself, and the Army refused to tell them where he'd gone.

"Go to bed, lass," Connor said softly when they reached the back door, his Irish accent rising to the fore in the way it did every now and then. "Everything is going to be okay."

"I hope so," she said as they made their way inside, Max trotting obediently after Connor, but she didn't believe it for a minute, and although she did go right back to bed, she didn't fall asleep again.

Several hours later, she was sitting in her favorite spot in the kitchen on top of the refrigerator, eating a slice of toast and petting her white cat, Tabitha, when someone knocked on the back door.

"Who could that be at this hour?" Cass asked. She was frying bacon, her hair tucked into a messy bun at the back of her head, an apron tied over her jeans and thick sweater.

"The plumber, I hope." Connor sprang up from his breakfast to answer it. He wore jeans, too, with a red plaid flannel shirt over the top of a gray long-sleeve T-shirt. Alice had noticed that the men had adopted a kind of uniform even though they were far from the military bases where they usually served. In the warmer weather it had been jeans and plain color T-shirts. Now they added flannel shirts. In their work boots and thick outer gear, they were hard to tell apart from behind when they were outside.

"This early?" Alice asked.

"I called, and he said he'd be over, but you're right—it is early." Connor pulled open the door.

It wasn't Walter. It was Wyoming Smith, Cass's best friend. A decidedly unhappy Wyoming. Wye was short, with a mop of light brown curls. She unbuttoned her dark blue wool coat and kicked off her boots.

"Wye—what's wrong?" Cass asked. She set down her spatula and turned off the stove, moving the pan to a cool burner. She crossed the room to meet her friend as Connor went back to his breakfast.

"You weren't supposed to notice. It's Lena's wedding day, and I don't want to cast a pall on it," Wye said as she unwrapped a scarf from around her neck and hung it up on the same peg as her coat. Cass led her to the table. "I lost my job yesterday. I'm still in shock."

"Oh, no. What happened?"

"They can't justify keeping me on—they simply aren't getting enough cases. They let me go effective immediately, and now I don't know what to do. It isn't exactly easy to find work as a paralegal around here. I might have to move to Bozeman."

"You are not moving," Cass decreed. "You're my best friend. I need you here."

"Let's not worry about it today," Wye said. "Where's Lena? I wanted to congratulate her on the big day."

"Out in the barn, where else?" Cass sighed. "I gave her a to-do list, though. She'll be back soon."

"Then feed me and point me to my first job," Wye said, putting her shoulders back and lifting her chin. "Cass, no—we're not going to figure out my future right now."

"I was only going to say that if you aren't working, you should spend the week with us. You could use cheering up, and I could definitely use the help. Not only will we have to clean up from the wedding, it's also time to do our pre-holiday clean up."

Alice, still on top of the refrigerator, groaned. Cass's pre-holiday clean-ups were legendary. "Please stay, Wye, and do my work for me," she begged. "I have to get my gowns done before Landon Clark gets here to view them." The movie producer was due in three weeks, and she was racing to finish the three elaborate Civil War–era ball gowns he'd commissioned to get a feel for her design capabilities.

Wye smiled a little. "Sure. I could use something to keep me busy. Otherwise I'll just sit around and worry. I haven't been out of a job since I was twelve!"

"I've got plenty of work for you," Cass said. "Sit and eat. We have a lot to do to get ready for the wedding. Where is that plumber, anyway?"

It was nearly ten by the time Walter showed up with a younger man in tow. Alice, who'd been in and out of the kitchen all morning, helping with the wedding preparations, was relieved to see them. Cass had been working herself into a tizzy that they wouldn't get the job done before their guests arrived.

"Heard you have a problem," Walter said, knocking the snow off his boots as he came inside. He was a gruff old man who had to be close to retirement. His shock of white hair tended to stand up on end, and he had a thick white mustache, too. "This is my new assistant, Will Beck. Will's just signed on to help me catch up on all the work."

"I'm glad you're here then, Will," Alice said brightly. In her experience, it wasn't good for anyone when Cass got stressed out.

"Glad to be here. Just got to town. Was happy to find work so fast." Will was taller than Walter, with a square face and a shock of wheat-colored hair. His blue eyes shone when he smiled, which he was doing now.

"I'll bet," Wyoming said gloomily.

Will considered her, his gaze lingering on her pretty face. Alice bit back a smile; Wyoming had an admirer.

"What seems to be the trouble?" Walter asked.

"Let me show you." Cass led them to the basement and came back a few minutes later. "Thank God Walter found Will," she said to Wye. "I hate to think what would happen if we let that valve leak for weeks. I don't know why Walter didn't hire someone sooner."

"Because Walter's a man who believes if you want something done right, you have to do it yourself. Just like me," Will said from the doorway, startling all of them. "He sent me to find out if you've got another bucket," he went on with a grin. "It took a lot of persuading to get him to agree to sign me on, but all I heard from everyone I asked when I got to town was how desperately Chance Creek needed another plumber. Good thing that's what I'm trained for."

"I've got a bucket." Cass went to the pantry and returned with one. "How do you like it here?"

"It's great. I already feel at home." He was appraising Wyoming frankly. "A lot more pretty girls around these parts than where I came from."

Wyoming perked up under his scrutiny. "Must be a pretty small town if Chance Creek has more women."

"Sometimes it sure felt small," he said with another grin. "But I'm here now. Better get back to work." He took the bucket from Cass and winked at Wyoming.

Cass looked from him to Wye and back again. She stepped forward to detain Will with a hand on his arm. "We have another problem. It doesn't need to be solved today, but maybe you could come back after the wedding?"

"What is it?"

"The pipes knock upstairs."

"I could take a look at them in a day or two, when I've finished up another few jobs."

"Good." Cass beamed. Wyoming looked like she wanted to melt into the floor. Alice tried not to laugh as Will disappeared down the hall.

"Looks like you made a conquest," Cass said to Wye.

"He must be starved for company. And you're shameless making up a fake job like that."

"It isn't fake," Alice put in. "Those pipes have knocked as long as I've been alive. I doubt he can fix it, though."

"I don't see why he couldn't," Cass said. "You need to stop talking yourself down, Wyoming Smith," she added. "Any man would be happy to go out with you."

Wyoming rolled her eyes. "Yep, they're beating down the doors. I'm surprised he wasn't flirting with you, Alice. Usually men can't even see me when you're around." She got back to work helping Cass polish the silverware they'd use to serve their guests later.

Alice didn't know how to answer that. She hated it when other women compared themselves unfavorably to her. Cass came to her rescue.

"Alice probably already has a *taken* sign around her neck that only men can see."

"What's that supposed to mean?" Wyoming asked.

"Her fiancé is arriving today. After all, Lena's getting married, and Alice is the only one of us left."

Wye smiled. "Forgot all about that. I wonder what

he'll be like? I guess it doesn't matter: you'll have to marry whoever your father sends through that front door tonight. It's tradition, right?"

Alice didn't mind Wye's banter, but she wished Cass hadn't brought it up. Wye was right; the General had sent each of her four sisters a man. She could only assume he'd send her one, too.

As for having to marry him…

The back door swung open, and Lena tromped in, scattering snow everywhere.

"The to-do list Cass gave me said I have to have a last fitting," she said ungraciously to Alice. "I don't see why. I haven't gained any weight since yesterday." Lena wasn't one to fuss over her appearance much. Alice knew it would take some cajoling to get her done up for her big day.

"Come on." Alice joined her at the door and began to pull on her outer things. "It will only take a minute, and you'll thank me later." She was grateful for the interruption. She might be able to glimpse the future sometimes, but she'd never seen her own wedding. She had no idea what would happen next.

And it was driving her crazy.

IT WAS LONG past dinner time when Jack arrived in Chance Creek, and as he pulled up and parked his rental car outside Two Willows, it was obvious Logan and Lena's wedding reception was in full swing. He patted his pocket to make sure he still had the small gift the General had left behind at USSOCOM for him to take to Lena, opened the door and climbed out, taking a moment to appreciate the cheerful, brightly lit windows of the house that shone through the winter darkness. Snow lay in a pale blanket on the ground. Above him, stars winked in the firmament. He savored the quiet. Two Willows was a full house at the best of times. Tonight it looked packed to the gills.

The wind had a bite to it, and he pulled his coat more firmly around him as he popped open the trunk and pulled out his bag. These next few minutes were crucial for the path his life would take. Soon he'd meet Alice in the flesh. He couldn't help but wonder how that would go.

He was especially worried about the confrontations that were sure to come when Alice realized he didn't believe in her ability to see the future. He'd often been accused of having that same ability. That didn't make it true. People's behavior tended to follow predictable tendencies. Once you made a study of it, it was regrettably easy to guess what would happen next.

Was Alice the same? Did her eyes notice things others didn't? Did she study people until she'd learned them well? Was she plagued by the details no one else seemed to notice? Did her mind whirl and click through images and facts late at night when she was supposed to be asleep?

Jack had met only two other people whose ability matched his. One was the man who'd brought him up. The other was a young girl. He'd saved her life seven months ago—

And lost his career as a result.

If he wanted his good name back, he needed to convince Alice to love him. Or at least to decide he was enough of an asset to her and Two Willows that she should spend her life with him.

Which was going to be a challenge, since he hadn't set foot on a ranch since he was seven.

His only hope was that all Alice's sisters had come around to the idea of marrying the men the General had sent. Maybe the General had some piece of intelligence he didn't.

Jack sure hoped so. He slowly walked up the path to Two Willows. Only one way to find out what would happen next.

He knocked on the door.

And waited for someone to answer.

"WHY AREN'T YOU dancing?"

Alice Reed pushed down the familiar sense of dread that still swirled in her gut and turned to see her youngest sister. Jo, petite, with an elfin face, was dressed in a spring green bridesmaid gown, identical to the one Alice was wearing. She was flushed in the heat of the room; there were far too many people packed into the house tonight. Alice was sure she was glowing as well. It was time to crack a window even if it was below freezing outside. At least the wedding had been a success so far—even the leak in the basement had been fixed. Walter had left Will behind to handle the job once he'd inspected the problem, and Will had left an hour later with the job completed and a promise to be back in a day or two to fix the knocking pipes.

"Any chance you'll be around?" she'd heard him ask Wyoming on his way out.

"Maybe."

"I don't have anyone to dance with," Alice said to Jo.

Jo raised an eyebrow. "Really?"

Alice only shrugged. She could have danced if she'd wanted to, as Jo knew well. A smile would raise a willing partner from any corner of the room. Alice wasn't vain, but she wasn't stupid, either. She'd been blessed with her mother's beauty, and men liked beauty. What they didn't like was finding out she had a mind of her own.

Alice had learned over the years that the combination of her ambition and her ability to see the future tended to turn men off. Not that she had a lot of experience with them. She and her sisters had spent their teenage years trying to drive away the guardians and overseers the General sent to watch over them—and then laying low on the ranch as long as possible before some other adult realized they were on their own and let the General know. This meant she hadn't gotten around to dating much until she was older. Howie Warner was her first serious boyfriend, but before him there was Matt Gordon.

Matt was two years older than her. He'd played baseball in high school before taking his place on his family's ranch. Alice had been twenty-one when they'd met up at the Dancing Boot one night and he'd asked her to dance. One thing led to another, and they'd gone out a few times. At first it had been fun—

Until Matt asked her about her costume designing business. He wasn't interested in the techniques she used or the research she did to make her creations period-accurate. "What do you get paid for something like that?" he'd asked at dinner one night.

Alice, thrilled at a commission she'd landed for a specialized movie costume, had told him, expecting him to be as excited and impressed as she was. Turned out the commission for the single outfit was double what he made in a month.

Matt wasn't amused.

"You think you're real hot shit, don't you," he'd spat at her as he stood up, his chair scraping the floor. "With all your money and your 'special abilities.'"

"I don't think I'm hot shit, but I am proud of my work," she'd countered, aware that everyone in the restaurant was staring at them.

"Your whole seeing the future thing is a crock of shit. Everyone knows it." Matt had left Alice to finish her meal and pay the bill. She'd never felt smaller, and when Howie had come along, she'd done her best to stay that way and let him feel like a big man.

That had been a disaster.

Now her future husband was due to arrive any minute. She had no idea what to do about it.

"What's wrong?" Jo asked. "Have you had a vision? Is something bad going to happen?"

Alice shook her head. "It's the same feeling I've had

since before—" She broke off, pulled herself together and tried again. "Before we all left the ranch." Since before *she'd* left it without checking to make sure one of her sisters was still at home. Whatever happened next would be her fault.

"The General is fine," Jo assured her.

"We don't know that. No one's been able to get in touch."

"Because he's overseas and his mission is confidential. We would know if anything had happened to him."

Alice wasn't reassured. That was the problem; she was supposed to be able to see the future, but her gift—her curse, Alice thought—was a sad, sorry, intermittent kind of thing that rarely told her anything useful. She was nothing like her mother, Amelia, who'd seen so clearly.

"You sure you aren't just nervous?" Jo asked. "After all, your husband's due to arrive any minute. Maybe that's why you've been feeling off these past few weeks."

"I'm going to get started cleaning up." She forestalled her sister when Jo would have joined her. "Enjoy dancing with Hunter."

"Can't wait to meet your new man," Jo teased but turned away.

Alice made her way through the crush of bodies to the relatively quiet kitchen. Dishes had been scraped and stacked when dinner was done and the tables cleared away. They sat in piles on the counter near the sink, which Alice now filled with hot water and dish soap.

She was grateful to be alone, but without the distraction of conversation, she found it harder to defend against the dread. It was an awful, stifling blankness where the future was supposed to be. She couldn't see it. Couldn't even get a read on it. Knew something was coming—something bad.

Not just a husband, although that was part of it. Something else.

Something—

Big.

The only other time she'd felt like this was in the months leading up to her mother's death. Alice didn't like to think about that, for obvious reasons, and rarely did she allow herself to probe that part of her past. She wondered if she'd actually known what was coming but had suppressed it, or if there were certain things too big to know.

What was coming now?

Alice slipped a number of glasses into the sudsy water and began to wash them carefully. She hated to admit it, but Jo was right: she was nervous. Not just about the bad feeling, but about her husband-to-be. When she tried to picture the man the General would send, she couldn't see him. Fate wasn't giving her even a glimpse of him, which made it hard to decide how she would react when he rang the bell.

She should rebuff him, of course, and if she'd been the first daughter to whom the General had delivered a husband, she would have, but she was the fifth, and she was beginning to wonder if it was even worth her time to fight against something so obviously preordained.

That was just the problem, though; everything was preordained. Her life. Her success. Her husband… and whatever this sense of dread portended.

Fate doled out glimpses of everything. Not especially helpful glimpses, but enough to derail her from making her own choices sometimes. It had shown her that she would make costumes for a living—and do well at it.

Fate had also told her Two Willows would always be her home. For most of her life she'd cheerfully accepted that, too, but lately she wasn't so sure that's what she wanted. Oh, eventually she'd settle here, but did she have to live in Montana every day of her life?

That didn't seem fair.

Then there was the case of her husband. If it was preordained that she marry the man the General sent for her, shouldn't she have seen that in her visions?

She hadn't. Not even once.

As far as Alice was concerned, her special gift kind of… sucked.

Alice rinsed a glass and set it down harder than she meant to, stifling a curse when she cracked it but grateful it hadn't shattered. She transferred the pieces into the trash carefully and took a deep breath.

She wished Amelia could have been here today to see Lena married. It had been breathtaking to watch her prickly, independent sister exchange vows with the man she so obviously loved.

Amelia had died when Alice was only thirteen. For months beforehand, Alice had been both restless and consumed with a desire to stay close to home at the same time. She'd heard her oldest sister, Cass, discussing it with Lena. "Hormones," Cass had said disdainfully, and Lena had snickered.

It hadn't been hormones.

On the day Amelia had been struck down, Alice hadn't wanted to go out riding, but Amelia's word was law on the ranch. Always had been, even when the General had been home. Alice hadn't even thought to contradict her when Amelia ordered them all to go out for a ride. They'd always been homeschooled, and riding was gym class. Everyone knew gym class was mandatory.

They were a quarter mile from the house when a blinding pain had nearly knocked Alice off her horse. She'd cried out and known instantly her mother was in trouble. Wracked with pain and terror, she hadn't been able to move; Cass had maneuvered her horse as close as she could, leaned over and supported her, while Lena and Jo had streaked home atop their mounts.

By the time Alice saw Amelia again, the paramedics had arrived. Amelia had lived a couple of days, and Alice had her chance to talk to her in the hospital—

But that was a long time ago.

She'd give anything for the chance to talk to her mother today.

If her dread back then had portended a death, what did it mean now? Was death stalking her family again?

If so, who was its intended victim?

A loud knock on the front door made Alice clutch the counter.

He was here.

The man the General had sent.

She couldn't breathe. Couldn't see the future. Couldn't see anything. Did this dread have to do with the man standing on her front step? Was he wrong for her? Would he hurt her?

No.

She didn't know how she knew, but she did. He wouldn't hurt her.

But something else was wrong.

Alice's hands shook as she dried them, then reached up to pat her hair. She made herself walk out of the kitchen and down the central hall.

This was it.

Taking another deep breath, she opened the door to find a handsome man with sandy brown hair and blue eyes on the other side. He stood at ease like a soldier, hands clasped behind his back, legs spread in a strong, ready stance. There was a rugged duffel bag on the porch to one side of him.

He was handsome. Oh, so handsome. Alice was unprepared for the desire that surged inside her. How could she feel like this when—

She gave up trying to understand anything. The universe was unfathomable, even to someone like her. All she could do was meet the day where it met her, and today fate had brought her a man to reckon with.

That didn't mean she'd make it easy on him. She fixed him with a steady gaze.

"I knew it would be you," she said.

"I knew you'd say that," he answered. "I'm Jack. Jack Sanders. The General sent me."

"I knew that, too," she assured him. She didn't want him to think she was dumb.

"Do you know what I'm going to say next?" He wasn't yanking her chain, Alice decided; he was actually curious. Someone had told him about her abilities, that was clear in his challenge.

Alice was used to that. She shook her head.

He stepped closer, and suddenly the soldier filled the doorway. His gaze held hers, and she read concern—and a searching hope she couldn't fathom. He swallowed. Cleared his throat.

"I've got some bad news."

Of course. She'd known that. Alice nodded, steeling herself. Whatever came next, it would be hard.

"The General's been hurt. He's coming home."

Chapter Two

BEAUTIFUL DIDN'T BEGIN to explain Alice Reed. Jack had been staring at her photo for months, but no likeness could convey the way Alice inhabited her loveliness. She left him breathless with her blue eyes, long ash-blond hair and otherworldly air. For the first time, the phrase "hauntingly beautiful" made sense. Men must be beating a path to this door.

She'd be aloof, he decided. The kind of woman who set herself above men. How the hell could he get through to a woman like that?

Did he even want to?

She stared back at him, assessing him the same way he was assessing her. The news about her father didn't bring tears to her eyes. She didn't faint, either. Instead she stood ramrod straight, taking it in.

"When?" Her clipped tone reminded him of Janet. His adopted mother reacted to news the same way, consuming every bit of information before coming to any conclusion about the matter.

Jack knew why Alice asked the question. He'd interrogated the other men about every detail they could muster about her. It was Brian who'd told him she blamed herself for leaving the ranch when all of her sisters had already gone. She wanted to know if she was to blame.

"It's that superstition they have," Brian had said. "They think one of them always has to be on Two Willows land. They've all been jumpy as cats ever since they broke the rule. They think something's going to happen to the General."

Jack didn't believe in superstitions, but the Reed women had been right; something had happened to the General. Jack had spent hours at the airport trying to sort through the information coming from abroad. The attack had happened about forty-eight hours ago. The General had been stabilized, then evacuated to Germany right away for surgery.

Early reports were skimpy on details but made it clear he wouldn't be returning to active duty anytime soon—if ever.

Jack hesitated, knowing what he was about to say would change everything, and possibly end any chance he had with the woman standing in front of him. There was no sense holding back, though.

"Yesterday. Early. No one could tell me the nature of his injuries, but they're serious."

Alice paled.

"I left the ranch." Her words were almost a whisper, and she shook her head, as if realizing that wouldn't make sense to a stranger, but Jack was no stranger, and he knew exactly what she meant.

"It was an accident," he assured her automatically. "You didn't realize the others were gone." He'd expected tears, not this stillness. It unnerved him.

"Who told you that?" Something deeper than wariness crept into her face. Something that increased the distance between them, although she didn't move.

Jack saw no reason not to tell the truth. "Brian. He was worried about you. He said you took it hard."

For the first time, her veneer cracked. She touched the doorframe as if to steady herself, although she hadn't swayed. "I left the ranch—and now the General's hurt."

"But he's alive—that's the main thing, isn't it?"

"Tell me everything," Alice demanded.

"Maybe you should get your sisters, so I can tell everyone at once."

It was a moment before she nodded, but then she hesitated. They still stood in the doorway, icy wind blowing past them into the overheated house. She glanced down at the threshold between them. Jack knew what she was thinking. If she invited him inside, she would let him into her life. She knew what it meant when the General sent a man to Two Willows. When her gaze went beyond him to the snowy darkness outside, he held his breath. People's eyes tracked where their thoughts did. She was thinking of sending him away.

"Can I come in?" He edged forward, knowing the farther he made it into the house, the harder it would be for her to send him back outside. Knowing, too, a woman like Alice, raised to be hospitable despite her carefully crafted veneer, would find it hard to say no.

"*Should* I let you in?"

Her question caught him off guard. Jack swallowed. That was direct. It shifted the onus of the conversation back onto him. Strengthened her boundaries. He took in the hall behind her, knowing it led to a warm country kitchen with a bullet-scarred wooden table. Glanced to the left where the formal living room was packed with guests.

A white cat appeared in the hall, padded toward them and wound around Alice's legs.

She bent down absently and picked up the animal, touched noses with the feline, then turned to lean her cheek against the cat's fur. "Tabitha," she whispered and closed her eyes. "The General's hurt."

Jack heard a world of pain in her words, and something shifted in his chest. He was judging her too harshly. Alice wasn't as immune to the news he'd brought as she pretended. She was simply hiding her feelings in front of a stranger.

He understood that.

A sharp breeze wafting through the door brought the age-old smell of cattle and ranch, and something deep inside him tightened with a hunger so cellular he couldn't even think to fight it. He remembered his home, and the longing he felt was almost a physical thing.

Tabitha, still in Alice's arms, turned his way, her golden eyes assessing him. Without thinking, Jack reached out to stroke the cat's head.

Alice lifted her gaze, caught his, and they shared a moment acknowledging how much comfort a cat could give when the people around you were causing you pain.

There was far more to this woman than he'd given her credit for, Jack thought. She wasn't cold; she was human, and he'd just brought her bad news about her father. What had he expected? A welcome wagon?

He needed to give Alice a chance.

Wanted to give her one.

"Yes," he said. "You *should* let me in."

Something shifted in her eyes. He saw uncertainty, surprise—

Hope?

He took a step over the threshold, and Alice moved aside to make way for him.

He'd done it. He was inside Two Willows.

It was a start.

"YOU WERE DOING dishes? Why weren't you with the others?" Jack asked as they made their way to the kitchen. Alice set Tabitha down, and the cat ran lightly up the stairs.

"How did you know I was doing dishes?" Alice hurried to keep up with Jack, the skirts of her bridesmaid gown rustling. The General was injured. She couldn't get her thoughts to stop traveling in circles. Meanwhile, Jack kept going. He entered the kitchen and gestured at the stacks of dishes and soapy water, which he couldn't have seen from the hall.

"The guys say you ladies always do the dishes after the wedding reception."

"The reception isn't over."

"Your skirt is damp where you must have wiped your hands," he said a bit apologetically.

Alice looked down. The dampness was hardly visible. But that didn't matter. The General was coming home—after being gone eleven years.

Alice couldn't fathom it.

At one time he had come home often, of course, but she'd been a little girl then, and she—

Alice straightened, staring at Jack, remembering why he was really here. "You didn't come here to tell me about the General." She wasn't going to play games with this man. If the General had sent him to be her husband, that needed to be said out loud.

"You're right. That's not the only reason." Jack had crossed the room to look out the back window for a long moment before he realized she was watching him and turned to her.

But she'd seen the way he'd focused on the tall green hedges of the maze. Another piece fell into place in her mind. "You're the one with the drone," she accused, her temper flaring unexpectedly. "The one always spying. The one so insecure he has to cheat with the hedge maze!" The drone had appeared last summer, coming back daily and hovering over the tall hedges out back until Alice had told Lena to shoot it out of the sky. This was the man the General had sent for her? Someone who was trying to make a mockery of the maze—

and the standing stone at its heart?

Her mother had planted the maze around the stone, which had stood here longer than anyone's memory. Jack's idle curiosity was a threat to her mother's memory, and Alice didn't take kindly to that.

"The General sent me to help keep Two Willows safe. All of it. I can't protect something until I understand it."

"There's no understanding the maze," she told him. "That's the point of it."

"That doesn't make any sense."

"If you're looking for sense, you've come to the wrong place." Nothing about Two Willows was normal, least of all her.

The General was injured. Coming home.

Jack frowned. "If you can't understand something, it just means you haven't tried hard enough. I'm the kind of person who keeps trying until he figures things out."

Alice shook her head. Maybe the General had sent the right men for her sisters, but if he thought Jack would suit her, he'd made a major miscalculation.

Which was almost too bad, because Jack was… hot.

Not hot enough to marry, though. Not if he thought the whole world could be explained. She didn't have time for anyone who didn't believe in her abilities.

"Look," Jack said. "The General gave me something to give Lena before he went overseas. Can you get her for me? And everyone else, too." He showed her a little box, and Alice knew it would contain a locket like the ones the General had given Cass, Sadie and Jo.

It wasn't the gift that made Jack require her sisters' presence in the kitchen, though. It was his news.

The General was hurt.

Alice's heart beat hard as she threaded her way through the crowd to where Lena and Logan stood in front of the fireplace, chatting and laughing with guests. Each of them held a champagne flute in their hand and they looked so happy, Alice hated to intrude.

Lena spotted her first. She frowned. Set her glass on the mantel. "What is it?"

"The General—" To Alice's chagrin, now that she was away from Jack, tears filled her eyes. Her sisters and their husbands were the only ones she trusted enough to share her emotions with. "He's—"

Lena grabbed her arm and pulled her back the way Alice had come. "Logan," she snapped, and he blinked, drawn out of a conversation with one of the local cowboys. "Kitchen. Bring everyone."

In a moment the man was all business, and he'd already crossed to grab Brian and Cass by the time Alice and Lena made it back to Jack.

"Who's this?" Lena demanded.

Jack opened his mouth to answer, but Logan burst into the kitchen behind them, followed by the rest of the members of her family. Cass and Brian. Sadie and Connor. Jo and Hunter. "Sanders! You made it!" Logan cried.

All conversation in the house hushed at his loud exclamation, then picked up again quickly. Alice was glad no one but family had followed them into the room—well, except Wyoming, who was lurking in the doorway. But then, she was pretty much family, too.

"I see you've met Alice." Logan grinned and clapped Jack on the shoulder. He thought this all was a big joke, didn't he? Alice burned to think he expected her future was wrapped up and tied with a bow. It wasn't like that at all.

She couldn't explain the next words that came out of her mouth, except to blame them on the hysteria building in her throat. The General had been hurt, and she was sick of fate, sick of foreknowledge and the lack of it, sick of the forces that ran her life no matter what she wanted or tried to do. She was especially sick of men not believing her. Of them thinking they knew better than her.

The General had sent this man to marry her. Her own damn stupidity was bringing the General home, too. Together, he and Jack would close in on her. Determine her future. Herd her where she was supposed to go.

To hell with that. She was taking charge.

"Lena, this is Jack Sanders, the man I'm *not* going to marry. Jack, this is my sister Lena." There. Let them stew on that for a while.

"*Not* going to marry?" Lena said. "But—"

"You asked her already?" Logan demanded of Jack. "You just got here. What were you thinking?"

"You've got no sense of timing," Sadie told him.

"Alice, are you sure—?" Cass began. Wyoming was fighting a grin. Alice knew Wye thought all of them were stark raving mad but loved them just the same.

"I'm positive." Alice crossed her arms, but as she did so, images chased through her mind, coming so quickly she couldn't stop them. A snowstorm. The hedge maze. Jack touching her cheek. Thayer's Jewelers. A ring. Her mother—

Alice forced the vision from her mind, met Cass's commiserating look and straightened her shoulders. She had a feeling Cass had guessed the direction her vision had taken.

"I didn't ask Alice to marry me. She's jumping the gun turning me down. She doesn't have all the facts yet, and as she knows darn well she should wait until she does."

Alice pulled back. What was that supposed to mean?

"What's the news from USSOCOM?" Logan asked heartily, obviously trying to shift the mood. Jack blinked, as if he'd forgotten why he was here, and a fresh wave of regret washed through Alice. The General was hurt. And she was playing games.

She opened her mouth to answer but found she couldn't put the news into words. As the others crowd-ed around, her lungs tightened in her chest. There were too many people in the kitchen. Too much chaos in her mind. Images sped through her brain again, glinting like shattered glass, too sharp and too many to grasp. The General. Desert heat. Drifts of snow. An explosion. A gunshot. Alice couldn't tell if she was seeing past or future—or both.

"Alice?" Cass cried as Alice wavered.

Jack appeared at her shoulder. "Hey, you okay?" When she couldn't answer, he put an arm around her, steadying her as she fought for air.

She should have pushed him away, but his strength was somehow comforting. Alice found herself breathing with him, wondering how he'd known she was panicking almost before she did.

"What's going on? Are you sick?" Cass asked her.

"I'm fine—" Alice gasped.

"It's my fault," Jack said. He kept his arm around Alice but faced the others. "I brought bad news."

"What is it?" Cass's sharp tone made Alice wince.

"The General was wounded in a missile strike," Jack said bluntly. "He's alive but injured," he rushed to add. "I'd imagine he'll have a long recovery ahead of him, but it could have been worse."

As he talked, Alice fought to get her emotions under control. She wasn't a clingy woman, but right now she was struggling to stay on her feet. The room was dipping and swaying, the blood rushing in her ears as she imagined the blast that took down the General—

It could have been worse. Jack's words echoed in her mind. It could have been deadly, that's what he meant. She could have lost her father—

Darkness clouded her vision.

"Woah, you'd better sit down." Jack lifted her suddenly, as if she weighed nothing. Alice, startled, could only link her arms around his neck and hold on. His jacket was rough under her cheek. He smelled of soap and something masculine. The muscles of his arms supported her as if he was used to carrying women around from place to place.

He set her down on one of the chairs, and Lena moved swiftly to prop open the back door, letting in an icy breeze. Cass fetched her a glass of water.

"You okay?" Jo asked, crouching beside her.

This was the explanation for her dread. She'd known something bad was going to happen; she just hadn't been able to pinpoint it. Of course the General had been injured—she'd left the ranch without making sure any of the others were home.

"You don't know what kind of injuries the General has sustained?" Cass asked Jack.

Jack shook his head. "I'm afraid not."

"He's coming here?" Lena asked.

Jack nodded. "Eventually. I'll help you get ready for him."

Lena turned to Logan. "We can't leave—"

"Of course you can. Go to the Bahamas. Relax and recharge," Cass said. Alice, taking another sip of water and setting the glass down on the table, agreed with her; Lena deserved her honeymoon.

"From the sound of it, it'll take some time before the General is transferred stateside," Jack said. "Plenty of time for you two to go on your honeymoon."

So there was at least a week before the General came home, Alice thought, relaxing a little. Her vision cleared and her breathing slowed. Lena and Logan weren't due back until next Sunday.

Lena nodded. "I can't picture him here."

"I can't picture you in the Bahamas," Alice told her, trying to break the tension. This was Lena's wedding. She didn't deserve this kind of drama. "Have you ever relaxed a day in your life?"

"Nope." Lena grinned, but her smile quickly faltered. She pulled herself together. "Is he really going to be okay?" she asked Jack.

"The General? He's a tough old goat. His wounds will heal."

Alice couldn't help exchanging a look with her sisters. The General's physical wounds would heal, but what about his emotional ones? The pain that had kept him away from his home for so many years?

She had a feeling Jack was right; the General would come home, but would he stay?

She had no idea.

"We need to look to our guests," Cass said suddenly. "We need to end this wedding on a positive note. No talk of the General until after. Logan, dance with your bride."

Logan jumped into action, but Lena hesitated.

"Go on," Jack urged her. "As soon as I hear about the General's progress, I'll pass it on. I don't think there's going to be any more news tonight."

"Do it for your guests," Alice told Lena, but she hoped her sister could manage to enjoy the dance herself.

Lena and Logan headed for the living room, and a minute later a jaunty pop song started up. Alice wondered if Cass's ban would work. She had no doubt news of the General's injuries would spread fast. Speculation about what would happen next would spread even faster.

In the past few months she and her sisters had finally taken their true place in town, entering into relationships with other folks after an upbringing that kept them mostly on the ranch. Still, people were curious about the Reeds. How could they not be? In a sleepy town like Chance Creek, gossip ruled supreme.

"Hey," Jack said softly, bending down and taking her hand. "How about we go join them?"

The touch of his fingers fired off a trace of awareness through her body. As much as she didn't want to react to the man, Jack stirred her senses. He was handsome. Alert. Assured. "I don't—"

"Come on. You love dancing."

He didn't give her a chance to say no. She let him pull her up and lead her into the living room, but that last phrase kept running through her head. What did Jack mean by that? Did he think she loved dancing because lots of young women did? Or did he know she loved dancing—

The way he'd known she was doing dishes when he arrived.

Did he get hunches, too?

A frisson of cold, then heat surged up and down her spine. Was Jack psychic?

She nearly pulled away, but when Jack swept her into his arms and tugged her in tight against his body, Alice forgot everything else. Images cascaded through her brain one after the other, almost too quickly to comprehend. Reverend Halpern standing at an altar, Jack standing close by, waiting. A starry night. A ring on her finger. Jack's mouth on hers—

Was her future sealed already? Did she have to marry him?

When Alice pushed him away, several other couples turned toward them. Jack came after her. Caught her hand.

"Alice."

She took a deep breath, aware of everyone looking. Aware Lena's happiness was already on thin ice.

"Easy," Jack murmured. He drew her into the circle of his arms but held them apart, as if they were in junior high at their first dance. "We can take it slow."

Alice laughed, but tears stung her eyes again. Slow? If that vision was to be trusted, it was already a done deal. The same fate that never told her the important things—like when her mother might have a stroke or the General might be struck by a missile—had just made it clear what her future held. Jack would be her husband, no matter what she wanted.

Jack slowed, although he didn't stop. He bent closer. When he spoke, his voice was far gentler than it had been so far.

"I'm sorry I brought such upsetting news. I'm glad to meet you. I should have said that before."

Alice looked up. "Why?"

"Because I'm beginning to think you're not the woman I thought you were at all."

HELL, WHY HAD he said that? He was losing his touch, Jack thought. You didn't give information like that to the enemy; not if you didn't want them to—

He stopped. Enemy? Alice wasn't the enemy.

At least, she shouldn't be.

Alice's eyes widened. "What kind of woman did you think I was?"

Jack shifted his hands, appreciating the feel of a woman in his arms. It had been a while. "The kind who holds back."

Alice thought this over. "I do hold back. Not everyone is to be trusted."

"Too true." Jack chuckled. "Come on, let's just dance for a bit. We've got to start somewhere if we're going to get to know each other." He tugged her a little closer, until she was back in the circle of his arms. He could just about feel her mind working overtime, though. He was right, she was just like him. She was analyzing what he'd said. Trying to find the patterns that explained him, the same way he sought for order in a chaotic world.

She wasn't the cold fish he'd expected, though. Neither was she haughty. Beneath her beauty there was fire, but you only got to see it if Alice trusted you.

Jack realized he wanted to earn her trust.

Nestled against his chest, she was soft and more entrancing than he cared to admit. His body was stirring in anticipation of getting closer to her. He'd spent half a year at USSOCOM unsure about his future. Keeping to himself.

Maybe a bit too much to himself.

When Alice relaxed against him, he murmured, "That's more like it," but when she chuckled softly, he went on high alert. "What?"

"The General and his matchmaking. Do they teach that in the Army?"

"They didn't teach it to me."

"Did you have to audition for the part?"

"Which part?" He slowed down again.

"The part of my husband."

Jack's gut tightened. That simple sentence told him he hadn't made as much progress as he'd thought. She'd already drawn the battle lines between them. "Not quite."

"How'd you get it, then?"

"You really want to know?" He began to move again, and Alice fell in with his rhythm as if they'd done this many times before.

"I asked, didn't I?"

He supposed she had. Jack chose his words carefully. "I did the right thing, instead of the thing I was supposed to do."

Alice thought that over. "So the General's criteria for my husband was that he had to be a renegade?"

Jack laughed out loud, making people turn toward them again. "Pretty much," he murmured against her ear and allowed himself to enjoy the rest of the dance.

Lena and Logan left early, Lena still protesting that they should stay, although from what he knew of Reed family history, she resented the General even more than her sisters, so it wasn't an overwhelming desire to see the man that prompted her concern. "The General had better not steal the ranch back from me while I'm gone," she kept saying as Logan ushered her into the taxi that would take them to the airport. Jack knew she'd waited years to run the cattle operation her way, and she was adamant no one else could do it as well.

"You'll be home before he is," Jack assured her, although he had no idea if that was true. Logan whisked her away, and the celebration broke up soon after. When Jack found his way into the kitchen again, the women were cleaning up.

"Where is the General going to sleep when he gets here?" Cass exclaimed suddenly.

"His bedroom," Jo answered, then slowed her motions as she finished drying a plate. She turned to her sister, and Cass shook her head.

"It's full of Mom's stuff. He won't want to see that."

"If his injuries are serious, he won't be taking those stairs, anyway," Jack said. "Do you have a room on the first floor?"

Cass frowned. "It'll have to be his office, I guess. But there's so much furniture in there, we'll never fit a bed."

"We can swap it with the furniture from your parents' bedroom," Brian said. He turned to the other men. "Let's get to it."

"Now?" Connor asked.

"No time like the present. There's too many of us to

all fit in the kitchen." He sent Jack a significant look, and Jack got the message: give the women some time alone to process the news.

Jo and Alice collected all the champagne flutes and dessert plates from the living room and brought them into the kitchen. The tables and chairs they'd used for the dinner had already been folded up and stacked out in the carriage house. Alice grabbed a broom and started sweeping the room.

Jack followed Brian and Connor upstairs, but when they entered the master bedroom, they both stopped. Connor gave a low whistle. The room was as tidy as a hotel room, every surface dusted, but its cleanliness couldn't cover the disused feeling that emanated from it.

"When do you think is the last time anyone slept here?" Connor asked.

"Eleven years ago." Jack was certain he was right. By all accounts, the General hadn't set foot on the ranch again since Alice's mother's death. "It's a shrine," he went on. Alice and her sisters must have left it exactly as it stood that day. He wasn't sure it was right to move anything, and he didn't know what he would have done if Cass hadn't come into the room, too.

"It's okay," she said. "You can move the bed down."

"I'm sorry for your loss." It was a stupid thing to say eleven years late, but Jack still felt compelled to say it.

"Thank you. My mother is still as real to me as she ever was. It's a good idea putting the General downstairs. He never wanted to come home. I'm not sure how he'd stand seeing this."

"Coming home might be the first step to healing."

"Maybe." She slipped out.

"Let's get going," Connor said, and Jack moved to help him. He was relieved when they maneuvered the mattress out of the room. He could breathe better out here in the hall. "When I said yes to this gig, I never thought about the fact the General would be my father-in-law."

"Can't say I did, either."

"Still worth it," Connor added with a grin. "Wouldn't trade my life here for anything."

Jack's chest constricted. He wanted to feel that, too, but Alice had already refused him—before he'd gotten the chance to propose. Not an auspicious beginning.

"LENA TOOK ME aside before she left and made me promise not to let the General take over," Alice told Cass when her sister came downstairs again. "I was sure she'd make that taxi turn around before they even made it down the driveway. She's positive the General only got hurt as an excuse to come and take control."

"That's not true," Cass reproved her.

"It's what she said."

"I'm glad it's November," Sadie said. "He won't be able to see the gardens. I know they're nothing like they were when Mom was here."

"I just can't imagine how I'm going to run the house with him underfoot. We've barely talked in years. It'll be like living with a stranger," Cass added.

"A stranger who thinks he owns the place," Jo said darkly.

"Well, in his defense, he does," Cass pointed out.

"He gave up his right to call the shots here a long time ago," Alice said. "He must know that."

"He just sent you a husband." Sadie lifted her hands. "There's no telling what he thinks he's allowed to do."

Alice's phone vibrated in her pocket, and she pulled it out. "It's Landon Clark." She shushed everyone else and answered it. In all the excitement she hadn't thought about the movie producer all night, and she certainly hadn't expected to hear from him this late, although this wasn't the first time he'd called at an unusual hour. He tended to check in once or twice a week.

"Alice? How are those costumes going?"

"Just about done." She slipped out of the kitchen and ran lightly up the stairs to her room, flattening her back against the wall as several of the men, including Jack, carried a box spring past her. In her room, Tabitha was curled on her bed. "My sister's wedding was today," she reminded him. "I planned to finish my gowns in the next few days, but I might have to push that back. I'll still have them done in plenty of time before your arrival, of course." Landon wasn't due to come see the costumes for several more weeks.

"What's the hitch in your plans?" Below the courteous question, Alice caught a thread of displeasure, and her grip tightened on the phone. She wanted this commission so badly she could taste it. Landon was new to the movie industry, but he was intent on bursting onto the scene with a blockbuster hit. He'd scored big with cryptocurrency, or so he'd told her—Alice wasn't entirely sure what that was—and now he was pursuing his real dream. The script he'd optioned was a Civil War drama with a cast of thousands, and it called for scores of historically accurate costumes, which was where Alice came in. He'd invited her to apply for the position of lead costume designer and had given her an ample allowance with which to create the three ball gowns to showcase her skills.

It was all highly irregular.

Alice was thrilled.

The Civil War meant hoopskirts. Alice loved hoopskirts. The sheer audacity of them fired up her imagination. She'd spent weeks designing the dresses and was almost done sewing them—

"The General. My… father," she clarified. How strange to use a term she hadn't spoken in years. "He's been wounded in action. He's coming home in a few days, and we need to get ready." Surely he'd understand that.

Landon didn't answer, and the silence stretched out so long she would have thought he'd hung up if she hadn't been able to hear him breathing on the other end of the line. "I see," Landon said finally. "The thing is, Alice, my plans have changed, too. I've had to move up my visit."

"To when?" Alice's stomach twisted. This couldn't be happening.

"Saturday."

Alice did the math. "You're coming here… in seven days?" She paced across the room and peered out into the darkness at the carriage house across the way, which contained her studio. "You weren't supposed to come for another three weeks!"

"Alice, I hope you weren't waiting until the last minute. That doesn't bode well—"

"Of course not," she rushed to say. "The gowns are done except for some detail work," she lied, "but… my sister just got married. And like I said, my father's been injured—"

A long pause greeted her explanation, and Alice braced for another lecture on professionalism. What did Landon care about the General?

"What day does he arrive?" Landon asked finally.

"I'm not sure. Next week, maybe." She really had no idea.

"Then that's settled. Saturday it is. I'll be there and gone before you know it, and you can give your father your full attention when he arrives. Don't you think that's best?"

"I… guess so." She couldn't lose this chance, but she'd have to work 24/7 to finish off the gowns. So be it, she told herself. No wonder she'd felt doomed. First her father's injuries. Now this. "What time will you be arriving?"

"Around noon."

"Then I'll be ready by noon on Saturday," she said resolutely. "Where will you be staying?"

"In town. I'll send you all the details."

Just like that, he was gone, leaving Alice to stare out her bedroom window. Landon Clark in Chance Creek?

A swooping feeling made Alice clutch the back of her desk chair as images filled her mind. The General. Shouting. Gunfire.

The vision cleared, leaving Alice slightly ill. She closed her eyes and forced her breathing to slow down. The General was in Germany. He was safe, she reminded herself. Still, the last thing she needed was for Landon to come now.

Opportunity knocked when it knocked, though. Time to get out to her studio and get to work.

Chapter Three

"WHO'S SHE TALKING to?" Jack asked no one in particular as he lugged his end of the box spring awkwardly down the stairs.

"Be careful," Wyoming said, meeting them at the bottom. "And that was Landon Clark on the phone for Alice. The movie producer guy."

"You should have known that, Jack. Aren't you keeping tabs on everyone?" Connor crashed into the wall, shifted his grip on the box spring and swore. They made it into the living room and put it next to the mattress they'd already carried down.

"Let's go get the frame," Brian said. "Then we can lug some of the office furniture up there."

"What do you think about this Landon guy?" Jack asked.

"Haven't met him. Only heard a few things from Cass, but Alice sure seems excited about him. Sounds like it could be her big break."

Connor followed Jack back upstairs. "What's it going to be like having the old man around, do you think? Will he stay?"

"That's the million-dollar question," Brian said.

Hunter nodded. "Sure is going to be interesting around here."

Jack couldn't help wondering how the General's presence would affect his chances with Alice. He wished he had more time to get to know her before the man arrived. Jack could only imagine how things would play out. A woman who'd been feuding with her father for years wasn't going to be in the mood for romance under these circumstances.

Which meant he'd better woo her now.

By the time they'd shuttled the office furniture upstairs and replaced it with the bed, bed stands and dresser, however, Alice was nowhere in sight.

"She's gone to her studio," Wyoming said when he came looking for her in the kitchen. She and Cass were still washing and drying dishes. Sadie was running a broom around the room. Jo was getting ready to take out the trash. "So you're Alice's husband-to-be, huh?" Wyoming scrutinized him.

"You'd better treat my sister right," Cass said to him as she handed a glass to Wye. "What made the General pick you?"

Jack had no idea how to answer that. It was a question he'd asked himself plenty of times. "Maybe he thinks we're alike."

Cass exchanged a look with Sadie. "Are you psychic?"

"Hardly." Jack shifted uncomfortably. "But then I highly doubt Alice is either."

"Oh, this is going to be fun." Wyoming turned to Cass. "I'm definitely staying for as long as you'll have me."

"Where should I sleep tonight?" he asked Cass. "Any couch will do." When in doubt, play the gentleman, he thought.

"We're putting Wyoming in Jo's old room," Cass said. "Jack, you'll take the spare room."

"Are you sure?" Jack asked.

"Works for me." Wye grinned at Jack. "Getting to watch you chase Alice almost makes up for getting canned yesterday."

"Don't forget Will's coming back soon. Maybe it'll be a double wedding," Cass told her.

Wyoming rolled her eyes. "Will's cute, but we haven't determined he's marriage material yet." She looked Jack over again. "We're reserving judgment on you, too, so behave yourself."

"Yes, ma'am." Jack saluted and got the hell out of there.

ALICE LOOKED UP from the lace she was stitching onto a lilac gown when she heard footsteps on the carriage house stairs and sighed when Jack came into view, ignoring the little extra thump her heart gave at the sight of his handsome face. She wished she could study him without him knowing. Get a good long look at the man the General had thought she should spend the rest of her life with.

"Am I interrupting?" Jack moved into the large studio and looked around him. She wondered what he thought about what he saw. Racks and racks of costumes she'd designed and sewed ringed the space. Large worktables filled the center. A long row of floor-to-ceiling windows lined one wall. In the daytime, sunlight poured through them, making the space delightful—and hot in the summer. Tabitha had joined her and was sleeping on an easy chair that sat in one corner.

"I'm trying to finish some work that's due in a few days."

"For Landon?"

Alice let her needle drop. "How do you know about Landon?"

"Brian told me."

Brian seemed to have told Jack everything. She picked up her needle again and got back to work, but it was hard to ignore the man prowling around her workroom.

"Did you sew all of these?"

"Yes."

He turned, taking in all the racks. "That's a lot of sewing."

"It's what I do."

"Did your mother teach you?"

Alice's stitches slowed. "Yes, the basics, anyway. I taught myself the rest."

Jack came to stand nearby and looked the mannequin up and down. "You'd look pretty in that dress."

"It's not meant for me." But he was right; it would fit her well, except for its length. Marlene Avarro, the actress Landon wanted to sign on for the lead female role, was far taller than her, but their proportions were about the same.

"Is it for someone specific?"

She chose her words carefully. "Landon has an actress in mind for the lead. He wants to bribe her with costumes. I'm supposed to make three ball gowns so he can get an idea of my work—and in the hopes one of them will prove irresistible to her."

"You're not going to say who it is?"

"I signed an NDA." She shrugged and bent back over the hem, glad for the excuse to hide her face. It was hard to disguise what she was feeling—a mixture of curiosity, resentment and… well… lust, if she was honest. Jack was… lustworthy.

Had the General realized that?

Ick.

"Got it." He sat down on the edge of a nearby table and watched her work. "Do you like it here? In Chance Creek?"

Alice's fingers slowed again. "Of course. It's my home."

"You never think of leaving?"

"Sometimes."

Was it her imagination, or was Jack turning her answer over in his mind? "Where would you go?"

"Hollywood. That's where all the work is, right?"

"You're a city girl at heart? Is that it?" He was teasing her, but she had a feeling the question was more serious than he was letting on. What did he really want to know?

A vision struck her, and she got a glimpse of the two of them riding horses over snowy ground.

Then it was gone.

But the scene left a feeling behind Alice was all too familiar with. An aching kind of bittersweet pleasure that came with living on a property your family had owned for generations. On the one hand, it held you in place, whether you wanted it to or not. On the other hand, it was so sweet when you knew your home through and through. She loved this ranch. Always had.

"No, I'm not a city girl. I'm just… looking for a change, I guess. I've lived here all my life."

"How about I take you somewhere special on our honeymoon, and we call it good?" She turned on him, and he raised his hands in a placating gesture. "Right, right—I forgot. I'm the man you're *not* going to marry."

"That's right."

"Why not?"

"Maybe I don't want to."

"Why don't you want to?"

"Maybe I feel trapped," she said, then wished she hadn't. "Maybe I don't want a man calling the shots. Maybe I want to be able to go where I want to."

Jack stilled. He was paying her far too much attention. Alice felt he could see right through her. "That's more important than family?"

Alice felt like he'd kicked her in the gut. That was the dilemma, wasn't it? Freedom or family. "I don't know," she said honestly, although the idea of ever leaving her sisters behind left her gutted.

He nodded after a moment. "I've had enough of travel. I want a real home."

"What about family?"

"I want that, too."

JACK WANTED ALICE. Wanted to get to know her, anyway. Wanted the rest of the bargain the General had offered him: part of a ranch, the camaraderie of living with the other men and their wives.

But Alice wanted to leave.

"When do you have to get this done by?" He nodded to the dress, trying to steer the conversation to safer ground.

She sighed. "Saturday. Noon. That's when Landon's getting here."

"Why's he coming here?"

"I think he wants to see my studio and get a feel for how I work. This is a huge commission. He needs to know I'm up for it. I'm not sure I am," she admitted. "I'm going to have to hire out a lot of the work. I've never done that before."

"Landon's coming here in seven days," Jack repeated. Which meant all Alice's time would be taken up trying to impress the man. "How long is he staying?" When the General arrived home, he figured Alice's attention would be taken up by her father.

Jack couldn't help wondering if the General would change his mind about this mission when he got here and made up with his girls. Why would he need Jack then? If the General sent him away, he'd be right back where he started from—in trouble with the Army, unsure about his future. He didn't want to backtrack like that.

"I don't know." Alice tied off the thread and snipped it close with a tiny pair of scissors. She got to her feet. "I've got to get these dresses done, and I need to help Cass get ready for the General, too. It's going to be a busy few days."

Her meaning was clear. It was time for him to leave.

He didn't want to. Being close to Alice was reminding him he was a man who hadn't been with a woman for far too long.

"If I lived on a ranch like Two Willows, I'd never leave," he confessed. Montana was different from New Mexico, but that didn't matter. He didn't need to return to the ghosts of his family; he wanted to move forward, taking along with him all of the happy memories.

He wanted to make some new ones.

"If?" Alice asked him. "So you're not sure about marrying me either?"

"No one knows what the future will bring."

Alice stilled. "I do."

THAT WAS THE whole problem, Alice thought. The General had sent Jack to marry her, and judging by what had happened with her sisters, chances were she would, even if she didn't want to. Then there was the vision she'd had of Jack standing at the altar, Reverend Halpern ready to perform the ceremony. She hadn't been in that vision, she realized. But Jack was going to marry someone in Chance Creek. It didn't take a psychic to guess who.

If there wasn't so much pressure on the situation, maybe she'd be able to enjoy getting to know this handsome man, Alice reflected. Maybe she'd fall for him bit by bit. Maybe he'd turn out to be exactly the kind of sexy, funny, smart man she would have picked for herself—if she'd been allowed to pick for herself.

Or maybe he wouldn't, and they'd drift apart.

That was the way people were supposed to find their husbands. Their father wasn't supposed to send them a man. Visions weren't supposed to make the outcome a foregone conclusion.

Am I attracted to Jack because I think I'm supposed to be? Or because I really am? She couldn't be sure.

Which made it impossible to simply follow her instincts—especially the ones urging her to close the distance between them.

"You're thinking about kissing me."

Jack's assertion brought her back up straight. "No, I'm not!"

"You leaned toward me. Your gaze was on my mouth. Doesn't take a mind-reader to know what you wanted. That's the way you work, too, right? Reading the cues that people give you?"

Alice recoiled. "That's not it at all."

"Come on, Alice. I won't tell."

He was serious, she realized. He thought she'd spent years cultivating a reputation that was a lie. "I'm not like you," she spat out. "Spying on people and using what you learn against them."

It was Jack's turn to pull back, but before he could defend himself, she waved him away. "Landon's coming in seven days, and I've got a lot of work to do."

After a moment Jack nodded. "Fine. I'll let you get back to it, but you don't know as much about me as you think you do."

"And you don't know me at all."

Chapter Four

IT WAS AFTER two in the morning when the knocking woke him.

Jack surged awake and found his feet on the floor, his hands reaching for his firearm—which was locked away in a safe. He nearly knocked Alice's photograph off his bedside table before he realized he was in Montana. He took another second to listen for the source of the knocking. He could swear it hadn't come from the direction of the door.

Had it come from the wall he shared with Alice's bedroom?

He listened hard and heard the quiet sound of a door shutting. Had Alice been in the hallway after all?

Did she want him?

Jack pulled on a pair of sweatpants, opened his door quietly and padded the few steps to Alice's room. "Alice?" he asked softly.

"Who's that?"

He heard a flurry of movement from his left as he opened her door and moved into the room, and he could make out Alice's form on her bed in the dim light.

She was clutching her covers to her chin, her shoulders bare. Did Alice sleep in the nude?

Interesting.

"It's Jack. What did you want?"

"What do you mean?" She relaxed—a little, but still clutched at her covers.

He shut the door behind him so as not to wake everyone else. "You knocked on the wall."

"No, I—" Alice laughed softly. "It's the pipes. They do that when someone uses the water in the upstairs bathroom. I just came in from my studio. I was getting ready for bed."

"So you weren't trying to lure me over here for salacious purposes?"

"Alas, no." Her voice was softer in the darkness than it had been earlier in the carriage house. Jack warmed to the sound of it. He found he wanted her to keep talking.

"But what happens if you want to someday?" he asked. "How will I be able to tell your salacious purposes knock from the knocking of the pipes?"

"My salacious purposes knock is very distinctive," she assured him. She was a vision with her hair tumbled about her bare shoulders. He liked discovering she had a sense of humor.

"You'll have to demonstrate."

"I'll do that. Tomorrow, when everyone is awake."

"I'll demonstrate mine, too."

"I'm pretty sure men don't get to have salacious purposes knocks."

"Huh. That seems unfair."

"Men would just overuse them."

Jack chuckled. Too true.

He knew it was time to let Alice sleep, but he hesitated, a hand on the doorknob. "See you in the morning."

"Good night." She shifted down under the covers, and Jack thought he'd carry the image of her nestled in her bed for the rest of his life. His whole body ached to join her there. Back in his own bed, it took him a long time to fall back to sleep.

All too soon, though, Jack woke to the smell of a delicious breakfast cooking. When he made it downstairs, Cass was presiding over the stove, frying eggs. A pan of sausages was already on the table, along with orange and apple slices and a plate of toast. Wyoming was setting the table. Sadie was pouring herself some coffee.

"Help yourself," Cass said. "Sit anywhere. We don't stand on ceremony at breakfast."

"Thanks." He took a seat across from Connor and began to fill his plate.

Brian was seated at the head of the table. Sadie was on the other side of Connor.

"Where's Jo and Hunter?" he asked, before he remembered they'd be in their own little house they'd built together before the snow came.

"They eat breakfast on their own," Cass said crisply, and Jack wondered if that was a bone of contention. Cass seemed the mother-hen type. Had it bothered her when one of her sisters escaped the nest?

"What about Alice?"

"She's already in her studio." Cass sent a worried look out the window toward the carriage house. "There was a plate in the sink when I got up. She must have grabbed a bite early this morning."

"She's worried about Landon," Sadie said. "She shouldn't be; who wouldn't hire Alice after they see what she can do?"

"Have you looked into this guy?" Jack asked Brian.

Brian shook his head swiftly, and Jack got the message. Not here, in front of the women. Save that conversation for another time.

"Just wondering what other movies he's made." Jack tried to cover his tracks.

"He hasn't made any other movies," Sadie said. "He's new to this, but he seems to have a lot of cash to throw around. Alice is going to be rich."

"Alice is already rich."

When everyone looked his way, Jack realized he'd said that out loud. "She's got all of you. This ranch. A job she loves."

"You're right," Cass said softly. "It's a good life. But you missed something. She's got ambition, too. She's a master at what she does. She deserves recognition for that."

"I guess." He didn't like the idea of Alice's ambition taking her away from Chance Creek—and him. After their conversation last night, Jack realized he'd utterly misjudged Alice. She could be warm. Funny.

Sexy.

The kind of woman he'd love to spend time with.

Would her ambition get in the way?

He finished his breakfast, thanked Cass, pulled on his outer gear and followed the other men outside, just in time to see a sheriff's cruiser pull up and a tall bear of a man climb out.

"Morning, Cab. You're out early," Brian called as they went to greet the sheriff. Jack had heard about the man from the others. Had looked him up on the internet, too. In person, the sheriff was imposing, but Jack knew he was on their side and took the trouble that had plagued Two Willows seriously.

"Wanted to get a word in with you before my day starts. Got another update from my associates out East."

From Tennessee, Jack thought. This had to do with the attacks on the ranch.

"I knew you were busy with the wedding yesterday, so I saved the news, but when I heard about the General, I knew I'd better come fill you in. Ron Cooper died about a week ago. So did Duke Manson, who we've learned headed the organization that's been targeting Two Willows."

Jack straightened. "Do you think that's the end of it?"

"No," Cab said bluntly. "I don't. Paul Ramsey and Beau Ellis are still out there somewhere. We don't know who's going to fill Manson's shoes, but someone will. That someone's probably coming after you." He turned to Jack. "Heard you're a whiz with surveillance."

"That's right. I'll be installing a security system. General's orders."

"Good to know."

When Cab was gone, Jack and the other men walked on to the barn.

"I'll get that surveillance system up ASAP," Jack told Brian, Connor and Hunter. "Motion detectors, cameras. We'll be able to keep an eye on everything from our command center."

"This is a big ranch," Hunter pointed out.

"It'll be a big surveillance system," Jack assured him. "Twenty-four/seven coverage of the whole damn ranch."

"The whole ranch?" Connor guffawed. "Just don't bug the bathrooms. A man's got to have a little privacy."

"Or the bedrooms," Hunter put in. "Already punched one guy out for trying to film Jo."

Jack brought the conversation back from going too far astray. "Just figure if you're outside, you're being watched."

Brian scratched his head. "Not sure if I like that."

"Doesn't matter if you like it. All that matters is we catch this guy—before he does any harm to Two Willows."

No one could argue with that.

"SINCE THE GENERAL is coming home, does that mean we can all leave the ranch?" Jo asked suddenly. Alice's sisters had appeared in her workshop mid-morning, except Lena, of course, whom Alice hoped was already lounging on a hot beach—or maybe still in bed with her brand-new husband. Wyoming was perched on one of the worktables, playing with a scrap of silk. She glanced up at their conversation but didn't say anything. She knew all about their superstition.

"Do you want to leave the ranch?" Alice asked. She couldn't pretend she hadn't asked herself the same question. They'd already broken their mother's promise, and the General had already paid the price. What else could happen?

"You agreed to stay," Cass reminded her. "We all did."

She was right. Alice went back to work, joining a rosette to the peach-colored gown she was working on with tiny stitches. They'd made their promise in front of the standing stone in the hedge maze the day that they'd all mistakenly left the ranch at once. At the time Alice had thought she was the only one wrestling with the decision. If she wanted to advance her career, she'd have to be willing to travel.

Her hunches, as usual, were of no help whatsoever. She got flashes of sewing elaborate costumes, but nothing concrete. When she tried to picture the movie itself, her vision gave her as little information as Landon's emails did.

She turned at the sound of heavy footsteps on the stairs. It had to be one of the men. Was everyone going to spend the morning in her workshop? She needed to get these dresses done.

"It's too early for lunch," Cass called out as Jack came into the studio.

"I know. Just giving you a head's up. I'll be installing a—"

"Surveillance system," Alice finished for him, a vision taking over her sight. Drones. Cameras. Sensors. "You'd better not surveil my maze."

"*Our* maze," Cass said.

Wyoming lifted a brow but didn't say a word. Alice had a feeling their antics often amused her.

"What's in the maze?" Jack challenged her.

"Why don't you go find out?" She folded her arms over her chest.

He hesitated, and she suppressed a smile. Was he afraid he couldn't make it through there? Afraid to make a fool of himself by not being able to find its center without cheating first?

She had another flash—he didn't like not knowing. Because not knowing was dangerous.

Alice faltered.

Jack had known danger before.

A second later she was scoffing at herself. Of course he'd known danger. He was in the military. Special Forces, she guessed.

But what she'd felt was different. Personal. What had happened to him?

"Well?" she asked again, but her bravado was sinking fast. "Why don't you go find out?"

"Fine. I will."

GOING IN BLIND. If there was one thing Jack hated, it was proceeding without a plan. What made him a good analytics officer was the fact that he always had all the information, always factored in everything that could go wrong and always stuck to the objectives, no matter what the heat of battle threw at him.

At least, he had until his last mission.

In his mind he could see Lila's dark eyes, her watchful expression, her small form waiting in the back room of a compound in Afghanistan, as if she'd already tallied up her chances and decided she had none.

Jack knew sometimes you had to go rogue. Break the rules. But he still didn't like it.

He had no idea how Alice had managed to block his drone from flying over the hedge maze when he'd been trying so hard to see inside it. He'd managed to hire a local kid, who was short on cash and long on time, to operate the drone remotely and fly it over Two Willows. He'd been able to map out every square acre of the property, except for the square that comprised the maze.

Brian, Connor and the others had all told him about Alice's hunches and the way she foretold the future sometimes. They were trained, competent men who shouldn't have been the kind to believe in fairy tales. He'd looked into the matter further and managed to find other people in Chance Creek willing to talk about Alice. They, too, believed in her abilities.

It wasn't until he'd watched the footage from the drone, seen it approach the maze again and again and be stopped each time by some invisible, implacable force, that he began to wonder if more was going on.

He wished he knew what the General thought about Alice and her abilities. People apparently had believed Amelia could tell the future, too. In fact, many said she'd been far better at it than Alice was. Did Amelia Reed have more to her story than people were saying? Was she involved in the intelligence community somehow? Had she used the claim that she never left Two Willows to cover up for some secret life?

Jack shook his head. He couldn't square that with what he'd experienced with Janet. Ask anyone about Amelia, and you'd get a litany of praise about her gentle ways, her devotion to her family and her herbal cures. Janet had never been able to cultivate that kind of cover. She'd barely been home.

Still, even if Amelia wasn't secretly a spy, Alice had somehow managed to jam the drone. He wanted to know how. It had nothing to do with psychic abilities, though. He was sure of that.

Hell, if either woman could really see the future, a good soldier like the General would have reported their capabilities to the military. Wouldn't that be a coup?

"Well?" Alice challenged him.

"Let's go."

"Fine. I don't have time for this, just so you know."

"We'll be quick."

"That's our cue, ladies," Cass said. "Time to get back to work."

Everyone put on their outer gear and trooped outside. Jack was afraid all the women would follow them to the maze, but Cass ushered Sadie, Jo and Wyoming into the house. He was happy to be alone with Alice finally, despite their showdown. Sunlight was glinting off the snow. The evergreen hedge maze loomed tall above them, its green walls so high that you couldn't even see into them from the upstairs windows of the house. Alice led the way to an entrance into the broad green expanse and gestured for him to go forward.

"You're the one who knows the way to the center," he told her.

"You're the one with the drones," she replied sweetly.

"Which you managed to prevent from flying over the maze. How did you do that, anyway?" He didn't really expect her to answer.

She simply shrugged and stepped through the opening into the maze. Jack relaxed a bit; he'd been afraid she'd leave him to take the lead and would laugh at him as he blundered through it, taking all the wrong turns. Not a great start to a relationship.

Jack shoved his hands in his pockets as the idea of a relationship with Alice solidified in his mind in a way it hadn't previously. Alice had turned out to be far more compelling than he'd expected. They were all wrong for each other. That didn't stop him from wanting to know more about her.

Alice turned back, waiting for him, watching him through beautiful, inscrutable eyes, and he wondered what was going on in her mind. Last night she had announced she wouldn't marry him. Was there anything he could do to change her mind?

He wanted to change her mind, he decided. Wanted at least to spend enough time with her that they both could make a sensible decision about their future.

"Are you coming?" she asked, watching him curiously.

Was he? He had the feeling that when he crossed the boundary into the maze, his life would change. If he stayed where he was, he might be single forever. He remembered Lila again, the way she'd shot from his arms to run to her parents when he'd delivered her safely home. The way her family had swallowed her with hugs and kisses, had burst into song and dance, had celebrated her return all night long. Her entire village had rallied around her. They'd rallied around him, too, but he was an outsider, a stranger, and in that moment he'd realized he'd been an outsider and a stranger since he was seven. He didn't have a village.

He wanted a village.

"I'll show you the way," Alice said. "We always show people the way." She smiled, and Jack's throat went dry. When she held out her hand, he stepped forward to take it gratefully.

And the entrance to the maze disappeared.

"JACK!" ALICE STARED at the wall of green where Jack had been a moment before. He had been about to take her hand, and for one minute she'd forgotten all the disasters that had befallen her lately. Her father's injuries, his imminent return home, the loss of the time she needed to finish her gowns. For that moment Jack had just been a man, a visitor to the ranch. Someone to spend time with. Someone to get to know.

"Alice?"

Alice breathed a sigh of relief. He was still there, which meant that she was still… here… too. But the maze—it had shifted somehow.

How was that even possible?

A chill tingled down her spine as she remembered coming across Cass exiting the maze several months ago and having the strangest feeling that her sister had come back from somewhere very far away. Cass had run through the maze, upset to her core, and had gotten… lost. She hadn't been able to explain what had happened to her.

Alice reached out and ran a hand over the stiff branches of the hedge. It felt real. She was still at Two Willows.

"Alice, what just happened?" Jack called.

"Can you see it, too? The hedge?"

"Of course I can see it. Come on, open up. I'm not buying this mumbo jumbo stuff for a minute."

Alice looked around her. She didn't know how to open it. The maze was blocking him out and keeping her in.

Her throat tightened. Keeping her in, like usual. She loved her home, loved her ranch, but this was the story of her life. She was hemmed in by the people in her life, the glimpses she got of the future—by the ranch and her responsibility to it. Where was the spontaneity—the fun—in that?

Suddenly, she needed to get out of the maze. "There must be an opening somewhere," she called back through the hedge. "I'm going to find it."

She hurried along the snowy path, turned and turned again, but in every direction the outer walls remained unbroken. She travelled all the way to the center of the maze, stood glaring up at the standing stone for a long minute, but resisted the urge to place her hands on it and ask the obvious question. Fate thought it could dictate everything, but she was sick of that. She traced her way back out, following familiar corridors she'd walked in, run down countless times during her life. "I can push my way through, you know," she said out loud, but even as she spoke the words she knew she wouldn't. That was one of the unwritten rules. Her mother had planted this maze. She wasn't ready to turn her back on Amelia and damage it by forcing her way through.

"Alice?" Jack called. "Come on. Stop playing games."

"I'm not! I can't find an opening anywhere," she called back. "The maze doesn't want you in here. Probably because you tried to cheat," she added.

"You just said you and your sisters show everyone the way to the center. So what's the big deal?"

Alice wasn't sure, but somehow it was a big deal. Peering into the heart of the maze was like peering into Amelia's heart. He didn't just get to fly over and see everything all at once.

"I'm not doing this," she repeated. "It's the maze. It's not going to let you in."

"And you can't get out, either," he pointed out. "So I'm going to stand right here until you open it again."

"Jack!" He wasn't listening to her.

"I'm a lot more determined than you give me credit for. You think you can run me off this ranch with a little hocus-pocus and a lot of attitude?"

"Attitude?" This wasn't attitude. This was... Alice didn't know what it was. This was the way things worked at Two Willows.

"You can't keep me out of there forever." She could hear the frustration in his voice, and while his words should have annoyed her—and did—his tone somehow endeared him to her. He was a man. Human. And he wanted to be in the maze with her.

She got a glimpse of them holding hands. Jack leaning down and kissing her. A surge of desire swept through her, surprising Alice with its strength. It had been a long time since she'd wanted a man's touch.

"I'm not trying to keep you out, but I think... I think for now you have to go away," she said reluctantly. "I don't think it's going to open again if it means giving you the chance to get in."

"I could just shove my way through it."

"Don't!" Alice caught herself. He'd think she'd lost her mind. "Don't push through it, Jack. This is a slow-growing hedge. You'll break branches and ruin it." She didn't add she wasn't sure what it would do to him if he tried.

"If you want me to leave Two Willows so badly, just say so."

Alice stepped forward. "It's not that," she heard herself say.

"Then what is it?" He sounded closer. Right on the other side of the hedge.

What did the maze want? That was obvious. "You have to have a little faith. I'm not lying to you, Jack. About anything." She wasn't sure he'd heard. It was quiet for a long time.

"How can I believe you when what you're saying is impossible?"

Alice chuckled. That was the question, wasn't it? "Welcome to my world. Just go back to the house for a minute, okay?"

She thought she heard him sigh. Would he leave Two Willows? Why did she hope he'd stay?

"Will you come back to the house, too?" Jack asked.

Alice touched her gloved hand to the wall of the hedge again, knowing Jack was on the other side of it. "Yes, I'll be right there."

Chapter Five

"SO? WHAT DID you think of the standing stone?" Cass asked when Jack met up with her in the kitchen. She was peering into the refrigerator at all of the leftover food from the wedding. None of the other women were in sight, and the rest of the men were still at their chores. No one had noticed Alice slamming the maze's door in his face, so to speak.

Just when he'd thought he was making progress, she'd made it clear she wasn't interested.

Although she'd sounded almost apologetic at the end.

Jack shrugged. "It's a stone," he said gruffly.

He couldn't forget the way Alice had held out her hand and the way his heart had lifted as he stepped forward to take it. To be denied that contact, that connection with her, frustrated him more than he could say. He hadn't pegged Alice as the kind of woman to torment a man. He'd seen plenty of cruelty in his career, sucked it up and kept moving without a second thought, but that outstretched hand just before she'd slammed the door in his face had cut him to the quick.

Would she come back to the house? He didn't want to turn around and see. Instead, he busied himself hanging up his winter things.

"It's a pretty special stone," Cass said.

The door opened again, and Alice came inside. Jack straightened, turned and caught her eye. She lifted her brows, and he knew what question she meant to ask. Had he told Cass?

He shook his head no. She might want to play games, but he wasn't interested. Wasn't going to be the butt of her jokes.

Cass shut the refrigerator. "I'm going downstairs. I won't need to cook for a week with all those leftovers, which is good because Wye and I are cleaning this house from the bottom up." She headed for the basement. A moment later they could hear her talking to Wye.

Alice faced Jack. "I've never seen it do that before," she told him. "The maze."

Was that supposed to make him feel better—or worse? Jack shook his head impatiently. "The maze didn't do anything. You did. Message received, Alice."

She sucked in a breath. "You think I'm lying?"

"I don't know what to think. I'm going to town. Should be some deliveries there for me. Gear I ordered for the surveillance system. You may not want me here, but I've still got a job to do."

"Jack, I—" She didn't finish the sentence. Couldn't pretend she wanted him, even for a minute, he thought.

"Be back in a while," he said curtly and went back

out the door.

Several hours later Jack's pride was still bruised, but he'd recovered his sense of humor somewhat, and he was satisfied with the start he'd made on what would be a big job. He intended to have visuals on almost every part of the perimeter, just as Alice had said. He was rigging up motion detectors to control the start and stop of the video feeds. No sense in amassing hours and hours of footage of nothing.

There was a lot more to do, but if he was honest with himself, he was grateful for that. It kept his mind off his disastrous attempts to connect with Alice. On the other hand, working on the ranch brought up memories of his parents. His family's ranch had been sold when they died and the money placed in trust for him. Some of it had been used for his education. The rest he had saved. He'd thought one day he would use it to purchase a ranch of his own.

He'd put that off, though. Year after year, he'd stayed in the military, as Richard had kept after him to join him in the intelligence world. He realized now he'd put off making a decision between the two possibilities for several reasons.

He'd always wanted to return to ranching, but that meant disappointing Richard. He hated to contemplate that after all the man had done for him. On the other hand, buying a ranch meant facing up to the fact he didn't know how to run one. He'd been far too young when his parents were killed to have known anything about running a spread. He knew he could hire overseers and hands, or even work on somebody else's spread for a time to learn the skills he needed, but it had been too much to face on his own. It had been easier to remain in the Army.

Getting sent on this particular mission was like being handed a pair of training wheels. The other men knew what they were doing. Alice and her sisters did, too. He wouldn't have to start from scratch, wouldn't have to try to oversee a bunch of men to do jobs that he didn't know how to do himself.

The only problem was… his pride. When the task of setting up surveillance for the ranch was over, he would need to take his place beside the other men. And then would come a day of reckoning. He would have to admit that while he was pretty sure he still knew how to ride, he was far less certain he knew how to saddle a horse or care for the tack. He knew almost nothing about cattle, except for the most basic aspects of their care. He had repaired a fence or two with his father, but only in the way that a boy helps a man.

The truth was, he was worthless around a ranch. And he took pride in his competence.

He supposed he was going to have to face the truth, get over himself and learn what he needed to know. He owed that to Alice if he was going to be her husband.

Her *husband.*

That was a joke. So far his chances seemed slim to none. Alice didn't even want to stay on the ranch. Could he stand a marriage like that, with him staying in Montana and her flying to California all the time?

Would the camaraderie with the others make up for the lack of connection between them?

Jack couldn't imagine it.

In a few days, the General would come home. His time was running out.

LANDON WOULD BE here soon.

And Jack thought she hated him.

Alice wasn't sure which of these situations was causing the ache in her gut. That sense of doom still haunted her. When she'd heard what had happened to the General, one part of her had been relieved to know the worst. He was alive. He would heal, that's what Jack had said. So why couldn't she shake the feeling that disaster still lurked around every corner?

The disaster had already happened.

Back in her workshop, Alice surveyed the three gowns she'd slipped onto dressmaker dummies in preparation for Landon's arrival. Was she feeling this way because she was afraid they weren't up to snuff? Was she going to botch this chance for a dream job?

Or was it Jack's insistence that she was lying that was the problem? If the man the General had sent to marry her didn't even believe in her abilities, what kind of marriage would theirs be?

Alice stopped herself. Just because the General had sent Jack didn't mean she had to marry him, tradition be damned. She might have seen Jack waiting at the altar in one of her visions, but that didn't mean anything conclusive. Maybe he would marry someone else.

She couldn't say why that caused her stomach to twist. She barely knew Jack. Handsome features and determination were too little to go on when it came to making a good choice. One thing tugged at her, though—his frustration at being blocked from entering the maze.

Alice figured that many men would have been furious at being barred from entering. Some might have threatened her. Others might have pushed through and damaged the hedge. She never could be with a man like that.

Still others might have given her the silent treatment, made her pay for the perceived slight.

Jack hadn't done any of that. He'd been frustrated—and hurt, if her suspicions were correct—and he'd left for town abruptly afterward, but she'd sensed his hurt outweighed his anger. There was something in Jack. Something… lonely.

She understood that.

Maybe some people would think loneliness was impossible when you shared a ranch with four sisters and four brothers-in-law, but they would be wrong. All her life Alice had been a little different from everyone else. She'd always had to bite her tongue. Keep her knowledge to herself. Or risk the consequences. People didn't really want to know the future—especially not in shards and pieces the way it was transmitted to her.

She wished she'd done a better job explaining things to Jack.

He was running his errands, though, and she didn't

have time to chase after him. Landon was coming on Saturday, and she had a lot of work to do.

Alice had spent long evenings perched on top of the refrigerator, sketchbook in hand, daydreaming about balls and beaus. She loved beautiful things and relished the chance to work with such splendid fabric and trimmings. This was a costume-maker's dream. She didn't know what she'd do if she lost the contract.

She wasn't sure what she'd do if she won it, either, though. She'd have to leave Two Willows—for a while. Some of the prep work could be done here in Chance Creek, but there'd be countless fittings for the cast. Countless alterations. She'd be expected on site for the filming, and that could take many months.

Alice stilled a qualm. She'd cross that bridge when she came to it. All four of her sisters would remain on the ranch indefinitely. Who cared if she left once in a while?

Wasn't she allowed a life, too?

When she looked out the window again some time later, Jack had just pulled up and parked his truck. When he climbed out, he paused for a minute, scanning the ranch. What was he doing now? Was he looking for someone?

For her?

She knew it was impolite to watch him, but she couldn't stop, and when he headed off not toward the house but for Sadie's snow-covered garden, Alice craned her neck to follow his progress.

Suddenly she knew his destination.

The hedge maze.

She grabbed her coat and hurried down the steps, bursting out of the carriage house in time to see him try to step inside it.

Just as before, the entrance vanished, and a wall of shrubbery confronted him.

Alice blinked.

She had no idea how it was doing that.

Jack's shoulders slumped. He waited a moment, but the maze didn't alter, and finally he turned around.

Alice scurried back into the doorway. Jack was the kind of man who wouldn't want her seeing him defeated. He was far more human than she'd given him credit for being at first. He wasn't cold and calculating at all.

She waited until he'd disappeared into the house—then quickly slipped back into her workshop.

It was late again when she finally gave up for the night, locked the carriage house and let herself quietly into the main house.

Upstairs, she got ready for bed quickly in the hall bathroom and had just made it to her room, stripped and gotten under her covers when a quiet knock sounded on her door.

"Come in." She was pretty sure who it was.

"You knocked again," Jack said, coming into the room and shutting the door.

"No, I didn't, and you know it."

"I don't know it, because you never demonstrated your salacious purposes knock. I didn't want to leave you hanging."

He was only wearing sweatpants, his chest and feet bare. Jack looked cold; they turned the heat down at night to save energy. Alice knew she should send him packing, but it was good to talk to someone after so many hours alone in her studio.

"Come here." She patted the bed, and when Jack sat down, she pulled the afghan from the bottom of her bed and handed it to him, still holding her covers close for modesty. She sat back against the headboard and tucked them around her. Jack wrapped the afghan around his shoulders. "Tell me one thing I don't know about you, Jack Sanders."

Jack thought a moment. "I can speak Mandarin. And Arabic."

"Show me."

He said something and then repeated it again. Alice had heard enough of both languages on television to know he'd switched from one to the other. "What did you say?"

"Home is where the heart is." He shrugged. "Just the first thing that came to mind."

Alice considered his silhouette in the dark. She appreciated having this moment to look at him without the glare of daylight making her scrutiny obvious. He was a powerfully built man, but there was a stillness at the core of him she found unusual. "Do you miss your home?"

"I've been gone a long, long time. The thought of it doesn't hurt. It's more like a dull ache. I miss the dust," he admitted. "The heat. The smell of the place. Its essence, I guess you could say."

"That's what I would feel like if I left Two Willows."

"But you don't have to."

"No." But she'd have to spend a lot of time in Hollywood to fulfill this contract if she got it. If that job led to another one, who knew when she'd be back. She tried to picture herself walking down city streets, going out clubbing with the A-list, shopping in pricey boutiques. It was a silly train of thought. Even in Hollywood, she'd just be the costume designer. No big deal at all.

Would she be lonely?

She knew a few people from previous work she'd done, but only to speak to on the phone. They weren't friends. It would be a whole new world.

Did she want a whole new world?

"You're thinking," Jack said.

"Always."

He took her hand, and to her surprise she let him. Jack's fingers were warm and dry. Masculine. She had the sense of strength held in check. "After everything I've seen, Two Willows is paradise."

"Even in November?" Things were pretty bleak here in November.

"The house is warm, the food is delicious, the company is pretty wonderful." He squeezed her hand.

"You barely know me," she reminded him.

"You're right. But I like what I've seen so far."

It would be a nice compliment if he hadn't previously dismissed what he'd seen of her abilities so far. "Like what?" she asked lightly, thinking he would remark on her looks, as if they represented anything about her.

"I like the way you care about details. I like the way you stick to something to get it just right. I'm like that, too, and it frustrates me when other people do things haphazardly."

She took this in. He'd been watching her.

"I like the way you treat Tabitha."

"My cat?" She tugged the blankets higher with her free hand. That was a strange thing to focus on.

"You treat her as if… you love her."

"I do love her." She wondered why he sounded surprised by it.

"Not everyone is open like that."

Alice wasn't sure what he meant, but perhaps he was alluding to some people's callousness around animals. "I think we should treat the living things around us as if they mean something."

"I do, too."

"Justice is important to you," she said.

"Isn't it to everyone?" he countered.

Alice tilted her head against the headboard. She needed sleep, but she liked these nocturnal conversations. She appreciated that Jack hadn't made a move on her, even though a tiny part of her couldn't help wishing he would. He was handsome. Kind to cats. She let her fingers brush the inside of his palm.

Jack didn't move, but she felt him go on alert. They

sat like that a moment.

"Alice—"

She waited for him to go on, but he didn't.

He squeezed her hand again and stood up. "I'll let you get some sleep."

Her heart sank. Had she put him off? Had she been misreading this situation all this time—

When he bent down and kissed the top of her head, Alice sucked in a breath, and her heart soared again.

"Good night," he said.

"Night."

As she snuggled down under her blankets, Alice knew she wouldn't sleep for ages.

"HOW'S MONTANA?" RICHARD asked several days later when Jack took his call. He'd been working on the surveillance system and had come back to the house for a break. He was alone in the kitchen for the moment and leaned against the counter to talk. "You going to tell me about this mission you're on?" Richard's tone told Jack he didn't believe his story for a minute. Jack wasn't sure he believed it either, but here he was on a ranch, chasing a woman who claimed to have magical powers, dealing with hedges that moved.

"Montana's great," Jack said heartily.

"And…?"

"Can't tell you more than that. Sorry, Pop." Jack had called his biological father "Dad" and his mother "Mom." He'd appreciated it more than he could put into words that Richard and Janet had never tried to co-opt the names when they adopted him. Richard had been Pop and Janet had been Ma. He didn't care if he sounded old-fashioned when he addressed them; it allowed him to keep his memory of his parents sharper in his mind.

"I had another reason for calling, anyhow," Richard said. "There's an opening coming up in the department. Wondered if I should put your name in. They'd be willing to work with you if they knew you were interested. We're always looking for a few good men."

Jack swallowed. This was the only place he disagreed with Richard. "I'm not ready for that," he said.

"Not ready? Or not interested at all?"

"Are we going to do this now?" Jack asked.

"Not if you don't want to," Richard answered evenly, "but I'd appreciate an answer soon."

"You'll get one. This mission—it may lead to an opportunity."

"In Montana?"

Jack could almost picture Richard in his office. He'd be leaned back in his chair, his feet crossed, resting on his desk. He'd probably be shaking his head, too. Jack had spent plenty of time in that office growing up, doing his homework while Richard took care of business, stopping when Richard came to show him something.

"Look at this." He'd put a photograph in front of Jack, or a data printout, or a list of numbers. "What do you recognize? What's out of place?"

What's out of place?

It was a mantra now. Jack scanned his surroundings out of habit, like every other person with a military background, but his gaze went even deeper. His mind sorted through information, lists, articles he'd read, everything he'd stored in the computer that was his mind. He spotted the incongruities. He figured out the patterns.

Every time he'd done it back then, his pop had smiled. "That's it. I was right about you."

It was meant to be praise, but every time Richard had uttered the sentence, Jack had wondered what would happen if his pop had been wrong about him. If Jack hadn't been the same kind of savant Richard was when it came to spotting clues.

Would Richard and Janet send him back to New Mexico? Would he have to live alone in the empty house where his parents had been murdered? Alone with the wind and the fading footsteps of gunmen—

Jack wrenched himself back to the present. When he was seven, he'd been afraid his return to that empty ranch was imminent, and he'd applied himself to Richard's teachings as if his life depended on it. He'd thought it had.

Soon enough he'd realized that wasn't the case.

"Yeah," he made himself say into the phone. "In Montana. Could be something good for me."

Richard hesitated. "Jack—you can't go back, you know. You can only move forward. You weren't meant to be a rancher. That mind of yours—"

It was another of Richard's frequent themes. "I

know I can't go back," Jack said. He wasn't looking to move back. He hoped to move forward.

Loud voices approaching warned him he wouldn't be alone long. Sure enough, the other men burst into the kitchen, all talking at once. They seemed in high spirits, and Jack told Richard, "Gotta go. Talk soon." He pocketed his phone. "What's going on?"

"Taking a break. Need to warm up; it's cold out there today," Connor said. He turned back to Brian. "We did it there once, you know. Sadie and me."

"Had sex? In the maze? Hell," Brian said. "Cass and I did, too. Our first time."

"Ours, too," Connor guffawed. "What are the chances?"

Hunter was looking green. Connor spotted him. Scowled. "You, too?"

Hunter just nodded and kept going out of the room.

"Wonder about Logan and Lena," Connor said, watching him go.

"We know they did. Remember that scream?" Brian asked.

Connor's face split into a grin. "Lena yelled like the house was on fire," he told Jack. "We all came running out to see what was the matter. They were in the maze. Logan said everything was fine."

"Made it clear he didn't want company, either." Brian chuckled. "Was a damn cold night. I'll bet there was contact between snow and skin."

"Maybe," Connor agreed. He peered out the window at the high walls of the hedge. "Guess if you want to make the magic happen with Alice, you should try in there." He elbowed Jack. "Glad I was courting Sadie in the summertime. Brr! Is that coffee ready yet?" He crossed to hover by Brian, who was fiddling with the machine.

"Not yet. Jack, how's that security system coming?"

"It's coming," Jack said slowly. He was still processing everything the other men had said. They'd all made love to their wives in the maze? Before their wives were their wives? Connor said he had his first time with Sadie in there. So had Brian. Had that been the case for all of them?

If so, what did that mean for him? He looked at the maze's implacable walls. The entrance stood wide open now, but what would happen if he approached it again?

And how was the damn thing moving? Was it one of Alice's tricks? She was doing a good job pretending she knew nothing about it, but that didn't make sense.

Too many questions. Not enough answers.

"Jack, I need to fix a bit of fencing in the north pasture," Brian went on. "Thought you could give me a hand with that this week sometime. But if you're busy—"

"I'll be busy for a while," Jack said shortly, distracted by this new problem. He didn't know how to fix fences.

"All right." Brian nodded. "I'll find someone else then."

I'm going to get in there, Jack told himself, still looking at the maze. *I'm going to get in there, and I'm going to figure out how Alice makes it move.*

And then I'm going to marry her—and convince her to stay right here.

"WILL'S BACK," CASS said that afternoon, looking out the kitchen window.

"Where?" Wyoming joined her.

Alice, just grabbing an apple from the fridge, shut the door and came to look, too. The man had pulled up in a truck outside and was unloading gear. He turned, saw them and waved.

Wyoming ducked, then covered her face in her hands as she crouched by the cabinets. "What am I doing?"

"Flirting with a cute guy. Now stand up and pull yourself together," Cass ordered.

Wyoming did so and busied herself wiping an already clean counter while Cass went to open the door and let Will in.

"Good afternoon. Sure is a beautiful day," Will said, looking at Wyoming.

"Sure is," Wyoming said and blushed.

"It's a freezing day." Cass shook her head at them.

"The kind of freezing day that makes you think about cozying up to a fire with your best girl," Will said.

Those two needed to get a room, Alice thought grumpily.

"Ladies, I'm going to have to turn the water off when I work on those pipes. You going to be okay without it for a while?"

"I'll be in my workshop," Alice said. She'd been

plagued by that doomed feeling again all morning, and she was beginning to think that no matter how much work she put into her dresses, she'd never get them right. Why was she even trying for this contract? Lord knew there had to be so many other designers far more talented than her.

"I'll tell the others, and we'll join you there," Cass said to her. "After we get Will all settled in. Right, Wye?"

"Uh… right."

Alice left them to it. Cass was becoming as ardent a matchmaker as the General was.

Once in her studio, she quickly lost herself in her work. It was down to getting the details exactly right. When Cass and Wyoming came in a while later, letting Tabitha in with them, she blinked, realizing she'd forgotten everything else while she'd been buried in her work.

"That's beautiful, Alice. You'll definitely get the job," Cass said when she sat down wearily in the chair across the worktable from where Alice was fixing one of the puffed sleeves of a light blue gown that hung on a dressmaker's dummy, a hoopskirt in place so she could see it the way it would ultimately be worn. This was the fanciest of the three dresses she was attempting.

"It really is something," Wyoming said. "But then everything you make is gorgeous."

"I hope so." She figured she might as well tell them the news. "Landon will be here in three days."

"Will you be ready?" Cass lay a hand on her belly.

She was nearly five months pregnant now, her stomach slightly rounded.

"You should rest more," Alice told her sister, but that was like telling a tumbleweed not to roll.

"I'm trying. There's so much to do. By the way, we're talking about making Jo's old room the nursery."

"That's a good idea." Alice kept making tiny stitches. The work was painstaking, and she'd been at it long enough she thought her eyes would cross.

"Do you think you'll have children someday?"

Alice dropped the fabric in her lap. "Children?" She closed her eyes as a vision swooped over her. A baby—she couldn't say whose—nestled in her arms. Her sisters around her—

"Alice?" Cass reached over to touch her. "You okay?"

Alice nodded. "The usual." She met Cass's gaze. "I saw a baby. I don't know if it was mine or someone else's," she added as Cass brightened. "Could have been yours."

"Or yours."

"I'm not having babies any time soon." And she wasn't ready to think about them today. She needed to finish these dresses. Alice got back to work again.

"What do you think about Jack?" Cass pretended to be engrossed in a detail of the dress hanging on the dummy, but Alice hadn't been born yesterday.

"I'm not marrying him." Her heart gave a little throb as she said the words, but she ignored it.

"You really think the General got it wrong this

time?" Cass didn't look convinced.

"Just because he got it right four times doesn't mean he's right again." She bent close to the gown and continued making tiny stitches.

"I have to agree with her," Wye said acidly.

"It's just—Jack seems kind of right for you. He's smart and dedicated, and pretty cute," Cass pointed out.

"We've only known him since Saturday," Alice said.

"But the General sent him, like he sent all the others." Cass shrugged.

"Oh, my god, Cass," Wyoming broke in. "Would you listen to yourself?"

"The General sending him is what makes him wrong for me," Alice said. She took another two stitches, but it was difficult to concentrate with Cass trying to marry her off.

Cass just smiled. "Every one of us has thought that about the man the General sent, and every one of us was wrong."

"You aren't listening to me, are you?" Wye asked. "It's like I'm not here."

"I'm not wrong." But Alice couldn't help sighing.

"You like him," Cass asserted.

"So what if I do? I still can't marry him. I can't have every choice made for me ahead of time. I can't stand it."

"Maybe that's the explanation," Wye said. "Maybe I'm not really here at all. Maybe someone's slipped something funny in my drink, and this is all some strange, psychedelic dream. It would explain a lot." She looked at the mug of tea she'd carried out from the house.

"You don't see everything, do you?" Cass asked Alice. "You said yourself recently you can't see your own future right now. You said it was getting too close. So if you fall for Jack, it's you that's doing it."

"Maybe the General should send me a husband," Wye said exasperatedly. "I could be a test case. See if his luck extends to people outside the family."

Cass gave her a hug, and Alice was glad Wye had finally succeeded in distracting her. Cass simply didn't understand.

Sadie came in, shrugged out of her coat and crossed the room to join them. "What's going on? Alice, this gown is gorgeous. I want one."

"I know, right?" Wye said to her. "In the meantime, try the tea. It's pretty trippy." She took a long sip from her mug and grinned. Cass chuckled, and even Alice had to smile, despite her irritation.

"You are really here, I'm afraid, even if we aren't paying attention to you," she told Wye. "And I don't think the General is in any shape to send anyone husbands right now."

"Oh well." Wye looked at her tea philosophically. "I guess you ladies are better than drugs."

"What is she talking about?" Sadie asked Cass.

"Wye thinks we're weird," Cass said.

"She always thinks we're weird," Sadie said. "This dress is really something." She stepped closer to it and examined the bodice.

"Alice is hitting the big time," Cass said with a sigh. "Meanwhile, I'm getting fat."

"You're not fat," Sadie said.

"Jo said I could use her old bedroom for a nursery—if no one else minds."

"I think that's a good idea," Alice said. "But what about you, Sadie? What will you do when you get pregnant?"

"We're not having kids—yet. Maybe next year," Sadie said. "For now, Connor and I plan to move into Jo and Hunter's little house when they build their bigger one. We'll live there and have some privacy until we're ready to start our family. That will give the rest of you more space in the house."

"It will feel so strange if everyone moves out," Cass said.

"We'll still be close by," Sadie said. "Alice, where will you and Jack live? How many kids are you going to have? I want two, I think."

Alice felt a chill, a draft coming from one of the old arched windows. Would she ever have children? Was it fair to take a chance of burdening one with the "gift" Amelia had passed down to her? "I have no idea what the future will bring," she said primly.

Sadie rolled her eyes.

"What's going on? Are you all throwing a party without me?" Jo asked when she came in. Champ and Isobel, her McNab breeding dogs, followed her, their nails clicking on the wooden floor. The dogs came to check out Tabitha, who got to her feet, arched her back and puffed up her fur to make herself look big. Getting the message, Champ and Isobel went to explore, and Tabitha settled down again.

"We're just hanging out." Cass passed a piece of cloth to Wyoming. "That color would look good on you, don't you think?"

"Maybe."

"We're grilling Alice about Jack," Sadie said.

"He's cute," Jo said. "Not as cute as Hunter, but not bad. When's the wedding?"

"I met him four days ago!" Alice struggled to finish the puffed sleeve as Jo admired the gown hanging on the dummy.

"I think you should wear this to your wedding," Jo said.

"She has to wear Mom's dress, like everyone else," Cass pronounced.

Suddenly Alice couldn't take it anymore. All these traditions—these foregone conclusions—were crushing the air out of her lungs. She put down her needle. "I'm going for a walk." She crossed the room, grabbed her coat and gloves, and clattered down the stairs to the door.

Outside, she pulled great gulping breaths into her lungs until she satisfied herself she wasn't being suffocated. She'd never felt so hemmed in before. Was it Jack's presence triggering this? Or the General's imminent arrival?

She stumbled to a stop when she caught sight of Jack near the entrance to the maze, charging toward it and then backpedaling just as quickly over and over again. She nearly groaned when she realized what he was doing. Each time he rushed forward, it closed, presenting an unbroken wall of green. Each time he moved back, it opened again.

"Jack!"

He was going to break the maze if he kept that up.

Jack reared around, spotted her and came to an abrupt halt. "I was just—" he began when she came near.

"I know what you were doing." Maybe she could kill two birds with one stone. Get Jack away from the maze and herself out of reach of everyone else. "Come on; we're going on a ride." She grabbed his arm and tugged him toward the stable, afraid one or more of her sisters would follow and deter them. She needed air, motion—a good gallop, but they wouldn't get that today. Too much snow; they'd have to stick to the nearby tracks that wound through the ranch.

Jack followed her without a word. In the stable, she saddled Priscilla, her usual mount, then led out Button. She was surprised that Jack didn't pitch in when she saddled Button. She noticed he stuck close, watching everything she did until she wondered if this was some kind of test.

If it was, it seemed she'd passed. After they led their horses out into the wintry air, Jack was quick to mount. A few minutes later, she looked back to find him smiling broadly. Her chest tightened. So did her hands on the reins. Jack was something to see.

"You look happy."

"It's been way too long," he called back.

"Really? How long?" Alice felt her irritation slip away. Out here, the wind in her face, she could breathe easily. Nothing about this ride seemed preordained.

He was quiet so long she thought he wouldn't answer. "Twenty-five years."

Alice straightened in her saddle. "That is a long time. You're doing really well." A dozen other questions came to mind, but she didn't want to be rude. All the other men the General had sent home were experienced with ranching. They'd taken to the work like old hands.

Was that why Jack hadn't saddled his own horse? She did the math in her head; he'd have been quite young the last time he'd ridden. She kept going, keeping a slow pace. Riding in snow could be dangerous, and she wanted to give Priscilla time to pick out a safe trail. Wanted to give Jack time to find his seat again, too.

"Grew up in the saddle until then. I was born on a spread twice this big in New Mexico. Don't mean to brag," he added with a sheepish smile. "Just stating facts."

"Your parents threw in the towel?"

He was quiet again. "They… died."

The vision that hit her nearly knocked Alice off her horse. She couldn't tell where she was seeing the action from—somewhere down low. Closed in. Under a bed? From this vantage point she couldn't make out much. A wooden floor. The edge of a blanket. Footsteps.

Gunfire.

A burst of it. A scream. Another burst that cut off

all sound.

"Alice! Alice? What's going on?" A strong arm just caught her before she slid off Priscilla. "Alice?"

She blinked, caught her breath and pushed Jack away, resettling herself in the saddle as Priscilla side-stepped and danced. She needed space. Room to clear her head of the vision.

"Easy," she told the mare. "Easy now." She was talking as much to herself as to the horse.

"What happened?" Jack pressed her.

She passed a hand over her face, rubbing away what she'd seen. "You were under the bed when they were killed. You… heard everything."

Jack scowled and busied himself getting Button under control. His gelding was sidestepping, too, jittery at their unexpected behavior. "Who told you that?"

"No one." Alice shrugged. "I… saw it."

He looked away, his jaw tight. She saw indecision and something else on his face.

Sorrow.

"You don't believe me."

"Come on, Alice. How could I? I'm not some ignorant, backwoods hick. You can't magically know things. That's not real."

Alice winced, then scolded herself. She was used to denial. She didn't blame people for not believing her. It was different with Jack, though.

She wanted him to believe.

Chapter Six

HOW COULD SHE know what had happened when he was seven? The question chased Jack's thoughts round and round until he could barely concentrate on the path they were taking.

Alice had urged her mount forward after his last remark and kept going without looking back. She was angry, or disappointed, or… something. He couldn't start their relationship off on a lie, though. Maybe she'd fooled everyone else in Chance Creek, but not him. He simply couldn't play along with some mumbo jumbo ruse.

Not for a whole lifetime.

The truth was too important. The truth righted wrongs. Explained puzzles. Caught criminals. It was lies that left things in the dark—

But he didn't want to lose his chance with Alice. Surely there was some way to make her see she could tell him anything.

He urged his own gelding forward, hoping she wouldn't try to get away. To his surprise, Alice slowed down and waited for him.

"I'm not lying," she told him matter-of-factly when he caught up. "I don't expect you to believe that now. You have to figure it out for yourself. When you do, just remember I was always telling the truth."

There wasn't any answer to that, so Jack kept silent. Alice sighed, and they rode on for a time without speaking.

"Are you ready for your father to come home?" Jack asked finally.

"No. I thought it would never happen. And to come now of all times, when I'm so rushed. I should probably be getting back," she added, looking up at the sky as if there might be answers to all her problems there. "I need to finish those dresses."

"This is a big deal for you, huh?" Jack asked, urging Button even closer. The crisp air was doing him good as they moved through the snowy landscape. Ahead of them, the land fell away to reveal mountains in the distance. There was something about an open vista that put things in perspective, Jack thought.

"The biggest. I'm usually called on by local and regional theaters. Occasionally I'll get a commission from a movie company for something unusual. My costs are low in comparison to Hollywood costumers. This takes it to a whole new level. I really want this job. I'll be in charge, for once," she explained. "The lead designer."

"I'm sure you'll get it," Jack said cautiously. It was what he dreaded.

"If I do, I'll have to leave." She studied the mountains, too.

"Isn't that what you want?"

"Yes." But she didn't sound at all sure, and Jack's heart began to beat faster. He'd mistaken her as being aloof when he'd first come and had been quickly proven wrong. Now he was assuming she wanted to leave Two Willows for good. Was he wrong about that, too?

"How long would you be gone?"

"Months. Possibly more than a year."

"What about us?" He couldn't help himself. He had to know.

Alice turned on him. "Us?"

"You. Me. Wedding bells. I'm supposed to marry you, remember? I've already sent out my save the date cards."

"No, you haven't." The corner of Alice's mouth quirked. "At least, I hope not."

"All right, I didn't send out cards. Still a bit of a letdown." He liked to see her smile. "I was getting excited for our wedding night."

Alice blinked. Her mouth opened, but no words came out, and Jack laughed long and loud, until he realized she'd gone funny again. She was gazing into the distance, but he'd bet she wasn't seeing those mountains.

"Alice?"

She snapped back, blinked again, took in his proximity and blushed furiously. Jack cocked his head. "What were you thinking about just now?"

Alice turned her horse around and began to ride back the way they'd come.

SHE'D NEVER HAD a vision like that.

When they overtook her, Alice saw, smelled, heard—even tasted things. They were so realistic it was jarring to come out of them and find herself back where she started.

This time, though—

This time her vision had been all about touch. Jack touching her. Undressing her.

Pulling her close.

She'd been cold, and Jack's body had been fiery hot.

Her body had ached with need for him. She'd wanted him inside—

"Hey, what's wrong?" Jack called, struggling to get Button to turn around so he could come after her. "Another one of your *visions*? Did you get a glimpse of our wedding night or something when I mentioned it?"

Heat flushed through her again, and she thought her cheeks must be scarlet. Of all things to guess—although she had no idea if it had been their wedding night. As usual, the vision was far from clear.

She urged on her mount, but Jack kept pace. "You're blushing. You did see us together!" he crowed. "I didn't know you were that kind of clairvoyant—"

"Shut up!" He was insufferable. He didn't even believe in her visions, and he was mocking her.

"Where were we? In bed? In a hotel? In a tent?" He was still laughing. "In the maze?"

Another vision tried to catch hold of her, but Alice kept it at bay through sheer will. They *had* been in the maze. She didn't know how he knew that, and she tried not to let her face confirm his suppositions, but—

"You sure blush a lot."

Alice let out a sound between a groan and a cry of rage. "Leave me alone!"

"I want to know everything. What position. How many times. Was I—"

"Come on, Priscilla. Home." Amelia had taught Alice to never, ever, *ever* insert a vision into someone else's mind. She hoped her mother would forgive her this one time. She conjured up an image of the stable, a bucket of oats, a warm rub-down and a comfortable stall. Priscilla leaped into a gallop. Soon they'd left Jack far behind.

"Meet you in the maze!" he called out, struggling to keep up.

"Good luck with that!" Alice yelled back and left him in the dust.

SO SHE'D PICTURED them doing it in the maze. And then tried to pass it off as a vision.

If she thought he was going to let her get away with pretending some higher power had sent her the image, she was wrong. Jack directed Button back the way they'd come. If she wanted him, she needed to own it. At least her thoughts were tending in a positive direction. If she saw them together in the maze, sooner or later she'd let him in, wouldn't she?

In both senses of the word.

The thought tugged at him, turning him on. If Alice was thinking about being with him, she wasn't as immune to him as she was pretending to be.

He caught up with her at the stable and pitched in to help with the horses, watching her for clues and copying her motions.

"So, what else have you seen us do together?"

"Nothing." Alice worked at the buckles of Priscilla's saddle, turning her back to him.

"I think you're lying," he pushed on. "You're supposed to know the future. So—when's the first time you'll see me naked?"

"Never, if I can help it." She kept working.

"We were fully dressed when you saw us on our wedding night? Interesting."

"I didn't say that."

"We weren't dressed?"

"You are so annoying." She got Priscilla's saddle off and put it away. Jack followed her.

"I was dressed but you weren't?" he guessed.

"Oh, my god, would you let it go? I did not see our wedding night!"

"You're going to be so hot for me you won't even let me get my clothes off?" Jack persisted. A stirring beneath his belt warned him he'd better not let this go too far if he didn't want to get uncomfortable.

"How do you know you won't be so hot for me you'll be the one who can't wait?" Alice faced him down.

"I could see that," he admitted.

Alice flushed again.

Jack couldn't help himself. "Are we really going to

do it in the maze?"

"Seeing as you can't get into it, I highly doubt it."

"OUCH," JACK SAID and clapped a hand to his chest. "Direct hit." He staggered a few paces before straightening again.

Despite herself, Alice laughed. It would be easier to keep her distance from Jack if he wasn't kind of fun to be around. Her body was thrumming with all this talk about sex. They'd both been partially dressed in her vision, because it looked like it was damned cold in the maze, but other flashes were seeping into her mind—other encounters—

And Jack was naked in those.

Naked and… gorgeous.

There was something about a man who was as at ease in his body as Jack was. His strong shoulders strained his shirt and jacket as he moved. His grin came easily around her, although she wasn't sure that was always the case for Jack. He was a serious man.

Serious about trying to get in her pants, she thought wryly.

She couldn't write him off as a good-time guy, though. He wanted more than that, and despite herself, the idea of a long-term relationship with him was more intriguing than she'd like to admit.

She stole a glance his way. Ran her gaze over his body. Getting close to him could be heavenly.

But they weren't there yet.

"I thought you said you weren't going to marry me,"

Jack went on.

"I'm not. You can't even get in the maze, so there isn't going to be any sex—or any wedding, either." She had to keep her head about her, no matter what her body was saying.

"Is that what it'll take to change your mind? I need to find my way into the maze? I'm going to figure out how you're closing the entrance, you know."

And there they were, back at the problem again. Alice got back to the job at hand. "I'm not doing anything. I've already told you—"

"It isn't magic. That's not how the world works."

Ouch, Alice thought, but she didn't say it out loud or stagger around to make her point. Instead she finished with the horses in silence. Jack took the hint and did the same. She'd been right all along. He wasn't the man for her and wouldn't ever be—not if he refused to see what was right in front of his face.

When they were done, she headed for the door.

"Alice—"

She half turned. "What?"

"When's our first kiss?"

The vision hit her too fast to prevent. Standing in the stable, the horses in the background, the smell of manure and wood. Jack stepping forward, cupping her chin—

When his mouth met hers, vision and reality coalesced in a shock of sensation, and Alice, light-headed, lifted her hands to brace them on his shoulders. Jack tugged her closer, slid his hand to the nape of her neck, and she went up on tiptoe to lean into the kiss.

As his mouth moved over hers, Jack filled her senses. The masculine smell of him, the roughness of his jacket under her hands.

When he finally pulled back, she was breathless.

"Sorry," he said huskily.

"Sorry?" she echoed.

"I… that wasn't fair."

What did fair have to do with any of this, Alice wondered, and went up on tiptoe to kiss him again.

Chapter Seven

JACK'S ARMS TIGHTENED around Alice, and he gave himself up to the sensations her proximity was arousing. Like parched earth opening to water, he found himself soaking in the feel of her—the wonder of her in his arms.

He wasn't sure what he'd thought it would be like to come to Chance Creek and meet Alice. He supposed he thought it would be like fulfilling any other mission, a matter of going through the proper sequence of steps to reach an objective.

This was nothing like the other missions he'd run. Being with Alice was like being handed a fascinating enigma wrapped in the most stunning package he could ever have imagined. To put it mildly, Alice was his type. His body responded to hers with a desire so strong it made him struggle to control it. He'd known that would be the case from the first time he'd seen Alice's photograph, and if he was honest, back at USSOCOM, he'd consoled himself that maybe that physical connection would get him through marrying her if they didn't click on a deeper level.

He'd been sorely mistaken. Jack doubted he could have agreed to a life with a woman he couldn't love, but the glorious thing was he didn't have to learn the answer to that.

He could love Alice.

He couldn't quite explain it. Her insistence on having mystical abilities should have made it impossible for them to be together. Still, there it was. She intrigued him with her ability to take the barest hints and turn them into predictions. She was his match for that, and there was something more.

Alice was a woman who loved her family, who had opened her heart to her sisters' husbands, too, even if her estranged father was the one who'd sent them to Two Willows. He had seen how gentle she was with her cat—and Jo's dogs. How often she checked in with the other inhabitants of the ranch to make sure all was well with them—even in the middle of her panic about getting her dresses done. She loved her family the way his birth mother had loved hers. Her face brightened when she saw the people she loved.

Would she ever brighten like that for him?

Alice broke the kiss this time, staring up at him through eyes so lovely he wanted to look into them for hours.

"What was that for?" Jack asked her slowly, afraid to break the connection between them.

"You're… yummy." She smiled, and his heart constricted.

"Yummy?" He'd been called a lot of things in his

life, but never that before.

"Yummy in a dumb way," she amended, her tone turning tart. "I wonder if you'll taste better when you smarten up." She strode away and left him standing there.

Yummy in a dumb way?

"I'm not dumb," he called after her, but he didn't bother to try to catch up. He had a feeling Alice could run rings around him.

ALICE WAS HALFWAY to the house when the vision overtook her, and she staggered a few steps before sinking to her knees. Images sliced through her mind like so many knives thrown through the air, every painful snapshot of past and future intersecting mid-flight. In her mind, she ran through the maze as a child, first aware of the power of it; she walked through its passages slowly, stiffened by age; she cried out and pushed a baby into the world; she stood over her mother's grave; she crossed a stage to receive an award; nursed Lena's black eye after her ex-boyfriend Mark hit her; watched Jo grab a knife and stab a man; danced under the stars—

All the visions, all the snapshot images, all coalesced into one continual thread that both led to and branched from something coming at her right now.

No, not something.

Someone.

"Alice?"

Dimly she heard someone call her name. She was

panting for breath, her heart throbbing like it was being wrung out to dry.

"Alice!"

A touch brought her out of it, and she stared up into Cass's frightened face. Wyoming was close behind her, eyes wide with concern. Neither of them wore jackets. They must have seen her from the kitchen and run outside.

"What is it?" Cass hissed.

"The General. He's here."

"But—" They both turned at the sound of an engine and watched a large black car pull around the house and park between it and the carriage house, near the other vehicles.

"No," Cass breathed, but Alice knew she was right, even when the driver's door opened, and a man she didn't recognize got out. He had short-cropped dark hair and a bearing she recognized.

Military.

But when he took a few steps forward, he was limping.

"Who is that?" Wyoming asked.

Alice just shook her head. "I don't know."

He looked the house up and down until an angry bellow from the interior of the vehicle had him spinning around to duck back into the car.

Alice stiffened. Cass did, too. They'd know that voice anywhere.

"He's not supposed to be here yet! Why didn't anyone warn us?" Cass asked.

Alice was already doing the calculations. Landon was coming on Saturday. She wasn't done with her gowns. Now the General was here—

"Call Brian." As usual, Wyoming was practical. "Get the men up here to help. Your sisters, too."

Cass scrambled to pull out her phone, and Wyoming helped Alice stand. "You okay?" she asked.

"I guess." But she found herself clutching Wyoming's wrist and had to force herself to let go. "I don't know. It's been a long time—"

"And now it's time for your family to sort this out—once and for all," Wyoming said sternly.

Alice had no doubt if it was up to Wyoming, she'd solve all their problems in a jiffy, but it wasn't up to Wyoming, and the Reeds were nothing if not good at prolonging a fight.

A moment later footsteps pounded up behind them, and Brian arrived from the barn. Connor, Hunter and Jack weren't far behind. Jo trailed after them.

"The General's here?" Brian asked. Cass pointed to the black car and the stranger who was straightening up again and looking around.

Brian waved to him and led the way forward. Alice held back until Jack took her arm. "Come on; best to get it over with," he murmured. Alice wasn't sure if that was true, but she walked with him. Jo caught up with them, her dogs following at her heels. Sadie opened the back door and came out on the porch, hugging her arms over her chest against the cold.

Cass twined her fingers through Alice's free hand,

and Alice knew she wasn't the only one whose nerves were skipping and jumping inside her.

"I can't believe this is happening," Cass whispered.

"Me, neither."

"No matter what happens, we stick together. This is our house," Cass asserted.

"Our ranch. We have to stay strong for Lena, if nothing else," Alice agreed. The knowledge stiffened her spine. Lena had waited years to run the cattle operation. Now that she was doing so—with the men's help—Alice wouldn't let the General mess with that.

What would he be like?

She hadn't seen him in person since she was fourteen, since the last time she'd attended a military function. During the first year or so after her mother's death, he'd commanded her and Cass to attend several such events, before Cass and the General had a major set-to at one of the functions and the General put an end to the exercise. A lot of water had passed under the bridge since then. She'd grown up.

Had he?

It struck her now, as an adult, that he'd let his grief overcome his better nature at her mother's funeral, and maybe that was embarrassing, or awkward, but his refusal to come home since was downright childish, and she still found it hard to forgive him.

Had he ever thought what it had been like for them? He'd hidden himself away from his wife's memory. Buried himself in work. They'd stayed in Amelia's house, on Amelia's ranch, tending all the things Amelia loved—immersed in her memory.

Alice thought they'd gotten the better end of the bargain. Yes, it had hurt back then to be reminded of her everywhere, but as time passed and their grief healed, her memory stayed strong.

The chance to be reminded of Amelia's spirit was worth the occasional pain of a wayward memory or a longing to see her again. Alice's mother was the kind of woman who made the world special, and Alice did her best to pattern herself after her.

She failed miserably, of course.

"There he is," Jo whispered, coming up behind them. Alice strained to get a glimpse of the man. Jack squeezed her other hand, let go and went to help Brian and the others who had clustered around the passenger side of the strange car.

Brian was reaching in to help, and Alice's breath hitched when she caught sight of the passenger's face.

The General.

He looked… old.

He shrugged Brian off, bellowed something—Alice couldn't make out the words—and took a step. When his legs buckled under him, Brian and the stranger caught him and steadied him between them.

"I'm not an invalid!"

Alice understood the General's words that time, and despite the gathering sense of dread that was tightening her stomach, she bit back an aching smile. He never changed.

The men conferred, and a second later, Brian and

Connor made a seat of their clasped hands. They picked up the General, climbed the steps and went right through the back door. Jack rushed ahead to open it as Sadie hung back. The stranger followed them past Sadie more slowly, with a pronounced limp. Alice wondered if he had been hurt in the missile strike, too.

Cass increased her pace, and the women caught up with Sadie on the porch.

"He's home," Sadie whispered. "Why is he home?"

"We don't know," Cass told her. She straightened her shoulders, took a deep breath and followed the men inside.

Alice exchanged a glance with Sadie and Jo and shrugged helplessly. Her premonitions were going off like sirens. Whatever she'd dreaded was coming. Alice couldn't understand it. The General had already been injured. Was already home. Why was she still feeling this sense of doom?

"Should I leave?" Wyoming asked in a small voice.

"I think Cass would want you to stay," Alice said. Wyoming nodded.

They went inside, too, Champ and Isobel underfoot, and Jo shut the door behind them. As the men deposited the General on his feet in the kitchen, catching hold of him again to keep him upright, the General fumed, "You will treat me with respect! I just said I can walk!"

"Doctor's orders, sir," the stranger said. "You aren't supposed to climb stairs. Not for a month, at least."

"That doctor is a—" The General bit off his words when he caught sight of his daughters. He straightened.

"Cass." His gaze ran down the line of them. "Sadie. Jo." His voice softened a little. "Alice."

Alice fought the urge to curtsey. It all sounded so formal. Instead, she nodded.

The General's gaze lingered on Wyoming. "You're not Lena. I know because you aren't trying to assassinate me."

Wyoming laughed, startling all of them, especially the young man who'd accompanied the General and was hovering behind him. "I'm not Lena. I'm Wyoming Smith. Cass's friend. I hope you don't mind that I'm here; I've been staying for a couple of days to help her."

"I'm Corporal Myers." To Alice's surprise, the young man stepped out from behind the General and shook Wyoming's hand. "Pleasure to meet all of you." His gaze stayed on Wyoming's face, though.

The General elbowed him out of the way, but as he turned back to the women, his glance rested on Wyoming, and a cunning expression crossed his face. It was gone in an instant, and Alice wondered if she'd seen it at all, or if she was reading into the situation. Lord knew her heart was beating so hard she could barely think straight.

"Don't leave on my account. Seems like there's lots to do to clean this place up. Never seen a barracks so ramshackle in all my life." His gaze traveled around the kitchen, and Alice could see what he meant. Poor Cass. It looked like she and Wye had just pulled everything out of the cabinets.

Cass's chin went up. "We're in the middle of pre-holiday cleaning," she said. "You have to take everything out of those cupboards before you can scrub them right."

"Besides, this isn't a barracks," Sadie pointed out. She had a stubborn look in her eye Alice recognized.

"We need to get the General to his room. Can you show me the way?" Myers asked.

Alice realized he'd directed his question at Wyoming. Wyoming deferred to Cass, but Alice noticed Wye's gaze rested on Myers as they spoke.

"We've put you in your office," Cass said to the General.

"Hmph."

Brian moved quickly to the General's side before he could say more. Connor joined him, and together they assisted him to his office, Myers trailing behind.

"He shouldn't be walking yet, should he?" Jack murmured to her, coming to stand near Alice. "He's had surgery. He needs to recuperate."

"That won't come easy to the General."

"I need coffee," the General bellowed from his office. "Myers, stop hovering around, and get me some! And where's my briefcase?"

"I'll get both of them in a jiffy, sir."

"That's my cue," Cass said and moved to the coffeepot. "Wye, I understand if you don't want to stay. I doubt we're going to get much more done today."

"I'll stay," Wye said cheerfully as Myers came back into the room.

"The General would like some—"

"Coffee. On it," Cass said. "Then I'll get the General settled in."

"I'll get the General settled, ma'am," Myers said firmly. "I know what he needs." He limped to the back door and let himself out. A few minutes later, he was back, a briefcase in his hand. "Good thing this made it through the blast," he said. "Don't know what he would have done if it didn't."

"The coffee will just be another minute," Cass told him.

"Yes, ma'am."

Alice, not knowing what to do with herself, climbed up onto the refrigerator. At least up here she was out of the way. Tabitha joined her a moment later, and she lifted the cat into her lap, grateful for her calming presence.

She still couldn't believe her father was home, an event she'd half hoped for, half dreaded for years.

"Think I've got a read on the problem," Will said, appearing suddenly in the kitchen and startling all of them. He caught sight of the gathered crowd and hesitated. "Sorry. Is something going on?"

"I forgot you were here." Cass pressed her hand to her heart. "The water's back on."

"That's right. I'm going to need some parts to get things fixed up. Thought I'd come back tomorrow if you don't mind." He winked at Wyoming, who flushed a little.

"Oh," Cass said. "The General—my father—just arrived home a few days early. I'm not sure what kind of recuperation he'll need. He was injured."

Corporal Myers was assessing Will frankly.

"Your father's here?" Will asked. His smile slipped for once. "The Army general? I've heard about him."

"That's right." Cass visibly gathered her thoughts. "I guess it's fine if you come back tomorrow. Just don't come too early."

"I won't." Will's voice was gruff. "Don't worry; I'll keep out of the way." He frowned, and Alice realized he was watching Corporal Myers, who was now watching Wye.

Myers must have felt his gaze. He looked up, noticed Will's expression. Alice thought the younger man might blush, but Myers held firm, and her estimation of him rose a notch. If she wasn't mistaken, Myers had just issued a challenge, and Will seemed ready to take it.

May the best man win.

Neither of them had spoken the words aloud, but somehow they were hovering in the room.

Cass had noticed. Wyoming, too. She was pretty sure Sadie had. What about Jack?

Yes, he'd noticed. Standing quietly to one side, observed by no one but her, he was watching the little drama play out around him. But then he saw everything—or thought he did.

"Well, I'll be off then. See you tomorrow," Will said to Wyoming.

"See you."

Will left. Myers took the cup of coffee Cass handed to him. Wyoming didn't seem to know what to do.

"The General is going to need to rest now," Myers said on his way out.

"I guess I should get back to work, then," Alice said. Tabitha jumped down when she shifted, and Alice followed her more slowly, sliding down to stand on the countertop before leaping to the floor.

"Guess we should, too," Cass said to Wye.

Jack touched Alice's arm when she reached him. "The worst is over, right?" he asked in a low tone. "The General's home."

Alice laughed out loud. She had a feeling the worst was yet to come.

JACK WAS RELIEVED to hear Alice laugh. He'd been afraid the General's homecoming would upset her far more than it seemed to have done.

"Let's get back to work," Brian said to him and the other men, coming into the kitchen again, followed by Connor. "Myers kicked us out. He's got the General in hand. Smells good in here, by the way." He went to give Cass a peck on the cheek. "What's cooking?" He was trying to normalize things, Jack knew, but it was going to take a lot more than a kiss to do that.

"A nice roast pork."

"Yummy," Brian said.

"Yummy in a smart way or in a dumb way?" Jack asked before he thought better of it. He looked up, caught Alice looking back at him from where she was tugging on her outer things. A wry smile quirked the corners of her mouth.

Cass turned on Jack, her hands on her hips. "My pork roast is not dumb."

Corporal Myers reappeared in the doorway and cleared his throat. "The General—"

"You calling my wife's pork roast dumb?" Brian swaggered up to Jack, puffing out his chest. "Them's fighting words, Soldier."

"Knock it off," Cass said when Jack puffed his chest right back and the two of them slammed together, then careened off each other, Jack bumping into the counter and upsetting a glass of water. "Out of my kitchen, both of you! Come back later. There's enough going on here today without you two acting up."

"The General wants you—"

"Why are you calling Cass's pork roast dumb?" Brian asked Jack conversationally as Jack grabbed a dish cloth and began to clean up the spilled water. Wye took the cloth from his hands and pushed him toward the door.

"Out of here. You all are a menace."

"Long story," Jack told Brian. "Involves a girl and a maze."

"Don't they all," Brian said.

"The General wants you all to muster in the office—NOW!"

Everyone turned to Myers, who filled the doorway. "Now," he said again, more quietly, and stepped back.

Jack exchanged a look with Alice. She shrugged and began to take off the jacket she'd just put on.

"I'll clean up here," Wyoming assured Cass.

"You, too," Myers said implacably.

"Me?"

"That's what the General said."

Jack followed the others as they filed toward the office. It was a tight fit with the General's bed in the room. He sat on it, a mass of pillows at his back and a few more under his knee. The General was in his fifties, his hair peppered with gray, but his eyes clear and bright. His face held more lines than Jack remembered, but the pain from his injuries might be exacerbating that. He watched them from under bushy eyebrows as they took their places. Soon all of them stood in a semi-circle around his bed.

"From now on, I expect to see you all first thing in the morning," the General said.

"We have chores," Jo began.

"Right after breakfast."

"We'll make a point of it, sir," Brian said.

Jack couldn't interpret the look Cass sent him. From what he'd seen, Cass liked things to be peaceful, and he was pretty sure she would work for a rapprochement with the General, but like all the women, he knew she harbored a lot of anger toward her father for the way he'd acted these past eleven years.

"Was there something you wanted to say?" Sadie was more challenging. Jack thought he knew why the rancor between her and the General was worse. From what Brian and the other men had told him, unlike Cass and Alice, after their mother's death Sadie hadn't ever received an invitation to accompany the General to a military event. According to Connor, she took the slight personally.

"Seems to me there'd be something you all need to say to me." The General waited, but no one spoke up. He sighed. "Lake, status report."

Brian straightened, and understanding rippled around the room. Jack caught Sadie's flare of anger, Jo's surprise and Cass's consternation. If Lena had been here, Jack figured she'd have probably exploded. Just as she'd feared, the General was taking over. They all reported to him now.

"The ranch is doing well, sir. We rebuilt the stable, and the horses are all home. We're working with Lena to improve the cattle herd and making plans for spring."

"O'Riley, you're up next."

Connor shrugged. "Same as Brian. Doing my chores, keeping my wife happy."

"Keeping my wife happy, *sir*!" the General said reprovingly.

"Yes, sir." Connor looked sheepish.

"Powell?"

"Why are the men going first?" Sadie asked suddenly.

"Drawing up plans for Jo's house, sir," Hunter said. "We'll build come spring."

"Sanders?"

"Why are the men going first?" Sadie repeated. She stepped closer to the bed, positioning herself between the General and Jack.

The General scowled. "It's how it's done. Sanders?"

"Why is it done that way?" Sadie demanded.

"Because it is. Sanders?"

"Started building the surveillance system, sir," Jack said hurriedly. Sadie shot him a disgusted look.

"Cass?" the General said.

"I think Sadie has a good question. Why *do* the men go first?"

The General crossed his arms and waited until Cass blew out an irritated breath and said, "Fine. Everything's fine. House is fixed. Baby's fine. You're home for the first time in eleven years. It's all fine."

"Fucking fine," Sadie said. "Jo, you're up."

Jo was caught off guard. "Uh… Isobel had some nice puppies this year. Oh, and I killed a guy. Alice?"

The General was scowling again.

Alice shook her head. She looked pissed. "I keep seeing visions. Some of them are kind of nice, like the ones where Jack's naked—" Sadie laughed. Jack choked. He was pretty sure the General growled. "But the others are pretty rough. I think trouble's coming again."

The General held her gaze a long time, then turned to Wyoming. "Your turn."

"Me?" Wyoming squeaked. "Uh… well… no one's sent me a husband, so my life's been kind of boring. Except for the plumber. He's sort of cute."

Corporal Myers frowned, but Jack saw the General's mouth twitch. Had he just suppressed a smile?

"If you're joining our ranks, I suppose I'll have to look into that husband oversight. You don't need a plumber. You need a soldier. Dismissed."

No one moved, then everyone moved at once, creating a bottleneck in the doorway.

"Who does he think he is?" Jack heard Sadie say.

"Going to be a rebellion if he keeps that up," Connor was muttering to Hunter.

"He's not really going to send me a soldier, is he?" Wye was asking Cass.

"I wouldn't put anything past him at this point."

DINNER WAS A quiet affair, with everyone conscious of the General in the office nearby. Corporal Myers served him his food and seemed to anticipate the General's needs before the man himself. In between times he sat at the table with the rest of them and ate up Cass's roast like he'd been starved for months.

When the General bellowed for him again, and he excused himself to see what was needed, Cass sighed. "Thank goodness Corporal Myers is here. I don't think I'd have the patience to fetch and carry the way he's doing."

"Do you think he was with the General when the missile struck?" Jo asked. "The way he limps—"

"Must have been," Alice said.

"He's certainly devoted to him," Cass said.

"Always has been. Was his shadow back at USSOCOM," Jack said. "Pretty sure the General is some kind of hero to him."

"More like father figure," Alice said.

"That one of your hunches?" Sadie asked.

Jack rolled his eyes. "Doesn't take a hunch to see

that."

"You didn't see it," Alice said.

"Course I did," he asserted. "But that's personal. Just because he lost his own parents—" Jack broke off. Alice looked up to see Corporal Myers in the doorway again.

"The General needs more coffee," he said grimly and limped across the room to fill the cup he was carrying.

Jack pinched his lips together. Cass looked desperate to change the conversation. Wyoming was tracking Myers's movements with her eyes.

When Alice's phone rang, she grabbed the excuse to push back her chair and run upstairs to her room. It was Landon. Of course. With all the hubbub around the General's arrival, she'd forgotten about him.

"Hello?"

"Alice, it's me. Just wanted to give you my information for Saturday."

"Oh." Should she tell him about the General? Alice figured she had to. She didn't know what was going to happen now that he was home. "I have some news on my end, too. Remember I told you about the General? That he'd been injured and was coming home?"

"Of course."

"Well…" She took a deep breath, hoping he'd understand and not think she was asking for an extension. "He came home early. He's here now. I'll still be ready for you on Saturday," she hastened to add, "but—"

"You said he wasn't coming home until next week."

It sounded like an accusation, and not for the first time Alice realized that managing Landon's moods was going to be one of the harder aspects of the job if she got the contract.

"He wasn't supposed to, but he did. My father is impatient."

"So am I." Landon paused and seemed to pull himself together. "He's staying at the house?"

"That's right."

"Then we won't want to meet there."

That was considerate, Alice thought. "You said you wanted to see my workshop."

"Of course I do. It's critical you have the facilities to pull this off. But everything's changed now, hasn't it?"

She was losing him. Landon didn't like changes once he'd made his plans. "I can come to you. Where will you be staying?"

"I'll get back to you." He hung up, leaving Alice to stare at the phone. She was the one having to juggle her obligations to the General with her need to finish her costumes. How did it impact Landon at all?

"Something wrong?" Jack asked from the doorway.

She shoved her phone back in her pocket. "Just Landon. He's… cranky tonight."

"Sounds like your boyfriend rather than an employer."

"He's neither… yet." She knew she should qualify that. Landon would never be her boyfriend. She was sick of men, though. Sick of the General's high-handedness. Sick of Landon's temper. And sick of not knowing how Jack fit into her life. Now that the General was home, she couldn't pretend he wasn't trying to force her to marry the man. "Excuse me, I've got work to do." She was relieved to escape to her studio in the carriage house. If only life could go back to what it used to be, when she'd known exactly where everything fit.

There was no going back, though, was there?

All she could do was muddle forward the best she could.

Chapter Eight

ALICE WAS FINALLY heading to bed.

Jack, who was working on several nights short of sleep, had gone to bed early, trying for a few hours of rest before Alice returned to the main house. He hadn't slept at all, though. Instead, images had run through his mind. His family's ranch. The desert in Afghanistan. USSOCOM. Two Willows.

A chain of events had led him here, and the culmination should be a wedding. How could he get from here to there, though?

He'd heard Alice's light footsteps pad past his room a few moments ago, and the bathroom door down the hall close. When the pipes in the wall knocked several times, he got to his feet but waited until he heard Alice return to her room.

When he knocked softly on her door, a frustrated "What?" greeted him. Undeterred, Jack slipped into her room and closed the door behind him. This time she didn't sit up in bed, or pat the mattress, or hand him the afghan. Wary of her mood, he sat on the floor with his back to the bed. He could stand the cold.

He'd stood much worse.

"I'm tired," Alice complained.

"Me, too, but you knocked, and I came."

Alice turned on her stomach and buried her head under her covers until her voice was muffled. "I didn't knock."

"I choose to believe otherwise. I won't stay long. Just wanted to know how you were progressing with those gowns. You're working hard."

"Not hard enough. How do you do three weeks' work in six days?" She peeked out again, her eyes shining in the dark. "Landon told me he hoped I hadn't left it all to the last minute, but I did. He's right; that's totally unprofessional."

"You'll get them done, and you'll blow him away. Everyone says you're a master craftswoman."

She was quiet a moment. "I try my best."

"I know you do." He turned, reached up and rubbed her back.

Alice groaned appreciatively. "I'm so stiff from sitting there all night."

That was his cue. He moved onto the edge of the bed and began to massage her shoulders, his fingers working out the kinks in her muscles. Her skin was silky smooth, and every touch woke the hunger within him, but Jack knew he had to be patient. After several minutes, Alice relaxed. After several more, her even breathing told him she'd fallen asleep.

He'd gotten something right.

He dropped a light kiss on her head, adjusted her

covers and snuck out of her room, shutting the door softly. Now if only he could sleep.

He dropped off faster than he'd thought, but he woke up thinking this was the calm before the storm. For the moment Myers was acting as a buffer between the General and his daughters, but that couldn't last. The General might take a few days to get over his surgery and the long trip home, but soon he'd be rested enough to set the full force of his attention on them.

Landon was coming soon, too, which meant Alice might get caught up in a contract that would leave her little time for thoughts of the future—or marriage.

Jack knew he had to work faster to get Alice to fall in love with him, because the writing was on the wall. The General had sent him and the others here to protect his daughters and increase his influence over them while he was far away at USSOCOM. Now he was here at Two Willows.

What use did he have anymore for someone like Jack?

"Want to come help me install the surveillance equipment?" he asked Alice before breakfast.

"I don't have time. I'll be working all day to get those dresses done."

He couldn't very well offer to help her, having no skill whatsoever with a needle or sewing machine. Jack was stumped, but he vowed to himself he'd try again later.

They were hardly done with breakfast when the General bellowed from the office, "Muster up!"

Just like the day before, they trooped into his room and arranged themselves around his bed. The General was dressed and although still sitting with a leg up on pillows, somehow managed to be ramrod straight.

"Lake, report."

"Not much new since yesterday, sir. Winter chores," Brian said.

"O'Riley?"

"The same, sir."

"Powell?"

"Working on those plans for Jo's new house, sir."

"Good, good. Too many people under one roof never works out. Sanders?"

"Still working on that surveillance system, sir."

"A little too hard," Alice added.

"What's that supposed to mean?" the General asked.

"No one likes to be watched all the time any more than they like to be told what to do."

"Just doing my best to keep everyone safe, sir," Jack put in hurriedly. He didn't like the way she'd lumped him in with the General. She viewed her father as the enemy, after all.

"Keep up the good work."

Alice sighed.

"Cass?" the General asked.

"Still pre-holiday cleaning with Wyoming. Today we're working on the living room."

"How's that baby?"

Cass touched her stomach. "It's fine."

"Sadie?"

"Everything's fucking fine with me. Jo, you're up!"

Jo, prepared this time, said, "Dogs are great. Horses are great. Everything's great."

"Alice?"

"I'm… good."

"You got a phone call last night. Who was it from?"

Alice hesitated. At first Jack thought she would refuse to answer. "Landon Clark. He's a movie producer. I might be getting a really big contract."

The General thought this over. "Good for you," he said.

Alice's brows lifted, but she didn't answer.

"And you." The General turned to Wyoming. "Ready for your husband?"

"Uh…"

"Dismissed."

"LANDON?" ALICE GRIPPED her phone anxiously, pacing her studio. "Glad to hear from you. I was—" She didn't want to tell him she was worried he'd decided to forgo his trip to Chance Creek altogether. "Hoping we could solidify our plans for Saturday. I'm so excited to show you my work."

"There's been a change of plans."

"Again?" Alice hurried to cover her dismay. "I was really looking forward to meeting you."

"You will meet me. I'll be in Chance Creek tomorrow."

"Tomorrow?" There was no way her costumes

would be done tomorrow. "Landon—you're already showing up weeks early. I need more time." She held her breath. Would he hang up on her again? "What if… what if you came by and see my workspace tomorrow, and then I'll show you my three costumes the day after, like we planned. I can even come by to your motel room early if you need to make a plane."

"I'll be staying for several days," Landon said to Alice's surprise. She'd assumed this would be a quick visit.

"Then that will work fine. You can tour my studio tomorrow. I have lots of costumes I've made for other productions I can show you. Then I'll get back to work and finish everything for Saturday."

"What about your father?" Landon asked gruffly. "I don't have time for family gatherings. This is business, Alice. I'm a busy man."

Alice wasn't sure what to say. "The General is confined to his room at the present. He's still healing from his injuries."

"What about your sisters and their husbands?"

Alice hesitated. She'd only mentioned Lena. Had Landon been checking up on her? Her discomfort grew. "I'll make sure no one bothers us," she assured him.

"Fine. I'll arrive tomorrow at four. See your studio and take you to dinner." He hung up.

Alice let out a breath. She'd nearly blown her chance. Thank goodness she'd found a way to turn it around.

She turned to find Jack standing near the door again. He hung around a lot.

"Who was that?" he asked, coming in.

"Landon. He's arriving tomorrow."

"Thought he was coming on Saturday."

"Plans change." She shrugged, but she was still discomfited by Landon's phone call and his gruff tone.

"I look forward to meeting him. Never shook hands with a Hollywood producer before."

"He's not a Hollywood producer yet," Alice said. "And you can't meet him. No one can."

"ALL I'M SAYING is I don't trust him," Jack said to Hunter later that afternoon. "What kind of a man visits someone's home and refuses to meet her family?"

"You're not her family," Hunter pointed out. They were in Hunter and Jo's small house, which sat next to the much larger main house. It was cute and tidy. Architectural plans were spread over the kitchen table. Hunter had been showing them to Jack with evident pride.

"The rest of you are. He doesn't want to meet you either."

"It's a business meeting."

"Something's off about him."

"Have you checked him out?" Hunter waved off Jack's answer. "Of course you have; you check everyone out."

"His record is too clean. Everything about him is perfect. Every post. Every website mention. He's hardly on social media at all. He doesn't pick fights on forums. What's this guy been doing with himself for the last twenty years?"

"Buying cryptocurrency."

"Maybe. Don't you think it's fishy that a man who can make millions trading money that barely exists is going to blow it all on a Hollywood bet? I mean, when's the last time a historical drama paid off big? Why isn't he making a superhero flick?"

"Maybe it isn't about the money. Maybe this is his ego trip. His effort to put a long-lasting mark on the world."

"After all the attacks on this ranch, we need to be careful."

"We will be," Hunter assured him. "You're getting your surveillance system in place. We'll all be here tomorrow. Meanwhile, we can look into him some more."

"Be my guest. I've exhausted all my resources. All I can do now is keep tabs on the man himself. Starting tomorrow. He's supposed to take Alice to dinner. I'm going, too." He thought again about his need to woo her—especially before Landon got a hold of her. When he'd looked into the man, the first thing he'd realized was that someone like Landon could hold a kind of charm for a woman like Alice.

Not that he was jealous.

Well, maybe just a little.

"See you later," Jack said to Hunter.

"Tell Alice I said hi."

ALICE'S FINGERS WERE shaking as she stitched a ribbon

to the bodice of the blue gown. She was never going to finish on time. There was no way. Landon was going to hate her costumes. She was going to blow a chance she'd probably never get again.

When she heard footsteps on the stairs, she bit back a groan of frustration. All she needed was another interruption.

"Hey, Alice." Jack almost bounded into the room. As usual, her heart sped up at the sight of him, but that didn't change the fact that she didn't have time for even a short conversation. "How about you and me have dinner tonight? Just the two of us—I'll take you to town."

Alice blinked at him. Dinner? Tonight? "Are you out of your mind?" She didn't have time for dinner. She barely had time to breathe.

"Not the last time I checked."

"I told you Landon's coming tomorrow."

"But I'm here today. We've barely spent any time together, and you know your dad sent me here to—"

"I have three dresses to finish!" Alice burst out. "Three. And none of them are done. And none of them are anywhere near good enough. And Landon keeps changing when he's coming. And I'm going to have to hide them tomorrow, show him a bunch of costumes that aren't what he wants to see, then sit through dinner with him and then come home and stay up ALL NIGHT to finish them—"

"Okay, okay, I get it. How about this?" Jack held up his hands. "I'll go to town and get takeout. I'll light a candle, bring out some dishes. We'll have a picnic right here—"

"What part of THREE DRESSES don't you understand?"

"Fine," Jack growled. "I'll get takeout and just toss it to you from the doorway!"

She'd toss him something, Alice thought. A bomb, maybe. She pointed toward the stairs.

"You've got time to eat out with Landon—"

"Get. Out."

Jack looked like he had more to say, but to her relief he clamped his mouth shut, turned on his heel and left.

Alice didn't let herself think about the look on his face as she got back to work. She didn't let herself think about anything other than her stitches until her fingers cramped so badly and her eyes grew so weary, she couldn't see straight anymore. It was nearly four in the morning when she dragged herself back to the house, got ready for bed and climbed under her covers.

When the light knock sounded and her door opened, she groaned. She couldn't deal with Jack again tonight.

He didn't say a word, though, just sat on the side of her bed, the mattress sinking under his weight, and eased her over onto her stomach under the covers. When she realized what he was doing, she went along with it, too tired to fight.

Just like the night before, his powerful fingers began to knead the tension out of her shoulders. Alice wasn't sure when she began to weep, but her tears slid down her cheeks and dampened the sheets.

Jack didn't comment on them, although she was sure he knew she was crying, and for some reason that opened the floodgates wider and she started to sob.

Jack gathered her up in his arms, wrapping her in her covers to preserve her modesty and letting her rest her face against his chest.

The tears wouldn't stop. All her fears about failing pressed into her throat as if they would choke her, and she couldn't hold her sobs back. The bleak weight of the sense of doom that had weighed on her for weeks now left her unable to process her anxiety any other way. It was all too much—

Jack rocked her gently, simply holding her and letting her cry. She felt no judgment. No intention to use this against her in the future, either. Just… safe. Jack was strong. Steady. Dependable.

Alice got the barest glimmer of the future. Jack's arms holding her, the whisper of his breath against her ear as he encouraged her, the weight of a different kind of pressure way low in her body. "Push, Alice! You can do it."

She tore away from the vision, not nearly ready for what it betrayed.

Did she have a future with Jack?

A future that included—

Without realizing it, she'd tilted her face up to look at Jack, and now he was leaning down toward her. He was going to kiss her.

Alice didn't pull away.

When his mouth brushed hers, she sighed and met him eagerly, her body acting for her before her mind could even sort out what she meant to do. Her arms went around Jack's neck, and she rose to get closer to him. The blankets slipped down, but Alice didn't care.

The brush of her nipples over Jack's chest sent desire racing through her veins, and when Jack skimmed a hand over her skin to cup one breast, Alice moaned and leaned into his touch.

"Alice—" Jack whispered.

She knew what he meant to say. This felt so good. So—right.

Their kiss went on and on. Alice wanted far more, and she knew Jack did as well, but he was holding himself back. When she turned to straddle him, no longer content to be half-sitting in his lap, Jack groaned and broke off the kiss.

"I want you," he said, wrapping the blanket around her gently. "But not like this, when you're overtired, overstressed—not able to make a decision you'll be happy with in the morning."

"But—"

"I don't just want you once, Alice. I want you forever." He kissed her again before she found her words. "We have to do this right, one step at a time." He smiled suddenly. Was he laughing at her horrified expression? Alice didn't think she could wait. She wanted him now.

"I don't want to do this right."

"Neither do I," he admitted, "but we have to. You

have to know what you really want. As soon as you're sure about me, use your salacious purposes knock."

Alice laughed despite herself, and realized her tears—and her tension—were gone. "Okay," she said, her voice wobbling a little but not too badly.

"Sleep, now."

She made a disbelieving noise as he helped her into her bed again, his hands taking all kinds of liberties as he did. He pulled up the covers.

"I know," he said, a smile in his voice. "It isn't going to be easy for me, either. I can't believe I'm being this much of a gentleman."

"What if I don't ever knock?" she asked.

"For the love of god and all that's holy, Alice—knock. Soon."

Chapter Nine

JACK STIFLED A yawn as he gathered with the others in the General's office after breakfast. Sooner or later he was going to have to sleep, but last night had been worth it. His body was still thrumming with the desire to make love to Alice. The feel of her naked body against his skin had been almost more than he could bear. He'd had to take care of matters himself—several times—before he'd finally managed to fall asleep.

The General couldn't have found him a better match if he'd tried, Jack thought as he took his position in the General's office. The man had a surprising knack for matchmaking. When Alice came in, he caught her eye and lifted his eyebrows slightly. She half smiled and turned away, blushing a little.

They were better together in the dark than in the daylight, he mused. Either that would have to change, or they'd have to become nocturnal.

Cass bustled in, wiping her hands on a dishtowel. She'd been distracted this morning. Had burned the sausages she'd cooked for breakfast and dropped a handful of silverware on the floor.

"The General's throwing her off," Jo had murmured to him at the table. "She thinks of this as her house. Now he's home. She doesn't know what it means."

"You're still here," the General said to Wyoming, pulling Jack's thoughts back to the present.

"I'm still here," Wyoming agreed. "For the moment."

"And *you're* still here, more to the point," Cass said crisply. "What do you have to say for yourself, taking eleven years to make it back home?"

Jack straightened. Cass was going on the offensive.

"I had a job to do—"

"Your job was to raise us," she snapped. "That's what Mom wanted. Instead you sent us overseers, guardians—and random men."

"Hey," Brian protested. "I'm not random."

"Well?" Cass demanded of the General. "Do you know how hypocritical you are? When I was a teenager and I accompanied you to one of your military functions, I tried to tell you our guardian was misbehaving with one of the ranch hands. You banished me back to Two Willows for talking about sex, but then you sent me a man to have sex with!"

"Hey!" Brian said again. "He sent me for more than that."

"Do you know how awful you made me feel, never inviting me to another function again?" Cass went on. "It was like I was the one who'd done something wrong instead of our guardian—or you! That wasn't fair."

The rest of the men and women in the room held

their breath. Jack braced himself for an explosion.

"You're right," the General said gruffly, surprising them all. "That wasn't fair. I was upset. I took it out on you. I was trying to keep up appearances at USSOCOM. Convince everyone—including myself—that nothing had changed after Amelia died." He shook his head. "Everything had changed. I couldn't keep up."

Cass's shoulders slumped. "We needed you. I needed you. When you stopped inviting me along, it was like I lost another parent."

The General shut his eyes. "I never meant for you to feel that way. You were so angry. I thought… I thought you hated me."

Cass made a sound, pressed her lips together, but her eyes shone with tears. "I didn't hate you," she whispered.

The General put out his hand. Jack wasn't sure she would take it, but Cass moved as if propelled by an invisible force to the General's side and let him grasp hers. "You remind me of Amelia," he said. "Keeping everything on the ranch running shipshape. I'll stay out of your way." His voice got husky, and he shook his head again, scowling. "Damn doctors trying to get me retired. We'll see about that." He squeezed Cass's hand again. "Lake?" he snapped. "You're up."

Jack supposed the man couldn't take more emotion than that. Cass pulled herself together, wiped her cheek and moved away. The General's gaze when it followed her was remorseful, but you'd never know how the man felt if you listened to his voice. "Lake? What's taking so long? Make your report."

ALICE WAS BACK in the kitchen later that afternoon with Cass when Wyoming returned from an appointment in town. Alice had spent the day in her studio and had just popped in to refresh her coffee and for the excuse to stretch her legs. She'd never sat for so long for so many days in a row. Still, she was wide awake. Jack's visit to her bedroom last night had done that. Ever since he'd cupped her breast, her body hadn't stopped aching for more.

Jack would feel amazing inside her. She knew that with a certainty that even a vision couldn't give her. Maybe the General had sent him. Maybe fate was playing with her again, dictating her future, but she couldn't deny what she'd felt when he touched her.

That was a connection worth pursuing.

Still, a thread of unease had nagged at her all morning. She couldn't shake the feeling her family was still in danger. Sometimes she felt like the danger was getting closer. Other times it felt like it was already here. She was so anxious about Landon, the General—and Jack—she couldn't untangle one set of fears from the others.

Wyoming's shoulders drooped, and she shook her head before Cass could even ask how things went. "Don't ask. My interview was a disaster. I don't even want the job, anyway. It's not in my field. It would have bored me to tears."

"Will's due back soon," Cass said encouragingly. "That'll cheer you up."

"I guess."

Alice filled her coffee cup and noticed Wye did perk up when the man's truck pulled around the house a few minutes later. By the time Will knocked on the back door, she was smiling.

"I think I've got the right part this time," he said cheerfully when Cass let him in. "Come on, Wyoming. I'll show you how it's done." He led the way to the basement.

"How what's done?" Wyoming asked, already following him.

"Manly plumbing work."

"Sounds like a handy skill."

Corporal Myers appeared in the kitchen. "Wyoming? The General needs you."

"Me? What for?" Wye stopped. Will stopped, too.

"Yeah, what for?" he asked. Wye elbowed him.

"You'll have to ask him."

Wye hesitated, and Alice could almost see her sorting through her options. Miss out on the chance to spend time with Will, or ignore the General's summons and risk offending her host. Finally, she sighed and crossed the kitchen. "I'll be there in a minute," she told Will and followed Myers out of the room.

"That father of yours seems determined to get in my way," Will said to Cass and Alice.

"The General doesn't even know you're here," Cass said primly.

Will's ready smile slipped. "Well, guess I'll get to it. Without my pretty helper." He made his way to the basement.

"I hope Will and Corporal Myers don't come to blows over Wyoming," Cass said, getting back to work. "I think she likes Will better, but I can't help being a little partial to the corporal."

"Poor Will. A man in uniform always wins out, doesn't he?" Alice quipped.

"Jack will be happy to hear you think that," Cass said.

"DUDE, YOU'RE SPYING on your girlfriend?" Connor asked when he caught Jack in Alice's workshop. Jack, having just rigged up a video surveillance camera behind a rack of her costumes, simply nodded. He'd heard footsteps on the stairs but had known the tread was far too heavy for it to be any of the women arriving. The men would understand. He'd watched the carriage house patiently all morning until he'd seen Alice go back to the house, probably to get more coffee, judging from the mug she'd carried in her hand. He'd hoped to slip in and out of the carriage house in her absence with no one the wiser.

"Landon Clark keeps changing plans, and he refuses to meet any of us. Even the General. You'd think the man could take a minute to shake the hand of a fallen hero."

"She's not going to like that." Connor pointed at the tiny camera Jack had hidden. He'd parted the costumes on the rack position in front of it just enough to see through but not so much that the camera would be visible from any distance.

"I'm not trying to invade her privacy, just keep her safe."

"By invading her privacy."

"What if this guy is really from Tennessee?" Jack demanded as he packed up the gear he'd used to install it.

"Landon Clark? No way; he's been in touch with Alice since before the last round of trouble here."

"So?" Jack tweaked the costumes again, trying to make them look normal, while still leaving enough space so as not to block the camera.

"So the two-bit outfit that's been sending these people wouldn't have two plays going on at once. They weren't that organized," Connor argued.

"Maybe. Maybe not. Let's get out of here before Alice gets back."

"You're making a mistake," Connor said, but he followed Jack downstairs and out the door. They'd made it halfway across the grounds toward the house when Alice burst out of the kitchen and hurried their way. Jack was surprised when she grabbed both their arms and turned them back the way they'd come.

"I need your help."

"Thought you wanted me to stay out of your way." Jack wished he could take his words back. "Glad to help, though."

"Landon's on his way, and my studio is a mess. You two can help me straighten it."

"Sure thing." If she cleaned it herself, she might

spot his camera.

"I need you to pull out costumes. Good ones I can feature to show Landon what I'm capable of." She led the way inside and up the stairs.

"Will do," Jack said.

"Connor, grab a broom."

"Already ahead of you." Connor twirled one he'd found in a corner and started to work his way around the room. Alice began to take her Civil War–era gowns off the dressmaker dummies to stow away. Jack began to peruse the costumes, unsure which ones would be best to showcase.

"Find complicated ones to demonstrate the breadth of my capabilities." She pointed to an intricately beaded 1920s-style flapper dress at the end of one rack. "Like that."

"What about this one?"

Jack looked up to see that Connor was perilously close to where he'd installed the tiny camera just minutes ago. He'd propped his broom against a table and pulled one of Alice's costumes off a rack. Jack sent him a look that should have reduced the man to a puddle, but somehow Connor still stood there.

Alice crossed the room to look at the delicate fabric of what he guessed to be a ladies' sheer cotton gown from the Roman era. "That is pretty."

"This one is cool." Connor edged even closer to where the camera was and picked out something vaguely medieval. Any minute he was going to expose the camera to view.

"I think this one is badass." Jack grabbed the closest costume to hand, a plain pink ballerina's tutu.

Alice shook her head. "Jack, be serious."

With a satisfied smirk, Connor went back to pushing his broom. Jack did his best to find costumes that were extra special. When he got close to Connor, he stuck a sharp elbow in Connor's ribs. "Stop fucking around."

"You stop fucking around." Connor elbowed him back.

"Oh, my god—can't you be serious for two minutes?" Alice sighed. "Out. Both of you. I can't think with this much testosterone in the room." When neither man moved, she clapped her hands together. "Now! Beat it! I'll clean up myself!"

Reluctantly, Jack moved toward the door, relaxing a little when Connor came, too. He waited until they were out of the carriage house before turning on the man. "What was that about?"

"Just trying to help," Connor said innocently.

"You're an ass."

"And you're still single. Better get cracking before that Hollywood producer steals Alice away."

Jack gave up, hustled across the yard and into the house. In the guest room, he pulled out his tablet and opened the video feed. There was Alice whisking around the room, pulling out costumes, putting some of them on the dressmaker's dummies from which she'd just taken the ball gowns.

When an expensive car pulled up outside a few minutes later, he moved to the window to watch as a man in his late thirties stepped out, surveyed the ranch in one sweeping glance, took in the house and then the carriage house, and proceeded toward the latter. Jack was struck all over again by the man's appearance. Instead of being an overweight middle-aged man with a Steven Spielberg complex, like he'd hoped when he'd first heard of Landon, the movie producer was muscular, sharply dressed in a suit and a wool coat, and gave off an impression of tightly coiled energy.

Alice opened the door before Landon could knock. Even from here Jack could tell she was a little breathless. She beamed at Landon and ushered him inside.

Jack returned to the video feed, an emotion twisting in his gut he couldn't name. He was rewarded a minute later when she and Landon came into view. He turned up the volume in time to hear Landon proclaim, "Love the space. It's perfect for an up-and-coming costume designer."

Jack's shoulders tightened. Prickles moved up his spine, and if he'd had hackles, they'd be raised, he thought as he zoomed in closer on the couple. When a man praised a woman like that, he wanted something from her. And it wasn't a bunch of costumes.

"She's digging him."

It was Connor again. This time his dog, Max, was with him. "How the hell did you get in here?"

"That weaselly little lock on your door isn't going to keep me out."

Connor had been far quieter than Jack had given him credit for. Far more skilled, too. He moved closer.

Max prowled around the room.

"She's hanging on his every word."

"More like the other way around," Jack said sourly. "Look at him. He's not even pretending to look at that dress she's showing him. He's looking at her."

"Do you blame him?" Connor chuckled. "Even Sadie admits Alice is stunning."

"She wouldn't fall for that jerk." Jack rested his elbows on his desk and watched the action on screen.

"You don't think so? I don't know—he's got looks, money, style… a film studio."

"You think he's got looks?"

"Hell, you're jealous."

"Go fuck yourself."

Connor chuckled and moved closer, peering at the small screen over Jack's shoulders.

Landon worked his way around the studio, Alice in his wake. He touched the costumes she'd put on display. Commented on them. Engaged her in a discussion about authenticity and fabric choices. Connor was right. Landon had the scruffy good looks of an artist or rock star, and he was talking Alice's language.

"There's something off about him," Jack said.

"Yeah, he's trying to bag your girl."

As they watched, Landon touched Alice's arm. Jack half stood. Connor pushed him down again. "Woah, boy. Let this play out. Let's get a sense of him."

Jack knew he should be the voice of reason, but Connor was right; the man's actions were hitting him at a visceral level. He didn't want anyone touching Alice.

"Alice, your work is fascinating. I can't wait to see the big reveal. Are you sure you won't show me a peek today?" Landon asked on screen.

"Not today. Not until they're perfect." Alice smiled charmingly. Jack clenched his fists.

"Let's go to dinner then, and we'll talk over the film some more. I'd love to hear your thoughts."

"Say no," Jack ordered Alice. "He doesn't give a crap about your thoughts."

"I'd love to," Alice said. "And you'll love Fila's. It's casual, but the food is to die for."

"Sounds perfect," Landon said.

"Sounds like a nightmare. Fuck. I don't have surveillance in place there," Jack said to Connor. "I can't beat them there, either."

"What are you going to do?"

Jack remembered how Connor had interfered earlier. "Never you mind about that. Get out of my room."

"Hell, no. I'm staying. Look, Alice is leaving to get her things. Let's see what Landon does while she's gone."

"EVERYTHING OKAY?" JO asked when Alice slipped inside the house past Jack's closed door to her bedroom to grab her purse.

"Of course." But it wasn't. So far things had gone swimmingly with Landon, and she thought she had made an excellent impression, but that was only because he hadn't seen her dresses yet. She'd been so nervous she could barely breathe since the minute he'd stepped into her work room and surveyed it with a critical eye. He'd said nice things about her costumes, but she'd spent the whole time seeing them from the point of view of a stranger, and suddenly every flaw and imperfection had seemed to glow like they were illuminated by a spotlight.

There was something else, too. Now that she was alone, Alice could admit it. When she'd opened the door to let Landon in, she'd been taken aback by the gleam in his eye as he ran his gaze over her. She'd seen that same gleam in many a man's eye, and it always prefaced trouble. Was Landon the kind of man who viewed women more as conquests and playthings than living, breathing human beings with thoughts and wants of their own?

She remembered her last boyfriend, Howie Warner. The way she'd played the doormat to his forceful personality. She was never going to make that mistake again. But how to let Landon know that without losing the opportunity he was offering her?

"Are you having visions?"

Alice shook her head. "Not visions…" It didn't take visions to tell her what Landon was after. Maybe he'd pursued her originally for her costume-making ability. The moment he'd seen her, his objective had changed.

Or maybe it hadn't. Maybe he'd drawn up that list of designers to interview, and she was on it because of her looks rather than her talent. He could have found her photograph on the internet. Would he spend all this time and money to come make a play for her if he wasn't serious about giving her the job? Or was he hoping for a two-for-one deal?

"Hunches?"

Alice wasn't ready to talk about it with Jo. "I just feel like… I feel like something really bad is going to happen, and I don't know what it is," she said instead. That was true, anyway. In the last fifteen minutes, her stomach had tightened with dread. "I'm afraid I'm going to fail completely."

"You won't fail. He'll love your work; everyone does."

"What if he doesn't?" What if he wasn't even interested in her work?

"Then you'll find another opportunity. You're Alice Reed."

"Who does that car belong to? And who's pulling in?" The bellow came from the General's office, and Alice stiffened. When she turned to look outside, she saw Will's work truck parking next to Landon's fancy town car.

"Landon's waiting in the carriage house. I can't deal with the General right now," she said to Jo. "Run interference, would you?"

Myers appeared at the bottom of the stairs as Alice and Jo ran down them.

"The General wants to know—"

"I don't have time. See you later!" Alice kept going, ignoring him. "Jo, do I look all right?"

Jo laughed. "Do you ever not look all right?" She followed Alice into the kitchen. So did Myers.

"Alice, the General wants to know—" Myers began again.

"She's busy," Jo said, getting between them. "Have a good dinner. Be safe," she added to Alice.

"I will." Alice shut the door on Corporal Myers's questions and quickly covered the ground to the carriage house, where Landon was waiting for her. She passed Will, who was heading toward the house, tools in hand. He was either stumped by the problem of the knocking pipes or was extending the job with the hope of wooing Wye. Alice wished him well, knowing that Corporal Myers wouldn't be happy to see him again.

When she reached her workshop, Landon was seated at one of her tables, but she had the uncomfortable sense he'd been picking through her costumes while she'd been gone.

Trying to find the ones she'd made for him?

Good thing she'd hidden them away.

"Ready?" he asked.

"Ready."

Landon ushered her to his town car, and soon they were on their way. He drove a little faster than Alice cared for, but she had to admit he handled the car well and followed her directions. Halfway to town, however, he slowed down. "I'm in no rush to eat. You could show me around a little."

"Oh." Alice was embarrassed. She hadn't foreseen this request. "Fila's doesn't usually take reservations, but I called ahead, and they're saving a table for us. It's kind of a big deal, given how crowded they usually are."

She quailed at the silence that followed her answer, but a moment later, Landon nodded. "Of course. You keep country hours. I'm used to eating a little later."

"Sorry." Alice hated how small her voice had gotten. She was falling all over herself trying to impress Landon, and all she'd done was irritate him. This was like being with Howie all over again. She needed to assert herself, but if she was honest, she found Landon intimidating. When they'd first begun to talk, she'd assumed he would be much older than he'd turned out to be. In person he was far more… masculine… than she'd expected. He filled the car, all muscles and long legs, and his energy was relentless. This was a man who got what he wanted, and she wondered what he would be like if he was crossed.

"Don't worry about a thing. You went out of your way so we wouldn't have to wait. I can't argue with that," he said, and Alice let out the breath she'd been holding. She hadn't pissed him off too badly yet.

The rest of the drive to Chance Creek would have been awkward if Landon hadn't smoothed over their silences with stories of his business career. She'd already known he was new to movies, but she'd never met a man who'd worked so many different jobs before.

"Car lots, real estate, franchises, day trading… import/export. What haven't you done?" They were just coming into town, slowing at a four-way stop before heading into the main shopping district. Landon hesitated, his hand resting on the turn signal, as if he'd changed his mind about their destination and was about to take a hard left. That way would take them north of town, out into ranchland.

"Fila's is straight ahead," she reminded him.

He waited just a moment too long, and a truck to their left sounded its horn before surging forward into the intersection. Alice gritted her teeth. Landon would think this was a hick town.

Instead, he chuckled. "Was trying to think of something I hadn't done," he said smoothly before accelerating forward. "Guess there isn't anything."

"Costume designing," she teased him and was rewarded with a smile.

"Got me there. Costume designing. That's where you come in."

Chapter Ten

"I CAN'T BELIEVE he was casing the joint," Jack said as Connor gunned his truck's engine and roared down the country highway after Alice and Landon. They'd both watched in shock as Landon photographed every angle of Alice's studio and many of her costumes while she was getting ready in the house. Jack was more determined than ever to stay close to Alice as long as Landon was around, and they'd hopped into Connor's vehicle just moments after Landon pulled out and headed for town, leaving Max at home.

"He might have been trying to steal Alice's costume designs," Connor pointed out.

"Shh!" Jack fiddled with his tablet and turned up the volume in time to hear Alice say, "Turn here."

"You bugged your girlfriend?" Connor said.

"I bugged her purse. What else was I supposed to do?"

"She's not going to be happy."

A crackling sound made them both wince. It continued, and Jack swore. "It's not going to pick up enough. I'm going to have to go into the restaurant when they get there."

"I'm coming, too."

"Like hell—"

"You need me."

"Really. In what way?"

"If you show up at Fila's alone, Alice will know you were tailing her, which is creepy. If we show up there together, we're just two hungry guys picking up dinner for the family."

Jack had to admit he was right. "Fine. Don't talk to them, though. Leave that to me."

"This should be fun. Better call Cass," he went on. "Tell her we're taking care of dinner."

When they entered Fila's fifteen minutes later, it wasn't hard to spot Alice and Landon. It was a small restaurant, which meant Alice spotted him just a moment after he walked in. Her eyebrows shot up. Jack feigned surprise right back. He crossed the restaurant to their table.

"Small world, huh? We're getting takeout. Hi, I'm Jack Sanders." He put out his hand to Landon, who shook it, giving him a long, assessing look. Jack moved close to Alice. "What did you get?" He attached a bug to the underside of the table.

"Enchiladas." She shot him a look he couldn't quite decipher, but it definitely wasn't "come join us."

"Nice. See you back at home. Good to meet you, Landon."

"Nice to meet you, too."

Jack had a feeling Landon would be asking some

pointed questions after they left. Good. He figured the man had gotten the message. Alice was his girl. Hands off.

They ordered, and when their food was ready, Jack waved to the couple and sauntered out the door.

"Where are you going?" Connor asked him when Jack angled away from his truck and toward Landon's fancy black car.

"Be right back."

Connor caught up to him as he tested the car's handle and found it locked. Connor pulled out a shim from under his jacket and popped open the lock a moment later. "Make it quick."

"Where the hell did that come from?"

"Thought it might come in handy."

"You're full of surprises." He ought to have brought one, Jack thought as he fastened a few more bugs in the car's interior. At least a vehicle like this would run smoothly. Should be easy to hear their conversation in here.

"Still think this could backfire if she catches you," Connor said as they finished up and made for their truck. "Alice won't appreciate the interference."

"Leave Alice to me."

"TERRIFIC MEAL." LANDON wiped his mouth, set his napkin down and pushed away his plate. "Have to admit, I wasn't sure what to expect."

"I'm glad you liked it." Alice tried to smile, but it was hard when she was scanning the room. Someone was listening. She was sure of it. And yet, all around them, people chatted and laughed, thoroughly involved in their own conversations.

Jack was long gone, but she kept getting a flash—almost a vision, but not quite—of him gazing intently into the distance…

Listening.

But Jack was nowhere near here.

A quick text to Jo while she was in the ladies' room confirmed that the men had brought a huge takeout dinner home. "We're all stuffing ourselves silly," Jo had texted back.

Which meant whatever her intuition was trying to tell her about Jack, she wasn't getting it right.

"That's why Keith Baker is my hero. He's a venture capitalist who's a total genius when it comes to raising funds," Landon was saying.

Alice tried to pay attention. "My hero is Kate O'Dell. She did the costumes for *The Passing Hour*," she said distractedly. She loved that Regency film.

"Never heard of it," Landon said.

That got her attention. "Never heard of *The Passing Hour*? I'd think anyone interested in period dramas would know it."

Landon frowned. "I'm interested in blockbuster movies, Alice. I know what's good when I see it."

"Well, *The Passing Hour* is good. You should watch it."

"Sure thing." He flashed her a smile. "Maybe we can watch it together." He touched her hand.

Alice squirmed. She didn't want him touching her. She was already uncomfortable enough without that additional pressure on the situation. She had the horrible feeling she was about to fail monstrously, and she couldn't shake the persistent image of Jack—

Listening.

For some reason Alice thought about the drone. It had been persistent, too, in its attempt to film the maze. When Jack wanted information, he tried to get it by any means necessary.

Landon took her hand in his. "I think it could be a real pleasure to work with a professional like you. You perform miracles, don't you?"

"What? Uh... I guess." She tugged her hand free and reached for her purse, pretending to look for something, still trying to get a handle on what she was feeling. How could Jack be eavesdropping when he wasn't even here?

Had he planted a listening device of some kind?

A bug. That's what they called it in the movies. That had to be it. But how could she find it without alerting Landon?

She put her purse aside and clasped her hands in her lap. Where would Jack have put it? She ran through his quick visit to their table in her mind and remembered the way he'd leaned in close. Keeping her upper body perfectly straight, nodding and acknowledging Landon's continued praises, she ran one of her hands under the table.

Bingo. All her senses told her she'd found the culprit.

Alice plucked the small round device off, dropped it, found it with her foot and crushed it, never taking her gaze off Landon.

What had he been saying?

"How many more people do you need to interview for the position?" she managed to ask, kicking away the remnants of the bug.

"Only a couple. I've narrowed the field down to the best."

He took her hand again, and Alice, uncomfortable, and still distracted by the thought that maybe there were more bugs around, decided it was time to leave.

"Alice, I—"

"It's been a long day," she announced suddenly and got to her feet, gently but firmly extricating her hand from his grasp. "I think I need to get home. Country hours, you know."

"Of course." Landon hid his annoyance well as they exited the restaurant and walked to his car, but Alice knew she now had a mark against her. She had far too much experience with this type of behavior from men not to know the signs. It couldn't be helped. She had no plan to get intimate with him, and the sooner he knew that, the sooner he'd bring things back to a business relationship. Men seemed to have to try with her. Once they knew the answer was no, most of them behaved themselves.

She hoped Landon would, too.

Landon opened the door to his car and handed her

in, before getting in on his own side. He didn't start the engine, however. "Beautiful night," he said conversationally.

"It is."

"I don't get to see so many stars in the city."

Alice pitied him for that. She loved the stars. "They sure are a sight, aren't they?"

"Bet they're even better out of town."

She wasn't dumb enough to fall for that trap, but as she raced for a way to deflect the conversation, nothing came to her, so when her phone buzzed, she answered it quickly.

"Alice? Coming home soon?" Jo asked.

"I'm on my way right now." She was thankful for the chance to say that out loud. Now Landon knew someone was waiting at home for her. Maybe he'd stop flirting.

"Awesome." Jo cut the call.

What had that been about?

"That was my sister," she explained to Landon, grasping at the excuse eagerly. "They're expecting me."

Landon covered his displeasure again quickly, but Alice caught the anger in his eyes. This time her feeling of foreboding made sense. If he was the kind of guy who didn't take kindly to a brush-off, it was a good thing she was learning that now. Maybe this sense of dread had more to do with Landon's character than her job prospects. She could arrange not to be alone with him. Easy enough with everyone around her, and her quiet life at Two Willows.

She silently thanked Jo for her call. It was as if her sister had known she'd need the excuse—

No. Not Jo.

Jack.

He'd been listening in the restaurant, which meant he'd probably gotten the sense Landon was hitting on her. Still, Jo's timing—

Was he still listening? He was, wasn't he?

Landon turned on the engine. "If they're expecting you, I suppose we'd better get you home. Your family keeps you on a short leash, don't they?"

"I've never felt that way." Not until Jack had arrived. She directed Landon back out of town.

"I'm an only child. Can you tell? No one's ever reined me in." He grinned at her, and Alice relaxed a little. Maybe she was overreacting. Landon had hit on her. So had a hundred other men, many of them with far less panache. He was lonely. Traveling. Starting a new business against all odds.

"I suppose siblings can be troublesome," she said. "But you know what's worse?"

"What?" Landon asked.

"Soldiers. They're the lowest of the low."

Landon shot her a puzzled look. "Your father's a soldier. He's served for over thirty years, right?"

Caught by surprise, Alice didn't know how to answer. "How did you know how long he's served?"

She braced herself as Landon took a turn a little too fast. He slowed down. "Sorry. Alice… look, I check up on all my possible employees. Old habit. I've been burned more than a few times in the past. This venture is important to me. I'm not going to let just anyone work on my first picture. When you mentioned your father, I looked him up. Impressive career."

His explanation made sense, she supposed. "Yes, he has had a long career." One that was probably over now. She knew a storm was looming in that direction, too. The General had been quiet so far—most of the time—but soon he'd get restless.

"Let's get you home," Landon said. "Family comes first." There was an irony in his tone that contradicted his words, though. He was impatient, and he didn't like being put off.

Back at Two Willows, Landon parked, opened her door and helped her out, but he didn't linger. "I'll be in touch tomorrow about seeing your costumes."

Alice bit her lip, hoping she hadn't ruined her chances for the contract but at a loss for how else she could have handled the situation. She didn't want Landon to think the relationship between them could be anything other than a business one. If he was only here to hit on her, best to know it now.

Landon must have read her worry on her face. He stepped closer and lowered his voice. "Don't worry, Alice. I've been given the brush-off before. I've always lived to fight another day."

He was gone before she could think of an answer, and as she turned toward the house, Alice told herself she was making a mountain out of a molehill, but when she saw Jack near one of the columns holding up the porch roof, all her anger returned.

"What the hell was that?" she asked without preamble, climbing the steps to face him.

"Not sure what you—"

"You forget you aren't the first man to try to control me. The General's made it his life's work. It stops now—from both of you."

"Alice—"

"No. Don't make some lame excuse, and don't pretend you don't know what I'm talking about. I deserve better. If I want to talk to Landon in private, I'll talk to him in private. Even if I have to take him to the center of the maze to do it."

She headed for the carriage house. She still had to finish her ball gowns—even if it took all night.

IT HAD BEEN past one in the morning by the time Alice returned to the house to make herself a snack, giving Jack the chance he'd been waiting for to slip into the carriage house and remove the camera he'd hidden in her studio. Back in the guest bedroom, he'd lain awake for several more hours before he'd finally fallen asleep. He woke again just after four-thirty in the morning to the knocking of the pipes and lay staring into the darkness, unsure what to do. Alice would barely get to rest before she had to get up again, and this was her big day. She was due to unveil her creations to Landon in a matter of hours, and even though he disliked the man, he didn't want to ruin her chances at the contract.

On the other hand, he hated that they were fighting.

He especially hadn't liked what she said about soldiers to Landon on their car ride home. He didn't know how much time he had to win her over—and beyond any concern about clearing his name, or winning a fifth of the ranch, he didn't think he could stand the thought of moving on with his life and leaving Alice behind.

He looked forward to their trysts all day. A glimpse of Alice made his heart lighten and his pulse kick up. He liked listening to her.

Liked touching her.

Wanted a chance.

A soft knock on the wall had him surging up to a sitting position. It came again a moment later. A single rap.

That was her salacious purposes knock?

Jack slid out of bed, pulled on his sweatpants and went to the door. Out in the hall, he paused, but the house was quiet. When he opened Alice's door, she was sitting up, her covers wrapped around her.

Her shoulders were bare, as usual. He liked that Alice slept nude.

"You need to work on that signal," he said as he shut the door behind him, but when she lifted the covers, he forgot everything else. Without thinking through the consequences, he shucked off his sweatpants and joined her under them. Alice came into his embrace with a sigh, and for a moment, Jack lost himself in the feel of her.

He was hard, and she was all soft curves and silky skin. Jack cradled her head, found her mouth with his own and kissed her thoroughly, until every fiber of his body strained to get closer to her.

It would be so easy. A shift of his hips, a thrust. He could bury himself inside Alice where he belonged.

But not yet.

Tonight was all about her.

He gently rolled her on her back and moved to position himself between her thighs, fighting against the instinct to push inside. Instead, he shifted lower and took his time exploring her breasts with his hands. Their soft smoothness felt good against the rough skin of his palms, and when he bent to take one of her nipples into his mouth, Alice groaned and arched, bringing herself closer.

His thorough but slow investigation of her body soon had her urging him on. Her fingers dug into his skin, her breathing became rapid, and when he slid lower still, exploring the core of her with his tongue, she tangled her fingers in his hair and held on.

Jack took his time bringing her to a fever pitch, and when she came, her soft cries made it all the harder for him to restrain the desire that coursed through him. When she finally sank back against the mattress, breathing hard, all the tension in her melting away, he moved back up to cover her, stealing a kiss.

"What about you?" she said.

"Another time. You need to sleep. Today's a big day."

"How come you're so… wonderful… at night and such a pain in the ass during the day?" she complained, turning on her side and snuggling into her pillow.

Jack slipped out from under the covers, aching from his hardness but determined to let her sleep. He pulled the covers over Alice. "I don't know," he said honestly. "I'm trying the best I can."

"Do better. And stop spying on me," she commanded and yawned.

He dropped a kiss on her head and left, once again spending quite a bit of time with himself before he was finally able to drop off to sleep. He hadn't made so much use of his right hand since he'd been a teenager.

It was worth it, he told himself. Someday soon Alice would be his, and he'd make up for lost time.

The morning came all too soon.

"Lake," the General said when they mustered in his office after breakfast.

"All quiet on the western front, sir," Brian said smartly.

"O'Riley?"

"Ditto, sir."

"Powell."

"Everything's good, sir."

"Sanders."

"Been keeping an eye on the surveillance system. So far, so good, sir. No one's come onto the ranch we don't know."

Jack thought the General hesitated before moving on to the women. Was he bracing himself?

"Cass?"

"Wye and I are cleaning the bathrooms today. Good

times."

A muscle worked in the General's jaw. "Alice?"

"I'm exhausted, and I don't have time for this." She sounded cheerful, though. Jack hoped he'd contributed to her good mood.

"Sadie."

"Fucking fabulous."

"That's fucking fabulous, sir, Soldier!" the General barked.

Sadie cocked an eyebrow, and Jack steeled himself for what was to come. She didn't disappoint.

"You know what isn't fucking fabulous? The way you turned your back on this land—when it was your wife's deal with it that kept you safe all these years. Mom never once stepped foot off Two Willows. And when she died, you couldn't even do a drive-by of the ranch?"

"You don't know what you're talking about."

"Like hell I don't. I did it, too. So did we all. None of us have left Two Willows in eleven years without making sure one of our sisters was going to be at home. We gave up our freedom for your safety. What did we get in return? Nothing!"

"You didn't keep me safe." The General slapped his hand down on his leg. "Look at me, all busted up."

Alice stiffened by Jack's side, and Jack reached for her hand. Squeezed it.

"That was an accident," Sadie said, "and it makes no difference. Two Willows was part of Mom. When you turned your back on it, you turned your back on her."

"I turned my back on it because it was part of her. I couldn't stand to be so close—and so far—" The General broke off. "You think I wanted to stay away?" His voice cracked, and the room became silent.

Sadie's face was a study of pain. "Two Willows is part of me, too," she said. "It's part of all of us. When you turned your back on it, you turned your back on us. You left us. I nearly—I nearly gave up. The garden started dying. The hedge started dying."

The General straightened and scanned her face as if looking for more information. "The hedge is dying?"

"Not anymore. Not since Connor came. He helped me… find my way."

"So I did one thing right at least."

Sadie huffed out a breath, but Connor put his arm around her shoulders. "I didn't do anything but hang around you. You did all the work."

"Couldn't have done it without you," she told him.

The General observed them with approval. "You're right; Amelia did love this land and everything that grew on it, including the five of you."

"But you hate it here," Sadie said.

The General shook his head. "No. I don't hate it. I just… hate that she's gone."

Sadie seemed to digest that. When she spoke, her voice was unsteady.

"I hate that, too."

A moment passed. The General cleared his throat. Nodded at Sadie. "At least we agree on something."

"Is there anything else here you don't hate?"

"Sadie." The General reached for her. Jack held his breath. When Sadie moved toward her father, finally taking the hand he offered, Jack's throat tightened in sympathy with father and daughter's anguish. "I don't hate… I… You're my girl. You're all my girls." He gripped her hand tightly. When he released it, Sadie's eyes were bright with unshed tears. She stepped back into her place. The General cleared his throat several times.

"Jo? Report."

"Everything's fucking fantabulous," Jo said, and the tension cleared. Jack let his shoulders relax.

The General straightened again. "Where's that Wyoming woman?"

Myers looked up, as if interested to know the answer, too.

"She's at an appointment in town. Another job interview," Cass said.

"Make sure she comes back," the General said.

"Don't worry, she's coming back." Cass sighed. "I don't think she's going to stick around in Chance Creek much longer, though. Not unless she finds a good job."

"She'll stick around," the General said darkly.

"Good," Myers said. "I mean… goodbye," he stammered. "I mean… everybody's dismissed."

The General looked at him curiously. "Since when do you give the orders around here, Corporal?"

"Since it's time for your physical training, sir. Everyone out."

AN HOUR LATER Jack was staring at the implacable green wall where the maze's entrance should have been when he heard footsteps. He turned to see Jo approaching from the direction of the stable. Champ and Isobel followed her, like usual.

When he turned back, the entrance was open again.

"I thought you'd be with the other men doing chores," Jo said as she approached, shaking him from his thoughts. "Something wrong?"

"I have… other things to work on." He kept an eye on the entrance, wondering if he darted forward if he'd be able to make it in. Would the maze close up if Jo was here to witness it? He decided not to chance it.

"Your spy stuff?"

Jack turned to face her. "Surveillance. It's important work. Don't you want to know if someone's sneaking up on the ranch?"

"What I really want to know is why you're so keen to get out of mucking stalls. This is a ranch, Jack. If you're going to marry Alice, you'd better be willing to help out."

"I'm willing to help out. It's just—" Time to face the music, he guessed. "Look, I haven't mentioned this to anyone else but Alice, but—it's been a while since I did much ranching. I'm… rusty."

"How rusty?" She cocked her head, waiting for his answer.

"Like… I haven't been on a ranch since I was seven rusty."

"Oh, wow." Jo straightened. "Got it. Well, in that

case, you're going to need some practice."

"Guess I will. As soon as I've made sure Two Willows is safe."

"Not good enough, Soldier. Come on. Let's get started."

ALICE WASN'T SURE whether to be worried or grateful that Landon didn't call until mid-afternoon. She was sure he was sending her a message: if she could brush him off, he could brush her off, too. She'd spent the morning racing to make some last-minute changes to the gowns, beginning to second guess all her decisions as a creeping sense of dread sprouted in her gut, soon blossoming to full-on panic.

She thought he'd have called first thing, and as the hours passed she'd grown edgier and edgier, until her fingers shook when she tried to make her trademark tiny stitches. Will had arrived at breakfast time to take another look at the pipes, which were still banging. While Corporal Myers stood grimly by replenishing a cup of coffee for the General, the plumber told them he had several ideas about how to fix the problem, but that it might take a few more return visits. He and Corporal Myers had both perked up when Wyoming came into the kitchen.

Alice's growing sense of impending doom was preventing her from getting any helpful flashes about anyone's future, however. She was as curious as Cass seemed to be about how the Will–Wyoming–Corporal Myers triangle would turn out but couldn't get a read on the situation at all.

Back in her studio, she fussed with the gowns until the phone finally buzzed. She was proudest of the lace that edged the bodice and the sleeves of the lilac gown. She'd had to call in some favors to find the authentic, period-accurate edging. As far as she was concerned, it made the dress.

She braced herself when she answered Landon's call. "Good afternoon." That sounded too stilted. "How is Chance Creek treating you?" That sounded far too breezy.

She was really batting a thousand.

"Chance Creek is treating me fine," Landon said, his warm baritone soothing her worries. He didn't sound angry. Maybe she'd read too much into things last night. "How has it been treating you?"

"Good. In fact, really good. I'm ready to show you the gowns."

"Glad to hear it. When should we meet?"

"Any time."

"I have an errand to run, but I'll be back at my motel in an hour."

Alice realized her mistake. The last thing she wanted was to end up alone with Landon in his motel room. What was the alternative? He'd made it clear he didn't want to come back to the ranch, and she'd volunteered early on to bring the gowns to him—before she'd realized what kind of man he was.

"Landon—"

"Is there *another* problem?" His slight emphasis on

"another" stopped her from suggesting a different venue.

"No. I'll be there."

"Good." Landon cut the call.

Alice heaved a sigh of frustration. What was wrong with her? She was acting like a schoolgirl. She needed to get this situation in hand.

"Is your boyfriend coming over?"

Alice jumped when Jack spoke behind her.

"He's not my boyfriend. And he's not coming here. I'm going to him."

"He wants to be your boyfriend."

She wished she could deny it. "I think he does," she admitted. "I've made it clear that's not going to happen."

"You need to be more direct."

Alice remembered Jack had listened to the whole conversation at the restaurant—and on their ride home, if she was right. "You'd better not be planting bugs in here."

Jack held up his hands. "I'm just talking."

She doubted that.

"Your sister sure put me through the wringer today."

"Which sister?" Alice turned back to the lilac gown, arranging and rearranging the folds of its full skirt, making sure it was perfect.

"Jo. Decided to make a rancher out of me."

Alice had to laugh. "I'll bet." She glanced at Jack, and when she took in his answering smile, her stomach gave a little flip. Now that was a man.

She caught herself. That was a snooping, interfering man.

"I listened in on your conversation because I was worried about you."

A flash of intuition caught her off guard. She saw a girl dressed in foreign clothes. Sand stretching in every direction.

"You were in the desert," she said.

Jack stilled. "I was. That's classified, though. Did your dad tell you?"

Alice made a big deal of scanning the workshop. "You see the General anywhere?"

"You could have talked to him any time."

"You've been there every time I've talked to him so far."

"I don't buy that you're psychic, Alice. I'm sorry; but I don't believe in that kind of thing."

"Then we're even. I don't believe in snooping into other people's business. If you'll excuse me, I have to get ready to go see my boyfriend." She turned back to the business of peeling the dress off the dummy and a moment later heard Jack's tread going down the stairs. She couldn't say why she felt let down that he hadn't risen to her teasing, but she did.

Chapter Eleven

JACK WAS REELING from Alice's revelations as he walked to the house. How on earth had she known he'd been in the desert last time he was overseas?

Or was that just another lucky guess?

He bumped into Wye on the back porch. She was just returning from an errand, her arms full of groceries. Jack took them from her and followed her inside.

"I'm beginning to feel like I live here," she said, taking the groceries from Jack and unloading them.

"I think Cass likes having you here. We all do," he hastened to add. "Especially Corporal Myers."

"Emerson? He just sees me as a fellow outsider, that's all."

Jack didn't think that was all, but he let it slide. "Emerson?"

"That's Corporal Myers's first name. You all should know that by now; he's living with you, too."

"I don't suppose you could do me a favor." He took several boxes of pasta and put them away in the pantry.

"Depends on what it is. I don't want to spy on anyone."

Cass must have been talking about him. Or maybe Alice. "Not spy. More like chaperone."

"I'm intrigued."

He appreciated Wyoming's sunny disposition and the fact she had a good head on her shoulders. As far as he was concerned, she was a welcome addition to the offbeat Reed clan. "Alice is about to bring her gowns to Landon's motel room to show him. Something about that guy is rubbing me the wrong way. I can't go with her—although I do plan to be close by. I'm wondering if you would. Maybe you could volunteer to help carry the dresses."

Wyoming thought this over as she put away several cans of beans. "I'm not going to force her to bring me, but I will offer. If she takes me up on it, I'd be glad to help. Otherwise I'll come along with you and stay close."

"Okay. With everything that's happened at Two Willows—"

"I get it, Jack." Wyoming caught his gaze and held it. "I agree with you, too. I don't think Alice should go alone."

"And I don't think you should put Wyoming in danger," Corporal Myers—Emerson, Jack corrected himself—said from the doorway. "Maybe I should go with Alice."

"She's not going to let you go with her either. You're the General's man," Jack said, recovering from surprise that Emerson had managed to sneak up on them.

"I'm my own man," Emerson countered.

"Jack's right. I need to be the one to ask, and I'll be fine," Wyoming said.

"I'll come with you then," Emerson said to Jack.

"The more the merrier. One more thing, Wye."

"What's that?"

"How do you feel about wearing a wire?"

"YES," ALICE SAID, "I'd love it if you came along." When Wyoming had wandered into her studio, bored because Cass was busy with some task she couldn't share, Alice had almost been annoyed at the interruption. Now she was anything but.

Here was her solution to the problem of Landon's libido. He wouldn't hit on her with Wyoming present.

"I'll be your assistant," Wyoming said. "This is probably my one chance to get a glimpse of a real movie producer up close. I'll be quiet as a mouse, I swear. I'll just hold up the dresses when you say to."

"That'll be perfect. Go ahead and speak up as much as you want if he gets…" Alice trailed off, suddenly embarrassed.

"If he gets…?" Wyoming echoed.

"Landon's been making plays for me. He wants more than a business deal."

"Ugh. I mean… unless you want it to be more than a business deal, too."

"Not at all. He's handsome in his own way. He's successful, obviously, but other than that we have nothing in common."

"Other than your love of movies."

Alice hesitated. "Right."

"That wasn't very convincing." Wyoming touched a piece of blue silk that lay on the nearest table.

"I'm starting to get the idea that maybe Landon is more interested in the idea of being a movie producer than he's actually interested in movies." Alice hadn't really put that together until she said it out loud, but how could a serious producer not know about *The Passing Hour*? "God, I hope I'm wrong."

"I hope so, too." Wyoming patted her arm. "I'll listen to everything he says, and when we're done, I'll give you my honest opinion of the situation, okay?"

"Okay." Alice appreciated it. Wyoming would tell her the unvarnished truth. "It's just… I haven't seen an opportunity like this before, and who knows if one will come around again."

"I know it's important to you. My coming with you will send a signal to Landon that you're all business. I bet it will work out just fine."

"I hope you're right."

An hour later Alice knocked on Landon's door, Wyoming close behind her, carrying the dresses. She'd instructed Wyoming to make a production out of helping, so Landon wouldn't complain.

She had a feeling he wouldn't be pleased, though, which made her that much more grateful Wyoming had volunteered to come along. She was far more nervous than she cared to admit, still feeling that generalized sense of doom she'd been feeling for weeks, and something else was tugging at her. She had the sneaking suspicion Jack was… listening… again.

She looked down at her purse, but before she could check it for bugs, the door opened.

"Alice," Landon said, but his welcoming smile quickly faded into a frown. "Who is this?"

"This is Wyoming Smith, my assistant. Wyoming, take the dresses straight inside. Landon and I will follow shortly."

Wyoming nodded and brushed right past Landon into the room. Alice relaxed a little. She and Wyoming had agreed that once Wye was inside, she wouldn't leave again until Alice was ready to go, too. Alice, carrying the requisite underthings for an 1860s ball gown, brushed past Landon, as well. "What a lovely room!"

It really wasn't. The Evergreen Motel was homey, if anything, but clean and well run. It probably didn't stack up to Landon's usual digs.

"I'm so excited for you to see my creations. I hope you'll agree they were worth the wait." Alice also hoped she wasn't overdoing this. Her heavy sense of dread was back. What if she failed? What if Landon, thwarted at trying to lure her to bed, simply sent her home?

"I hope so, too," Landon said tightly.

"Let's start with the lilac gown," Alice commanded Wyoming, deciding not to engage in any more banter.

Wyoming hung the other gowns over the back of the closet door, slipped the lilac one out of its cotton wrapper and off its hangar, and held it up against her body on display.

"This gown, like all three of them, is patterned with exacting correctness to authentic ball gowns that have survived since the 1860s. Notice the neckline," Alice began.

"I can't view it properly like this," Landon interrupted. "The gown needs to be modeled."

"I… uh…" Alice turned to Wyoming, but Wye wasn't even close to the proper measurements. "I'm sorry. You didn't say. I don't have a model—"

"You can model it yourself. You look about the same size as Marlene Avarro. You can change in my bathroom if you're shy." Somehow Landon's tone implied that only a prude would be shy enough to need to close a door while changing.

"I can't demonstrate the techniques I used if I'm wearing it," Alice sputtered.

"You can do a better job demonstrating what makes it special by wearing it than by talking about it."

Wyoming opened her mouth, and Alice knew she was about to tell Landon off. Alice took the lilac gown out of her hands before she could do so. "Wye? I need your help." She jerked her head toward the bathroom, and Wye followed her inside—and locked the door behind them.

"Why are you doing this?" Wye whispered as Alice stripped and pulled on the 1860s-style corset.

"Because I have to." She presented her back, and Wye did her best to do up the ties. When she was done, she helped Alice step into the wide hoopskirt and laced that up, too.

"Landon's creepy."

She was right, but Alice had come this far. She couldn't simply leave now.

Wye lifted the heavy lilac gown over Alice's head and helped her with the fastenings when she got it on. It took a bunch of fussing to get it right—and the gown was still far too long for Alice.

"Ready?" Wye said when they were done.

"Ready as I'll ever be." Her stomach was fluttery when Wye opened the bathroom door and preceded her out. Landon was sitting on the bed. He watched Alice's progress dispassionately as she pushed in the sides of her hoopskirt with her hands in order to make it through the bathroom door, then let the skirt plump out again.

Alice squared her shoulders. She wasn't going to let Landon get to her. She was an expert at what she did, and she deserved respect.

"This gown is modeled after a dress currently displayed in the Smithsonian museum," Alice began, and she was off and running. Landon listened carefully and allowed her to go through the whole description she'd practiced ahead of time, his expression unchanging. Several times she thought his gaze rested on her décolletage, which the gown rendered ample and exposed.

Alice kept going. If she was honest, she'd expected nothing but praise from him, despite the little tiffs they'd had so far. She considered this gown some of her best work. All hand-stitched, historically accurate—and beautiful, if she did say so herself—it deserved a standing ovation.

Not this—silence.

When she'd finished, she must have fidgeted, because Landon straightened. "It's quite… lovely," he said, as if it wasn't really beautiful at all. Was his gaze resting on her cleavage again? "It needs alterations, of course."

"Of… course," Alice managed. Alterations? Where? The way he kept focusing on her chest made it seem like he was implying the problem might be with her body rather than the gown.

"Something's off." Landon pointed at the bodice—and her breasts. "I'm not entirely sure what." He let the statement hang, all the while considering her. Alice stiffened, and despite herself, her cheeks grew hot. Wye stood equally rigid nearby, her face a study of anger and indecision.

"Maybe it's the lace," Landon said slowly. "Something's wrong in that area," he added, drawing a circle in the air that indicated her bosom.

Alice fought to keep her voice steady. "It was difficult to locate this lace—"

"And the sleeves. I don't know… there's something unattractive and overdone about them."

Alice gazed down at the sleeves. She loved the little puffed sleeves, but… maybe he was right. Maybe they weren't quite the thing—

Or maybe it was her. Was she overdone? She'd put makeup on before coming to see him—a touch more than usual, but not that much—

He caught her expression. "Hey, Alice, you're doing great for an amateur. I don't expect your first attempt to be on par with one of the pros. You just need to try a little harder. Get in my head. See what I see. I mean, I know you aren't psychic or anything—"

Wyoming snorted. She clapped a hand to her mouth. "Sorry."

Landon sent her a curious look. His sudden grin made Alice relax, just a bit. Maybe she was being oversensitive. Maybe he had been looking at the dresses—not her body, or her face. Had she been reading him all wrong?

"Alice, you don't think you're psychic, do you?" he teased. "That would be just a little too small-town gothic for me."

Irritation flared within her again. She was getting sick of him treating her like a dilettante when she was anything but—as a seamstress or a psychic.

"I am psychic," she said matter-of-factly before she could think better of it. "I get hunches. They're often accurate. But that's something I only share with family and close friends."

Landon studied her for a long moment, then chuckled. "You know, I actually heard a rumor in town about that, but I never guessed you'd make a claim to it. That's a handy talent. You should tell me who's going to win the football game tonight."

"The Raiders." Hell. Alice stilled. She shouldn't have said that. Why had Landon been talking about her in town? What had people said? This had all gone too far. "Wyoming? Help me change. We'll show Landon the peach gown now."

Wyoming entered the bathroom with her again.

"He's an idiot," she hissed. "Why's he cutting you down like that? The gown is gorgeous, and so are you."

Alice wasn't so sure of that, and the peach gown, which was exquisite if she did say so herself, wasn't a color that suited her. Back outside in the room, her fears were confirmed. While Landon kept nodding as she explained the details, it was plain he didn't like what he saw.

"That isn't quite right either. I need something showstopping. No man would look twice at you in that dress, Alice," Landon said. Wyoming opened her mouth. Alice rushed to intercede.

"Marlene has much darker coloring than I do. It will look spectacular on her," she asserted.

"Maybe. But it leaves a lot to be desired. It's dowdy. There's no spark—no sexual promise. You look like someone's aunt. I want you to be a bombshell."

"I won't be wearing the dress," she reminded him.

Landon frowned. "You're wearing it now."

"Wyoming? Let's do the blue one."

Alice's hands were shaking by the time Wye closed the bathroom door behind them and she tried to get out of the gown. Wye took over.

"Don't you listen to a word he says. He's read that book."

"What book?"

"The one that teaches men how to control women

by criticizing them. I saw a show about it once."

"Does that work?" Alice raised her arms and let Wye pull the gown up and over her head, then replace it with the light blue one.

"Look at you—you're playing dress up for him in his motel room, and you're practically in tears. Alice Reed, you are the most beautiful woman anyone in Chance Creek has ever seen. The most talented, too. Everyone knows you're going places—and he's making you feel like shit."

"Chance Creek's a small town. Landon's used to city girls."

"City girls aren't any prettier—and they're definitely not better at designing costumes." Wyoming finished doing her up and turned her around. Placing her hands on Alice's shoulders, she gave her a little shake. "Snap out of it. You put this asshole in his place. No job is worth this. You go out there, show him what you can do and make it crystal clear who's in charge. You hear me?"

Alice straightened her shoulders. Thank God for Wye. "You're right, and I hear you."

This time she was ready for Landon's brutal comments, but they still hurt more than she wanted to admit. After nitpicking the cut, the drape and every other design choice she'd made for the gown, he finished by saying, "Come on, Alice. That dress is straight out of central casting for a '40s musical. These simply aren't good enough."

"Then I'll take them home—" She turned away.

"Let me finish. They're close enough I want to give you another chance. You can sew, Alice, I'll grant you that."

Alice gripped her hands together to hide that they were shaking. Of course she could sew.

"When I come back, I want to see these gowns fixed."

"When you come back?" she repeated.

"I've got to catch a plane tonight."

"You said you would stay a few days." She was merely pointing out the way his story kept changing, but she realized after she'd said it how weak it sounded. Like she was begging him to change his mind.

"Don't worry—I won't desert you. I'll give you five days. If you've made the changes I've asked for, we'll talk more. Can you do that?"

"Of course."

Wye huffed out a sigh, but Alice knew she had to give this another chance. Landon was an ass, but he was an ass who was producing one of the biggest period dramas of the decade. Wyoming's expression was thunderous as they withdrew into the bathroom and she helped Alice undress a third time, but Alice had gotten her mojo back. Now that she knew what Landon was looking for, she could do better.

When they emerged again, Landon stepped in Alice's way.

"Hold on a moment. I planned for us to go to dinner tonight. I'll drive. She can take the dresses home." He nodded at Wye.

"I'm sorry; I have a prior engagement," Alice said loftily. "Have a safe trip."

"Break your prior engagement," Landon demanded.

"With my father? The man with a thirty-year career in the Army who was just injured in a missile attack? I don't think so."

There was that pinched look again. "Of course. Next time."

"GLAD TO SEE you home," Jack told Alice when she and Wyoming finally returned. As soon as he and Emerson had seen them safely get into Alice's truck at the motel, he'd gunned the engine and driven home as fast as he could, so that now it would look like he'd been there all along. He was still fuming about the way Landon had spoken to Alice. He'd known guys like that—men who used psychological tricks to manipulate women. He'd been ready to storm the motel door, but Alice had rallied. He'd nearly cheered when she'd walked out on Landon.

But she was still trying to get the contract. He was sure that was a mistake.

"Glad to be here." She looked over her shoulder at Wyoming. "Thank you so much for coming along. You were a lifesaver."

"Any time." Wyoming had lectured her all the way home about never being alone with Landon. Alice assured her she had no intention of ever doing such a thing.

"Why was she a lifesaver?" Jack asked. As if he

didn't know.

"None of your business," she said tartly. "Even though you seem to think it is."

"All I want is to keep you safe."

"From Landon? He couldn't hurt a fly." Alice waved off that idea.

"Yes, he could." Jack wasn't going to let her get away with that. "He could hurt you if he wanted to."

"But that's not what he wants." Alice looked away. "He's been hitting on me, okay? That's why I brought Wyoming with me."

Wyoming raised an eyebrow at Jack, as if daring him to admit he'd asked her to go. Jack wasn't going to do that, though.

"Next time you should bring me."

Alice narrowed her eyes. "Next time? How did you know there'd be a next time? You haven't even asked me if I landed the contract. Because you know I didn't. You were listening again, weren't you?" Alice pulled open her handbag, searched inside it and pulled out one of his bugs. She dropped it on the floor and squashed it. Jack winced. Those were expensive. "You're as bad as the General, you know that?" she added, heading for the stairs. A moment later they heard her door slam.

"If she'd spotted my wire, do you think she would have crushed me like a bug, too?" Wye asked Jack.

"I'm not going to apologize, if that's what you want. I heard how he was talking to Alice."

"You're right," Wye said, becoming serious. "I'm glad I was there. If I hadn't been, he would have applied a lot more pressure to get her into bed with him."

"Thanks for everything you did."

"Any time. I'm going to go get changed." Halfway to the door, she paused. "These Reed women. They're so strong and so… hurt… at the same time. A person looking to do damage can really get to them."

"I don't want to hurt Alice," Jack said. That's what she was asking, wasn't it?

"Just make sure you don't do it accidentally."

She went upstairs, too, leaving Jack to think over her words. Hours later, when Jack went to bed, he lay awake and listened for a knock that never came.

When he couldn't stand it anymore, he got up, pulled his sweatpants on and went to Alice's door.

It was locked.

ALICE WAS STILL out of sorts when Cass found her in the kitchen very early the next morning. It was still dark out, and she didn't think anyone else was up, but she hadn't slept well. Up on her perch on top of the refrigerator, Alice knew she should be getting on with her day. After all, she had three costumes to fix. She couldn't seem to calm down, though.

She couldn't say what made her angrier, Landon's attempts to cut her down, or Jack's continued attempts to surveil her entire life. When Tabitha meowed, Alice pet her. Things were so much simpler for cats.

"What's wrong?" Cass asked.

"Men are driving me crazy."

Cass chuckled as she began to pull breakfast fixings

out of the refrigerator. "Maybe that's only fair. I think you've driven a fair number of them crazy over the years."

Alice made a face. "You know what I mean. Jack's as bad as the General, following me around, listening in on my conversations, telling me who I should be hanging out with."

Cass's eyebrows shot up. "When did the General ever do any of that? Maybe if he'd been here waiting at the door for us the way Jack was waiting for you last night, things wouldn't have been so hard."

"Jack isn't my father." But Alice knew what Cass meant, and she was right; there'd been times it would have been nice to have someone around who cared like that. That didn't give Jack the right to pry, though. "He's been bugging my purse."

Cass blinked. "Bugging your purse?"

"That's what I said."

"That's not okay."

"Exactly."

Her sister let out a breath. "I'm sorry; I wasn't taking you seriously. It's just… as much as the General has always driven me crazy, too, the men he's sent have worked out pretty well. I just figured…"

"Maybe five out of five is too much to ask from a man who knows nothing about us." She didn't want to spend a lifetime with a man who didn't trust her to take care of herself—or believe what she told him. "Jack's as bad as Howie."

Cass made a strangled sound. "Hardly." When Alice

huffed, she went on. "Come on, Howie was a two-bit criminal. He didn't care about you at all. Jack's problem is he cares too much."

"All he cares about is controlling me."

"Are you sure that's true?"

Alice wasn't ready to back down, but she knew what Cass meant, and she knew she was reading Jack's actions in the worst way possible. Bugging her crossed every line in the book—until you took into consideration what had happened at Two Willows during the last four months.

"He thinks Landon could be involved with the guys who attacked us," Cass said quietly.

"That doesn't make any sense."

"That's what I told Brian, and Brian agrees," Cass acknowledged. "But that doesn't mean Jack's wrong."

"If he wants to be with me, he'd better back off." Alice went back to petting Tabitha.

"Is him being with you still a possibility?" Cass was pretending she didn't care about the answer, but Alice knew she did.

Alice had a glimpse of a vision. Cass clinging to her and sobbing. The image was gone as fast as it had come, but it left her shaken. She realized she'd been trying to convince herself that since the General had already been hurt—and was home—her premonitions of danger had been fulfilled.

But that wasn't true.

"What?" Cass asked, straightening. She could read Alice too well.

"Nothing. I'd better get to work. Landon didn't like the lace on the lilac dress."

"He didn't like the lace?" Cass's frown deepened. "I love that lace."

"I know, right? But what the client wants, the client gets." She shifted, and Tabitha jumped down from the refrigerator. Alice followed her, gave Cass a hug and headed for the door. "Don't worry about me. I've always been fine without a man. I don't need to get married."

She didn't think she'd convinced either of them, though.

Chapter Twelve

"I'M SORRY."

Jack caught up with her when she was halfway to the carriage house. He'd seen her from the maze, where he'd been attempting to enter it again. It was still dark—and he'd figured no one would see him trying to get in. At this time of the year, the sun wasn't up until seven-thirty, but their day started closer to five. He'd been up extra early this morning and had slipped outside while the others were still sleeping.

"Did you get in this time?" She ignored his apology.

"I mean it. I shouldn't have listened in without you knowing." Jack touched her arm.

"You're right, you shouldn't. I can't be with a man who doesn't trust me."

"And I can't be with a woman who's dead."

"That's a little overdramatic, don't you think?" Alice's breath plumed in the cold air, but she didn't move away.

"Your ranch has been attacked four times in four months. I'd say I was being practical." He hoped she understood what he really meant: that he couldn't take any chances with a woman he cared about.

When she didn't answer, he braced for trouble, but when she spoke, her words surprised him. "You're right," she admitted. "They're coming back. I can feel it."

"That's what Cab thinks, too."

She rolled her eyes, and he realized that had sounded like he thought Cab's opinion meant more than hers. Not what he meant at all. "What do you feel about Landon?" he asked to change the conversation.

Alice narrowed her eyes, as if she knew he wasn't asking if Landon was dangerous; he was asking if he had a rival.

"I'm not sure yet," she hedged, then bit back a smile. She was teasing him.

"I didn't get into the maze." Another diversionary tactic.

Alice's smile widened. "It hasn't forgiven you yet."

"Alice—come on, how are you doing that?" Jack's frustration grew. She was laughing at him for wanting her—and for worrying about Landon. He didn't like that one bit.

Alice shrugged. "It's not me."

He studied her. "I don't like things I can't explain." He'd looked all over the hedge that formed the perimeter of the maze and seen no evidence of a mechanism that could move thirty-foot trees around in the blink of an eye.

"No, you don't, do you? You're a careful man."

"Especially with the things I care for. And people."

Alice looked down, and the moment stretched out between them. When Jack stepped nearer, she didn't move away. He remembered the way her mouth had felt under his, remembered the curves of her body as he'd explored it the other night. His blood thrummed in his veins. He'd like to experience that again.

He touched her shoulder. Bent to kiss her once, twice, and then tugged her nearer and deepened the connection. Alice braced her hands on his chest, rising up on tiptoe.

Did she want more? He sure did.

When they broke apart, they were both breathless.

Jack grinned down at her. "That works."

"What do you mean?"

"I'm too inquisitive, you're too cautious, but that… that works between us."

"I've got to get back to my dresses." She turned away, but Jack caught her hand.

"I think Landon's wrong, you know. Those costumes are perfect the way they are. So are you. When I heard the way he was talking to you, I wanted to bust in there and—" He balled the fingers of his free hand into a fist. "Here's the thing, Alice. When a guy talks that way, he doesn't mean any of it. It's not that anything is wrong with you—or your gowns. It's that everything is far too right. He wants you. Probably wants your dresses, too—if he's really a movie producer at all. He's afraid he's not going to get either."

"You really think it's just a business tactic?" she asked.

"Absolutely. Are you sure you want to go through with meeting him again? Do you really want to work with this guy?"

She hesitated. "I have to give this my best shot. Maybe he won't hire me. Maybe you're right; maybe he's not even who he seems. But maybe he is. This still could be my chance. I have to give it everything I've got."

He didn't want her taking any chances. Knowing he had to choose his words carefully if he wanted her to listen, Jack moved closer. "Alice, I'm not saying this as the man your father sent to marry you. I'm saying this as… just a man. Someone who's gotten to know you and wants you to be safe. You feel controlled when I bug you. But Landon could hurt you if I'm not there to protect you. Isn't there any common ground we can meet on?"

She thought about that. "If I say yes, will you take it as permission to try to run my life?"

"No." He sighed. He didn't want to run her life. He just wanted to share it.

"Then go ahead."

"Really?"

Alice nodded. "If I'm honest, I'm having doubts about him, too. I don't want to lose this opportunity, but I don't want to be stupid, either. Next time I see him, I'll let you bug my purse. I'll take Wyoming with me, too. I don't want you to surveil me again without my agreement up front, you hear? But when it comes to Landon, do your worst."

"Okay," he agreed quickly. All of that was fair. "Just remember when all this is said and done that you know costumes a hell of a lot better than he does. Do what you need to do, and then get back to your own vision. Because yours is a hell of a lot better than his."

SHE'D ALMOST MADE it to the carriage house when she heard the back door shut behind Jack. Alice hesitated, suddenly feeling the urge to see the standing stone. It had been too long.

She couldn't pretend she wasn't worried about Landon. On the one hand, she didn't think he was lying about who he was, and she thought he was far more likely to be a man used to getting his way with women rather than anything else, but the pit of dread in her stomach had been there for weeks. She had to admit trouble was on the horizon.

She slipped back across to the maze's entrance and traversed the paths quickly. The standing stone stood tall in the starlight, for all the world like it had stood there since the dawn of time, although of course that couldn't be true. No one knew who'd put it there. Her own mother had planted the maze around it. Sadie tended it. It was one of Alice's favorite spots on the ranch.

Alone with the stone, peace filled her, and she drew her gloves off so she could touch it with her bare hands. It was icy cold as she rested them on its bare surface. Soon the sky would lighten, but for now it could be midnight it was so dark. In the quiet, away from the warm glow spilling out of the kitchen's windows, she felt far from anyone else—in her own world.

She didn't know what to think about her attraction to Jack. He'd pushed her buttons from the minute he arrived—in both senses. When he was close, she couldn't think about anything else, and even if she'd brushed off his apology earlier, he had apologized.

That's more than most men did.

She thought she understood why he was like he was—or at least had a hunch. Something had happened to that girl she'd gotten a glimpse of in her vision. Something bad.

Now Jack was trying to prevent the same thing from happening to her.

He'd have to stop surveilling her without her permission, but she supposed she could understand the sentiment.

Without thinking, she flattened her hands against the stone. "Should I open my heart to Jack?"

She didn't expect to receive an answer. The stone spoke in mysterious ways, and she knew she'd have to be patient. Alice looked up into a sky where the stars shone like chips of ice.

It was quiet here, and Alice realized she'd been so taken up with her racing thoughts these past few weeks that she hadn't slowed down to simply be. She felt her shoulders relax and knew she must have been holding them stiff and high. Her fingers ached from sewing. Her back hurt from bending and stooping. It felt good to let go all the tension for a moment.

A glint of metal at the base of the nearest row of hedge caught her eye. Curious, Alice went to see what it was. The link of a chain. She tugged at it gently and unearthed a necklace of some kind from the snow.

No—not a necklace.

A pair of dog tags.

A memory seized her, and Alice sank down on the nearby wooden bench, clutching the dog tags in her hand.

Lena had been the one to take them from their father's bedside table. The General had been home for one of his fleeting visits when they were little girls, but he'd been about to leave again, and Lena had been so determined to make him stay for once that she'd stolen his dog tags and raced away with them through the maze. Cass, ever the little mother, had given chase, screaming at her to put them back before they got in trouble. Alice, Sadie and Jo had followed, caught up in the excitement.

Alice remembered Lena flinging the dog tags. She'd always had a strong arm. Cass had been in tears at the rebellion. Lena had been in tears of rage that the General kept leaving her behind. By the time their parents came to see what was the matter, they'd all been crying.

Alice remembered the way the General had gathered them in his arms. Back then he'd made such displays of affection unconsciously, and they eagerly turned to him for comfort. When they'd settled down, they all searched the maze from top to bottom, but the dog tags had never been found, and the General had to leave without them.

What was the stone trying to tell her?

She thought she knew.

Maybe it was time to open her heart—not just to Jack, but to her father, too. Maybe healing was possible.

Maybe family was possible.

She pocketed the dog tags, retraced her steps, feeling lighter somehow, and when she was ensconced in her workshop, she found herself whistling as she began to unstitch the lace.

She didn't care about Landon. The important people were here on this ranch. If she was taking apart these gowns and fixing them, it was because she was doing it for herself.

But Landon was right—the gowns could be better.

And she knew just what to do.

JACK SPENT THE morning helping Jo with her chores as she gave him a running commentary about everything she did.

"Won't Hunter be suspicious about why we're spending so much time together?" he asked as they set out on the tractor to bring hay to the cattle.

"Hunter's at the dentist this morning. We have a few hours."

Alice joined the rest of them in the house at lunchtime but returned to the carriage house after twenty minutes. She seemed almost luminous in her determination, and Jack found it hard not to watch her, but he didn't know how to help.

"How are those dresses?" Cass called after her as she tugged on her outer gear.

"Coming along" was all Alice said. Jack decided to let her be for now, although he'd have loved to follow her to her studio to spend some time with her.

"Let's get back to work." Jo roused him from his reverie.

"Sure thing, boss."

Will was back when they stopped for a snack mid-afternoon. Jack had run upstairs for a moment and found the hall full of plumbing equipment. Wyoming was leaning in the doorway to the bathroom, where Will was hard at work.

"Any luck?" He didn't really want those pipes fixed, but of course he couldn't say that.

"Not so far. I've tried every trick in the book. Wyoming is going to think I don't know my trade." Will flashed him a grin. He was always smiling, Jack thought. Neither life nor stubborn plumbing problems ever got Will down.

"I'm not thinking anything in particular. Just enjoying watching a man at work," Wye said contentedly.

Heavy footsteps behind them had them both looking to see who was coming. Emerson was mounting the staircase.

"The General wants a report about the plumbing," the corporal said. "Should have been done by now."

"It'll take as long as it takes," Will said caustically, scrambling out from under the sink. "Tell the old man to relax. He's just like my old man—always rushing. Never getting anything done right."

"Maybe you should tell him that."

"Maybe you should keep your nose out of my business."

Jack stepped between them. "How long will it take for you to finish your current set of repairs?" he asked the plumber.

"Another half hour, tops." Will relaxed back against the cabinet and crossed his arms over his chest.

"Go tell the General that," Jack ordered Emerson. "Wyoming, maybe we'd better let Will get to it."

She looked like she would argue, but then she shrugged and gave Will a little wave. "See you later."

"Yeah, later." Will looked like thunder as they left. Emerson, on the other hand, held his head high, Jack noticed. Had he just stacked the cards in the corporal's favor? He hadn't meant to, although there was something about Corporal Myers that he could sympathize with.

Of course, Wyoming should be the one to choose.

When his phone buzzed, and Richard's name showed up on screen, he went into the guest room and answered the call quickly, although he knew there might be awkward questions. While he was there, he tapped on his tablet and checked the various feeds from his surveillance equipment. Nothing was amiss.

"Pop!"

"Hey, Jack. How's it going?"

"Pretty good. How are things in DC?"

"Lots of work for you here whenever you're ready for it."

Here they went again. Jack looked at the tablet again and paged to the sports website he followed. He tended to cycle through news, a military forum and a couple of video bloggers who were constantly showing off new gear. When he was done with the heavy stuff, he switched to sports to take his mind off things.

"How about those Raiders?" Alice had been right; they'd won last night. What would Landon make of that?

Pure luck, if you asked him. Anyone could call a game when the odds were 50/50.

"You know I don't watch football. I don't have time," Richard said.

"Maybe you should make time now and then." Not that he got the chance to catch many games, either. "You need to relax more, Pop."

"I will when you will."

One point for Richard. Jack tapped his fingers on the desk. "Was that why you were calling? To tell me about work?"

"Just calling to chat." Richard was trying to sound casual but failed. Jack understood. Their conversations were getting more and more awkward, something neither of them wanted. Jack wasn't ready to cave, though. Richard had been pushing too hard lately. He'd orchestrated much of Jack's life, and now Jack was old enough to make his own decisions.

"Then let's chat. I met a girl."

Richard hesitated. "I wondered if you might have. I've heard some rumors about that task force you're on. Something about all the participants ending up married."

Jack didn't know how to answer that. He should have known Richard would be digging for dirt.

"Well, she and I just met, so I don't know about marriage," he hedged. He wouldn't tell Richard that was the whole point.

"Gonna give me a name?"

"Alice."

"Alice—"

"That's all you get to know until things are serious." He hoped that would be the end of it but knew it wouldn't be.

"You've just given me a challenge, you know." Richard chuckled. "Like waving a red flag in front of a bull."

"She deserves her privacy, Pop. And respect." Not that he'd given her much of either lately.

"Hell, you've got it bad. You've only been there a week. It can't possibly be serious. Neither can your insistence on privacy, since I already know you're at Two Willows, and I know the General has a daughter named Alice."

Hell. Richard had him there. Jack was losing his touch—that was a rookie mistake.

"It can be serious." Jack kept his tone light, but he figured it made sense to give Richard a head's up. He was serious about Alice.

"Why do I get a feeling there's more to this story than you're letting me know?"

Richard was too damn perceptive.

"I've got to do this on my own. Can't let my father call the shots on this one."

An edge crept into Richard's voice. "Sometimes fathers know best, son."

"And sometimes they don't. Sometimes they have to take things on faith." He hadn't meant to get into all this tonight. Jack was beginning to wish he hadn't answered the call.

"I've taken things on faith before. I took you on faith. Last thing I expected when I came along on that call to your parents' ranch was to come home with a seven-year-old child."

"I know, Pop."

"I've never regretted a minute of it, either."

Jack closed his eyes. "I know that, too."

"YOU WERE RIGHT about those Raiders. Should have laid down more money," Landon said when Alice took his call.

"Lucky guess." She wished she'd never mentioned it. It wasn't like her to show off her abilities. Besides, it wasn't like she could count on her hunches. Sometimes she got them; most times she didn't.

She wondered where Landon was now. In some city where some professional costume designer had shown him her creations? Was she even still in the running?

Someone was coming up the stairs. One of her sisters, since the tread was light. Jo popped around the corner and waved when she noticed Alice was on the phone.

"Who's going to win tonight?" Landon asked.

"I don't know. I don't even know who's playing." She carefully kept her mind blank. She wasn't going to tell him a thing. "I've been too hard at work on the dresses," she added. Jo crossed to stand before the gown she was working on and looked it up and down.

"I'm sure you have. Just wanted to check in. I'll call again later. See how you're doing."

"Okay." She wondered why he was being conciliatory now when he'd been such a bear yesterday.

"It's hard to be alone all the time on the road."

"Hm." She wasn't going to fall for that trick. Landon probably wanted some phone sex. She stepped back to survey the lilac gown now that she'd removed the lace.

"Guess I'll turn on the game," he said glumly.

"More football?" She kind of liked the neckline without the lace, now that she'd had a second look at it. Maybe she should edge it with—

"Basketball."

"The Celtics," she murmured, deep in thought.

"What was that?" Landon's sharp tone recalled Alice to herself. What had she said?

Celtics. Crud. Why had she done that?

"I didn't even tell you who was playing," Landon said.

"The Celtics are the only basketball team I know,"

she lied. "Who's your favorite?"

"How did you know—"

"Gotta go. Talk to you later."

She nearly dropped her phone in her haste to cut the call. Jo lifted an eyebrow. "Handing out hot tips now?"

"I didn't mean to."

"Who was that?"

"Landon." She sighed again. "I screwed up. Mentioned the Raiders winning last night. When he told me he was going to watch another game, the winner just slipped out."

"Wish you'd told me about the Raiders." Jo grinned and ducked when Alice tossed a tape measure at her. "That's not like you, though."

"He rattled me. He's not taking it seriously. At least, I hope not."

"What are you going to do to it?" Jo gestured to the gown.

"I'm still working on that." An idea had taken shape in her mind, but she was still refining it. Alice was beginning to give Landon credit for seeing her work better than she had. When she was done, the dress would be better.

"I bet Mom could have made a mint making predictions. I wonder if she was ever tempted?" Jo mused.

"She was a lot better at managing her gift than I am, that's for sure." Alice had always wondered how Amelia did it. Had her foresight plagued her the way it did Alice sometimes? How did she know when to speak up about what she'd seen and when to keep quiet?

She didn't realize she'd asked that last question out loud until Jo said, "You know what animals do?"

"No." Alice took a seat and gave her sister her attention. Jo had a feeling for animals—a special way of relating to them.

"Animals listen to their gut. That's all they have to go on. They can't ask questions or do research or consult with their friends, so they have to rely on their observations and their instincts. Humans are so unhappy all the time because they ignore their gut—and because they fight against their fate."

"Do animals have fates?"

"Sure they do." Jo was serious. "So do we. I don't think it's your fate to wind up with Landon."

"I don't think so, either," Alice said sharply.

"But you're spending a lot more time thinking about his opinion of your gowns than you are wondering what Jack thinks about you."

"I know what Jack thinks." She plucked at a length of cotton fabric nearby.

"Then you know he likes you."

"He likes me. But he doesn't believe me." She met Jo's gaze. "I don't want to be with a man who doesn't believe me."

"Give him a chance. I think he'll change his mind. Speaking of Jack, I'd better go find him. I'm supposed to teach him about pasture management."

"Sounds like a good time."

Chapter Thirteen

JACK JOINED THE rest of the men in the barn at the end of the afternoon, trailing Jo.

"Well, would you look who's come calling," Connor called out. "It's about time. Was thinking you were one lazy son of a bitch."

"I've been making sure no one's prowling around this ranch," Jack pointed out. It had taken days to get his surveillance system up and working. And more days to learn his way around the chores with Jo.

"Whatever. We've got a sick critter, looks like. Come with me, and let's see what we can figure out before we go in for dinner."

Jack cast a look back at Jo, willing her to step in and deflect Connor, but she had already grabbed a pitchfork and was headed for the stable.

"Well? You coming?" Connor asked.

"Don't know a lot about sick critters," Jack said uncomfortably.

"Your folks have some magic formula to keep them all well?" Connor scoffed.

Brian looked up from where he was sorting through

some tools. "I'd like to know that trick."

"Wouldn't we all?" Hunter said.

"No trick." He'd backed himself well and good into this corner, hadn't he? Jack braced himself against their derision. "Just haven't spent that much time on a ranch."

"Thought you grew up on a ranch." Brian straightened.

"I did. Until I was seven."

"What happened then? Folks have to sell out?" Connor asked.

Jack hated the sympathy in his face. Hated what would come next more. "Died." He would have walked out of the barn, but Connor blocked his way.

"Your folks died when you were seven?"

"Yep." Jack stood his ground, but it took doing.

"Hell, why didn't you ever say that?" Brian asked.

"Never came up."

"And that's why you're trailing around my wife like a lost puppy dog?" Hunter drawled. "Thought I'd have to teach you some manners."

Just like that, the heaviness lifted. Jack allowed a smile to tug at his mouth. "Only one Reed girl has my interest."

"Better not be Sadie," Connor said.

"You know it's Alice."

"Better come learn how to be a rancher then," Connor said. "I'm the best teacher you'll find."

The other men groaned.

"Better go find Jo again," Brian advised, "or you'll

have to unlearn everything Connor teaches you."

In the end Jack went with Connor, who proved to know quite a bit about sick critters, although he ended up calling in the vet to take a look, too. Jack knew he hadn't heard the last of the jokes, but he also knew he could take it. He liked this work.

Liked these men, too.

He was beginning to think he'd found a home here at Two Willows.

If only he could convince Alice to let him stay.

ALICE WAS SITTING on top of the refrigerator again when Lena and Logan arrived home from their honeymoon about an hour before dinnertime. She should have been in her studio working, but she'd hit a wall. Tabitha was curled up in her lap sleeping. Alice had been petting her, trying to get her racing mind to calm down, but it wasn't working, so she was happy to shoo Tabitha off her lap and climb down to greet her sister.

"Look how tan you are," Alice exclaimed jealously. Oh, to relax on a tropical island. Wouldn't that be heavenly? "I'm surprised you didn't extend your vacation."

"Missed the ranch too much. The sun was great, so was the water, but nothing beats Two Willows."

Alice had to smile. Lena would never change.

"Is the General really home?" Logan asked, lowering his voice, after allowing Alice to give him a welcome home hug.

"In his office. He's spent most of his time there.

Corporal Myers—Emerson—guards him like a dragon guards its gold. Emerson bunks down in the living room, but you'd never know it. He's got his bedding folded up and stowed away every morning and the room straight as a pin before breakfast." She touched the dog tags she carried in her pocket but decided this wasn't the time to bring them out.

"Is the General trying to run everything?" Lena asked.

"Trying, but not succeeding."

Cass came in, and soon the others joined them until the kitchen was full of talk and laughter.

"Well? Where is everyone?" The bellow jolted them all. A moment later Emerson popped his head around the doorway.

"Muster time."

"We already did muster time," Jo complained, but they all trouped into the office, including Logan and Lena, who looked like she'd rather be walking toward a firing squad.

"So. You finally decided to come home," the General said to Lena once everyone had arranged themselves around his bed. Like usual, he was dressed but sitting with his leg propped on several pillows. Alice wondered if his injuries hurt much. Neither he nor Emerson ever complained about them, but toward the end of the day she had noticed Emerson made more trips back and forth from office to kitchen. She had a feeling the General got crankier at night, probably because of the pain and enforced rest.

Lena sputtered for a moment before she found her voice. "Are you serious—?"

"I'm waiting for my report," the General said to Logan, ignoring her. "Status?"

"Uh… fine, sir. We had a great honeymoon. We're both rested and ready to get back to work."

"Good, good. Lake?" the General turned to Brian.

Lena's eyebrows shot up. "That's it? After eleven years, all you have to say is 'good'?"

"What do you want me to say?"

"How about, 'Great job running the ranch, Lena. I always knew you had it in you. Wow, you handle things way better than those assholes I sent—'"

"Lena," Logan said.

"No, I'm going to have my say." Lena shrugged off her husband's restraining hand. "You are a lousy father," she said to the General. "Always have been, always will be. This is my ranch, and I'm going to run it the way I see fit, and you just stay out of it!" Lena caught herself, took in the men around her, who'd all been helping to run things the last few months, and the wind went out of her sails. "You all know what I mean," she said.

"We do," Brian assured her. "We've been through this before, and we have a system in place that works. No need to rock the boat. Sir, with all due respect, we've got this ranch running shipshape."

"That's what I just said," Lena growled.

"I'm still the senior officer here," the General began.

"And what—you think you can do a better job than I can? When's the last time you even rode a horse?" She gestured at his leg supported on the pillows. "What are the chances you'll ever ride again? A cowboy who can't ride isn't a cowboy—and you aren't fit to run this ranch—"

"Lena!" Logan said again. "Think about what you're saying!"

Lena stilled. Alice couldn't remember ever hearing Logan raise his voice before—or her sister letting anyone restrain her temper. For a moment she thought Lena might walk out. Instead, she closed her eyes, turned back to the General. "I'm… sorry," she managed to say stiffly, although her anger was plain to hear. "I shouldn't have said that, but there are a lot of things you shouldn't have said or done, either. Maybe I'm not a man, but I'm your wife's daughter—"

"You're my daughter, too," the General snapped.

"Am I? You sure as hell haven't ever acted like it. Not since I got—" She gestured to her breasts and hips, making an hour-glass shape in the air with her hands. "Why do you hate women so much?"

"I don't hate women." The General pushed himself up straighter in the bed. "I've done everything I can to protect you—"

"I don't want protecting. I want respect! Why is that so hard to understand?"

The General searched for an answer but couldn't seem to come up with one.

Lena threw her hands up. "I'm so over this." And

she walked out the door.

"MOMENTOUS DAY," CASS said a half hour later when Jack walked through the kitchen, checking to see if it was dinnertime. The smells emanating from the oven had him salivating. "The General is joining us at the table for dinner."

"To celebrate all his daughters being home?" He wondered how Lena would handle that.

"Probably." She smiled at her friend, who was chopping vegetables to add to a salad. "Plus, I'm pretty sure he's trying to set up Wyoming with Emerson."

"Either that or he's sweet on her himself," Sadie quipped, coming in and opening the fridge.

Wyoming dropped her knife and faced her. "Don't even joke about that."

"You'd be our mom," Sadie teased her. "You could boss Cass around."

"Sadie." Cass's voice was sharp.

"Just kidding." Sadie reappeared with a soda and left the room again.

"If your father hits on me, I'm out of here," Wyoming told Cass while Jack crossed to grab himself a beer. "I'll be out of your way and back home in a couple of days, anyway."

"No hurry at all," Cass assured her. "I love having you stay here. We all do. You know that."

"It's true," Jack added. "You're not in anyone's way." Quite the contrary. He wanted her close in case Alice needed a chaperone again.

"I need to find a real job, though."

"Any new leads?"

Jack left them to their discussion. When he made it upstairs and bumped into Emerson coming out of the bathroom, he was pretty sure it would be the corporal hitting on Wyoming, rather than the General. Emerson's hair was damp. His face newly shaved.

"Dinner's almost ready," Jack told him. "Wyoming's here."

"Thanks."

"You all right with this? The General setting you up?"

The younger man flushed. "Why not? Wyoming's sweet. Pretty, too. This place—it'd be a good home."

"Where is your home?" He knew Emerson's parents were gone. Was pretty sure the man's only home was the Army.

Emerson's flush deepened. "Don't have one," he said and hurried away.

"DINNER IS GOING to be a disaster," Alice whispered to Cass when they met in the upstairs hall. She'd passed Jack a minute ago and had just popped into the bathroom to freshen up before the meal. She'd found Cass waiting for her turn when she got out again.

"Is that a prediction?"

"I don't need a vision to know it. Lena's furious, and the General is practically throwing Wye at Emerson."

"I think it's the other way around, actually." Cass

sounded amused. "Wye is getting a taste of what we've all gone through. After the way she's laughed at our expense these past months, I kind of think she deserves it. Besides, Emerson seems like a pretty nice guy. I don't know how he stands the General."

"He's a corporal. He signed up to be ordered around. We didn't."

When Cass announced that the meal was ready, Emerson helped the General to his seat at the head of the table, then took the empty chair by Wyoming. Alice thought he looked handsome tonight, although he had to be several years younger than Wye. She appeared rather discomfited by the situation, which was amusing, seeing as Wye was usually so practical and calm. Alice had long thought Cass had chosen her as a friend for those very characteristics.

She wasn't calm now. And Lena was practically smoldering.

When Cass passed Wyoming a bowl of green beans, Wye dropped the serving spoon on the table. She dropped her napkin later and nearly bumped heads with Emerson when they both bent to fetch it.

But it was when she spilled milk across the table halfway through the meal that Alice realized Wye was nervous.

Nervous—about Emerson?

Or the General?

The General was watching Wye and Emerson like they were two rats in a laboratory experiment. His avid attention seemed to unnerve Wye.

Lena watched the General the way a mountain lion watches a tethered goat. Alice was finding it hard to eat.

Emerson wasn't faring much better.

He remained silent through the meal, until the General barked, "Cat got your tongue, Corporal? Lord, you yammer all day long when you're with me. What's the problem?"

"Nice weather we're having," Emerson managed.

Wye's eyebrows shot up. "It's twenty-five degrees out there."

"Nice for Montana. I think."

"You have to give him that, Wye," Sadie said mischievously.

"Tell us about yourself, Emerson," Cass said kindly. "Where were you born?"

"Chicago."

Alice stopped with her hand outstretched to grab the salt shaker. "I didn't know you were a city boy."

"I'm not. Spent most of my childhood in Nebraska."

Alice had the feeling there was more he wasn't saying, and she stopped pestering him, afraid she'd hit a sore spot. Emerson focused on his plate, but a few moments later he went on. "My parents died in a car crash. My grandparents raised me. I'm grateful to them."

"Sorry for your loss," Alice said. Jack had lost his parents, too. She and her sisters had lost their mother—and the General for a number of years. They'd all lacked for parental love.

Still, they'd all survived. Thrived, even. Were here now.

Although Lena didn't look like she was thriving.

"What's got up your craw?" the General asked her when he noticed her glaring at him.

She just shook her head, stabbed a baked potato from the bowl Logan had passed her and let it drop on her plate.

"Didn't anyone teach you any manners?" the General asked. "We have guests."

"Guests?" Lena parroted. "All I see is your honorary son and my future honorary sister-in-law."

Wyoming choked. Emerson turned crimson.

"You always did want a boy," Lena added pointedly.

"Maybe I did. Maybe I thought I could have understood one better. Maybe with a boy I wouldn't have screwed up every time I turned around. Maybe a boy would have loved m—" The General broke off, cut another bite of steak and popped it in his mouth.

Alice held her breath. She noticed Jo touch the General's arm. The General noticed it, too.

"You're lonely," she pronounced.

The General stood abruptly, swore, grabbed the table to steady himself until Emerson leaped up and supported him. "Office. Now. Bring my food," the General managed. Emerson helped him out the room. A minute later he came back for his dishes.

"Of course he's lonely," he hissed at them. "He's always been lonely. And I've never tried to be his son—but if I did, I'd be a hell of a lot better at it than you all are at being his daughters." He strode out of the room, leaving Alice and her sisters each in their private shame. Even Lena looked nonplussed.

"Welcome home," she whispered to herself wryly.

Alice's heart sank. Would there never be peace at Two Willows?

Chapter Fourteen

"ARE YOU GOING to work all day every day?" Jack asked when he found Alice still in her workshop at a quarter to two in the morning.

"As long as it takes to get this done." Alice didn't even look up from her work. She was putting tiny tucks into a piece of peach cloth. Jack couldn't guess where that would go.

"If this contract doesn't work out, there will be others. The quality of your work won't be overlooked long," he told her.

"It's not everyday someone makes a movie like this."

"Maybe not, but is it worth killing yourself over?"

Alice finally turned his way. "Yes, it is. This is a chance, and whether I win out or not, I want to know I've tried my best."

He could understand that, but he hated to see her so tired and drawn. Her hair was piled on her head and pinned in place, but strands were coming down. She looked like she might simply fall asleep where she sat.

"Anyway, the work isn't stressing me out."

"Something else is?" He made a show of examining the blue gown worn by one of the dressmaker dummies, but he was listening intently.

"Landon."

"He hitting on you again?"

"No. But he called earlier. Was wondering who'd win a game tonight."

It took Jack a moment to catch up. "You predicted the Raiders game the other day."

"Exactly. Then I told him about the Celtics. I was right both times, of course. He called again a couple of hours ago looking for more predictions. He's pretty excited."

Jack bit back a laugh. Excited about a parlor trick? "Two for two is pretty lucky, but—"

"Luck has nothing to do with it." Alice dropped her work on the table and stood to face him. "Jack, you have to understand this right now. Luck has *nothing* to do with it. If you don't get that, you don't understand anything about me. Jack, I see the future. Hell, I can show you the future—" She cut off abruptly. "But that's not allowed."

She was trembling. She wasn't making any sense. Jack's heart sank. Alice was overworked, under too much pressure—

"Damn it." She shoved the chair out of her way and began to pace. "Cavaliers, Chicago, Raptors—are you writing this down?"

"Should I be?"

"Yes!" She scuffled among the things on the table,

pulled out a pencil and a pad of paper and slid them his way. "Write them all down." She started over and began to rattle off a list of teams that had Jack scrambling to keep up, starting with basketball, but moving to football, and then hockey and then curling, if he wasn't mistaken.

Jack had never followed curling.

"Those are the winners for the week. You tell me if I know the future or not." She grabbed the back of the chair she'd pushed away and leaned on it heavily, before wrenching it away from the table and sitting down hard.

When she hugged her arms across her stomach and bent over, Jack dropped the pencil and rushed to her side. "Alice? You okay?"

It took him a minute to realize she was crying. When he did, he felt like a heel. He'd done this. He'd disbelieved her, and now she was in tears.

"Honey, I—"

Alice pushed him away, covered her face with her hands and swayed with silent tears.

"Stop it." She beat her palms against her forehead. "Stop. Stop it!"

"Alice!" Cass appeared in the doorway suddenly, giving Jack a turn. He hadn't heard her coming. Hadn't expected anyone else to be awake this time of night. She wore a winter jacket over her pajamas, her feet shoved into a pair of boots. "I got up to use the bathroom, and I saw the lights out here. Wondered if everything was okay."

"It's not. She—" Jack gestured to Alice, who was

still beating her palms against her forehead.

"Alice." Cass rushed across the room, fell to her knees beside her sister and gathered her in her arms. "Alice, what's happening?"

"I can see—too much—there's too much!"

Cass turned on Jack. "What did you do to her?"

"Me? Nothing!"

"What happened right before I came?"

Cass's tone brooked no defiance, and Jack found himself answering. "She was telling me the winners of all the games—for the week."

Cass gaped at him. "For the week? She can't be that specific. She gets flashes, not—that's like Mom." She turned back to Alice. "Sweetheart, what happened?"

Alice had her eyes shut, the heels of her hands jammed against her face. She was concentrating hard. Wrapped up in some inner struggle. All Jack could do was watch along with Cass. It seemed like hours before Alice slumped forward and Cass caught her.

"Help me," Cass cried, but Jack was already there, scooping Alice into his arms. "Let's get her back to the house."

"She needs to go to the hospital."

"No, she just needs rest. This used to happen to Mom once in a while." Cass led the way. A few minutes later they tucked Alice under the covers in her room. Cass went to fetch tea. Jack sat on the bed and smoothed the hair back from Alice's forehead.

When she opened her eyes and took him in, she struggled to sit up, but Jack shushed her. "Rest. You're tired."

"The dresses—"

"You need sleep first."

Cass hurried back in and set a cup of tea on the bedside table. "You scared me, Alice. Jack said you told him all the winners in upcoming games. That's not like you."

Alice made a little sound, halfway between a laugh and a sob. "I just… got so mad. I lost control of it, Cass. It's like my mind cracked open, and I could see everything—"

"Shh. It's okay now."

"He doesn't believe me."

The look Cass turned on Jack could have melted lead, and he decided this was his cue to leave. "Rest up, Alice. I'll see you in the morning."

She let her head drop on the pillow and closed her eyes.

Back in his room he heard the sisters' voices murmuring for hours.

"IT'S NOT OPENING to it that's the problem. It's trying to block the flow," Amelia was saying when Alice woke up. She grasped at the fragments of the dream—sitting on the back porch on a summer's day with her mother, a glass of lemonade in her hand so cold, droplets of water condensed on the outside.

Opening. Flow.

Alice lost the context. Couldn't remember what her mother had been saying. It was important—but then all the dreams she'd been having about Amelia lately seemed important. If only she could remember what her mother was trying to tell her.

She'd evaded Jack as much as she could yesterday and spent almost every waking moment in her studio. Last night she'd locked her door so he couldn't invade her room. She missed his visits more than she could say. It was agony keeping away from him, but she didn't have time to sort out her feelings for Jack, or what to do about them. The dresses were almost done—again. This time she was sure Landon would like them—and if he didn't, at least she'd know she'd done the best she could.

She sat up and looked at the phone on her nightstand. Almost time to get up, but for the moment the house was quiet. She slid out of bed, pulled on her thick, old terry-cloth bathrobe and went down to the kitchen, glad to be alone to greet the day. She needed to get back to her workshop. But first she needed to eat.

This late in November, the sky was pitch black, the stars still out at this time in the morning. Soon Cass would be down to rustle up breakfast. The rest of her family would get ready to start their chores. She was blessed to have so many people around her who loved her.

That didn't make her ache for her mother any less. Amelia would have helped her negotiate the maze of growing up with a gift like hers.

Alice carefully avoided thinking too closely about what had happened last night when she'd collapsed in her workroom. She'd opened the floodgates of her mind wide, greedy to give Jack every proof she could that she wasn't lying. She'd never opened to her intuition like that. Had never given out such clear information.

Hadn't known she could.

She'd thought her foresight was a weak, uncertain thing in comparison to Amelia's.

Now she knew better.

It wasn't comforting.

Was it her anger that had made her gift more powerful? Or was it Jack's presence? Or something else entirely?

"Alice?" Jack prowled into the kitchen and turned on the lights, finding her staring out the window into the darkness. "Everything okay?"

"Everyone keeps asking me that, and the answer is never yes." That sounded defeatist. "I'm fine."

"Somehow I find that hard to believe."

"You find everything hard to believe."

He nodded. "But I also know how important it is to be believed."

She took this in. Crossed the kitchen to pour herself a glass of water, and then decided to start a pot of coffee.

"I was seven when my parents were killed."

She stilled. He'd said that before, but she had a feeling more was to come. Jack came and took over the process of making coffee, moving around the kitchen with ease. He was feeling at home here, she realized. She moved to the table and sat down.

"I was hiding under the bed, like you said. I wasn't a coward; I was following directions. My father had ordered me to hide in the spare room."

"What happened?"

"I didn't see it, and I didn't hear much, either. There were too many of them for my father to fight. He tried—he really tried, but they knew the layout of the house. They came in from several directions at once. My dad got a couple of shots off. He winged one guy, we found out later, but they killed him. Killed my mom. They looked in my bedroom. I heard swearing when they didn't find me. They checked a couple of other rooms and decided I must be staying somewhere else. They got sloppy there. Too greedy to get to the cash they knew my dad had on hand to pay his hired help the next day. They knew where the safe was—one of them was the nephew of a woman who came to clean our house every week. He'd tagged along with her once to help dig a new garden bed for my mom. That's how I remembered—" He broke off. "They blew the safe open. Took everything and got out of there. It was a big ranch," he added, seeing Alice's confusion. "A big payroll."

"They were caught?" She liked watching him move around the kitchen, but the pain in his voice was palpable. She couldn't imagine what it must have been like for a little boy to keep hidden while all that was happening. To hear his parents die—to wonder if he was next. She ached to take Jack in her arms, as if she could comfort the child he'd once been. That was impossible, as she knew too well. You took pain like that into your very cells, and it never went away.

He nodded again. "Almost weren't. The first idiots who questioned me didn't believe a word I said. Didn't think a little kid like me could keep calm enough to know any of the details. Didn't listen to me when I told them who did it."

"You recognized their voices?"

"I recognized the sound of the engine of the truck they drove in. I'd heard it once before."

"Once?"

He chuckled grimly. "Yeah, once—when the cleaning lady's nephew came to dig the garden. I remember things like that."

Alice considered his words. "You have a photographic memory?"

"More than that. It isn't just images—it's sounds, smells, details. It's like I know things I shouldn't know, because I piece details together other people don't notice."

"It isn't like that for me." She knew what he was doing. Trying to find common ground between them. A rational explanation for her foresight.

There was no rational explanation.

As close as she'd felt to Jack a moment ago, now the differences between them yawned like a chasm.

"What I'm trying to say is I know how it feels to be different. I want to believe you. It's just—" He shrugged and took out two mugs for the coffee.

"It doesn't fit with your rational worldview." She

could see how that rationality was important to a man like Jack. "Someone must have believed you eventually."

"My adopted father, Richard. Works in intelligence. I didn't tell you that, though." He grinned, but the grin slipped away fast as he poured out coffee for both of them. "He saw the potential in me right quick. Made sure I developed it."

Alice got the sense this was a touchy area. "He pushed you?" she hazarded.

His expression became inscrutable. "Yeah, he pushed me. He's a good man," Jack asserted.

"Of course."

"Didn't your mother ever push you to be the best you could be?" He set one of the cups down in front of her and joined her at the table.

Alice thought about that. Amelia had taught her many things, of course, and she still shone as a beacon in Alice's mind as the example of what a mother should be, but when it came to her hunches, Amelia had never pushed her.

"She always said I would come into my own at the right time."

When Jack's shoulders drooped a quarter of an inch, she knew he'd been searching for a connection again—and she hadn't played along. "Do you feel like your father pushed you too hard?"

"I don't know." Jack blew on his coffee, and she could sense that he was sorting through memories. Judging them. "Maybe he pushed me more than most men would. He prizes excellence. I'm excellent at what I do." He sent her a sheepish smile. "You're one of the few people who's ever figured out I bugged them."

"I've got an unfair advantage." She could tell Jack didn't know what she meant. "That day in the restaurant I could sense you listening. Drove me crazy until I found the bugs. I sensed it again in the hotel room."

"That's… impossible. You know that, right?"

"And yet it's true."

"I'm trying to accept what you say, Alice, but it's hard."

"I think that's how most people feel about me."

"But they tell you they believe you?"

Alice searched for a way to discuss this without triggering Jack's sarcasm or her own insecurities. If their roles were reversed, she'd want answers, and she wouldn't want to play games.

"They do believe me," she said quietly, "because unlike you, they've witnessed it. And I'm not the only one in town like this. You haven't met Rose Johnson, the sheriff's wife. She owns Thayer's Jewelers. She has a knack, too."

"A knack?"

"Not quite what I've got, and nothing like my mom had. A sixth sense. If she holds your engagement ring, she gets a feeling about whether you'll stay together or not. It's not a very comfortable ability—they never are—and she doesn't tell many people about it, but everyone knows in town. Sadie can sense what growing things need to flourish. Jo can sense animals'—and people's—emotions when she touches them."

He remembered the way Jo had touched the General's arm—and pronounced him lonely. "That's… bizarre."

"Here's the thing," she said, losing patience. "You can either trust me now that I'm telling you the truth, or you can look up that list of sports teams I gave you and prove it to yourself. It's up to you."

"You're asking—"

"For you to be my friend." Alice wasn't interested in a conditional relationship. "Do you want to be my friend?" She took a sip of her coffee.

"I want a whole hell of a lot more than that," Jack growled.

Wow, Alice thought, her whole body tingling. She wanted more, too. She set her coffee cup down.

"Then come on." She stood up and held her hand out.

"Where are we going?"

"Where do you think?"

THIS WASN'T GOING to end well, Jack thought when he realized where Alice was taking him. They'd pulled on their outer gear, and Alice had unlocked the back door and led him outside into the dark and cold. Dawn wasn't even a glimmer on the horizon. It would be an hour at least until they sky turned gray. Jack shivered, zipped his coat all the way up and crunched over the icy snow after her.

"It won't let me in."

"Have a little faith," Alice called back. "Above all

else, the maze is a romantic."

Now she was personifying shrubbery? Jack wasn't sure what to think of that.

As they approached the maze, the opening disappeared, replaced by an unending slate of green.

"Open up," Alice called and whacked the shrubbery when it didn't disappear again. "I said, open up. We need to talk to the stone."

The shrubbery didn't listen.

"Isn't there a lever to pull or a button to push?" Jack said—and swore the shrubbery bristled and became even denser.

"Would you knock it off?" Alice asked him. "You aren't helping."

Jack pretended to zip his lips and throw away the key. "How's that?" he asked.

"Completely ineffective." She turned back to the wall of the maze. "I want him to see the heart of Two Willows. I'm marrying this man—you know that—so you have to let him in."

Jack straightened. She was marrying him?

The hedge stayed where it was.

"It's going to take something more," she said in frustration.

"A sacrificial lamb?" When had Alice decided to marry him? All this time he'd struggled to find a way to get to her, and she'd simply up and decided on her own to spend her life with him?

"A little respect!" Alice faced him, arms crossed. "When I envisioned us having sex, we were in there!

Don't you get it? In… there…" She was talking like he was either very slow or very stupid.

Suddenly Jack realized he was both. "Sex… in there?"

"Would you like me to restate that with an interpretive dance?"

Hell, yeah, he'd like that. But… "Are you saying you want to have sex right now?" And *marry him*?

"I give up!" Alice whirled away and stomped back toward the house. Jack ran over everything she'd said and done in the last ten minutes.

She wanted him to believe her—without proof. Wanted him to be her friend. Wanted him in the maze—because she'd seen them there in her vision.

Alice… wanted him.

Wanted to marry him, too.

And he was still quibbling over whether people could predict the future.

What the hell was he doing? Making sure he never got that village he was looking for, he realized.

Jack faced the maze. "I love her," he declared. "I love her, and I believe her, and I believe you. There are moving mazes and women who tell the future, and hold rings and know whether people are getting divorced or not. There are probably fairies and leprechauns and dragons, too, and I'm an idiot for not noticing—"

Jack stopped short. Before him stood the opening to the maze, as if it had always been there. He took a step. Then another. "Alice?" he called, refusing to turn around, afraid the entrance would disappear again.

"Alice, you seeing this?"

A second later she grabbed his hand and yanked him forward. "Hurry! Before it changes its mind!"

And they were through.

Jack quickly lost track of the twists and turns of the maze's passages and knew he'd need Alice to help him retrace his steps or it would take a long time to find his way out. He couldn't look for details or memorize their way and watch Alice at the same time.

In the fading light of the stars she looked luminous, and for a moment Jack could believe in anything. Maybe Alice wasn't entirely of this world. Maybe nothing on Two Willows was.

He stopped dead when they reached the center, and the tall gray expanse of the standing stone came into view.

"Hell. How'd that get here?" he asked, tipping his head back. It was old. Everything about it told him so. This hadn't been upended and buried in the ground anytime recently, but Jack knew Chance Creek's history only ran back a hundred and fifty years, give or take, as far as settlers were concerned. He had no doubt Native Americans had lived here for thousands of years, but he'd never heard of them building this type of monument.

"No one knows. It's something, though, isn't it?"

"I'll say." Alice was still holding his hand, and he curled his gloved fingers around hers. In front of an artifact so obviously ancient, he didn't mind showing his awe. It was good to remember now and then he didn't know everything.

Alice tugged away from him, drew her gloves off and placed her hands on the stone. "It always answers your questions. And it's always right."

Connor, Hunter, Logan and Brian had all mentioned that at one time or another. Jack had always brushed their stories off, but it occurred to him now that none of the other men were the type to sensationalize experiences—well, except for Logan, maybe. He supposed he should have listened to what they said.

Before he could respond, however, Alice closed her eyes. "Am I telling the truth?" She straightened and opened her eyes again. "Now you'll see."

Jack waited a bit. "I'll see wha—Ouch! Hell, what was that?" He dropped into a defensive crouch when something smacked him in the head. Alice's giggle brought him upright again as she bent to scoop something from the ground.

A newspaper.

"Where the hell did that come from? Who's here?" he called.

"No one's here," Alice chided him. She opened the paper and leafed through it to the sports pages, finally fishing out her phone and putting it in flashlight mode so they could see. "Read it and weep, Soldier."

Jack took the paper from her and peered at the tiny type as she held the light. A second later he fished the copy of her list from his pants pocket and compared the scores from overnight. On every game he'd checked so far, she'd gotten them right.

"Thirteen for thirteen," he said grudgingly.

"It'll be one hundred percent right when the week is up," Alice told him. "I wouldn't lie to you, Jack."

"I know you wouldn't." He rolled up the paper and stuck it in his back pocket.

"You're just not sure I'm sane."

Jack shrugged. "You're saying some pretty crazy stuff."

"I know."

"But I believe you, Alice Reed, because I want to be with you, and being with you means believing, doesn't it?"

"Same for you, right?"

Jack couldn't stop looking at her, drinking in the sweet contours of her face. Her wide eyes, full lips, pert nose—he loved everything about her. "Yeah. Same for me," he said huskily. "I guess in the end it doesn't matter how you're doing it. Just that you are. Can I kiss you?"

The corners of her mouth turned up. "Yes."

And he did.

ALICE CLOSED HER eyes and savored the feel of Jack's mouth on hers. Her toes were cold, but her heart beat so fast the rest of her was warm. When Jack tugged her closer, she came willingly, wanting more of him.

There was something about his hands on her hips that turned her on. Knowing he wanted to get close to her—to be inside her. So much he was willing to give up his beliefs for the chance.

She'd gotten glimpses of his deepest pain—and the questions he asked himself in quiet moments. Had he been pushed too far? And the question he hadn't voiced—would a father who loved him do that?

Jack wouldn't ever ask that out loud. Nor would he ask for what he needed: to be loved unconditionally. They were dancing around each other's edges, wanting to be vulnerable, fearing it at the same time. Alice was beginning to think she'd spent her whole life that way—holding back. Craving closeness.

Fearing it at the same time.

She wasn't willing to live her life like that. Wasn't willing to take the sensible steps with Jack, getting closer a bit at a time.

She wanted him now. Wanted this now. Wanted no boundaries between them.

If they weren't meant to be, she wanted to know that right away, because what she really wanted—

Was to stop going through life alone.

A flash of intuition hit her, and Alice staggered.

"What is it?" Jack caught her.

Alice finally understood something she must have known all along but had never faced head on. Someday she'd open to her gift—truly open to it—like Amelia had—like she had for a moment when she'd channeled that list of winning teams—and she'd need—

She'd need someone to ground her. To stand by her side. To be her rock.

That's what had made her compassionate, open-hearted mother fall for a man as flawed and mercurial as her father. The General had many faults, but inconstancy wasn't one of them. He dug his heels in, and he maintained his position.

Just like the standing stone.

Alice had always thought of the stone as a physical representation of her mother's love. Monolithic. Solid. Never-ending.

But Amelia was the one who'd built the maze around the stone. What had it represented to her?

Probably not her own heart.

Had it stood in for the man she loved? The man who might have spent more time away from Two Willows than at home, but for all that still counted as the rock who anchored her mother's life?

Alice had seen the love the General had for her mother. Knew it was his pain that had kept him far away from the ranch since she'd been gone.

His love for Amelia was as monolithic as the standing stone. As old as he seemed to her, Alice realized he'd been a relatively young man when he'd lost his wife. And yet never once had he taken a step to replace her.

He never would.

Alice searched Jack's face. Was he capable of a love like that? "Can you…" she found herself asking. "Can you be there? All the way? For someone like me?"

His expression changed from worry to something like… relief. "Yes." He cut her off when she tried to speak. "Yes—I can. No matter what happens, or what I believe or think is real or not real—I can be there for you. I will be there for you. Always, if you let me."

That was all she needed to know.

Alice stepped back, unzipped her jacket and shrugged her way out of it. A moment later she peeled her sweater off, tugged the hem of her shirt over her head.

Would Jack follow her lead? At first he watched, like a man unsure whether to trust his eyes. Then he unzipped his own jacket, flung it aside and started to strip.

"It's damn cold out here," he told her.

"You'll have to keep me warm."

He surveyed the snowy ground, the bench, the stone. "Where?"

Alice wasn't going to answer that. She'd gotten them here; let him do a little of the work. She had to unlace her boots and step out of one at a time to get her jeans off and shimmy out of her panties, but she stuck her feet right back in them afterward.

"Alice." Jack's wonder at her body was summed up in the single word. He shucked down his pants but left them pooled at his ankles. "Get over here."

He lifted her up the moment she was in reach, and Alice locked her legs around his waist. Contact with his body sent a surge of heat through her shivering form. She crushed her breasts to his bare chest. "You're right; it's freezing."

Jack shuffled forward, stooped to snag his jacket off the ground and draped it over her shoulders.

"I don't think it'll stay on," she began, but he moved her up against the standing stone, and Alice sighed. His jacket protected her from the worst of the cold, and Jack's hardness pressed against her was sending all kinds of sexy signals to her brain. "What about you? Aren't you cold?" she asked.

"Freezing." He didn't sound concerned, and he captured her mouth with his, putting an end to that line of questioning. When he skimmed his palms up to cup her breasts, Alice gave up thinking altogether and gave in to the pleasure of his touch, her skin humming under each caress.

She hadn't realized how lonely she'd been until Jack came along. It was a loneliness that went far beyond the normal wanting between a man and a woman. Howie hadn't slaked her need. Only someone like Jack—someone who truly loved her—could fill the void inside her.

She clung to him as he explored her curves, first with his hands, then with his mouth. Arching back as he took one nipple into his mouth, she gasped, aching to feel him inside her.

"Jack," she begged. He kept going, teasing her with his tongue, sliding a hand down to cup her bottom, bringing her hard against him.

"Jack," she said again.

"Do we need protection?"

She shook her head. She didn't care about protection—didn't care about the future. All she wanted was now. She wanted to be known—to be possessed, utterly and completely. She wanted to annihilate the space that loomed between her and everyone else, that kept her isolated and alone even when surrounded by the people she loved most.

Only Jack could fill that gap. She opened to him and gasped when he shifted and slid inside her, filling her until she nearly came right then.

Holding on for dear life, Alice closed her eyes and rode his movements, glorying in the exquisite pleasure of each slip of his skin against hers. She'd never felt this way with a man—like she could lose herself in the sensations between them. Forgetting the cold, forgetting the hard stone behind her, she urged Jack on, digging her fingers into his shoulders.

Jack didn't disappoint. He was strong—so strong. Holding her up like she weighed nothing. Pushing into her with control and rhythm that built the desire inside her into a dizzying peak.

When Alice thought she couldn't hold on any longer, his next thrust took her over the edge, and pulse after pulse of ecstasy rippled through her until she buried her face against his neck to keep from crying out.

Grunting with his thrusts, Jack slammed into her, gripping her so tightly she thought he'd never let go. Clinging to him, she gloried in his pleasure, his rough motions stirring desire inside her all over again.

Alice tightened her grip as her need built up to a dizzying level. She'd never come twice—not like this—and for a moment she feared losing control altogether.

"Alice," Jack panted, and his raw need for her knocked down the barrier she'd begun to build between them. Jack held her gaze, looking straight into her heart, and Alice realized this was the true test of her desire. She'd said she wanted to be known. If she let go—if she showed him the way he was making her feel—she'd expose herself utterly. "Alice, please," Jack breathed.

He wanted that. Wanted to know her.

She wanted it too.

Gazing back at him, letting go of her fears, Alice gave in and came with a cry. Jack's strong thrusts played her like a well-tuned instrument; his hands on her body urged her to higher heights as her release pulsed through her. When he lost control, too, Alice cried out again with him, then rode the wave of his orgasm until he finally slumped against her, pinning her against the standing stone, breathing hard, his heart pounding in her ear as she struggled with him to catch her breath.

"More," he said when he could breathe, and Alice laughed. She wanted more, too.

"Any time," she promised, but Jack had stiffened.

"What is that?"

Alice held her breath. Now she heard it, too. "Is that a… trumpet?"

Jack laughed. "Hell, must be time to muster." With a groan, he disengaged from her, set her on her feet with a kiss and hurried to pick up their clothes.

"We don't have to come when he calls," Alice told him, barely able to keep up. After such a connection, breaking apart took her breath away.

"You want Corporal Myers hunting us down—finding us like this?"

Alice laughed, too, and relaxed. "No, I guess I

don't." Although she'd give anything to make love to Jack all over again. "Where has he been hiding a trumpet all this time?"

"Who knows." Jack considered his clothes, then bent to scoop up a handful of snow. He swore as he cleaned himself off and pulled on his clothes as fast as he could afterward. Alice gingerly followed suit, the icy coldness bringing her back to the real world. She did her best to put her clothes and hair to rights, although she was sure anyone could guess what they'd been doing out here.

When Jack led the way back through the maze, she noticed that dawn had caught up to them. The sun wasn't up, but the sky was noticeably lighter. Had they missed breakfast?

"There you are," the corporal said accusingly, lowering the trumpet when he caught sight of them. "Been looking for you everywhere. You're late."

Inside, everyone had gathered as usual around the General's bed, although the man was perfectly capable of moving to another room, Alice thought.

"What's the hold-up?" the General said when she and Jack slipped in, Emerson following.

"Sorry, sir," Jack said.

"Lake, make your report so we can all get on with our day."

"Everything is shipshape, sir."

"O'Riley?"

"Snow's expected later today, so I'm making sure we're ready for it, sir."

"Powell."

"What Connor said. Snow's coming, sir."

"Hughes?"

"Looking forward to shoveling, sir," Logan said cheerfully. "And some hot chocolate later."

"Sanders."

"Banner day so far, sir."

Was he smiling? Alice was pretty sure he was smiling. The General gave him a dark look.

"Cass?"

"Laundry's piling up."

The General frowned. "Sadie?"

"It's a splendiferous day, sir!"

"Lena?"

Lena shrugged.

"Jo," the General growled.

"Fucking splendiferous!"

"Alice." She had a feeling he was losing his cool, but she simply couldn't help herself.

"Well, I just got laid—in the maze. So I agree with Jo and Sadie. Fucking-A splendiferous!"

When the General's face went purple, Alice felt a pang of remorse.

"Out! OUT!" he bellowed. "All of you! Before I—"

Alice didn't hear the rest.

She ran.

Chapter Fifteen

"I HEARD ANOTHER rumor about that task force of yours," Richard said when Jack answered his call later that morning.

"Oh yeah?" Jack's grip on the phone tightened. Couldn't Richard leave it alone?

His body was still buzzing from his incredible encounter with Alice this morning. He couldn't think about anything else.

"I heard that every man on the task force had gotten themselves in trouble. Something you want to tell me?"

Hell. Exactly what he'd hoped wouldn't happen.

"Might've had some trouble. I hope you know me well enough to realize my intentions were good."

"Is the Army going to kick you out?"

"Not if I do my job on this task force."

"The General's blackmailing you?"

This conversation was getting worse by the minute. "Let's just say he's offering me a way to expunge my record."

"I don't like this," Richard said. "None of this makes sense, Jack, and from what I hear, the men who landed in Montana before you are married and settled in Chance Creek. They're ranchers, not soldiers."

"They weren't soldiers to begin with."

"All the more reason this whole situation stinks. How's the General grabbing men from other branches of the military?"

"It's a joint task force."

"It's a joint scam, if you ask me. Probably illegal in fifty different ways. If I shine a spotlight on this—"

"You won't shine a spotlight on it," Jack snapped. "You'll back off and keep out of it altogether."

"If he's forcing you—"

"He's not forcing me. I want to be here. I want to marry Alice. I want to ranch, Pop. I don't want to be an intelligence officer, and if that makes you not want to know me anymore, so be it. This is the life I want. It's the life I've always wanted. Don't fuck it up."

Richard's silence left Jack sick with remorse. He hadn't meant to hurt the man who'd raised him. He couldn't live a lie anymore, either.

Richard hung up before he could apologize, and Jack thought about calling him back but decided to wait until they'd both calmed down.

"Jack?" Emerson poked his head into the kitchen. "General's got a doctor's appointment in town this morning. Mind driving us?"

"Sure. How's your foot?" Jack struggled to get his temper back under control.

"Healing. I'm seeing the doctor, too. Not sure it'll ever be quite right again."

"Sorry to hear that. You seem to be getting around okay." What was Richard doing now? Pacing, probably. Trying to connect the dots.

Emerson shrugged. "Career's over."

It was the first time Emerson had admitted that in Jack's hearing, and Jack focused on him, grateful to let go of his own problems. "Any idea what you'll do next?"

Emerson was looking out the window at the area between the house and the carriage house where everyone parked. Jack realized Wye had just pulled in and was climbing out of her truck. Will the plumber had just arrived, too. He still hadn't managed to fix those pipes. "Not really." Emerson caught Jack watching him. "Everyone knows I like her."

"She seems to like you, too."

"She likes him more. Don't blame her. What can I offer her? Thought I'd make something of myself, but now—"

"You've got the General on your side. That's something," Jack pointed out. "He's a man with a lot of connections. I don't think he means to see you sidelined."

"He can't fix this." Emerson pointed to his foot.

"Maybe not, but he'll do what he can. He's sure throwing you at Wyoming."

"So? Doubt she'll want a man who's going nowhere." He watched Will pull his tools out of the bed of his truck.

Jack straightened. "Know what? That might be exactly what she wants—and what the General wants for her."

Emerson scowled. "What's that supposed to mean?"

"It means Wye is Cass's best friend. Cass is staying here, but now the General is home. The General knows his girls are upset with him. What if they decide to move on?"

"I don't follow."

"Cass is the heart of this family, the way her mother was before her. If Cass stays, her sisters will stay. And if Wye stays, it's more likely that Cass will stay, right? Women like to be near their best friends."

"What's that got to do with me?"

"I think the General plans to marry you off to Wye so you settle down right here at Two Willows. He hasn't mentioned it to us, and he did promise us each a fifth of the ranch when he's gone, so maybe I'm completely wrong, but I don't think so. I think your future is right here if you want it."

"But—" Emerson shoved his hands in his pockets. "You all wouldn't want that. Like you said, wouldn't that diminish your shares?"

"This is a big ranch," Jack told him. "The more men we have to work it for free, the fewer we have to pay. Wouldn't bother me one bit to have you here. Besides, you're the only one who knows how to handle the General."

"That's true." For the first time since Jack had known him, Emerson grinned. When the back door opened and Wye came in with Will, the two of them chatting, Emerson went to meet her, ignoring the plumber, even as he blocked the man's way.

"Want to take a field trip with us, Wye?"

Jack took in Will's scowl and Wye's interest.

"Where are you going?"

"Doctor's office."

"Better let me talk to Cass first. I'm supposed to hang out with her."

"I thought you were supposed to hang out with me," Will said.

"I think the General is going to blow his top if you don't get those pipes fixed today," Emerson said.

"The General better be a little more patient. I'm the one getting this job done, not him."

"Except you aren't," Wye pointed out. "And we don't want the General to get upset."

Wye went in search of Cass. An hour later they'd made it to town, and Jack ushered the General and Emerson toward the doctor's office, trailed by the women.

When both men had been examined and the group left the doctor's office some time later, Emerson and the General were in good spirits, although the General was grumbling a bit about the changes in the physical therapy regimen he'd been prescribed. The doctor had only good things to say about their injuries. "Must be something in the water out there at Two Willows making you heal so well."

"Who wants a burger?" Jack asked. He was having a craving for a Burger Shack bacon cheeseburger.

"I'm in," Emerson said.

"Why not?" the General said.

"Sure thing," Cass said. "Wye, do you have time to join us?"

"Of course."

"Jack? Got a minute?"

Jack was surprised when a man who'd been loitering near the front of the building straightened and gestured with a tilt of his head for Jack to join him.

"Uh… sure thing. I'll catch up with you all at the Burger Shack. I'll just be a minute." He strode away after the stranger before anyone could ask questions or offer to accompany him.

The tall man disappeared around the corner. Jack followed him.

"Steel Cooper," the man said and offered his hand.

Jack shook it. "Jack—"

"I know who you are. Glad to see the General up and about."

"You know him?"

"My family goes way back in this town. So does his. Look, I've got a message for you."

"From who?"

"Can't say, unfortunately. But I know you're worried about trouble coming from Tennessee again."

"That's right." He wondered how Steel knew.

"I've got a tip. Don't know if it'll come to anything, but my cousin—Ron Cooper—got himself messed up in all of this. He's dead now."

Steel didn't sound too sorry about it. "Heard that,

too," Jack said.

"I heard Duke Manson pulled the trigger."

"That's right."

"Don't know if your people know this, but Manson's got a son."

That got Jack's attention. "I didn't know that."

"Might want to look into him. That's all I can say."

"Wait—what's your part in all this?" Jack asked.

"Wish I could say more, but I can't."

"Understood." Jack didn't understand, though.

The other man must have seen the doubts in his face. "Look," Steel said. "I'm on your side. That's all you need to know." He walked away, leaving Jack to wonder just how the man was involved in all of this. He resolved to ask Cab if he had the chance. For now, he'd take the tip and run with it.

He was deep in thought about how best to track down Manson's son when a movement across the street caught his eye.

Was that—Landon Clark? He wasn't due back until the day after tomorrow, according to Alice.

The man in question disappeared out of sight behind a van parked on the side of the street. By the time Jack crossed against traffic, Landon—if it was Landon—was gone. He checked both the hardware store and the clothing boutique next to it but didn't see Landon anywhere. He even ducked down an alley between them and searched behind the buildings. No one was there.

Had he been seeing things?

Jack didn't think so, and with Steel's message ringing in his ears, he couldn't help but worry. He called Brian next and filled him in.

"I'll keep an eye on Alice until you're home," Brian said. "I'm heading up to the house right now anyway."

"Thanks." Jack was beginning to doubt he'd even seen the man at all. It had only been the back of his head—maybe he'd been completely mistaken.

He didn't know if he should call Alice. It would stress her out to think Landon had arrived early if it wasn't really him. On the other hand, if he didn't tell her and she found out, she'd be pissed off.

And what if Landon wasn't who he said he was?

What if he was Manson's son?

"Jack—hurry up!" Cass called from the entrance to the Burger Shack. "We're ordering, and we've decided to get takeout. We need to get the General home."

Jack increased his pace, relieved. That solved his problem. If Landon was here, he was in town for the moment. Brian was with Alice at home. They'd order their food and be back at Two Willows in a half hour, where he could take some time to research this new piece of the puzzle without upsetting Alice or getting ahead of himself.

"Coming!"

"LAKE?" THE GENERAL barked the next morning at their muster session. Alice, tired to the bone, jumped, then sighed. She had one last day to fix her dresses, and while she was sure she was making progress, she was also beginning to feel like she'd done nothing but sew for weeks.

Probably because it was true.

She'd used her salacious purposes knock last night. Jack had been at her door before she was through. He'd joined her in bed, and they'd made love twice more. She was hooked. Alice couldn't imagine ever walking away from the soldier again.

She didn't know what had made her tell the General—and everyone else—about being with Jack in the maze. Maybe it was her way of putting them on notice. She didn't want to admit the General had done well with his pick.

Really well.

But he had.

"Working on that lead, sir. The one Jack got from Steel Cooper," Brian said.

"Well, Sanders?" The General turned to Jack. "What have you learned so far? Got a photograph of Manson's son yet?"

"You skipped O'Riley, Powell and Hughes," Lena said. Logan nudged her.

"I'll get back to them. I want to hear about this," the General told her.

"Not yet, but I will soon, sir," Jack said.

"Is his son part of the organization?" Lena asked.

"We don't know yet," Brian told her. "We're tracking down all the information we can."

"There's something else," Jack said. "It's possible that Landon's back."

Alice turned to him in surprise, the warm glow that had enveloped her all morning shattering in an instant. "Since when? He's supposed to come back tomorrow." She wasn't done with her dresses.

"I saw him yesterday—"

"And you didn't tell me?" Alice couldn't believe it. Jack knew how important this all was to her. But he considered Landon a rival, didn't he? Is that why he'd held the information back?

"I wasn't sure it was him. I didn't want to upset you if it wasn't." He was steeling himself, she realized. "I'm wondering if Landon is connected to Manson's son."

"Or maybe is Manson's son," Brian added.

Alice's temper flared. Not because what they were saying was impossible, but because she didn't want it to be true. Was it too much to ask for this opportunity to be real—and for her to have the chance to do her best work?

"Keep on it," the General said.

"Will do, sir," Jack said.

Alice burned with frustration. Just because Landon had come back early didn't make him Manson's son.

"Hughes?"

"Just helping Jack, along with my regular chores, sir.

"Powell?"

"The same, sir."

Jack didn't even look remorseful that he'd kept the information about Landon from her, Alice thought. He'd spent all night exploring every inch of her body and never said a word.

Just like a man.

"O'Riley?"

"Keeping out of trouble, sir."

"Cass?"

"Wye and I are finishing up the pre-holiday cleaning. Thanksgiving's coming up soon."

"Good job. Looking forward to a homemade turkey dinner."

"Me, too," Emerson said, then dipped his head and blushed.

"Alice, I—" Jack began, moving closer to her.

"Don't want to hear it," she snapped. She was furious at his betrayal. How could he have kept something so important from her?

"Sadie?" the General asked.

"Helping to turn Jo's old room into the nursery. I'm doing the painting since Cass shouldn't be inhaling fumes. We've moved Wye into the attic room for now."

The General's expression softened. "Will be splendid to have some young pups around here. Jo?"

"Uh… I'm okay."

The General narrowed his eyes. "Are you?"

Jo swallowed. "No, sir."

Alice, tangled up in her own thoughts, heard the sudden silence that followed Jo's pronouncement and played the last few lines of the conversation over again in her head. She held her breath. Out of all of them, Jo was the one who had missed their father the most. She'd been his shadow as a girl and had been hurt so badly when he'd stopped coming home.

"You always had a lot of spunk," the General said. "You'd fall off a horse and climb right back on it. You were as loyal and courageous as those dogs you always had following you around."

"That was a long time ago," Jo said, reaching down absently to pet Champ, who lay by her feet. "I've learned not everyone deserves that kind of loyalty."

Alice braced herself for an angry answer from the General. Instead, his shoulders lowered, and he leaned back against his pillows. "Isn't that the truth," he said wearily. "I guess you learned not to be loyal to me."

Jo wavered, and Hunter steadied her with a hand to her back. "I… tried to be loyal. For a long time," she said. "But you never came home."

"You gave up on me. I don't blame you."

Pain made Alice's throat raw. They'd all lost so much time to this rift between them.

"I didn't want to," Jo said baldly. "But I didn't want to be stupid, either."

"You never could be stupid." The General sat up. "You hear me, Jo? You are the smartest soldier I know. Worth a dozen of the recruits I see each year."

"Not smart enough to make it clear to you I needed you home."

Her assertion hung in the air. It was what they all meant to say but hadn't been able to find the words. Jo had made it plain. Now the General had to face it, Alice thought.

Would he face it, though? Or would he find another way to escape?

"I've made a lot of mistakes," the General said heavily, "But the worst was not facing all this sooner. I thought I was afraid to face your mother's absence. Now I know that wasn't it. It was her presence I was afraid of, and I see her here everywhere I look. Most of all in my daughters."

Jo bit her lip.

"Come here." He gestured her over, and Jo crossed the room to him. "Jo, I can't tell you how proud I am of you. Of all of you. You have an ass for a father, and you kept your stations, performed your duties. Accomplished the mission when your ranking officer was nowhere to be found."

"It was… hard," Jo managed.

"I know. I'm… sorry." When he opened his arms, Jo went to him, her shoulders shaking as she sat on the bed and leaned into his embrace.

Lena huffed out a breath, turned on her heel and left the room.

"I'M LOOKING FOR Landon Clark," Jack said into the phone again. "I know you're not supposed to talk about your clientele, but I've got a delivery for him. I know he was in room nineteen during his last visit. Has he taken his old room back?"

"I'm not at liberty to say," the young woman manning the phones at the Evergreen Motel said.

"Can you at least tell me if he's checked in yet so I don't waste a trip to town?"

"Can't tell you that either."

"Can you take a message for him?"

"Sure." He heard her fumbling through things and figured she was looking for a pad of paper. Jack hung up. He now knew everything he needed to know—if she was willing to take a message, Landon was definitely in town. Staying at the Evergreen Motel. Here when he wasn't supposed to be here.

He knew Alice was angry he'd kept that information from her. Maybe he should have told her—but he hadn't wanted to upset her. He'd been protecting her again. Alice had made it clear after the muster session she didn't like being protected.

He found the other men—and Lena—in the barn, and reported what he'd found out.

"I'm all for being cautious and checking this out," Connor said when he was done, "but none of this makes sense. Landon was dealing with Alice before the last set of men came to attack Two Willows. No one in the Tennessee operation has shown the kind of initiative to make a long play like this."

"Not since the first round of men, anyway," Brian said. "What Bob Finchley and his friends did took organization and planning."

Lena scowled but held her tongue. Jack figured she was still angry about that.

"If Landon is Manson's son, he's got a reason to have initiative," Logan said.

"Now. Two months ago he had no way of knowing Ron Cooper would kill his dad," Connor said.

"It's all we've got," Jack countered, "and I'm not

taking any chances. Not where Alice is concerned. Duke Manson has a son, and Landon Clark is hanging around Chance Creek when he's supposed to be off scouting costume designers. Something's rotten in Denmark. The guy isn't even a real movie producer. How do we know he's got the money he claims he does? He's never had anything to do with films before."

"All I'm saying is don't let your jealousy blind you to other possibilities," Connor said.

"Jealousy?" Jack bit back an angry retort, catching Hunter's smile and the look Brian and Logan exchanged. "I'm not being blinded by my jealousy. Alice has made it damn clear she's not interested in Landon, but this guy's got two strikes against him in my book. His past doesn't reconcile with the future he's pretending to aim for—"

"Does yours?" Connor challenged him. "I mean, you're in the Special Forces. A highly trained officer with all kinds of skill in intelligence. And you're going to spend the rest of your life on a Montana ranch… when you barely know how to do your chores?"

Jack went for him, but Brian and Hunter both stepped in his way.

"Easy, easy," Brian told him. "Maybe you should answer the question."

"I'm giving my all to this ranch—"

"I know. That's exactly my point," Connor said. "You're making a change because you want to make a change. How do we know Landon isn't doing something similar?"

"He keeps cutting Alice down. Trying to make her feel ugly and unskilled. He's an ass."

"That I believe," Connor said. "But being an ass and being a criminal are two different things. All I'm saying is let's not jump to conclusions."

Jack got his anger under control. Connor was right about that. "I've got my surveillance equipment set up to notify me if anything crosses the Two Willows border and comes onto the property." He'd been checking his phone every time it buzzed, watching all the vehicles that came in and out of the lanes—and a few critters that had crossed onto the property, too. So far he'd seen nothing out of the ordinary, but he wouldn't stop being vigilant.

"Let's get back to work. Keep an eye on that surveillance system of yours," Brian told him. "And on Alice. Lena, if you find out she's going anywhere, make sure to tell us. She shouldn't be alone."

Lena nodded. She'd been uncharacteristically quiet all afternoon.

"Something bothering you?" Jack asked. "Other than the General?"

Lena chuckled grimly. "Isn't that enough?"

ALICE PAUSED WITH her hand on the doorknob to the carriage house, taking a deep breath of the cold air to try to clear her head. The dread was back, which made sense given that she had less than twenty-four hours until she showed her gowns to Landon again, and she was on the outs with Jack. She couldn't get past the fact

Jack hadn't thought it was important to tell her about Landon.

As for Landon, she told herself his cutting comments hadn't affected her, but she was lying. She kept replaying them in her brain, wondering if there was any truth to them. She could wave away his criticisms of her looks; while they were hurtful, she figured they were part of his negotiation technique. He wanted her to feel small so he could push her around. Since she wasn't attracted to him, she didn't much care if he thought she was pretty. It was harder to explain away his criticisms of her work, though. She'd taken her sewing prowess for granted, and now she heard his comments in his head when she worked on the dresses, and they were undercutting her confidence. His stinging critique of her gowns had been far more difficult to stomach than his petty slights about her looks.

What if he was right? What if her work, which had always been praised locally, regionally—and even nationally from time to time—wasn't up to snuff for a real box-office hit? What if her talents were limited?

Could her pride take that?

Her fingers tightened on the doorknob. She was being silly. She was good at what she did, and her dread was unfounded. The General had already suffered the consequences of them all leaving the ranch at the same time. He was already injured. Already home. So what if Landon turned her down? Jack was right; there would be other opportunities.

But would any of them include hundreds of hoopskirt ball gowns?

Alice smiled wryly. Probably not.

Her phone buzzed in her pocket, and she pulled it out.

"Alice? It's Landon. I'm back in Chance Creek. Got some time? I'd love to see those costumes again."

She rested her head against the doorframe and shut her eyes. So Jack was right; he had come back early. What kind of game was Landon playing now?

"You gave me until tomorrow," she said flatly, unable to hide her irritation.

"I have to leave first thing in the morning again. Business."

"Why didn't you call me yesterday—I know you were here."

Landon hesitated, and she wondered if he would deny it. "Look, Alice—I'm having some problems. Nothing to concern you, but I've been on the road for weeks, and I needed to take a day to sort things out. I guess in a small town like this, people talk. I should have told you what was going on."

"Yes, you should have," Alice relented. "Is everything okay?"

"Not… exactly."

"Will this affect the contract at all?"

"No," he said hurriedly. "That's all on track. I'd really like to see those gowns again, now that I've visited the other candidates."

Alice's grip on her phone tightened. She wondered how he'd reacted to their work.

"I understand they won't be perfect," he said soothingly. "I'd still like to see them. Any chance you can bring what you've got to my motel?"

"I'm not trying them on again," she warned.

Another hesitation. "Fine. Just bring them."

"I'm bringing Wye with me, too." No sense beating around the bush. He needed to know she didn't like his games.

"Alice—"

"Not up for discussion."

"Fine," he said again. "Bring Wyoming. When will you get here?"

"When I get there." She hung up.

Now where the hell was Wye—and Jack?

Chapter Sixteen

"THERE YOU ARE," Landon said when Alice and Wye arrived at his room an hour later. He ushered them inside before closing and locking the door. It made Alice feel better to know that Jack—and Lena—were sitting outside in the parking lot in Jack's truck. They'd wanted to come in, too, but had settled for bugging Alice's purse. Jack had explained that the bugs didn't transmit well from inside her handbag, but they'd managed to arrange one under the purse's flap. Hopefully that would do the trick.

"Any hint of trouble, and I'm in there," Jack had warned her.

"I'm still pissed at you," Alice said.

"Understood," Jack said grimly.

"I appreciate you coming," Landon said. "Wyoming, what a pleasure to see you again."

Wyoming nodded. She hung the gowns over the back of the bathroom door and held up the first one against her torso, as she and Alice had planned. No more playing around with Landon. He could see the dresses and make up his mind.

Alice pointed to the neckline of the lilac gown. "I got rid of the lace, as you suggested, and replaced it with—"

Landon listened patiently through her descriptions of the alterations of each gown, until Alice began to think she'd made a mistake not trying them on again. They really required a hoopskirt and corset to be shown to their best effect. Unlike last time, Landon seemed interested in every detail, asked thoughtful questions and examined the gowns closely.

When they were done, Wye got to work putting the gowns away. Landon touched Alice's arm and led her across the room near the front windows.

"Listen, Alice, I'm sorry I was so hard on you before," he began.

"I didn't like the way you talked to me," she said honestly, "but I do feel that I improved the gowns in the meantime."

"Like night and day. You have a gift when it comes to costume design."

"Does that mean I've got the job?" she challenged him. She was losing patience with this process.

"I think you're the right person for the part. But I have to ask you—is it really the best use of your skills… and mine?"

"I'm not sure what you mean." Wye caught her eye from across the room and lifted an eyebrow. Alice nodded to let her know everything was all right.

"You are a very talented seamstress, but you have other talents, too." Landon stepped closer. "Alice, you have to know I'd like to get to know you better. I haven't made that a secret."

"I—"

"Don't answer yet. It seems to me we could form a different kind of partnership."

Oh no, Alice thought. He was going to proposition her. After everything she'd done to get this job—and to fend him off.

"I've got a lot of money," he added.

Alice stiffened. Was he going to offer to pay her to be with him?

"A lot of money," he repeated. "And you've got a hell of a talent for predicting winners. I think you and I could go places."

Alice gaped at him. He—wanted her to predict the outcome of sports competitions? She nearly laughed in relief. At least he didn't want to have sex with her. She caught the way he was looking at her and realized she was being naive. He wanted that, too.

"What about the movie?" she managed to ask.

Landon shrugged. "A movie is a risky bet at any time. Why take a risk when you can have a sure thing? What do you say? Horse races, sports, stock markets—the world is our oyster."

"No." She didn't even have to think about it before she answered.

"What do you mean, no?"

"I just worked for months on these gowns because you said you were making a movie—"

"Fine, we'll make a movie, too. Whatever you

want." He opened his arms wide. "I mean it, Alice. Whatever you want. We're sitting on a gold mine here."

"I am not going to make a movie with you now," she countered. "And I'm not going to help you cheat, either—at horses, sports or the stock market."

"Alice—"

"You just jerked me around for months, Landon. I don't play games like that. And I don't steal people's money.

"You've got a conscience? Is that the problem?"

"Of course that's the problem, plus I don't need a man in my life who thinks he can come around here, waste my time, talk shit about my body—"

Landon dropped his hands to his sides. "Is that what this is about? Did I hurt your feelings? Oh, sweetheart—"

He was insufferable, and she'd had enough. "Goodbye, Landon. Have a pleasant trip back from where you came. Wye, let's go." She headed for the door, sparing a helpless look at the three beautiful gowns, now cocooned in their cotton wrappers. She had to leave them behind. Landon didn't deserve them, but he'd paid her to make them, so they were his.

"You're making a mistake," Landon called after her.

"Then we're even, because you already made one."

"HE OFFERED ME the job."

Jack pulled out of his parking space, sparing a glance for Alice, who sat in the passenger seat. Lena was driving Wye back to the ranch in Alice's truck to give the two of them time to talk.

"I know."

She made a face. "I forgot you were listening."

"He's an ass."

"I told him no. I don't think we have to worry about him anymore." Her voice was tight.

Jack wished that was true. He was pretty sure they needed to worry more than ever. "He thinks you can predict the future."

"I can," she said tiredly.

"And he wants part of the action. I'm not sure we've seen the last of him."

Alice turned his way. "You're kidding, right?"

He didn't answer. She was smart enough to know he wasn't.

"I'm sorry you won't get the contract," he finally said. "I know it meant a lot to you."

"I don't want to work with a man like that. I'm not going to spend my time being pushed around. By anyone," she said firmly.

"I understand. You know I don't want to push you around—or control you," he added, heading toward Two Willows.

"You like to be in control, though," she pointed out. "You didn't even tell me he was in town." She kept her gaze out the window.

"I know. That was… dumb. I wish you could understand it from my point of view. I care about you. I don't want to see you hurt."

"That's the thing," Alice said. "You don't get to

make that call. I do. I have to have all of the information to do that."

"Don't you think we're on track to find a middle way?"

"What do you mean?"

"You agreed to be bugged this time," he pointed out.

"That doesn't mean you get to bug me when I don't agree, or that you get to make decisions for me. You aren't my father, Jack Sanders."

"I don't want to be your father."

"If you want to be anything else, you'd better smarten up."

She was quiet for the rest of the ride, and Jack let her be, although he wanted to make his case in the strongest way possible. There could be times in the future where he needed to override their agreement. On the other hand, he didn't want her to lump him in with Landon.

The minute Jack pulled in behind the house and parked, she got out and strode off toward the carriage house.

"Alice?" Jack called after her.

She didn't look back.

INSIDE THE CARRIAGE house, Alice closed the door and rested against it. She'd felt so strong when she'd made her decision back at the Evergreen Motel, but now her emotions were catching up to her. All that work—

For nothing.

She didn't regret her decision to refuse any kind of partnership with Landon, but she did regret the loss of her dream.

The stairs to her office never seemed so steep. The dressmaker dummies, without their finery, seemed to accuse her of letting them down. Alice slumped in a chair at one of her worktables, and for the first time her workshop didn't comfort her.

She felt a vision coming on—and pushed back hard. She didn't want them anymore. Didn't want hunches or foreknowledge. Didn't want to belong to a stupid family with gifts and mazes and pacts with the land.

She wanted to be normal for once. Wanted to succeed. Was that so much to ask?

Landon had been the key to that success—

Except he wasn't the key to anything.

Alice looked around her workshop again. How had Landon managed to poison her feelings about her haven? This space had been everything to her—especially since her mother died. It was where Amelia had taught her the basics of sewing and then set her free to create whatever she wanted. This was where she could take ideas and make them real. Where she expressed herself without compromise.

With Landon she'd begun to accept compromise as a given.

She'd almost sold out—sold herself.

Why had she done that?

She didn't need the money; was it fame she was after? Prestige?

Approval from a man, since she never got it from her father?

It was as if she was fighting against something. Alice stood up and crossed to the window. Fighting against the boundaries that always seemed to hem her in. She'd thought Landon offered a way out, but—

Did she need one?

Alice took in the house and the spread of the ranch around it. This was her home. These were her people. She loved it here. Loved what she did.

Loved Jack. As infuriating as he could be.

Maybe she even loved the General, though they had much to patch up between them.

So why had she been so intent on this commission?

Hoopskirts?

Alice shook her head, but she had to acknowledge it was partly true. At the end of the day, she loved hoopskirts. Their incredible exuberance. Their impracticality. The sheer audaciousness of them. She wasn't a Civil War buff. Hated that slavery was ever practiced in her country. Knew that for some people such dresses were inextricably linked to a past they couldn't forgive.

For Alice, hoopskirts were simply a three-dimensional challenge, a cross between architecture and fashion. They swished around when you walked. Swung wide when you danced. Popped up in embarrassing ways when you tried to sit down. They were… fun.

She wanted to go to a ball full of hoopskirts.

She wanted a dress like that for herself.

She wanted… fun.

Life had been so hard for so long. All those years since her mother died, she and her sisters had to hold everything together through sheer will. The caretakers and guardians her father had sent were no substitute for the loving presence Amelia had been. They'd all grown up so fast. Had banded together to build walls between them and the rest of the world.

Each time they'd kicked out their overseers and guardians, they'd held their breath every minute of the day, waiting to be found out. Waiting for the General to send more tyrants to dictate their lives.

All they'd really wanted was for the General to come home. Alice thought about Jack hiding under the bed and hearing his parents be killed. She knew exactly how it felt when you realized your parents were gone for good and you were truly alone.

All these years she'd kept her emotions in check. Had helped her sisters. Had tried to see the future. Had done her best—

Meanwhile Two Willows had been attacked again and again. She'd been shot at. Threatened. She'd nearly lost the ranch.

She'd kept her wits about her. Kept plodding on.

When was she going to get a break?

Alice stifled a sob that was very nearly a laugh.

That was her mistake—waiting for fate to hand her the chance. She couldn't wait for her life to settle down, as if the universe might simply solve all her problems some sunny day. She had to grab fun wherever she could find it. Make her own fun.

If she wanted a ballroom full of hoopskirts, she didn't need Landon or anyone else to make it happen.

In fact, she could sew one for herself tonight. She had the underthings already. She had plenty of fabric. She just needed to pick a style—

Alice stood up and turned in a circle, surveying the racks of costumes and the piles of fabric at the ready for whatever she wanted to sew next.

She came to a stop when her gaze rested on a dressmaker dummy she'd pushed aside into the corner; the only one clothed at the moment.

It wore her mother's wedding dress, which had been altered to fit first Cass, then Sadie, then Jo, and finally Lena.

It would be her turn next.

Would she marry Jack?

She had a flash of him pacing his room, his face drawn with worry, and knew she was seeing what was happening right now. He'd done everything he thought was right. He'd kept warning her about Landon—thinking the man wanted to do her harm. When she hadn't listened, he'd taken things into his own hands.

She remembered what he'd said, that keeping people safe was his job. He was right; she'd been in danger a number of times this year. What if instead of fighting him, she turned things around? What if she asked him to protect her?

When she put it that way, the idea was kind of sexy. It wasn't that she didn't appreciate that Jack cared for her. She simply wanted to be in the loop.

Meanwhile, she needed to take her mind off this disaster of a day. Needed a brand new project…

Alice crossed the room and examined the wedding dress she'd altered so many times. It would be hard to turn it into a Civil War–style gown, but if she could…

Chapter Seventeen

"WOULD YOU SEE if you can convince Alice to come and eat?" Cass asked several hours later.

"I'm not sure if she wants to see me," Jack told her, although he'd been dying to go to the carriage house. He knew Alice was sad about the way things had turned out, and furious at him. He wanted to comfort her, but he also knew sometimes you had to give a woman a little space.

"Try," Cass told him.

He let himself into the carriage house and climbed the stairs to the second floor, bracing himself against an unfavorable reception. He found Alice bent over one of her worktables, a long white gown spread out before her.

A wedding dress.

Jack stopped, unsure whether or not to proceed. Whose gown was it?

Hers?

His chest tightened. Maybe she wasn't so mad after all.

"You can come in." Alice didn't look up.

"What are you working on?" He took a seat nearby.

"My wedding dress. Seeing what I can do with it."

"Thinking about getting married?" he asked lightly.

She put down her sewing and faced him. "Maybe. But don't get too cocky."

"I won't. Look—" He sat on one of the tables. "I'm sorry things didn't work out with Landon. And I guess I should have told you he was here."

"You knew it wouldn't work from the start. Why are you always so sure you're right?" she asked.

"Because I usually am."

Her blue eyes studied him. She didn't look amused.

"I've made a career out of knowing things. Seeing patterns where other people don't. You know all this—I told you before."

"You saw things about Landon you didn't like?"

"Actually, I didn't. I think I've gotten a little gun-shy about my abilities." He hadn't put it into words before, but it was true. "Something happened about six months ago. I got into trouble."

"Tell me about it." She kept working, but Jack knew she was listening, and for once he felt ready to talk. Alice was different from the other women he'd known. He wanted her to understand.

"In my last assignment I was stationed in the Middle East and worked closely with an informant. I can't tell you where—sorry."

Alice waved this off.

"Got to know his whole family," Jack went on. "He had a wife, two sons and a daughter. Lila was the baby of the family. Sweet girl—but smart as a tack. My informant was proud as heck of her. She was like me," he added.

"She noticed things, too?"

Jack was grateful that Alice got it. "Exactly. Learning languages has always come easy to me. I have a great memory, and I catch the details of the way native speakers use words. She was like that. She knew some English from school, of course, but a few weeks around me and she was speaking like she'd grown up in the US."

"Sounds cute."

"She was. A little genius. I stayed with them for nearly a month. You're not supposed to get close to people, but it's hard not to when you're with them all the time. My informant's wife wasn't pleased I was there. His two sons were at school all day. Lila only went to school for a couple of hours a day. The rest of the time she was home, and she was curious about who I was and where I came from. We played games. I quizzed her on math problems, which no one else did, but she'd been listening to her brothers and had taught herself. You wouldn't believe how much ground we covered while I was there."

"What happened?"

"My informant and I were out of town when there was a raid on her school. The attackers took all the girls away. Her father was out of his mind with fear and grief. Her mother blamed me. My superiors ordered me not to interfere. That wasn't why I was there." Jack took a deep breath. "How could I not interfere?"

Alice nodded, her work forgotten in her lap. "Of course you had to."

"Thing was, the kidnappers wanted money. Thought the United States government might pay to get those girls back. They called up the village chief. Put one of the girls on the line to prove they were still alive."

"Lila," Alice guessed.

"That's right. She remembered a code I taught her. Used it right in front of her captors. Told me everything about what she'd seen on the way to where they'd taken her. She was amazing."

"What happened?"

"I got her out. Got all of them out. With Lila's information, the men in my informant's village were able to track down her kidnappers and mete out justice. What I'm trying to say is—"

"You sense danger. You thought Landon was a danger to me."

"That's right. Alice, I'm always looking for danger. That's my job—it's what I do. It's not that I don't trust your judgment—or your gift—it's that I don't trust anyone, really. And I need to keep the people I love safe. I already lost my parents. I nearly lost Lila. I can't… lose you. I just can't."

"Okay. Here's the deal. I'm hiring you to keep me safe. You work for me now."

"Are you serious?" She had his full attention.

She nodded. "Dead serious."

"How are you going to pay me?"

Alice just smiled.

WHEN JACK GOT up and came to kiss her, Alice met him halfway, her heart throbbing. He loved her.

To a man like Jack, loving and protecting was the same thing. She had an uncomfortable realization that the General might feel the same way. While he'd admitted he'd taken the wrong tack with them after Amelia died, in those first years when his wife was gone, when he couldn't find it in himself to return to Two Willows, had he felt that by sending overseers and guardians he'd been demonstrating his love for his girls?

If he had, he'd gotten it so wrong.

But so had she and her sisters. They'd viewed those interlopers as an expression of their father's loathing for them.

They'd begun to loath themselves.

By the time Howie Warner had come around, Alice thought he was worthy of her—although he never was.

"What?" Jack pulled back.

"For a species whose specialty is communication, we all suck at it," Alice said.

Jack chuckled. "Yeah, although I thought I did a good job of communicating just now."

"You did," Alice rushed to assure him. "Poor Jack."

"Poor Jack?" he repeated, eyebrows lifting.

"By saving Lila you lost your career and condemned yourself to marrying me. That's how the General got control over you, right? Because you didn't follow orders."

"That's right. Can't say I mind the outcome, though." He grew serious. "Unless I mess this up somehow. What do you see, when you look into the future... about us?" he asked hesitantly. He'd tangled his fingers in her belt loops, holding her in place as if afraid she'd run away.

Alice knew it was a miracle he'd asked at all. She couldn't fool herself into thinking Jack believed in her abilities wholeheartedly. He was trying because he loved her, not because he thought it was possible.

Images filled Alice's mind. Making love to Jack. Sitting side by side on a porch swing with him. Laughing together. Walking and talking.

"I see something wonderful," she whispered.

"Good." Jack braced his hands on her hips, took a deep breath, then suddenly pushed away. When he lowered himself to one knee, Alice sucked in a surprised breath. Was he... ?

"Alice, you know that your father sent me here, and you probably imagine that it was against my will. It wasn't. The first time I saw your photograph, I knew I could care for you. The first day we met, I knew I wanted to make you my wife. I keep waiting for the other boot to drop—for someone to show up and say it was all a mistake. I didn't know how a man like me could end up with a woman like you. All I know is, I never want to leave you—or Two Willows. I've dreamed of a life like this for years, but didn't think it was possible. Now I've begun to hope. Alice, it's too soon, and it's not fair, and you've had so much going on in your life these past few months, but I don't think I can take not knowing anymore. Would you… marry me?"

Alice thought of her mother. What would Amelia say if she knew Jack? Would she focus on his inability to fully believe in her foresight? Or would she focus on the man himself? The way he worked to keep the ones he loved safe. The way he'd dedicated his life to using his talents to help other people, rather than wallow in sorrow over his parents' murder. The way he'd opened up his heart to a new family, rather than keep his love locked inside him.

She had grown to love this man, despite the places they were different. She'd seen that he was someone she could depend on, too.

And she wanted to be with him. Desperately.

She felt a touch on her shoulder, as if her mother stood by her side and had just placed a hand there to offer comfort.

She waited to hear her mother's advice, but none came. Amelia simply stood by her in solidarity. A woman who'd loved a man with a vastly different way of seeing the world. A woman who'd found everything she'd ever wanted within the small sphere of a single ranch.

A woman who'd embraced her gift fully, no matter what anyone else thought.

Alice had wondered what guided her mother through her life. What made it possible for Amelia to handle such a powerful gift.

Now she understood. The answer was staring her in the face.

Love.

Amelia gave love and accepted it freely. Wholeheartedly. Without holding anything back.

Alice wanted that, too.

"Yes," she heard herself say. "Yes, I'll marry you." Accepting Jack was the path truest to herself.

Jack stood up, and she got the sense that her answer had begun to thaw the wall of ice he'd built around his heart so many years ago. As someone who'd also known loss and loneliness, she understood. It was hard to trust again—to love again.

But oh, so worth it.

As he took her in his arms and kissed her, Alice realized she was saying yes to life. To all of it—not just the parts she thought other people could understand. She was saying yes to herself as well as to Jack.

She wrapped her arms around his neck and met him kiss for kiss, happiness welling up inside her until she wondered how she could hold it in. Jack was hers, and she wanted to savor the feeling of him. Unlike her visions, he was real and present—not a ghost from the future, but a solid force in her life today.

And he was letting her know he wanted far more than kisses. His hands slid under her shirt to rest on her waist. Alice knew what he was asking. Wanted it, too.

She tugged her shirt up and over her head and tossed it aside.

"Now we're talking." Jack tugged her close again

and dipped down to kiss the tops of her breasts. Alice bit her lip.

"That feels good."

"It's going to get much better before I'm done."

"Really?"

Jack stopped. "Are you doubting me?" He lifted her up and sat her down on the worktable.

"Wouldn't want to make assumptions," she teased.

"Get your clothes off. Let me show you how it's done."

WATCHING ALICE STRIP, perched on her worktable, her hair tumbling over her naked shoulders, her motions slow and sensuous, was turning him on so bad Jack was losing his cool.

He shrugged out of his jacket and flannel shirt. Tugged his T-shirt over his head and nearly went to help her shuck off her jeans but decided to wait and enjoy the view instead.

It was a hell of a view.

Unbuckling his belt, undoing the button of his jeans, slipping them down with his boxer briefs and kicking the whole lot off with his boots, he stood in front of her, hard and ready.

"Look at you," Alice said as she tossed the last of her clothing to the floor, still seated on the edge of the table, one leg crossed over the other. She took her time doing just that until Jack burned to take her right then and there.

"Look at you." He moved closer, spread her thighs

and stood between them, running his hands from her hips to her breasts, palming them softly before bending to tease one of her nipples with his tongue.

Alice's hands went to his shoulders, and she braced herself as he caressed her, breath catching with the sensation of his hands on her skin.

The heat of her against his hardness made it difficult to go slow, especially when Alice leaned back, lifting her breasts into his touch, and moaned.

Jack slid his hands under her bottom, lifted her up, positioned himself—

And pushed inside.

Her gasp nearly took him over the edge, but he held on, wanting to bring her with him, and he began a slow rhythm moving in and out, knowing soon she'd be ready, too.

ALICE WORKED WITH him, meeting him thrust for thrust, moving her hips, clinging to his shoulders, until her breathing was as ragged as his.

"Jack—"

She arched back, cried out, and Jack bucked against her, Alice's release pulling him into his own. They crashed against each other again and again until Jack, winded, bumped the table and they both collapsed on it.

Alice wriggled beneath him. "You're heavy."

Jack savored the feeling of her body pressed against him one last moment before pulling out and sitting beside her. "Maybe we should head inside. Try this again—in bed."

Alice made a noise. "We'd have to get dressed, go out in the cold and get undressed again."

"What's the alternative?" He let his hand trace her hip. Alice moaned appreciatively and rolled over.

"We can do it again right here."

Jack let out a happy groan and ran his hand over her shapely bottom. Yeah, he could be persuaded to stay here. He got off the table and moved between her legs. Bent over the table, her position gave him so much visual stimulus he was ready all over again, straining to hold back from taking her hard and fast right now.

Instead he ran his hands over her body, appreciating every dip and curve. When Alice pushed up on her elbows, he cupped her breasts, savoring the weight and fullness of them.

Alice lifted her hips, telling him what she wanted, and Jack was only too happy to comply. As he pushed inside her, she pushed back against him, taking him deep until Jack had to fight for control. He moved a hand to tangle it in her hair, moved his hips to slide in and out of her.

"Oh god, that's good," Alice breathed.

He wasn't sure he could find the words to answer her.

It was good. She was slick and hot and moving with him in a way that was bringing him oh, so close to losing his mind.

"Faster," she coached him. Jack sped up. What else could he do?

Bent over her, moving inside her, one arm wrapped

around her, the other hand tangled in her hair, all Jack could do was hold on and go for it. Alice's moans told him she was right there with him, but Jack wasn't sure if he could have stopped if he tried. His body had taken over, moving of its own accord, desperate for relief from the tension every glimpse of Alice twisted tighter inside him.

"Jack!" Alice cried out, pushing back against him. Jack went over the edge into an orgasm that spun on and on until he thought he'd black out. He pumped into her again and again, praying he wasn't hurting her, reassured by her own cries of ecstasy as she bucked back, meeting him thrust for thrust.

When it was finally over, Jack could barely move. "Woman," he panted. "You're going to kill me."

Beneath him, Alice's shoulders shook, and for a horrible moment he thought she was crying.

When he slid out of her and turned her over in his arms, he was relieved to find her laughing.

"What?" he demanded.

"Like you said before. This… works."

"Hell, yeah it does." Jack gathered her close. "Am I wearing you out?" he added.

"Is that possible?"

Jack laughed. "I hope not. I want a lifetime of that."

"Me, too." She sighed when he palmed her breast with his hand, then bent to kiss it.

"But first there's something we have to do."

"What's that?" Alice leaned into his touch and caught his mouth with hers. "What do we have to do?"

she asked again a few minutes later when they broke apart.

Jack thought hard. What was it?

Oh, right.

"Go buy you a ring and make this official."

Chapter Eighteen

"ROSE JOHNSON IS like me, you know," Alice said on the way to town. "She can see the future—at least a little bit of it."

"So you told me before." Jack kept his eyes on the road. "What kind of ring do you want?" That seemed like a safer topic.

"Something flashy and ostentatious."

The truck swerved a little. "Really?"

"No—what do you take me for?" Alice grinned at him. "You were worried there a minute, though."

"I never know what to expect from you."

"Good. That's the way it should be, don't you think?"

Jack parked in front of Thayer's Jewelers, and when they went inside, Alice relaxed a little. The shop was cozy, one large wall filled with beautiful landscape paintings. "Rose did those," she told Jack. "That's Mia Matheson's wedding planning business." She pointed to an office.

"Engagement rings are in the left-hand corner," Rose Johnson said, not looking up from some documents she was filling in near the till.

"Thanks, Rose."

"Oh—hi, Alice! Sorry!"

"No worries. You look busy."

Rose bustled over to help them. "This is the part of my job I don't like: paperwork. Are you here for a ring?"

"Yes," Jack said. "Something beautiful."

"And ostentatious and flashy," Alice added with a grin.

Rose smiled at their banter. "I have just the thing." She unlocked a case and pulled out a tray of rings. "Try this on. I was wondering who it was for." She pointed to a lovely ring that sat alone on one side of the tray, then moved away and bent over her paperwork again.

Alice picked it up, slid it on her ring finger and clutched the counter with her free hand, the vision overtaking her almost instantly.

It was of the past, not the future. Of Amelia—a much younger Amelia than she'd ever known—standing with a tall, handsome man—the General, long before he was a general—and beaming up at him as he slid a ring on her finger.

"That's much too expensive," Amelia said.

"It is," the General told her. "We can't get it today, but I swear, someday—"

A shadow crossed her mother's face, but she straightened her shoulders and smiled harder, and Alice was sure the General didn't even notice. Amelia turned to another ring lying on a tray on the counter, one she'd tried on before, Alice thought. "No, Augustus. This is our ring." She slid the fancier one off her finger. "This one belongs to someone else. Someone special." She looked up, seemed to see Alice and smiled tenderly. "I hope she's as happy as I am when she wears it," Amelia went on. "I hope she knows I was always happy with my life and my marriage."

"Amelia?" The General bent closer to her, then turned to look in the same direction she was—right at Alice. "Who is it?" he whispered.

"We don't know her yet," Amelia told him, "but we will. We're going to be so happy, Augustus. And so blessed. Remember that."

"I don't have to remember." The General took Amelia's hands in his. "I already know. Now let's get married and get working on those five girls you promised me."

"Alice?" Jack's hand supported her elbow. "Don't you like the ring? Let me take it off—"

"No!" Alice snatched her hand away. "I mean… I'm sorry. I—" She realized she couldn't hide her visions from Jack anymore. If they were to be together, he had to know about them. "I… my mother's here," she said softly. "So's my dad. They saw this ring, too. Mom tried it on, but then she had a vision and knew it was for me. She's looking at me right now."

Jack followed her gaze. "I can't see her," he said, his voice low. But he didn't try to convince Alice she wasn't there. Alice loved him for that concession.

"I know you can't see her. Jack, she's—they're so in

love." And the General was so excited to be a father. He'd known he was going to have daughters. He'd wanted them.

Jack put his arm around her waist to steady her. "Of course they are. Anyone who's met the General knows he adored Amelia."

Alice's heart expanded. Jack was right. She'd never doubted her father's love for her mother.

Now she knew he'd loved her, too.

"She's smiling at me. She can't wait to meet me."

"Of course she can't. I wish I could meet her."

"I know. I'm glad you've met the Gen—my father," Alice corrected herself. Seeing the General so young and happy, so ready to face life, it occurred to Alice that he was just a man—

He'd made mistakes. Like everyone else.

That didn't mean he didn't love her. She knew now he did. He'd always loved her—and her sisters. Even before they were born. He'd looked forward to meeting them.

Why hadn't she realized that before?

It was time to heal those old wounds for good.

"I'll do my best," she told her mother.

Amelia only nodded, but Alice saw the knowledge in her eyes. Amelia held up the ring, made sure Alice was looking, then carefully put it down on the side of the tray, exactly in the position Rose had lifted it from.

Had it sat there all this time?

Somehow Alice knew it had.

Her mother had seen her wedding ring. Tried it on.

That made up—just a little—for all the times Alice had wished Amelia could share an event in her life.

Amelia waved and faded away, the General still close by her side.

"They're gone," Alice whispered. Jack still held her tight.

"What about the ring? What do you think?"

"I… I love it," she said to Jack. She looked down, only now seeing it properly. A beautiful diamond ringed with smaller stones that glittered like something that belonged to a queen. "But it's much too expensive—"

"No, it isn't. You're marrying a rich man." Jack's hand covered hers. "My parents' ranch was sold after they died, the money invested for me. Richard and Janet never took a dime to raise me. We can afford this ring. Will it make you happy?"

Her eyes filled with tears. Knowing her mother had touched it made it so special she'd be filled with joy whenever she looked at it. "Yes," she said.

"We'll take it," Jack told Rose. Alice handed it to her, and Rose clasped it in her hand a moment, closing her eyes. When she opened them again, she nodded. "There's trouble ahead. I wish I could say otherwise, but later there's happiness. Deep, deep happiness. You two are going to be blessed. Remember that when it gets tough."

"I don't have to remember." Jack took Alice's hands in his. "I already know."

LATER THAT NIGHT, the whole group, including Emerson and Wye, gathered at the table. The General sat at one end, Emerson on his right and Alice on his left. Brian headed the other end of the table, flanked by Cass and Connor. Jack sat by Alice, with Hunter, Jo and Sadie following along that side of the table. On the other side, Wye sat next to Emerson, with Lena and Logan beside her.

"Everyone, we have big news. Alice and I are getting hitched," Jack proclaimed.

Connor cheered. Hunter clapped Jack on the back. Logan raised his glass in a toast. Brian grinned like he'd known it all along, exchanging a pleased glance with Cass.

"Five for five," Jo said, toasting the General, who looked more surprised than Jack would have expected. "Good going, Dad."

Everyone turned to look at her, and Jo blushed a little. "Well, he is our dad," she said defensively.

"That's right. He is," Cass said softly.

"What do you say, General? Do I have your blessing?" Jack asked. Lena snorted but held her tongue.

The General shifted in his seat. "Of course you do. Welcome to the family." He turned to Alice. "Suppose you saw this coming all along."

"Not really," she said.

"But you do see things."

She nodded.

"Amelia found it a hard burden to bear sometimes. I tried to help—"

"I'm sure you did."

"And I plan on helping, too," Jack said.

Lena slapped the table suddenly and stood up. "Stop it!" she commanded. "Stop pretending everything's okay, because it isn't. Alice, Jack—I'm happy for you if you're happy together. Don't pretend the General had anything to do with it, though."

"He did send me here—" Jack pointed out.

"I don't care. After the way he's treated us, I don't care if he wins the Nobel Peace Prize." She turned on the General. "I'll never forgive you for what you've done. The way you doubted me. Undermined me. Overrode me. Never saw what I was capable of!"

"Lena," Logan began.

"No. Don't try to make this better. Let the man gloat. He's won, hasn't he?"

"Is that how you see our marriage?" Logan asked.

"This has nothing to do with our marriage. It has to do with the way my father can't see my sisters and me worth something on our own. I ran this ranch just fine without anyone's help. All of us worked our asses off to keep it up, and all he did was interfere! He had no right!"

"This is my ranch," the General said. "You may not like me, but I expect a little respect."

"I'll respect you when you show me some respect," Lena retorted. "This isn't your ranch. It belonged to Mom. She ran it first, and I've run it ever since. You were never here, and you didn't care, and you ignored us, and you lost any right you ever had to call the shots here—or when it came to us! You should be court-martialed for dereliction of duty. You're supposed to be such a hot-shot General. Why the hell couldn't you handle coming home and helping once in a while?"

Lena was pale. Her hands shaking. Maybe Alice had been wrong. Maybe the General's defection had hurt Lena even more than all the rest of them.

Alice fished in her pocket. Drew out the dog tags she'd found in the maze. Reached out and pressed them into Lena's hand.

"What—?" Lena broke off, staring at them.

"I found them in the maze. We have to let go of the past, Lena. Of our pain," Alice told her. "We're all here now. Mom wants us to be together."

"Alice is right. I'm home now, and I'm your father." The General got slowly to his feet. "Regardless of what you think of me, I'm still head of this house. I still own this land. I'm the one who calls the shots around here—"

"Sorry to barge in on a family squabble," a new voice said from the back door. Alice turned around in her seat to see that Will had come in. "But you're both wrong. I'm the one calling the shots around here—starting right now." He pulled out a pistol and swept the room, pointing it at each of them in turn.

"Will? What are you doing?" Wye gasped.

Alice sucked in a surprised breath. She hadn't seen this coming, but now her mind filled with images. The rat-a-tat-tat of gunfire. Screams. Shattering glass. It didn't take foreknowledge to know she was seeing the carnage that was to come. Will's hand was steady, but his eyes glinted with fury. How had she ever thought him easygoing?

Jack touched her leg under the table. "Stay calm," he whispered.

She was calm. She was caught like a fly in amber, the past, present and future swirling around her. She blinked away the visions, needing to stay in the present, but she had no idea what to do next.

"I'm getting what's mine," Will growled.

"I don't understand—" Cass said.

"I've been watching you. Watching all of you." Will swept the barrel of his firearm sideways to encompass everyone in the room. "Just like my father used to do."

"Duke Manson," the General said slowly. "You're his son? Ought to have known. Any plumber who takes weeks to do a simple job—"

I should have known, Alice thought. Why hadn't she gotten any indication…?

In a blinding flash, she realized she had. That creeping sense of dread that had haunted her—she'd pinned it on Landon—or the General coming home. That wasn't right at all, was it? It had surged every time Will came to work on the pipes.

"My dad hated you, General Augustus Reed. With good reason. You got him kicked out of the Army."

"Deserved it. Running drugs into boot camp. Getting recruits messed up and hooked on his wares."

"Just good business practices." Will shrugged. "It was a good gig until you got in the way. He'd planned to make a bundle, put in his four years, go home a rich man and make something of himself. Instead he had to start at the bottom back home. Claw his way up. Wasted years doing that, working for other men."

"Wasted his life, if you ask me." The General met Will's gaze squarely.

"You ruined him," Will said. "Made him half the man he could have been. Now he's dead, and that's your fault, too."

"I didn't kill him."

"You set the law on him. You sent that snitch Ron Cooper back to Tennessee to try to rat him out. You're not going to get away with it, though. My dad couldn't get the job done, but I can. I planned everything out. Cased this house until I learned it backward and forward. There's nowhere you can run from me."

Will must have broken the spigot that set off his whole series of visits, Alice thought wildly. What would he have done if Cass hadn't brought him back to fix the banging pipes—?

Alice saw Lena, on the other side of the table, slip her hand under her flannel shirt. She knew her sister wore a shoulder holster, and if she could reach—

Will took three steps forward and jammed the tip of the Luger to the General's temple. "I wouldn't do that, Lena. Unlike my father, I managed to serve my time in the Army. I know how to use this thing, and I won't hesitate."

"What do you want?" the General asked.

"I want everything, but I'll start with Alice. She's too good for Jack here. His silly surveillance system never stopped me, did it? And you, General, you wanted all your daughters married off, right? Well, coincidentally, I'm in the market for a wife, and Alice will do just fine. Sorry, Wye, you're cute, but you can't predict the future, can you?"

Alice cringed. How did he know?

Will chuckled. "Oh, come on, I've been listening to you all," he said. "None of you thought twice about talking in front of me. Neither did the other people in town. Hell, Walter never shut up. Told me all about you Reeds. I've heard everything."

"You aren't taking Alice," the General said.

"Yes, I am, and it'll be a fine life for your girl. You won't even need to worry about me running drugs anymore. With Alice helping me predict the stock market, I won't need to mess around with stuff like that. I'll treat her right, Augustus. I'll squire her around the world. We'll live on a yacht, party with the stars, visit every port. Not a bad life, eh? I can't believe none of the rest of you thought of it. Working your asses off on this stinking ranch for years—too moral to place a few bets on the game? Come on. Landon Clark had the right idea, didn't he? Oh, yeah—I know about all that, too. You aren't the only one who can bug a room, Jack. What kind of surveillance expert doesn't check to see if someone else is surveilling you?"

"You'll leave right now if you know what's good for you," Brian said. He was trying to distract Will, Alice thought. Trying to give the rest of them a chance to get to their guns and get a shot off. Lena sat tense, her fingers flexing, but she didn't make a move for her pistol again. Jack sat frozen, but she knew his mind was working overtime. He was looking for information, noticing details, making plans.

Will stayed cool. Kept surveying the room. Shaking his head at them. "I'll leave as soon as Alice is ready. Say your goodbyes, honey. We're going on a round-the-world tour."

Alice stood up slowly, knowing she needed to do something. Not knowing what that was. Why didn't her gift ever give her any real information—?

"Start predicting tonight's games, darling," Will added. "We need some cash for the road."

Games. She'd predicted all the games. *All* of them.

Jack looked up at her. He was trying to send a message with his eyes. Trying to tell her something.

But what?

"There's one of you and thirteen of us. You aren't going to get out of here," Logan said suddenly. "Give up while you still have the chance, Will."

"You think I came alone? You really must think I'm stupid. Boys? Get in here!"

Men streamed in from every doorway, and Alice's heart sank. She saw Jack's flash of surprise. Knew what he was thinking—how had they gotten past his defenses?

"Like I said, I know all about surveillance, too," Will told him with a grin. "I definitely know how to disarm a system. Don't forget, I've been in your house for weeks. You don't have many secrets left."

"You aren't taking my daughter," the General

growled.

"Oh, but I am. Come on, honey." Will gripped her arm as his men spread out through the room. Alice recognized Paul Ramsey and Beau Ellis among them. Hatred burned in Beau's eyes. Lena and Logan had killed his twin nephews.

He was back for blood.

IF IT WAS only Will, he could get off the shot, Jack thought. But it wasn't only Will. At least ten men had entered the kitchen, the room as crowded as if a party was going on. The quarters were close. If he drew his gun, people would die.

And they wouldn't all be his enemies.

He'd been in tough situations before, but none where the odds were stacked so highly against a happy outcome. Will held Alice's arm. Had his pistol still pressed against the General's temple. In the General's eyes was the knowledge he could very well see his family killed—or die himself first.

Jack knew every man on the ranch was armed. Probably the General and Emerson, too. Lena certainly was. Logan had told him long ago she wore her shoulder holster constantly. With some element of surprise, they could have taken on the intruders easily, but the intruders had all the surprise on their side.

Jack couldn't believe his surveillance network had failed so utterly.

Of course, it had been flawed from the start. Arriving after Will had started working at the Reeds' house, he'd failed to consider the man as a possible enemy.

Now he was going to lose Alice if he didn't think of something quick.

He scanned the room, looking for possibilities, no matter how slight or remote. Could he signal the men for a simultaneous attack? Maybe, but Will would take out the General at the very least before they could act definitively.

Beau Ellis looked like he wanted to murder Logan and Lena with his bare hands. The rest of the attackers looked just as hungry for blood. The Reeds and the men the General had sent had been decimating the ranks of their organization for months.

What else could he use against them? Could he pit them against each other somehow?

He didn't have time.

Could the men engage them long enough for the women to escape?

Probably not in these close quarters.

He turned to Alice, standing so rigid beside him, held in place by Will's hand, her eyes closed, like she was searching her mind for information—

No, Jack realized. Not searching her mind—searching the future.

A chill swept through him.

She couldn't see the future.

Except—all those scores. She'd gotten every single one of them right. That was statistically impossible from sheer luck, and he didn't think Alice had a way of rigging sports competitions in four different categories.

What if—what if she really could see what was about to happen?

What if she could see what these men would do before they did it?

He remembered what she'd said the night she listed all those scores—that she could show him the future—but it wasn't allowed. Did she mean—could she send him the images she saw?

If so—

"Alice," he heard himself say. "Show me."

Alice opened her eyes. Stared down at him uncomprehendingly.

"The future. Show me."

"What are you saying? Shut up," Will demanded, his pistol still pressed against the General's temple.

Alice glanced at Will, then back at Jack. "It's not allowed," she hissed.

"Sometimes you have to break the rules," Jack told her.

"I said, shut up!" Will glared at them.

Jack held his breath, his gaze on Alice.

When she nodded, his heart soared.

Chapter Nineteen

THE FUTURE. JACK wanted her to show him the future. To anticipate what Will would do—

And put the image in his mind.

That's right, Amelia's voice said.

But it was wrong—

Rules are made to be broken.

Could she do it?

Alice wasn't sure. She'd only tried once. It had worked, but…

Open your mind.

Alice shut her eyes, gripped the edge of the table, strained to see—

It wouldn't come—

"I've waited too long for this," Beau snarled from the far side of the room. He took two steps and struck the side of Lena's head with the butt of his gun. Logan roared and caught her as she fell. Half the men leaped to their feet.

"Goddammit," Will shouted. "What the hell did I tell you, Beau? Get yourself under control."

Rage, clean and pure, shot through Alice like a multi-bladed knife. No one hit her sister. No one—

"Hold your fire," Will barked at his men.

"Fuck that," Beau said. "I'm here for revenge." He raised his pistol and pointed it at Logan.

Time sped forward for Alice and her vision multiplied, images overlaid one on top of each other, the present and the future spinning out at the same time.

In the future, Beau stepped toward Logan, arm outstretched—

Alice sent the image to Jack.

Beau stepped toward Logan. Jack leaped up and over the table, sending dishes flying, hit the ground on the other side and knocked the pistol from Beau's hand.

In the future, Ramsey scrambled after it—

Alice sent the image to Jack.

Ramsey scrambled after it. Jack kicked the pistol across the floor. Wye grabbed it and leaped to her feet, pointing it at Ramsey.

Future Beau bellowed with fury, turned around and went for Logan—

Alice sent the image to Jack.

Beau roared with fury, turned—

But Jack couldn't get there in time. Beau's fist connected with Logan's face hard enough to knock Logan down.

All around Alice, chaos ensued. Will yelled orders, still holding his pistol to the General's head. The other men ignored him as Brian, Logan, Hunter and Connor all leaped to their feet and joined in the melee.

In the future, Will shook Alice. "Let's move, bitch!"

Alice sent the image to Jack—too late.

Will shook her. "Let's move, bitch—fuck!"

He crashed to the ground as Jo struck him over the head with a chair. Alice fell, too, the floor coming up to slam against her body. The air whooshed out of her lungs. Will swore and scrambled up again. Alice tried to push up, too, but the room swam, and it was all she could do to sit. She saw Emerson tackled by one of the strangers as he pointed a pistol at Will's prone form. Saw the General struggle to go after the man who'd tackled his corporal.

"Alice!" Jack shouted.

She couldn't do this alone. Jack couldn't—

"Alice—show me!" Jack shouted.

Alice swayed. Straightened. Her head filled with images cascading far too fast for her to catch and sort. The General falling. Emerson tussling with the stranger. Jo bringing her chair down again and again before being knocked down herself—

Her rage was back—and with it her vision.

Suddenly it was clear and strong. She was clear and strong. She didn't have to move. All she had to do was think—and send the images, not just to Jack—but to everyone.

In the future, Ramsey pointed his pistol at Jo—

She sent the image to Jack, and he drew his own weapon, aimed, fired and laid Ramsey out.

Beau would lunge for Lena.

Alice sent the image to Logan, who had his pistol in his hand in a flash and killed Beau with a single shot.

Beau dropped to the ground.

In the future, a man she didn't know went for Emerson.

Alice beamed that image to Wye, who wound up and swung a rolling pin she grabbed from the nearby counter like a World Series hitter and knocked the stranger sideways, his temple hitting the table with a crack.

Someone else would shoot off several rounds into the heart of the fray.

Alice sent that image to Connor, who whipped out a pistol of his own and shot the man dead.

The images came faster and faster, and Alice sent them winging their way with a precision she couldn't have dreamed of a few moments ago. She didn't know if she'd sped up or if time had slowed down. All she knew was that Jack figured in most of them.

He caught the images she sent far faster than anyone else, reacted to them almost instantaneously after she sent them. He disarmed man after man and put them on the ground until he was faced with Will again.

But Will didn't aim at Jack. He twisted around and pointed his pistol at the General once more, who clutched the back of a chair for support, Emerson by his side.

"This is for my dad," Will growled. "You can join him in hell."

"No!" Lena screamed as he pulled the trigger, bringing her pistol to bear on him—too late. The General crumpled in Emerson's arms.

"No! No! No!" Lena fired again and again, her shots ripping through Will over and over until he crumpled, too, his body hitting the floor with a sickening thud.

Lena ran to the General. Alice wanted to go, too, but the fight wasn't over, and present and future merged into a groaning stream of distorted images in her brain as she kept sorting them. Kept sending them out.

And when the rest of the strangers had all been disarmed—or killed—she couldn't seem to stop. Hands were tied, firearms disabled, men sorted, women consoled. Alice went on and on, sending images, directing the scene until she thought she'd be trapped in the slipstream of time forever.

Let go.

It was Amelia again.

Darling, let go.

But she couldn't. If she let go, time would stop. The future would become the present.

Her father would be dead.

The images went on and on.

Brian would console Cass. Hunter would tie the wrists of two strange men. Emerson and Wye would bend over the General's prone form. Logan would call Cab. Cab would grab his gun and his badge, and rush from his office. His secretary would call out a goodbye. An ambulance would drive past the sheriff's department, sirens blaring. Ellie Donaldson would alter a wedding dress for a customer. Maggie Lawton would hug her daughter. Ned Matheson would shrug into his winter coat and head outside to work on the Double-

Bar-K.

Let go!

She couldn't. The weight of all that future was crushing her. Forcing her down.

Alice, Amelia called. But her mother was slipping away, pushed aside by the images piling and piling up in her mind. A black dog would bark. A cow would low in a distant barn. A crow would wing its way over a meadow—

"Alice! Alice, come back!"

Something shook her shoulders, but she couldn't respond. Everything that was Alice was melting away, diluting in the deluge of futures. She tried to swim back upstream, but the current was too strong.

Lives spooled out all around her. Movements, dishes, eyes and breaths, stairs and driveways, cars and radios. People kissing, people laughing, drawing breath, reaching, grabbing, stepping—dying.

"Alice!"

A hand grabbed hers. Jerked her hard. "Alice—can you hear me?" It pulled again.

Alice clung to it, knowing it was her only hope. Knowing, too, that returning to the present would cause too much pain.

Fight, Alice! Amelia cried. *Remember your home. Remember your family. Your future.*

She tried to picture her sisters. Her home.

They were all sliding further and further away.

The future—

She didn't want to see the future.

"Alice!"

She knew that voice, but she couldn't place it. Knew the hand that held hers but couldn't remember the face that went with it. The images poured down over her, burying her alive until Alice, gasping and choking, flailing and kicking, went under one last time—

And everything went dark.

"ALICE! ALICE!" JACK yelled. "Come on, Alice. Wake up. Someone call an ambulance!"

"Already did," Logan called from across the room. He held Lena in his arms.

Several feet away, Lena knelt over the General's prone body, Emerson and Wye beside her. Brian joined Jack by Alice's side. He checked her pulse. Bent down to listen. "She's still breathing."

"Why won't she wake up?"

Cass joined them, taking Alice's hand and bending over her sister. "Is she hurt?"

"I don't think so." Jack kept running his hands over her. "I can't find any blood. She's unconscious."

"Did she hit her head?"

"I don't know."

Cass moved to the General. "Dad? Where was he hit?" she asked Emerson.

"I can't find the bullet."

"I hear sirens," Jo cried.

"Dad?" Cass asked again. "Dad, can you hear me?"

"He's dead," Lena said. "He's dead, and I never got to tell him—"

"Get away from my daughter!" The General surged up with a shout, thrashing and kicking until Emerson caught him and stopped him from trying to rise.

"General, it's okay. Where were you shot?"

The General pushed him away. "Shot? I wasn't shot! My damn leg—"

Relief flooded Jack. When Alice woke up, he wouldn't have to break bad news to her about her father.

If she woke up—

She lay so still on the ground it was as if—

No. She wasn't dead, either.

Lena still crouched by the General. "I thought… I thought you…" Her voice cracked, and tears flooded her eyes.

The General reached for her hand. Emerson helped him to sit up. "Not a scratch on me, thanks to you. You're a damn good shot. But that's because you're my girl. Come here."

Lena moved closer, and the General took her into his arms, supporting her when she began to sob. "That's my girl," he said again. "God, I've missed you all."

As the sirens neared Two Willows, Jack stroked Alice's hair and bent to kiss her forehead. "Come back," he whispered. "Please come back. I was wrong," he added. "So damn wrong. I should have believed you from the start."

Cab burst into the kitchen, followed by paramedics.

"What the hell happened here?" He gestured to the bodies, the men tied together, the scattered inhabitants of Two Willows fighting to recover their equilibrium.

"We put an end to it," Brian told him bluntly.

"Alice put an end to it," Jack corrected him as the paramedics surrounded them.

"Sir, we need you to let go now," one of them—a stocky woman with her hair in a twist and a no-nonsense air—told him.

"I'm coming with you."

"Sir—"

"Let's move," Jack barked. "This is my fiancée, and I'm not letting her go."

HOLD ON, AMELIA said. *Alice, you have to hold on.*

She was trying. Clinging to the hand that held hers. That one point of contact was the only thing preventing her from annihilation in the sea of images sluicing through her brain.

You are you. Inhabit yourself.

But Alice couldn't seem to feel where she ended and everyone else's lives began. So many futures—and pasts—and presents. So many people and lives and problems and joys.

So much pain.

You are Alice. Remember.

She tried to remember who Alice was, but there were so many other memories in her mind.

"Who—?" she tried to say. "Who… am… I?

Forming the words felt impossible with so many other words cascading through her. Her tongue was thick. Alien to her mouth. Or maybe her body had become the alien, separate from her consciousness.

"Who… who…?" she whispered, but her voice drowned in a flood of other voices. She wanted to let herself go. Give up the boundaries that kept her separate—

Allowed her to feel her own thoughts.

Her own hurts.

"Alice." The sound of her name came from very far away, but Alice strained toward it despite herself. Images rushed past her, swirled around her, lifted and floated her, then pulled her down again, and though she tried she couldn't seem to get closer to that voice.

Hold on, Amelia said. *Just hold on.*

"Alice," the other voice said again, a little closer this time. "Remember."

That was just the problem, though, she didn't want to remember—and yet she remembered everything. Everything.

"Your sisters need you," the voice said. "Cass. Sadie. Lena. Jo."

She had a flash of her sisters. Standing with them in the maze. Joining hands and making a promise. Was it past or future?

She didn't know.

"Your father needs you, too. He's alive, Alice. The General is alive."

Alive.

Her father—alive.

Her sisters—

"Remember Two Willows, Alice. Horses. Cattle.

Tabitha—"

Tabitha. A white cat. Her white cat.

Her father was alive.

Her sisters—

"Sitting on the refrigerator. Sewing in your workshop. Costumes. Hoopskirts."

Hoopskirts. Alice remembered squeezing through a doorway, bursting out the other side in a lilac gown.

"The General. He sent you a husband. A soldier."

Jack.

Alice clung to the hand more tightly.

The General had sent her Jack.

And she loved him.

"Alice, do you remember? We made love in the maze—"

Hold on tight, Amelia urged her. *As tight as you can.*

Alice clung to Jack's hand, because it was Jack's hand—she knew it. And she needed him. She needed Jack. Needed her sisters.

Her father.

She fought to speak—the words hard to form—to separate from the floods of words flowing past in the memories and futures that weren't hers.

"L-love," she managed. "I… love—"

The hand gripped her tighter. Jack's hand. "Please, Alice. Fight for us. Please come back."

"I… love… you."

Alice broke through the ocean of visions, floundering and gasping as if she'd come back from drowning. She came back fighting, surging up in the hospital bed she found herself in, ready to leap into action until Jack restrained her.

"Easy. Easy. You're attached." He cradled her in his arms, softly laid her back down and straightened out her IV as she gulped in deep breaths of air and scrambled to make sense of her surroundings.

"What—where—?"

"You're in the hospital. You've been unconscious," Jack said as the room filled with nurses and doctors. "You're okay."

"Dad?" She tried to sit up again, but an orderly restrained her. When she caught sight of a needle in one of the nurse's hands as the woman approached the IV in her arm, she flailed out again. "No! Jack—don't let them. I can't go back down!"

"Put that away," Jack ordered the nurse. "She has to stay conscious."

"She needs to rest—"

"Put it away, or we're leaving," Jack thundered.

The nurse looked to the doctor, who nodded after a moment. She put the needle away.

"Your dad is fine," Jack assured Alice. "Everyone's fine. What you did was amazing. We knew what would happen before it happened."

He seemed to take in the doctor's interest in their conversation, and when he went on, he lowered his voice. "We'll talk more later, but you did it—you saved us all."

"You saved us," she countered as memories—her own memories—flooded her mind. "You moved so fast."

"You were in danger," he told her. "I had to protect you. That's my job. That's always going to be my job."

Alice swallowed in a tight throat and nodded.

"I need to examine the patient now," the doctor said.

"Don't leave," Alice told Jack. "Please."

"I'll be right here," he promised her. "Always." He took a seat on one of the plastic chairs near the bed and kept hold of her hand, challenging the doctor with his gaze to say anything about it.

The doctor shrugged and put a stethoscope to Alice's heart.

"Is she going to be okay?" Jack asked him.

"I'm already okay," Alice said.

Chapter Twenty

IT WAS SEVERAL days before Alice was cleared to come home. By then the mess in Two Willows's kitchen had been cleaned up and everything put to rights again.

A new bullet groove scored the long wooden table, and one of the windows had been replaced—a cold job on a November day—but the room was surprisingly unscathed after the battle that had raged there. Will was dead. So were Beau and Ramsey. Cab agreed with Jack's assessment that the threat to Two Willows was most likely over.

Cass had dispatched Brian to town to bring home some pizzas. By the time Jack ushered Alice through the back door, Brian was pulling in, too. They decided to eat in the living room. Jack led Alice to a couch, wrapped a blanket around her and brought her a plate of pizza there. One by one, everyone else filed in holding a plate full of food and found a seat.

"Glad you're home," Cass told Alice. The others murmured their assent.

"Glad to be here." Alice still felt fragile but strong,

too, in a whole new way. She'd learned how to control her gift, and while the lesson had been harrowing, now that it was over she had a feeling it was like riding a bike—she'd remember how to do it from here on in.

"How did you do that back there?" Logan asked tentatively. "Put images in our minds…?" He trailed off.

Jack knew why he was asking. The whole thing had been uncanny. He'd gotten all the information just before he needed it. He'd seen what the attackers would do—and what he'd do in response—and then he'd done it. It was a kind of knowing that went well beyond the clues he was usually so astute at picking up.

It boggled his mind he'd ever thought he and Alice were the same.

A month ago, knowing they were so different would have set him on edge, and he would have worried it would make it impossible for them to be together.

He didn't feel that way now. On the contrary, he knew where he stood with Alice. He was her anchor. Her standing stone. His job was to keep her here—and now—and not let the slipstream of time take her somewhere else.

"I'm… sorry," Alice said, staring down at the plate of pizza in her lap. "I really am."

"Sorry?" Jack straightened. "What do you have to be sorry about? You have nothing to blame yourself for. I'm the one who kept insisting Landon was the one we needed to worry about. All along it was Will. I've never been so wrong."

"Neither have I," Wye said. Her eyes were red-rimmed, and it didn't take a psychic to know she'd spent much of the last few days crying. "I fell for that asshole."

Emerson winced but kept working to prop up the General's leg on a couple of pillows. Jack felt for the man, but he felt for Wye, too. It was never easy learning you'd been fooled.

"Mom told me never to put the future in someone's head."

"I asked you to," Jack reminded her. He nearly hadn't, and that knowledge haunted him. Two things had made him want to shy away from taking such an action. One, he'd known that if he asked Alice to show him the future—and she did so—he'd have to believe her utterly. Which would change everything about the way he viewed the world.

Two, he'd known it wasn't enough for Alice to send him an image of the future—he had to open his mind to it. To her.

After keeping his barriers up for so long.

He loved Alice. Planned to pledge his life to her soon. And yet—until that moment when they were surrounded by enemies, bullets flying, he'd still been patrolling the boundaries of his heart.

He was ashamed of that now.

"You asked me," Alice said. "But no one else did. I put those images there without their permission."

No one said a word for a long time.

"How did you do it?" Sadie asked finally. Jack noticed no one dismissed the notion. On the contrary, everyone was braced for Alice's answer.

Alice shook her head. "I opened all the way to it. I got so angry—" She broke off and set the plate of pizza on the coffee table. "I got so angry, everything.... clicked. I could see it all. Send it all."

"I didn't know that was possible." Sadie sounded shocked.

"I'm not supposed to do it," Alice said. "And then I couldn't stop. I nearly got swept away—"

Cass was pale. "That sounds dangerous."

"It was dangerous. I nearly didn't make it back. Mom saved me. She—and Jack."

Jack looked at her.

"You called me back," she said simply. "You held my hand. You helped me remember who I was."

"You saved all our lives," Jack said evenly. "And I didn't want to lose you."

"What about now?" Logan challenged Alice suddenly. "Are you still in my head?"

"No!" Alice got control of herself. "I've never done that before—well, except to Priscilla once." She sent Jack a look he couldn't decipher.

"Priscilla—the horse?" Hunter asked.

She nodded. "I needed to get back to the barn—fast."

Jack remembered the time she meant, and chuckled. "She needed to get away from me," he explained to the others.

Cass smiled. Jo laughed. They all relaxed a little.

"I would never do that again," Alice told Logan earnestly. “I don’t want to do it again. It… was awful.”

Jack’s arms tightened around her unconsciously. He didn’t like the idea of her being swept away. Didn’t want her to ever be in danger again.

“You’re right; you can’t ever do that again,” Cass said sternly. “When it was over, you weren’t here—it was like you’d gone somewhere else—”

“Like you did that day in the maze last spring,” Alice said softly.

Cass’s eyes filled with tears. “We all need to stay *here*.”

“That’s the plan, isn’t it?” The General spoke up for the first time, batting Emerson away. “Stop fussing, Corporal. Everyone is going to stay here. That’s why I sent you girls husbands.”

“Guess I should have let you send me one, after all,” Wye said miserably.

Emerson turned away. The General reached out and patted Wye’s shoulder. “Patience. Alice,” he went on softly and waited for her to lift her head. “Your mother had rules about her abilities. Strict rules. Made it mighty clear from day one what she’d do and what she wouldn’t. You’ll have to think of your own rules, and learn to abide by them. One thing she always said, though. Rules were made to be broken.”

“HOW ARE YOU holding up?” Jo asked when she slipped into Alice’s bedroom. Alice had come upstairs ostensibly to shower and settle in, but the real reason was that she couldn’t seem to stop thinking about what had happened the last time she was in the house.

"Not so well," she confessed.

"You're pale as a ghost." Jo came to stand beside her as she combed out her hair in front of the mirror. "Shaking, too."

"I keep… remembering."

Jo touched her arm. "You know, animals recover from danger and bad scares a lot better than we do. When they're frightened, they don't try to repress it. They react to whatever bad thing happens in the moment, and when it's over, they shake a lot. They let it all run through them. When they've had enough, they sleep."

"I'm not sure I'll sleep tonight." It had been easier in the hospital. There had been noise and light at all hours to keep her visions at bay.

"Why don't you try?" Jo led her to her bed. "Climb in. I'll make you a nest, and then I'll go get some tea—and Jack. Animals like to cuddle together to comfort each other," she added with a smile.

"I guess that sounds good," Alice said. She climbed under the covers and let Jo arrange pillows and blankets until she was surrounded in softness and warmth. Relaxing a little, she closed her eyes, but opened them again when images began to seep into her mind.

"Alice? Can I come in?"

"Yes."

Jack shut the door behind him and began to strip. Alice pushed up on one elbow. "I thought I was supposed to sleep."

"Jo sent me." He climbed into bed, too, and insinuated himself into the nest Jo had created. "It's warm in here."

"Comfy, too. Safe."

"You're definitely safe here."

"I keep remembering."

"Hmm. Turn over."

She did and sighed when he began to rub her back. "That feels good."

"Shut your eyes. Try to empty your mind." He kept up his massage. Alice focused on the motion of his hands. That helped. Jack kissed the back of her head. "Go to sleep."

"Aren't you going to seduce me? You know, payment for your services?" she teased.

"Not tonight. You need your rest, but tomorrow I'll be back to collect what you owe me."

"Good." She settled in.

"I love you, Alice," Jack said.

"Love you, too." His hands traveled up and down, up and down.

When she opened her eyes next, morning had come.

"I'M JUST GLAD everyone's safe," Richard said after Jack gave him a run-down of the attack. Jack had called first thing after he woke up and apologized for the way they'd left things after their last conversation. Even if they disagreed about his choices, he needed Richard in his life. Richard was several hours ahead in Washington, DC, and he didn't mind early morning calls.

"Me, too."

"Guess the General really needed men like you there."

"Guess so."

"What aren't you telling me?" Richard asked.

Jack, in the guest room, moved to his window and looked out at the snowy scene beyond it. The view had become familiar. Now it would be his home.

"Have you ever come across something… uncanny?"

Richard chuckled. "Like a seven-year-old who could identify a killer based on the truck he drove after hearing the engine only once before?"

"Something that had no explanation. Not even a far-fetched one."

Richard was silent a minute. "Yeah. When you work the kind of job I do, you come across stuff like that once in a while. We don't talk about it a lot. No one likes to admit some things can't be explained."

"So you think some things can't?" Jack pressed.

"I think some things have an explanation we just can't understand," Richard hedged. "I don't know, Jack," he added. "We live in a big universe, you know?"

"Yeah. I know. I'm getting married," he added.

"No shit," Richard said and laughed. "You serious?"

"Yeah, I am." Jack braced himself for Richard's reaction, but instead of the scolding he'd dreaded, Richard called out, "Janet—get on the phone. Jack's got big news!" He came back. "You're going to have to start from the beginning. Tell us everything."

Jack checked his watch. Other people would be getting up soon, but he did his best to fill his parents in, without giving away anything he knew he needed to keep secret. When he heard movement downstairs, he said, "Pop. Ma—got to go. I'll call you again in a few days. Watch out for your invitation, okay?"

"Will do," Richard said.

"Say hi to your bride—and everyone else," Janet said.

He couldn't believe how happy his parents were with the news. He was whistling when he entered the kitchen a few moments later. The General was already sitting at the table alone, nursing a cup of coffee.

"How are you this morning, sir? Feeling all right?" Jack asked.

"I suppose I can't complain: I fulfilled my mission, didn't I? All my daughters are taken care of now. My ranch is back under my control, and the enemy has been vanquished. Victory all around."

Jack smiled. "I'd agree with all of that—except the part about controlling the ranch. I'd say your daughters have control of it, don't you think?"

"What kind of treason is this?" The General gave him a baleful stare.

"It's the truth, and the five of us men can handle that. This ranch is more than a bunch of acres to Cass, Alice, Lena, Sadie and Jo. It represents their link to their mother. Surely you must understand that."

"Of course I do. Still think a woman does best with a man by her side."

"Some women do. I like to think that in my marriage to Alice, the total will be more than the sum of its parts."

"I hope so, too. Things have changed since my day."

"Yes, they have. For the better, I think, when it comes to treating men and women like equals."

"Maybe so. Amelia never complained," he grumbled.

"Amelia didn't have to—she had a good husband."

A strange look came over the General's face. Something like… gratitude, Jack thought. It couldn't be easy for the man to know his daughters held such harsh opinions of him. Jack had a feeling the man was all too aware of his own shortcomings.

"Eat your breakfast," the General said.

"Yes, sir."

The General was uncharacteristically quiet through the meal, and Jack was beginning to get worried by the time everyone else came down and ate, and they gathered for the muster session. He joined the others in the General's room when the time came. The General was back sitting on his bed, his leg raised. Jack found his place next to Alice, took her hand and dropped a kiss on top of her head.

"Well," the General said, looking around at all of them. "This is the last time we'll assemble like this."

Jack, about to steal another kiss, straightened. He felt Alice stiffen beside him.

"Why?" Brian asked.

"I've come to realize something." The General was as solemn as Jack had ever seen him. He got up from the bed slowly and stood as ramrod straight as he ever had back at USSOCOM. "You all worked like a well-oiled team the other day standing up to that rotten son of Manson's."

"Thanks to Alice," Connor said.

"Thanks to all of you. I thought I needed to get this ranch under control—and keep it under control. I thought you needed me. I was wrong." He linked his hands behind his back. "It's time to turn this ranch over to the next generation. Time to step back and let you all take control. You don't need any more muster sessions."

"What if we want them?" Lena said.

Alice looked at her sister in surprise. Jack couldn't blame her. This was a far cry from the Lena who'd railed against her father the other day.

Lena met their stares. "I don't know about everyone else, but I think this is a good way to start the day. It's given us a chance to air things out and make plans."

"You don't need me for that." The General waved a hand.

"Maybe we want you for that," Lena said. "Maybe we need—to make up for lost time." Her voice softened. "Maybe we need to get to know you again."

"That's right," Cass said.

"I agree," Jo said. Sadie nodded.

"We'd be honored if you'd help us," Alice said.

"Well." The General's voice was gruff. "I guess… if

you need me to keep things in line."

"We do, sir," Jack said, but the General was watching Lena.

She nodded. "We do."

"Then I'll retain my command," the General said.

And smiled.

"WHAT IS IT?" Alice asked when she met up with Jack in the upstairs hall later that morning. "You look… worried."

"Not worried. Just…" He shrugged his shoulders. "Just got word that I'm to receive an honorable discharge. I won't be in the Army much longer."

"Does that make you sad?"

"No, not sad. But I served a long time." He leaned against the wall. Tugged her closer until she stood between his legs. "Will you still be hot for me when I'm not in the military?"

"Always." She went up on tiptoe to kiss him. "Are you sure you're ready to be done with it?"

"I'm sure. I'm ready to stay here—with you."

"Good."

Brian came up the stairs and stopped when he caught sight of them. "Sorry—don't mean to intrude. I just got word—"

"An honorable discharge?" Jack asked.

"Yeah. You, too?"

"Yep."

"He didn't even wait for the wedding," Brian pointed out.

"Guess he's pretty sure I'm going to carry it off." Jack cupped Alice's chin and kissed her.

"More like he's sure I'm going to carry it off." She kissed him back.

"I'm going to find Cass." Brian kept going.

"Alone at last," Jack said to Alice and pulled her into his room.

Their lovemaking was slow and thorough, even though Alice felt guilty neither was helping with chores.

"Relax," Jack told her finally. "There's a lot of hands on this ranch making the work light. They won't miss us."

When he began to move inside her, Alice decided she didn't care if they did. As always, Jack spun her desire tight—and her release when it came nearly overwhelmed her. Like Jack had said before, this worked, and she was so happy she'd have a lifetime to make love to this man.

Soon he'd be hers forever.

When they were done, they lay side by side until a hunger inside Alice had her tracing Jack's muscles with a fingertip. He turned to her.

"I want you," she told him again.

"Okay."

"I want… to stop using birth control."

Jack went still beside her. "You want a baby?"

"Yes." She hadn't known how much she wanted one until now.

Or until her visions had started to show their baby to her.

It had been their baby she'd seen—she was sure of that now.

"What about your career?"

"I want that, too. But from now on I'm going to take more care with the contracts I choose, and I'm not going to let them interfere with my family. With you. What about you?" she asked. "Do you want children?" She held her breath.

"Hell, yeah." Jack gathered her in his arms. "I can't wait. How many are we going to have?"

Alice tried to close off to the vision that swamped her, but she was too late. "Three," she told Jack.

"Really?"

"Really."

"Let's get busy then."

LATER THAT AFTERNOON Alice entered the kitchen and found the General alone there. "Everything okay?" she asked him.

He grunted. "Everything's fine if you like sitting on your ass all day. Which I don't."

"It must be hard to be home—for all kinds of reasons." She moved to the fridge, took out a soda and popped the top of the can.

"It's harder and easier than I expected," the General said. "Easier because it's good to be with my girls, even if they are a pain in the ass. Harder because I can't imagine what I'm good for anymore. My hip's shot. So's my knee. Can't ride for months, if ever, the doctors say—"

A vision hit her. A phone call. A military uniform. Her father barking orders.

She smiled. "I know exactly what you're good for," she said over his continued grumbling.

"Oh yeah? What?" He sounded wary, as if afraid she might use the occasion to get in another jab. Alice supposed she and her sisters had been hard on him.

"Your job is to be a grandfather. Cass is pregnant. Jo's working on it, I think. I'll be pregnant soon. And the Army isn't finished with you either."

"The Army can't wait to be finished with me—"

"General? Phone call for you." Emerson appeared in the doorway and handed the General his phone.

"Hold that thought," he said to Alice. "General Reed here." He listened a moment. "Oh yeah? What's that?" He was silent again. "You sure about that? Can't get around like I used to. The drive? That doesn't bother me. I got five sons-in-law at my beck and call. Yes. Yes, you do that. Speak to you next week." He handed the phone back to Emerson. "Well, I'll be damned. You were right; the Army does want me. That was the reserve base in Billings. They've got a position for me. Part time, of course."

"Of course," Alice said. "Sounds perfect."

"As you were." The General got up and limped from the room.

Emerson lingered. "Do you think Wye will be all right? She seemed pretty down last night."

"She'll bounce back." Tabitha came into the room and wove around Alice's heels. "Wye is strong. She's just hurt because she misread Will so badly. Cass said she convinced her to stay the rest of the month. Told her she would need help cleaning up again after the wedding."

"Do you think she could ever—" Emerson didn't finish the sentence.

"I don't know, Emerson," Alice said. "But I sure hope so."

Emerson shrugged. "I'm glad the General's going back to work. That means I'm going back to work, too."

"Guess that is a good thing."

"You know what they say. A bored General is never a good thing."

"They say that?" Alice asked.

"They do now."

When her phone buzzed in her pocket, Alice was shocked to see it was Landon calling. She answered reluctantly.

"Hello?"

"Don't hang up," Landon hurried to say. "I'm not asking for any predictions."

"Good thing. I'm not making any," Alice said tartly.

"I'm calling to thank you."

"Why?" She noticed Emerson was sticking close. Gathering intel for the General?

Let him, she decided. The General was on her side.

"You got me back on track. Alice, I haven't been entirely honest with you."

Somehow she wasn't surprised.

"I did make my money in cryptocurrency. Thing is,

the market is volatile. I've lost half my net worth since we started talking."

"H-half?" She couldn't imagine it.

"I'll probably earn it back in a few more weeks. And then lose it again. I don't know—it's the nature of the beast. I thought I was prepared. Turned out, I wasn't. When the numbers started going down, I panicked. And then someone said you were psychic. Like, for real. I mean, normally I would have laughed, but—"

"You were desperate," Alice said.

"I lost my cool," Landon agreed.

"Thanks for letting me know what was really going on, but what does all this have to do with me?"

"I'm not panicking anymore. I still have plenty of money. I need to follow my heart and make a movie. I've got a new idea. It isn't a Civil War drama this time. It's an action flick. Set in the near future. There's been a pandemic—"

"And you're telling me because—?"

"You're still the champ when it comes to costumes, Alice. No one else I interviewed even came close. I was wondering—"

"No," she said gently. "I'm not looking for a contract at this time."

"But—"

"Sorry, Landon. Good luck, though," she said without a qualm. Landon was a man who was all vision and no follow-through. She was well rid of him. "I do have a favor to ask you, though."

"What's that?" he asked warily.

"I'd like my dresses back. I think you owe me that much."

He was quiet for a long time. "Yeah. Okay. I guess I do. The thing is… I already gave them to someone else."

Alice got a flash of an older woman with a wide smile and bright eyes—

"I checked out that movie you told me about. *The Passing Hour.* Called up Kate O'Dell to see… well, to see if I could hire her."

"You were going to dump me for Kate O'Dell?" That would have been ironic. "What happened?"

"She let me in on a little secret. She's already been hired to do a Civil War drama for a major producer with a major budget. Trying to compete with that would be a disaster. We got to talking about talent. I mentioned you. She was interested in seeing your work."

"You sent my gowns to Kate O'Dell?" Alice squeaked.

"Yep. You'll probably be hearing from her," he said glumly. "You'll probably say yes to her."

"I probably will," Alice said truthfully. "If she likes what she sees."

"She will. Well, guess I'll see you around." Landon didn't sound happy.

"Good luck with your movie." Alice could only pity him.

"Thanks."

Chapter Twenty-One

"WHAT DOES THE future hold? Any more attacks?" Jack asked when he and Alice were alone again that evening, curled up in her bed.

"No more attacks."

"Good. We could use some peace and quiet around here. So what happens next?"

"Like… now?"

"Exactly."

"That doesn't take a clairvoyant," she said dryly. "We're going to have sex."

"We are?"

"First you're going to kiss me."

"Like this?" Jack edged closer, tilted her chin up and covered her mouth with his. He took his time with it, as if they had all night. Which they did, Alice supposed.

"Then you're going to touch my breasts."

"Like this?" Jack palmed them both and squeezed like a teenager.

"Hey! Like you know what you're doing!"

"Oh. Sorry." He lightened his touch and spent a long time caressing her, teasing her with his hands and then his mouth, enjoying the way his touch made her respond. "Now what?"

"You're going to explore the rest of me," she said contentedly.

He did so, and soon Alice was clutching the sheets in her hands, her head thrown back, her hips lifting, legs opening. She moaned, and Jack struggled to stay in control. He wanted to make this encounter last.

Wanted to surprise her, too.

"But did you know I was going to—"

"Yes. Get in me. Now!" Alice commanded him.

"You know everything before I do it," he complained, but he got in position between her legs.

Alice pushed up on her elbows and regarded him seriously. "Okay," she said. "I've turned it off."

He hesitated. "Really? You can do that?"

"I can now." Alice lay back. Opened to him. "Go on and surprise me."

And he did.

ALICE COULDN'T SAY how she'd learned how to shut off the flow of her visions of the future. Maybe it had to do with concentrating on Jack. Last night the pressure of his hands on her skin had offered her relief. Today his caresses were doing the trick. As long as she stayed present, her mind on his hands, everything else faded away.

They'd have to make love a lot.

She still found her own future to be hazy, and she was all right with that. She didn't want to know everything that would happen to her. For now, Alice sank into the pleasure Jack was giving her, reveling in each sensation as his movements sped up. She knew he was concentrating on pleasing her. Knowing he was trying to make her feel good made his every touch that much more potent.

She wouldn't conceive today, but she would soon, and Alice looked forward to every attempt, knowing that the more they got to know each other, the better their lovemaking would be.

It was pretty good right now.

As she moved with Jack she realized they already knew a lot about each other. When they'd set a date, they'd both been worried they were jumping the gun. Now that seemed silly. It wasn't the length of the acquaintance; it was the depth of it. She understood Jack's fears, and he understood hers. Their goals matched. So did their desire to live here at Two Willows, to build a life with the others who lived here—and to throw themselves into their work.

Alice linked her legs around Jack's back and urged him on. Soon she could think of nothing else except the sweet friction building between them. When she cried out and clung to him, waves of pleasure rippling through her, Jack grunted and bucked against her, coming too. They rocked together until they were spent, then collapsed, Jack still inside her.

"This is where I want to spend forever," he said. "Right here with you."

"I want that, too."

JACK WAS POSITIONED in front of the mirror, fighting with his tie two weeks later when someone knocked on the door of the guest bedroom. He turned as it opened, and his parents came in.

"Pop! Ma—you made it!"

"Wouldn't miss your wedding for the world," his mother said. "Look at you, so handsome! No wonder Alice fell in love with you."

"We're proud of you, son. I hope you have as happy a wedded life as I've had," Richard said.

"You're not mad I'm not coming back to DC with you?"

"Can't say I'm not disappointed. I was looking forward to getting the chance to work with you, but after seeing this place, I guess I can't blame you. Must remind you of home."

"From the pictures I've seen it's even better in the warm weather," Jack said, "But I've already fallen in love with the place. And you're right; it does remind me of home. Guess ranching is in my blood."

"Guess so."

"Also...Cab Johnson came by and had a word with me the other day." He hadn't even told Alice this yet, because he wasn't sure what his answer would be. "He made it clear there might be work for me in the local sheriff's department if I'm interested."

"Are you interested?" Janet asked.

"I'm not sure. Maybe. After I get this ranch stuff figured out. Right now I want to concentrate on Two Willows."

"And your wife," Janet put in.

"That doesn't mean I don't appreciate everything you two have done for me, or that I love you any less. You know that, right?"

"Of course he does," Janet said firmly. "We really are proud of you, you know. You've served your country, and now you'll serve your family. That's how it should be."

"You'll have to visit as often as you like. Alice says there'll be grandkids around soon enough."

Richard beamed. "Another generation to train."

"Don't get ahead of yourself," Janet told him. "Another generation to *love*. That's what's important."

"You said a mouthful," Richard admitted. "Better let this generation get ready for his wedding. Good luck out there, son."

"Thanks, Pop."

"Your folks would be proud, too, you know," Richard said. "I'm sure they're with you today."

For a second Jack thought he was right. His memories of his parents had gotten hazy, but he could almost feel his father's hand on his shoulder, his mother's cheek pressed against his.

He nodded, suddenly finding it difficult to speak.

When they left, Logan slipped in. "Ready?" he asked. "It's nearly time."

Jack looked in the mirror. Gave his tie one last tug. "I'm ready."

"A HOOPSKIRT WEDDING was genius," Wye said,

"except we need more mirrors."

She craned her neck to try to see herself in the large mirror Alice stood in front of, but when she tried to move closer to see the rest of her body, their hoopskirts pressed together, making the far side of their dresses flare up.

"Are we going to fit down the stairs?" Jo asked. All Alice's sisters were her bridesmaids, and she'd invited Wye to participate, too. Alice had worked her fingers to the bone taking the spring green dresses they'd worn to the other weddings and turning them into period-accurate gowns. They couldn't all fit into the same bedroom, so they were taking turns moving from room to room.

"I sure hope so," Alice said. "Or the guests will have to come up here. Wye, you about ready?"

"I'm ready." Wye beamed at her. "This is so much fun. I always wanted to be a Reed," she confessed. She preened in her spring-green, hoopskirt bridesmaid dress.

"If you want to be a Reed, you'll have to take the oath," Alice said. "Pledge to stay here all your days. In front of the standing stone."

"I'm game," Wye said. "Not like there's anything else for me to do. Plus, I'm going to run out of money if I don't get a job pretty soon. I'll have to mooch off you all."

"Something will turn up," Alice told her. "Or else we'll put you to work on the ranch."

"It's time," Cass said, sticking her head in the room. "Line up. Wye first, then youngest to oldest. Jo, you're after Wye."

"As if I didn't know," Jo mumbled but followed Wye out into the hall. Sadie lined up after her, then Lena and Cass. Their wide skirts touched both sides of the hall as they made their way to the head of the stairs.

"Here we go," Wye said.

Alice waited her turn, her heart in her mouth. This was a new beginning. A new chapter at Two Willows. Soon their family would expand. Her business, too. Her experience with Landon had taught her she wanted new challenges. When the time was right, she'd go looking for them.

For now, she couldn't wait to meet Jack at the altar and start her life with him.

"Ready?" Cass whispered when it was her turn to walk down the stairs.

"Ready." Then Alice was alone. But not for long. She felt her mother's presence as she descended carefully, one step at a time. When she reached the bottom, her father was there to take her arm. He regarded her gravely before he did so.

"I keep waiting," he said in a low voice so only she could hear.

"For what?" she asked.

"For you to come at me the way your sisters did. Isn't there something you want to get off your chest before you move on?" He nodded at the altar at the far end of the room.

Alice didn't pretend not to know what he meant. "Yes, there is."

The General straightened. "Have your say." He braced himself.

Over the years she would have given anything to tell him all the ways in which he'd let her down, but Alice felt she understood her father too well for that now. "None of the pain this family has felt has come from a lack of love. It's come from an overabundance of it. The thing is we're all terrified of losing what we have. I've learned something, though."

"What's that?" The General's voice was gruff.

"We can't lose it. Mom has proved that. She's been gone eleven years, and her love surrounds us every day." Alice steadied herself. "Dad, I love you."

Her father stiffened. Blinked. Jutted his chin and swallowed.

Patted her arm.

Alice waited, wondering if he would manage to say the words back.

"I have something for you," he said finally. He took out a small box, opened it and showed her the locket inside, just like the one her mother had worn when she was alive. Like the ones her sisters had each received on their wedding days.

She allowed the General to help her put it on, knowing this was the only way he knew how to show what he felt in his heart. By giving her gifts, protecting her—

Sending her a husband.

Even though she longed to hear the words, she didn't need him to speak them. Alice took her father's arm. Guilt flared for a moment that she was the only one the General would walk up the aisle, but at the front of the room her sisters' faces were shining with joy—and hope.

And there was Jack. Wonderful Jack. The man who had seen all of her and loved her for everything she was. The man who believed her through and through. Alice's whole heart yearned for him. She couldn't wait to spend her days with Jack. Pledging her heart to him was a dream come true.

"Take good care of her," the General said to him when they reached the altar. "I love my girl." He raised his voice. "I love all my girls."

An expansive joy filled Alice's heart. Healing was possible. The General was truly home—

Where he belonged.

AS ALICE WALKED up the aisle on her father's arm toward him, Jack's heart stood still. She was beautiful, but that wasn't what stole the breath from his lungs.

It was the love that shone in her eyes as she met his gaze and held it. The moment she'd seen him, she'd brightened, pure joy shining in her smile.

She loved him.

Absolutely.

The shell that had formed around his heart when his parents had died finally cracked open, leaving him fresh and new. As Alice walked toward him, he knew he'd been given another chance at life, and he promised himself he'd spend the rest of it cherishing her.

When the General took his seat, Jack took Alice's hands in his, and he knew he'd finally found home again. He could belong to Two Willows the way he'd belonged to his parents' ranch back in New Mexico so many years ago. He had no doubt as the seasons passed he'd fall in love with the place, although he was already so in love with his bride he didn't know if it was possible he had any left to spread around.

"Dearly Beloved," the minister began, and Jack listened to every word, knowing the traditional ceremony would change his life forever. It made him happy to think that so many other couples had made the same pledges throughout time. How wonderful to find a partner in life, he thought as he slid the plain band onto Alice's finger, next to the beautiful diamond she already wore. When he thought of the vision Alice had in the jewelry store, Jack was happy to know that her mother, whom he was pretty sure had initially barred him from her maze, had worked on his behalf when he took Alice to pick out her engagement ring.

He was happy, too, to see the General making a place for himself at Two Willows. Healing was happening, and Jack had a feeling when the grandkids came along, the healing would speed up.

Meanwhile, he meant to enjoy every moment of the life he'd make with Alice. He had no qualms about their future.

He couldn't wait to get to it.

ALICE COULD BARELY form the words of her vows, she

was trembling so hard—with happiness. Only now did she realize what a strain the last six months had been. Finally, her family was out of danger, and when she looked into the future—just a little bit—she saw peace at Two Willows.

She and Jack planned to travel to Buenos Aires for their honeymoon and lie on the beach for a couple of weeks, soaking up the sun. That's where they would conceive their child, and Alice looked forward to every moment of their lovemaking as they tried.

She looked forward to coming home, too, and planning the house they'd build come spring. Two Willows was going to be busy for a long time. It would become a little community. There'd be lots more occasions for hoopskirts, she was sure.

"You may kiss the bride," the minister said.

As Jack bent down to do just that, Alice went up on tiptoe to meet him. She kept a hand on her skirt to keep it under control. But when Jack scooped her up for another kiss, she forgot all about it.

Jack was everything to her, and now she belonged to him.

"Happy?" Jack asked her.

"Ecstatic."

"After you, Mrs. Sanders," Wye told her, gesturing for them to head back down the aisle first.

"Hold on," Alice replied. Once again, she struggled to get her hoopskirt in hand. She had to admit these things weren't very practical.

"Hurry up before we starve," Logan called out.

"Some of us want cake."

Alice led the way, Jack squeezing in beside her huge skirt. "How on earth are we going to dance with you in that?" he asked.

"Very carefully."

Chapter Twenty-Two

Dear Augustus,

You are finally home. Finally. My heart would ring with joy if I didn't know what it took to get you there. But you're safe and so are our daughters, and that means the world to me.

Augustus, take it slow building your new life, and be patient with our girls as you all learn to live with one another again. You may be back at Two Willows, but the road home is a long one when you've been gone so many years.

Our daughters need tenderness, empathy and strength from you. They need knowledge of our lives together—a connection to their heritage. They need to see you happy, Augustus, and I hope you'll search for and find your happiness.

You and I had a life worth celebrating. We shaped the land together, built a business together, brought up our family. I'd have given anything to extend my time with you, but I am grateful for all the sweet moments I did have.

I am grateful for my children, too. For every moment

I got to hold them in my arms. For every accomplishment I witnessed—and for those I didn't. My girls are my heart, split in five and still living on this earth. Cherish them, Augustus, and keep them close, even if it takes time for them to get over past hurts.

Your road back to me is a long one, too, and I hope you'll be content to walk it slowly. Enjoy your life. I'm there with you even when you're not aware of me. Ours is a love that endures. We both knew that from the start. Nothing can change that fact.

I love you, Augustus. Always and forever.

Oh, and you have one more (honorary) daughter to marry off. I'm sure you have a suitable man in mind.

You're always in my heart,
Amelia

Epilogue

WYOMING CARRIED A stack of dishes into the kitchen, glad to get out of the heat and hubbub of the living room. All the Reed women's weddings had been crowded, but with the General home, all of their friends and neighbors had wanted to come and get a chance to commend him on his service to their country.

Alice and Jack had decided to turn the affair into a Thanksgiving wedding, and huge plates of turkey, stuffing, mashed potatoes and other holiday favorites had been passed around at dinner. She was so full she thought it was a miracle she still fit into her dress. Lord knew her dress barely fit into the house.

Everyone was married except her. Two weeks had given her enough time to play back over her brief courtship with Will and see all the times when the veneer of his cheerful behavior had slipped. The times he'd grown impatient with his work. The times he'd scowled when Emerson came near.

He'd fooled her, but he'd fooled everyone else, too.

That was small comfort, though. She'd always thought of herself as practical. The last person to be taken in by a quick smile and a false intimacy. Will had done worse than hurt her pride—

He'd undermined her confidence in herself.

It wasn't helping she couldn't seem to find a job, either. Without telling Cass, she'd begun to answer ads for positions in Billings and Bozeman. It wouldn't be the end of the world to move to the city, she kept telling herself.

So why did it feel like the end of the world?

A tear slipped into the sudsy water in the sink, and Wyoming impatiently scrubbed a hand across her cheek. There was no time for feeling sorry for herself. She had a wedding to help with. A job to find. A life to get on with.

When the knock sounded on the front door, it startled her out of her thoughts.

Someone was arriving late.

She hurried to answer it before one of the others did, wanting all the Reed women to have a chance to relax with their friends without having to play hostess. When she opened the door, she laughed.

The corporal stood in the doorway, so handsome with his dark hair and dark eyes. She'd been too infatuated with Will to notice that while lean, Emerson was as strong as the other men. His gaze had depths she hadn't plumbed yet. There were lines she hadn't noticed around his mouth and at the corners of his eyes. He wasn't as young as he'd looked at first. She knew from watching him with the General he was a man who took his responsibilities seriously.

"Emerson? What are you doing out here?"

"The General sent me. Are you going to let me in?"

Be the first to know about Cora Seton's new releases!
Sign up for her newsletter here!

www.coraseton.com/sign-up-for-my-newsletter

Other books in the Brides of Chance Creek Series:

Issued to the Bride One Navy SEAL

Issued to the Bride One Airman

Issued to the Bride One Sniper

Issued to the Bride One Marine

Author's Note

While Issued to the Bride One Soldier was meant to be the last book in the Brides of Chance Creek series, Emerson and Wye simply wouldn't let me go without telling their story, too. Go here to receive a special announcement newsletter when the pre-order for Issued to the Bride One Sergeant for Christmas goes live.
www.coraseton.com/books/issued-to-the-bride-one-sergeant-for-christmas

Meanwhile, if you enjoyed the Brides of Chance Creek, you will love the SEALs of Chance Creek! Check out A SEAL's Oath for free here, or read on for a short excerpt.

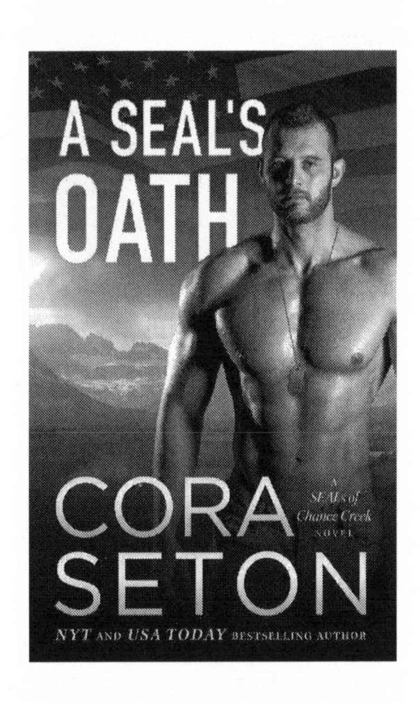

Read on for an excerpt of Volume 1 of **The SEALs of Chance Creek** series – *A SEAL's Oath.*

NAVY SEAL BOONE Rudman should have been concentrating on the pile of paperwork in front of him. Instead he was brooding over a woman he hadn't seen in thirteen years. If he'd been alone, he would have pulled up Riley Eaton's photograph on his laptop, but three other men ringed the table in the small office he occupied at the Naval Amphibious Base at Little Creek, Virginia, so instead he mentally ran over the information he'd found out about her on the Internet. Riley lived in Boston, where she'd gone to school. She'd graduated with a fine arts degree, something which confused

Boone; she'd never talked about wanting to study art when they were young. She worked at a vitamin manufacturer, which made no sense at all. And why was she living in a city, when Riley had only ever come alive when she'd visited Chance Creek, Montana, every summer as a child?

Too many questions. Questions he should know the answer to, since Riley had once been such an integral part of his life. If only he hadn't been such a fool, Boone knew she still would be. Still a friend at least, or maybe much, much more. Pride had kept him from finding out.

He was done with pride.

He reached for his laptop, ready to pull up her photograph, whether he was alone or not, but stopped when it chimed to announce a video call. For one crazy second, Boone wondered if his thoughts had conjured Riley up, but he quickly shook away that ridiculous notion.

Probably his parents wondering once again why he wasn't coming home when he left the Navy. He'd explained time and again the plans he'd made, but they couldn't comprehend why he wouldn't take the job his father had found him at a local ranch.

"Working with horses," his dad had said the last time they talked. "What more do you want?"

It was tempting. Boone had always loved horses. But he had something else in mind. Something his parents found difficult to comprehend. The laptop chimed again.

"You going to get that?" Jericho Cook said, looking up from his work. Blond, blue-eyed, and six-foot-one inches of muscle, he looked out of place hunched over his paperwork. He and the other two men sitting at the table were three of Boone's most trusted buddies and members of his strike team. Like him, they were far more at home jumping out of airplanes, infiltrating terrorist organizations and negotiating their way through disaster areas than sitting on their asses filling out forms. But paperwork caught up to everyone at some point.

He wouldn't have to do it much longer, though. Boone was due to separate from the Navy in less than a month. The others were due to leave soon after. They'd joined up together—egging each other on when they turned eighteen over their parents' objections. They'd survived the brutal process of becoming Navy SEALs together, too, adamant that they'd never leave each other behind. They'd served together whenever they could. Now, thirteen years later, they'd transition back to civilian life together as well.

The computer chimed a third time and his mind finally registered the name on the screen. Boone slapped a hand on the table to get the others' attention.

"It's him!"

"Him, who?" Jericho asked.

"Martin Fulsom, from the Fulsom Foundation. He's calling me!"

"Are you sure?" Clay Pickett shifted his chair over to where he could see. He was an inch or two shorter than Jericho, with dark hair and a wiry build that concealed a perpetual source of energy. Even now Clay's foot was tapping as he worked.

Boone understood his confusion. Why would Martin Fulsom, who must have a legion of secretaries and assistants at his command, call him personally?

"It says Martin Fulsom."

"Holy shit. Answer it," Jericho said. He shifted his chair over, too. Walker Norton, the final member of their little group, stood up silently and moved behind the others. Walker had dark hair and dark eyes that hinted at his Native American ancestry. Unlike the others, he'd taken the time to get his schooling and become an officer. As Lieutenant, he was the highest ranked. He was also the tallest of the group, with a heavy muscular frame that could move faster than most gave him credit for. He was quiet, though. So quiet that those who didn't know him tended to write him off. They did so at their own peril.

Boone stifled an oath at the tremor that ran through him as he reached out to accept the call, but it wasn't every day you got to meet your hero face to face. Martin Fulsom wasn't a Navy SEAL. He wasn't in the military at all. He'd once been an oil man, and had amassed a fortune in the industry before he'd learned about global warming and had a change of heart. For the last decade he'd spearheaded a movement to prevent carbon dioxide particulates from exceeding the disastrous level of 450 ppm. He'd backed his foundation with his entire fortune, invested it in green technology and used his earnings to fund projects around the world aimed at helping him reach his goal. Fulsom was a force of nature, with an oversized personality to match his incredible wealth. Boone liked his can-do attitude and his refusal to mince words when the situation called for plain speaking.

Boone clicked *Accept* and his screen resolved into an image of a man seated at a large wooden desk. He was gray-haired but virile, with large hands and an impressively large watch. Beside him stood a middle aged woman in a severely tailored black suit, who handed him pieces of paper one at a time, waited for him to sign them and took them back, placing them in various folders she cradled in her arm.

"Boone!" The man's hearty voice was almost too much for the laptop's speakers. "Good to finally meet you. This is an impressive proposal you have here."

Boone swallowed. It was true. Martin Fulsom—one of the greatest innovators of their time—had actually called *him*. "It's good to meet you, too, Mr. Fulsom," he managed to say.

"Call me Martin," Fulsom boomed. "Everybody does. Like I said, it's a hell of a proposal. To build a fully operational sustainable community in less than six months? That take guts. Can you deliver?"

"Yes, sir." Boone was confident he could. He'd studied this stuff for years. Dreamed about it, debated it, played with the numbers and particulars until he could speak with confidence about every aspect of the community he wanted to build. He and his friends had gained a greater working knowledge of the fallout from climate change than any of them had gone looking for when they joined the Navy SEALs. They'd realized most of the conflicts that spawned the missions they took on were caused in one way or the other by struggles over resources, usually exacerbated by climate conditions. When rains didn't come and crops failed, unrest was sure to follow. Next came partisan politics, rebellions, coups and more. It didn't take a genius to see that climate change and scarcity of resources would be two prongs spearheading trouble around the world for decades to come.

"And you'll start with four families, building up to ten within that time frame?"

Boone blinked. Families? "Actually, sir…" He'd said nothing about families. Four *men*, building up to ten. That's what he had written in his proposal.

"This is brilliant. Too brilliant." Fulsom's direct gaze caught his own. "You see, we were going to launch a community of our own, but when I saw your proposal, I said, 'This man has already done the hard work; why reinvent the wheel? I can't think of anyone better to lead such a project than someone like Boone Rudman.'"

Boone stifled a grin. This was going better than he could have dreamed. "Thank you, sir."

Fulsom leaned forward. "The thing is, Boone, you have to do it right."

"Of course, sir, but about—"

"It has to be airtight. You have to prove you're sustainable. You have to prove your food systems are self-perpetuating, that you have a strategy to deal with waste, that you have contingency plans. What you've written here?" He held up Boone's proposal package. "It's genius. Genius. But the real question is—who's going to give a shit about it?"

"Well, hell—" Fulsom's abrupt change of tone startled Boone into defensiveness. He knew about the man's legendary high-octane personality, but he hadn't been prepared for this kind of bait and switch. "You yourself just said—"

Fulsom waved the application at him. "I love this stuff. It makes me hard. But the American public? That's a totally different matter. They don't find this shit sexy. It's not enough to jerk me off, Boone. We're trying to turn on the whole world."

"O-okay." Shit. Fulsom was going to turn him down after all. Boone gripped the arms of his chair, waiting for the axe to fall.

"So the question is, how do we make the world care about your community? And not just care about it—be so damn obsessed with it they can't think about anything else?" He didn't wait for an answer. "I'll tell you how. We're going to give you your own reality television show. Think of it. The whole world watching you go from ground zero to full-on sustainable community. Rooting for you. Cheering when you triumph. Crying when you fail. A worldwide audience fully engaged with you and your followers."

"That's an interesting idea," Boone said slowly. It was an insane idea. There was no way anyone would spend their time watching him dig garden beds and install photovoltaic panels. He couldn't think of anything less exciting to watch on television. And he didn't have followers. He had three like-minded friends who'd signed on to work with him. Friends who even now were bristling at this characterization of their roles. "Like I said, Mr. Fulsom, each of the *equal* participants in the community have pledged to document our progress. We'll take lots of photos and post them with our entries on a daily blog."

"Blogs are for losers." Fulsom leaned forward. "Come on, Boone. Don't you want to change the world?"

"Yes, I do." Anger curled within him. He was serious about these issues. Deadly serious. Why was Fulsom making a mockery of him? You couldn't win any kind of war with reality television, and Boone approached his sustainable community as if he was waging a war—a war on waste, a war on the future pain and suffering of the entire planet.

"I get it. You think I'm nuts," Fulsom said. "You think I've finally blown my lid. Well, I haven't. I'm a free-thinker, Boone, not a crazy man. I know how to get the message across to the masses. Always have. And I've always been criticized for it, too. Who cares? You know what I care about? This world. The people on it. The plants and animals and atmosphere. The whole grand, beautiful spectacle that we're currently dragging down into the muck of overconsumption. That's what I care about. What about you?"

"I care about it, too, but I don't want—"

"You don't want to be made a fool of. Fair enough. You're afraid of exposing yourself to scrutiny. You're afraid you'll fuck up on television. Well guess what? You're right; you will fuck up. But the audience is going to love you so much by that time, that if you cry, they'll cry with you. And when you triumph—and you *will* triumph—they'll feel as ecstatic as if they'd done it all themselves. Along the way they'll learn more about solar power, wind power, sustainable agriculture and all the rest of it than we could ever force-feed them through documentaries or classes. You watch, Boone. We're going to do something magical."

Boone stared at him. Fulsom was persuasive, he'd give him that. "About the families, sir."

"Families are non-negotiable." Fulsom set the application down and gazed at Boone, then each of his friends in turn. "You men are pioneers, but pioneers are a yawn-fest until they bring their wives to the frontier. Throw in women, and goddamn, that's interesting! Women talk. They complain. They'll take your plans for sustainability and kick them to the curb unless you make them easy to use and satisfying. What's more, women are a hell of lot more interesting than men. Sex, Boone. Sex sells cars and we're going to use it to sell sustainability, too. Are you with me?"

"I..." Boone didn't know what to say. Use sex to sell sustainability? "I don't think—"

"Of course you're with me. A handsome Navy SEAL like you has to have a girl. You do, don't you? Have a girl?"

"A girl?" Had he been reduced to parroting everything Fulsom said? Boone tried to pull himself together. He definitely did not have a *girl.* He dated when he had time, but he kept things light. He'd never felt it was fair to enter a more serious relationship as long as he was throwing himself into danger on a daily basis. He'd always figured he'd settle down when he left the service and he was looking forward to finally having the time to meet a potential mate. God knew his parents were all too ready for grandkids. They talked about it all the time.

"A woman, a fiancée. Maybe you already have a wife?" Fulsom looked hopeful and his secretary nodded at Boone, as if telling him to say yes.

"Well…."

He was about to say no, but the secretary shook her head rapidly and made a slicing motion across her neck. Since she hadn't engaged in the conversation at all previously, Boone decided he'd better take her signals seriously. He'd gotten some of his best intel in the field just this way. A subtle nod from a veiled woman, or a pointed finger just protruding from a burka had saved his neck more than once. Women were crafty when it counted.

"I'm almost married," he blurted. His grip on the arms of his chair tightened. None of this was going like he'd planned. Jericho and Clay turned to stare at him like he'd lost his mind. Behind him Walker chuckled. "I mean—"

"Excellent! Can't wait to meet your better half.

What about the rest of you?" Fulsom waved them off before anyone else could speak. "Never mind. Julie here will get all that information from you later. As long as you've got a girl, Boone, everything's going to be all right. The fearless leader has to have a woman by his side. It gives him that sense of humanity our viewers crave." Julie nodded like she'd heard this many times before.

Boone's heart sunk even further. Fearless leader? Fulsom didn't understand his relationship with the others at all. Walker was his superior officer, for God's sake. Still, Fulsom was waiting for his answer, with a shrewd look in his eyes that told Boone he wasn't fooled at all by his hasty words. Their funding would slip away unless he convinced Fulsom that he was dedicated to the project—as Fulsom wanted it to be done.

"I understand completely," Boone said, although he didn't understand at all. His project was about sustainability. It wasn't some human-interest story. "I'm with you one hundred percent."

"Then I've got a shitload of cash to send your way. Don't let me down."

"I won't." He felt rather than heard the others shifting, biting back their protests.

Fulsom leaned so close his head nearly filled the screen. "We'll start filming June first and I look forward to meeting your fiancée when I arrive. Understand? Not a girlfriend, not a weekend fling—a fiancée. I want weddings, Boone." He looked over the four of them again. "Four weddings. Yours will kick off the series. I can see it now; an empty stretch of land. Two modern pioneers in love. A country parson performing the ceremony. The bride holding a bouquet of wildflowers the groom picked just minutes before. Their first night together in a lonely tent. Magic, Boone. That's prime time magic. *Surviving on the Land* meets *The First Six Months.*"

Boone nodded, swallowing hard. He'd seen those television shows. The first tracked modern-day mountain men as they pitted themselves against crazy weather conditions in extreme locations. The second followed two newlyweds for six months, and documented their every move, embrace, and lovers' quarrel as they settled into married life. He didn't relish the idea of starring in any show remotely like those.

Besides, June first was barely two months away. He'd only get out of the Navy at the end of April. They hadn't even found a property to build on yet.

"There'll be four of you men to start," Fulsom went on. "That means we need four women for episode one; your fiancée and three other hopeful single ladies. Let the viewers do the math, am I right? They'll start pairing you off even before we do. We'll add other community members as we go. Six more men and six more women ought to do it, don't you think?"

"Yes, sir." This was getting worse by the minute.

"Now, I've given you a hell of a shock today. I get that. So let me throw you a bone. I've just closed on the perfect piece of property for your community. Fifteen hundred acres of usable land with creeks, forest, pasture and several buildings. I'm going to give it to you free and clear to use for the duration of the series. If—and only if—you meet your goals, I'll sign it over to you lock, stock and barrel at the end of the last show."

Boone sat up. That was a hell of a bone. "Where is it?"

"Little town called Chance Creek, Montana. I believe you've heard of it?" Fulsom laughed at his reaction. Even Walker was startled. Chance Creek? They'd grown up there. Their families still lived there.

They were going home.

Chills marched up and down his spine and Boone wondered if his friends felt the same way. He'd hardly even let himself dream about that possibility. None of them came from wealthy families and none of them would inherit land. He'd figured they'd go where it was cheapest, and ranches around Chance Creek didn't come cheap. Not these days. Like everywhere else, the town had seen a slump during the last recession, but now prices were up again and he'd heard from his folks that developers were circling, talking about expanding the town. Boone couldn't picture that.

"Let me see here. I believe it's called… Westfield," Fulsom said. Julie nodded, confirming his words. "Hasn't been inhabited for over a decade. A local caretaker has been keeping an eye on it, but there hasn't been cattle on it for at least that long. The heir to the property lives in Europe now. Must have finally decided he wasn't ever going to take up ranching. When he put it on the market, I snapped it up real quick."

Westfield.

Boone sat back even as his friends shifted behind him again. Westfield was a hell of a property—owned by the Eaton family for as long as anyone could remember. He couldn't believe it wasn't a working ranch anymore. But if the old folks were gone, he guessed that made sense. They must have passed away not long after he had left Chance Creek. They wouldn't have broken up the property, so Russ Eaton would have inherited and Russ wasn't much for ranching. Neither was his younger brother, Michael. As far as Boone knew, Russ hadn't married, which left Michael's daughter the only possible candidate to run the place.

Riley Eaton.

Was it a coincidence that had brought her to mind just moments before Fulsom's call, or something more?

Coincidence, Boone decided, even as the more impulsive side of him declared it Fate.

A grin tugged at his mouth as he remembered Riley as she used to be, the tomboy who tagged along after him every summer when they were kids. Riley lived for vacations on her grandparents' ranch. Her mother would send her off each year dressed up for the journey, and the minute Riley reached Chance Creek she'd wad up those fancy clothes and spend the rest of the summer in jeans, boots and an old Stetson passed down from her grandma. Boone and his friends hired on at Westfield most summers to earn some spending money. Riley stuck to them like glue, learning as much as she could about riding and ranching from them. When she was little, she used to cry when August ended and she had to go back home. As she grew older, she hid her feelings better, but Boone knew she'd always adored the ranch. It wasn't surprising, given her home life. Even when he was young, he'd heard the gossip and knew things were rough back in Chicago.

As much as he and the others had complained about being saddled with a follower like Riley, she'd earned their grudging respect as the years went on. Riley never complained, never wavered in her loyalty to them, and as many times as they left her behind, she was always ready to try again to convince them to let her join them in their exploits.

"It's a crime," he'd once heard his mother say to a friend on the phone. "Neither mother nor father has any time for her at all. No wonder she'll put up with anything those boys dish out. I worry for her."

Boone understood now what his mother was afraid of, but at the time he'd shrugged it off and over the years Riley had become a good friend. Sometimes when they were alone fishing, or riding, or just hanging out on her grandparents' porch, Boone would find himself telling her things he'd never told anyone else. As far as he knew, she'd never betrayed a confidence.

Riley was the one who dubbed Boone, Clay, Jericho and Walker the Four Horsemen of the Apocalypse, a nickname that had stuck all these years. When they'd become obsessed with the idea of being Navy SEALs, Riley had even tried to keep up with the same training regimen they'd adopted.

Boone wished he could say they'd always treated Riley as well as she treated them, but that wasn't the truth of it. One of his most shameful memories centered around the slim girl with the long brown braids. Things had become complicated once he and his friends began to date. They had far less time for Riley, who was two years younger and still a kid in their eyes, and she'd withdrawn when she realized their girlfriends didn't want her around. She still hung out when they worked at Westfield, though, and was old enough to be a real help with the work. Some of Boone's best memories were of early mornings mucking out stables with Riley. They didn't talk much, just worked side by side until the job was done. From time to time they walked out to a spot on the ranch where the land fell away and they could see the mountains in the distance. Boone had never quantified how he felt during those times. Now he realized what a fool he'd been.

He hadn't given a thought to how his girlfriends affected her or what it would be like for Riley when they left for the Navy. He'd been too young. Too utterly self-absorbed.

That same year he'd had his first serious relationship, with a girl named Melissa Resnick. Curvy, flirty and oh-so-feminine, she'd slipped into his heart by slipping into his bed on Valentine's Day. By the time Riley came to town again that last summer, he and Melissa were seldom apart. Of all the girls the Horsemen had dated, Melissa was the least tolerant of Riley's presence, and one day when they'd all gone to a local swimming hole, she'd huffed in exasperation when the younger girl came along.

"It's like you've got a sidekick," she told Boone in everyone's hearing. "Good ol' Tagalong Riley."

Clay, Jericho, and Walker, who'd always treated Riley like a little sister, thought it was funny. They had their own girlfriends to impress, and the name had stuck. Boone knew he should put a stop to it, but the lure of Melissa's body was still too strong and he knew if he took Riley's side he'd lose his access to it.

Riley had held her head up high that day and she'd stayed at the swimming hole, a move that Boone knew must have cost her, but each repetition of the nickname that summer seemed to heap pain onto her shoulders, until she caved in on herself and walked with her head down.

The worst was the night before he and the Horsemen left to join the Navy. He hadn't seen Riley for several days, whereas he couldn't seem to shake Melissa for a minute. He should have felt flattered, but instead it had irritated him. More and more often, he had found himself wishing for Riley's calm company, but she'd stopped coming to help him.

Because everyone else seemed to expect it, he'd attended the hoe-down in town sponsored by the rodeo that last night. Melissa clung to him like a burr. Riley was nowhere to be found. Boone accepted every drink he was offered and was well on his way to being three sheets to the wind when Melissa excused herself to the ladies' room at about ten. Boone remained with the other Horsemen and their dates, and he could only stare when Riley appeared in front of him. For once she'd left her Stetson at home, her hair was loose from its braids, and she wore makeup and a mini skirt that left miles of leg between its hem and her dress cowboy boots.

Every nerve in his body had come to full alert and Boone had understood in that moment what he'd failed to realize all that summer. Riley had grown up. At sixteen, she was a woman. A beautiful woman who understood him far better than Melissa could hope to. He'd had a fleeting sense of lost time and missed opportunities before Clay had whistled. "Hell, Tagalong, you've gone and gotten yourself a pair of breasts."

"You better watch out dressed up like that; some guy will think you want more than you bargained for," Jericho said.

Walker's normally grave expression had grown even more grim.

Riley had ignored them all. She'd squared her shoulders, looked Boone in the eye and said, "Will you dance with me?"

Shame flooded Boone every time he thought back to that moment.

Riley had paid him a thousand kindnesses over the years, listened to some of his most intimate thoughts and fears, never judged him, made fun of him or cut him down the way his other friends sometimes did. She'd always been there for him, and all she'd asked for was one dance.

He should have said yes.

It wasn't the shake of Walker's head, or Clay and Jericho's laughter that stopped him. It was Melissa, who had returned in time to hear Riley's question, and answered for him.

"No one wants to dance with a Tagalong. Go on home."

Riley had waited one more moment—then fled.

Boone rarely thought about Melissa after he'd left Chance Creek and when he did it was to wonder what he'd ever found compelling in her. He thought about Riley far too often. He tried to remember the good times—teaching her to ride, shoot, trap and fish. The conversations and lazy days in the sun when they were kids. The intimacy that had grown up between them without him ever realizing it.

Instead, he thought of that moment—that awful, shameful moment when she'd begged him with her eyes to say yes, to throw her pride that single bone.

And he'd kept silent.

"Have you heard of the place?" Fulsom broke into his thoughts and Boone blinked. He'd been so far away it took a moment to come back. Finally, he nodded.

"I have." He cleared his throat to get the huskiness out of it. "Mighty fine ranch." He couldn't fathom why it hadn't passed down to Riley. Losing it must have broken her heart.

Again.

"So my people tell me. Heck of a fight to get it, too. Had a competitor, a rabid developer named Montague."

Fulsom shook his head. "But that gave me a perfect setup."

"What do you mean?" Boone's thoughts were still with the girl he'd once known. The woman who'd haunted him all these years. He forced himself to pay attention to Fulsom instead.

Fulsom clicked his keyboard and an image sprung up onscreen. "Take a look."

Letting his memories go, Boone tried to make sense of what he was seeing. Some kind of map—an architect's rendering of a planned development.

"What is that?" Clay demanded.

"Wait—that's Westfield." Jericho leaned over Boone's shoulder to get a better look.

"Almost right." Fulsom nodded. "Those are the plans for Westfield Commons, a community of seventy luxury homes."

Blood ran cold in Boone's veins as Walker elbowed his way between them and peered at the screen. "Luxury homes? On Westfield? You can't do that!"

"I don't want to. But Montague does. He's frothing at the mouth to bulldoze that ranch and sell it piece by piece. The big, bad developer versus the environmentalists. This show is going to write itself." He fixed his gaze on Boone. "And if you fail, the last episode will show his bulldozers closing in."

"But it's our land; you just said so," Boone protested.

"As long as you meet your goals by December first. Ten committed couples—every couple married by the time the show ends. Ten homes whose energy requirements are one-tenth the normal usage for an American home. Six months' worth of food produced on site stockpiled to last the inhabitants through the winter. And three children."

"Children? Where do we get those?" Boone couldn't keep up. He hadn't promised anything like that. All he'd said in his proposal was that they'd build a community.

"The old-fashioned way. You make them. No cheating; children conceived before the show starts don't count."

"Jesus." Fulsom had lost his mind. He was taking the stakes and raising them to outrageous heights… which was exactly the way to create a prime-time hit, Boone realized.

"It takes nine months to have a child," Jericho pointed out dryly.

"I didn't say they needed to be born. Pregnant bellies are better than squalling babies. Like I said, sex sells, boys. Let's give our viewers proof you and your wives are getting it on."

Boone had had enough. "That's ridiculous, Fulsom. You're—"

"You know what's ridiculous?" Fulsom leaned forward again, suddenly grim. "Famine. Poverty. Violence. War. And yet it never stops, does it? You said you wanted to do something about it. Here's your chance. You're leaving the Navy, for God's sake. Don't tell me you didn't plan to meet a woman, settle down and raise some kids. So I've put a rush on the matter. Sue me."

He had a point. But still—

"I could sell the land to Montague today," Fulsom said. "Pocket the money and get back to sorting out hydrogen fuel cells." He waited a beat. When Boone shook his head, Fulsom smiled in triumph. "Gotta go, boys. Julie, here, will get you all sorted out. Good luck to you on this fabulous venture. Remember—we're going to change the world together."

"Wait—"

Fulsom stood up and walked off screen.

Boone stared as Julie sat down in his place. By the time she had walked them through the particulars of the funding process, and when and how to take possession of the land, Boone's temples were throbbing. He cut the call after Julie promised to send a packet of information, reluctantly pushed his chair back from the table and faced the three men who were to be his partners in this venture.

"Married?" Clay demanded. "No one said anything about getting married!"

"I know."

"And kids? Three out of ten of us men will have to get their wives pregnant. That means all of us will have to be trying just to beat the odds," Jericho said.

"I know."

Walker just looked at him and shook his head.

"I get it! None of us planned for anything like this." Boone stood up. "But none of us thought we had a shot of moving back to Chance Creek, either—or getting our message out to the whole country." When no one answered, he went on. "Are you saying you're out?"

"Hell, I don't know," Jericho said, pacing around the room. "I could stomach anything except that marriage part. I've never seen myself as a family man."

"I don't mind getting hitched," Clay said. "And I want kids. But I want to choose where and when to do it. And Fulsom's setting us up to fail in front of a national audience. If that Montague guy gets the ranch and builds a subdivision on it, everyone in town is going to hate us—and our families."

"So what do we do?" Boone challenged him.

"Not much choice," Walker said. "If we don't sign on, Fulsom will sell to Montague anyway."

"Exactly. The only shot we have of saving that ranch is to agree to his demands," Boone said. He shoved his hands in his pockets, unsure what to do. He couldn't see himself married in two months, let alone trying to have a child with a woman he hadn't even met yet, but giving up—Boone hated to think about it. After all, it wouldn't be the first time they'd done unexpected things to accomplish a mission.

Jericho paced back. "But his demands are—"

"Insane. I know that." Boone knew he was losing them. "He's right, though; a sustainable community made only of men doesn't mean shit. A community that's actually going to sustain itself—to carry on into the future, generation after generation—has to include women and eventually kids. Otherwise we're just playing."

"Fulsom's the one who's playing. Playing with our

lives. He can't demand we marry someone for the sake of his ratings," Jericho said.

"Actually, he can," Clay said. "He's the one with the cash."

"We'll find cash somewhere else—"

"It's more than cash," Boone reminded Jericho. "It's publicity. If we build a community and no one knows about it, what good is it? We went to Fulsom because we wanted him to do just what he's done—find a way to make everyone talk about sustainability."

"By marrying us off one by one?" Jericho stared at each of them in turn. "Are you serious? We just spent the last thirteen years of our lives fighting for our country—"

"And now we're going to fight for it in a whole new way. By getting married. On television. And knocking up our wives—while the whole damn world watches," Boone said.

No one spoke for a minute.

"I sure as hell hope they won't film that part, Chief," Clay said with a quick grin, using the moniker Boone had gained in the SEALs as second in command of his platoon.

"They wouldn't want to film your hairy ass, anyway," Jericho said.

Clay shoved him. Jericho elbowed him away.

"Enough." Walker's single word settled all of them down. They were used to listening to their lieutenant. Walker turned to Boone. "You think this will actually do any good?"

Boone shrugged. "Remember Yemen. Remember what's coming. We swore we'd do what it takes to make a difference." It was a low blow bringing up that disaster, but it was what had gotten them started down this path and he wanted to remind them of it.

"I remember Yemen every day," Jericho said, all trace of clowning around gone.

"So do I." Clay sighed. "Hell, I'm ready for a family anyway. I'm in. I don't know how I'll find a wife, though. Ain't had any luck so far."

"I'll find you one," Boone told him.

"Thanks, Chief." Clay gave him an ironic salute.

Jericho walked away. Came back again. "Damn it. I'm in, too. Under protest, though. Something this serious shouldn't be a game. You find me a wife, too, Chief, but I'll divorce her when the six months are up if I don't like her."

"Wait until Fulsom's given us the deed to the ranch, then do what you like," Boone said. "But if I'm picking your bride, give her a chance."

"Sure, Chief."

Boone didn't trust that answer, but Jericho had agreed to Fulsom's terms and that's all that mattered for now. He looked to Walker. It was crucial that the man get on board. Walker stared back at him, his gaze unfathomable. Boone knew there was trouble in his past. Lots of trouble. The man avoided women whenever he could.

Finally Walker gave him a curt nod. "Find me one, too. Don't screw it up."

Boone let out the breath he was holding. Despite the events of the past hour, a surge of anticipation warmed him from within.

They were going to do it.

And he was going to get hitched.

Was Riley the marrying kind?

RILEY EATON TOOK a sip of her green tea and summoned a smile for the friends who'd gathered on the tiny balcony of her apartment in Boston. Her thoughts were far away, though, tangled in a memory of a hot Montana afternoon when she was only ten. She'd crouched on the bank of Pittance Creek watching Boone Rudman wade through the knee-deep waters, fishing for minnows with a net. Riley had followed Boone everywhere back then, but she knew to stay out of the water and not scare his bait away.

"Mom said marriage is a trap set by men for unsuspecting women," she'd told him, quoting what she'd heard her mother say to a friend over the phone.

"You'd better watch out then," he'd said, poised to scoop up a handful of little fish.

"I won't get caught. Someone's got to want to catch you before that happens."

Boone had straightened, his net trailing in the water. She'd never forgotten the way he'd looked at her—all earnest concern.

"Maybe I'll catch you."

"Why?" She'd been genuinely curious. Getting overlooked was something she'd already grown used to.

"For my wife. If I ever want one. You'll never see me coming." He'd lifted his chin as if she'd argue the point. But Riley had thought it over and knew he was right.

She'd nodded. "You are pretty sneaky."

Riley had never forgotten that conversation, but Boone had and like everyone else he'd overlooked her when the time counted.

Story of her life.

Riley shook off the maudlin thoughts. She couldn't be a good hostess if she was wrapped up in her troubles. Time enough for them when her friends had gone.

She took another sip of her tea and hoped they wouldn't notice the tremor in her hands. She couldn't believe seven years had passed since she'd graduated from Boston College with the women who relaxed on the cheap folding chairs around her. Back then she'd thought she'd always have these women by her side, but now these yearly reunions were the only time she saw them. They were all firmly ensconced in careers that consumed their time and energy. It was hard enough to stay afloat these days, let alone get ahead in the world—or have time to take a break.

Gone were the carefree years when they thought nothing of losing whole weekends to trying out a new art medium, or picking up a new instrument. Once she'd been fearless, throwing paint on the canvas, guided only by her moods. She'd experimented day after day, laughed at the disasters and gloried in the triumphs that took shape under her brushes from time to time. Now she rarely even sketched, and what she produced seemed inane. If she wanted to express the truth of her situation through her art, she'd paint pigeons and gum stuck to the sidewalk. But she wasn't honest anymore.

For much of the past five years she'd been married to her job as a commercial artist at a vitamin distributor, joined to it twenty-four seven through her cell phone and Internet connection. Those years studying art seemed like a dream now; the one time in her life she'd felt like she'd truly belonged somewhere. She had no idea how she'd thought she'd earn a living with a fine arts degree, though. She supposed she'd hadn't thought much about the future back then. Now she felt trapped by it.

Especially after the week she'd had.

She set her cup down and twisted her hands together, trying to stop the shaking. It had started on Wednesday when she'd been called into her boss's office and handed a pink slip and a box in which to pack up her things.

"Downsizing. It's nothing personal," he'd told her.

She didn't know how she'd kept her feet as she'd made her way out of the building. She wasn't the only one riding the elevator down to street level with her belongings in her hands, but that was cold comfort. It had been hard enough to find this job. She had no idea where to start looking for another.

She'd held in her shock and panic that night and all the next day until Nadia from the adoption agency knocked on her door for their scheduled home visit at precisely two pm. She'd managed to answer Nadia's questions calmly and carefully, until the woman put down her pen.

"Tell me about your job, Riley. How will you as a single mother balance work and home life with a child?"

Riley had opened her mouth to speak, but no answer had come out. She'd reached for her cup of tea, but only managed to spill it on the cream colored skirt she'd chosen carefully for the occasion. As Nadia rushed to help her mop up, the truth had spilled from Riley's lips.

"I've just been downsized. I'm sorry; I'll get a new job right away. This doesn't have to change anything, does it?"

Nadia had been sympathetic but firm. "This is why we hesitate to place children with single parents, Riley. Children require stability. We can continue the interview and I'll weigh all the information in our judgement, but until you can prove you have a stable job, I'm afraid you won't qualify for a child."

"That will take years," Riley had almost cried, but she'd bitten back the words. What good would it do to say them aloud? As a girl, she'd dreamed she'd have children with Boone someday. When she'd grown up, she'd thought she'd find someone else. Hadn't she waited long enough to start her family?

"Riley? Are you all right?" Savannah Edwards asked, bringing her back to the present.

"Of course." She had to be. There was no other option but to soldier on. She needed to get a new job. A better job. She needed to excel at it and put the time in to make herself indispensable. Then, in a few years, she could try again to adopt.

"Are you sure?" A tall blonde with hazel eyes, Savannah had been Riley's best friend back in school, and Riley had always had a hard time fooling her. Savannah had been a music major and Riley could have listened to her play forever. She was the first person Riley had met since her grandparents passed away who seemed to care about her wholeheartedly. Riley's parents had been too busy arguing with each other all through her childhood to have much time left over to think about her. They split up within weeks after she left for college. Each remarried before the year was out and both started new families soon after. Riley felt like the odd man out when she visited them on holidays. More than eighteen years older than her half-siblings, she didn't seem to belong anywhere now.

"I'm great now that you three are here." She wouldn't confess the setback that had just befallen her. It was still too raw to process and she didn't want to bring the others down when they'd only just arrived. She wasn't the only one who had it tough. Savannah should have been a concert pianist, but when she broke her wrist in a car accident several years after graduation, she had to give up her aspirations. Instead, she had gone to work as an assistant at a prominent tech company in Silicon Valley and was still there.

"What's on tap for the weekend?" Nora Ridgeway asked as she scooped her long, wavy, light brown hair into a messy updo and secured it with a clip. She'd flown in from Baltimore where she taught English in an inner-city high school. Riley had been shocked to see the dark smudges under her eyes. Nora looked thin. Too thin. Riley wondered what secrets she was hiding behind her upbeat tone.

"I hope it's a whole lot of nothing," Avery Lightfoot said, her auburn curls glinting in the sun. Avery lived in Nashville and worked in the marketing department of one of the largest food distribution companies in North America. She'd studied acting in school, but she'd never been discovered the way she'd once hoped to be. For a brief time she'd created an original video series that she'd posted online, but the advertising revenue she'd generated hadn't added up to much and soon her money had run out. Now she created short videos to market low-carb products to yoga moms. Riley's heart ached for her friend. She sounded as tired as Nora looked.

In fact, everyone looked like they needed a pick-me-up after dealing with flights and taxis, and Riley headed inside to get refreshments. She wished she'd been able to drive to the airport and pick them up. Who could afford a car, though? Even when she'd had a job, Riley found it hard to keep up with her rent, medical insurance and monthly bills, and budget enough for the childcare she'd need when she adopted. Thank God it had been her turn to host their gathering this year. She couldn't have gotten on a plane after the news she'd just received.

When she thought back to her college days she realized her belief in a golden future had really been a pipe dream. Some of her classmates were doing fine. But most of them were struggling to keep their heads above water, just like her. A few had given up and moved back in with their parents.

When she got back to the balcony with a tray of snacks, she saw Savannah pluck a dog-eared copy of *Pride and Prejudice* out of a small basket that sat next to the door. Riley had been reading it in the mornings before work this week as she drank her coffee—until she'd been let go. A little escapism helped start her day off on the right foot.

"Am I the only one who'd trade my life for one of Austen's characters' in a heartbeat?" Savannah asked, flipping through the pages.

"You want to live in Regency England? And be some man's property?" Nora asked sharply.

"Of course not. I don't want the class conflict or the snobbery or the outdated rules. But I want the beauty of their lives. I want the music and the literature. I want afternoon visits and balls that last all night. Why don't we do those things anymore?"

"Who has time for that?" Riley certainly hadn't when she was working. Now she'd have to spend every waking moment finding a new job.

"I haven't played the piano in ages," Savannah went on. "I mean, it's not like I'm all that good anymore—"

"Are you kidding? You've always been fantastic," Nora said.

"What about romance? I'd kill for a real romance. One that means something," Avery said.

"What about Dan?" Savannah asked.

"I broke up with him three weeks ago. He told me he wasn't ready for a serious relationship. The man's thirty-one. If he's not ready now, when will he be?"

"That's tough." Riley understood what Avery meant. She hadn't had a date in a year; not since Marc Hepstein had told her he didn't consider her marriage material. She should have dumped him long before.

It wasn't like she hadn't been warned. His older sister had taken her aside once and spelled it out for her:

"Every boy needs to sow his wild oats. You're his shiksa fling. You'll see; you won't get a wedding ring from him. Marc will marry a nice Jewish girl in the end."

Riley wished she'd paid attention to the warning, but of course she hadn't. She had a history of dangling after men who were unavailable.

Shiksa fling.

Just a step up from Tagalong Riley.

Riley pushed down the old insecurities that threatened to take hold of her and tried not to give in to her pain over her lost chance to adopt. When Marc had broken up with her, it had been a wake-up call. She'd realized if she waited for a man to love her, she might never experience the joy of raising a child. She'd also realized she hadn't loved Marc enough to spend a life with him. She'd been settling, and she was better than that.

She'd started the adoption process.

Now she'd have to start all over again.

"It wasn't as hard to leave him as you might think." Avery took a sip of her tea. "It's not just Dan. I feel like breaking up with my life. I had a heart once. I know I did. I used to feel—alive."

"Me, too," Nora said softly.

"I thought I'd be married by now," Savannah said, "but I haven't had a boyfriend in months. And I hate my job. I mean, I really hate it!" Riley couldn't remember ever seeing calm, poised Savannah like this.

"So do I," Avery said, her words gushing forth as if a dam had broken. "Especially since I have two of them now. I got back in debt when my car broke down and I needed to buy a new one. Now I can't seem to get ahead."

"I don't have any job at all," Riley confessed. "I've been downsized." She closed her eyes. She hadn't meant to say that.

"Oh my goodness, Riley," Avery said. "What are you going to do?"

"I don't know. Paint?" She laughed dully. She couldn't tell them the worst of it. She was afraid if she talked about her failed attempt to adopt she'd lose control of her emotions altogether. "Can you imagine a life in which we could actually pursue our dreams?"

"No," Avery said flatly. "After what happened last time, I'm so afraid if I try to act again, I'll just make a fool of myself."

Savannah nodded vigorously, tears glinting in her eyes. "I'm afraid to play," she confessed. "I sit down at my piano and then I get up again without touching the keys. What if my talent was all a dream? What if I was fooling myself and I was never anything special at all? My wrist healed years ago, but I can't make myself go for it like I once did. I'm too scared."

"What about you, Nora? Do you ever write these days?" Riley asked gently when Nora remained quiet. When they were younger, Nora talked all the time about wanting to write a novel, but she hadn't mentioned it in ages. Riley had assumed it was because she loved teaching, but she looked as burnt out as the rest of them. Riley knew she worked in an area of Baltimore that resembled a war zone.

Her friend didn't answer, but a tear traced down her cheek.

"Nora, what is it?" Savannah dropped the book and came to crouch by her chair.

"It's one of my students." Nora kept her voice steady even as another tear followed the tracks of the first. "At least I think it is."

"What do you mean?" Riley realized they'd all pulled closer to each other, leaning forward in mutual support and feeling. Dread crept into her throat at Nora's words. She'd known instinctively something was wrong in her friend's life for quite some time, but despite her questions, Nora's e-mails and texts never revealed a thing.

"I've been getting threats. On my phone," Nora said, plucking at a piece of lint on her skirt.

"Someone's texting threats?" Savannah sounded aghast.

"And calling. He has my home number, too."

"What did he say?" Avery asked.

"Did he threaten to hurt you?" Riley demanded. After a moment, Nora nodded.

"To kill you?" Avery whispered.

Nora nodded again. "And more."

Savannah's expression hardened. "More?"

Nora looked up. "He threatened to rape me. He said I'd like it. He got… really graphic."

The four of them stared at each other in shocked silence.

"You can't go back," Savannah said. "Nora, you can't go back there. I don't care how important your work is, that's too much."

"What did the police say?" Riley's hands were shaking again. Rage and shock battled inside of her, but anger won out. Who would dare threaten her friend?

"What did the school's administration say?" Avery demanded.

"That threats happen all the time. That I should change my phone numbers. That the people who make the threats usually don't act on them."

"Usually?" Riley was horrified.

"What are you going to do?" Savannah said.

"What am I supposed to do? I can't quit." Nora seemed to sink into herself. "I changed my number, but it's happening again. I've got nothing saved. I managed to pay off my student loans, but then my mom got sick… I'm broke."

No one answered. They knew Nora's family hadn't

had much money, and she'd taken on debt to get her degree. Riley figured she'd probably used every penny she might have saved to pay it off again. Then her mother had contracted cancer and had gone through several expensive procedures before she passed away.

"Is this really what it's come to?" Avery asked finally. "Our work consumes us, or it overwhelms us, or it threatens us with bodily harm and we just keep going?"

"And what happened to love? True love?" Savannah's voice was raw. "Look at us! We're intelligent, caring, attractive women. And we're all single! None of us even dating. What about kids? I thought I'd be a mother."

"So did I," Riley whispered.

"Who can afford children?" Nora said fiercely. "I thought teaching would be enough. I thought my students would care—" She broke off and Riley's heart squeezed at Nora's misery.

"I've got some savings, but I'll eat through them fast if I don't get another job," Riley said slowly. "I want to leave Boston so badly. I want fresh air and a big, blue sky. But there aren't any jobs in the country." Memories of just such a sky flooded her mind. What she'd give for a vacation at her uncle's ranch in Chance Creek, Montana. In fact, she'd love to go there and never come back. It had been so long since she'd managed to stop by and spend a weekend at Westfield, it made her ache to think of the carefree weeks she spent there every summer as a child. The smell of hay and horses and sunshine on old buildings, the way her grandparents used to let her loose on the ranch to run and play and ride as hard as she wanted to. Their unconditional love. There were few rules at Westfield and those existed purely for the sake of practicality and safety. *Don't spook the horses. Clean and put away tools after you use them. Be home at mealtimes and help with the dishes.*

Away from her parents' arguing, Riley had blossomed, and the skills she'd learned from the other kids in town—especially the Four Horsemen of the Apocalypse—had taught her pride and self-confidence. They were rough and tumble boys and they rarely slowed down to her speed, but as long as she kept up to them, they included her in their fun.

Clay Pickett, Jericho Cook, Walker Norton—they'd treated her like a sister. For an only child, it was a dream come true. But it was Boone who'd become a true friend, and her first crush.

And then had broken her heart.

"I keep wondering if it will always be like this," Avery said, interrupting her thoughts. "If I'll always have to struggle to get by. If I'll never have a house of my own—or a husband or family."

"You'll have a family," Riley assured her, then bit her lip. Who was she to reassure Avery? She could never seem to shake her bad luck—with men, with work, with anything. But out of all the things that had happened to her, nothing left her cringing with humiliation like the memory of the time she'd asked Boone to dance.

She'd been such a child. No one like Boone would have looked twice at her, no matter how friendly he'd been over the years. She could still hear Melissa's sneering words—*No one wants to dance with a Tagalong. Go on home*—and the laughter that followed her when she fled the dance.

She'd returned to Chicago that last summer thinking her heart would never mend, and time had just begun to heal it when her grandparents passed away one after the other in quick succession that winter. Riley had been devastated; doubly so when she left for college the following year and her parents split. It was as if a tidal wave had washed away her childhood in one blow. After that, her parents sold their home and caretakers watched over the ranch. Uncle Russ, who'd inherited it, had found he made a better financier than a cowboy. With his career taking off, he'd moved to Europe soon after.

At his farewell dinner, one of the few occasions she'd seen her parents in the same room since they'd divorced, he'd stood up and raised a glass. "To Riley. You're the only one who loves Westfield now, and I want you to think of it as yours. One day in the future it will be, you know. While I'm away, I hope you'll treat it as your own home. Visit as long as you like. Bring your friends. Enjoy the ranch. My parents would have wanted that." He'd taken her aside later and presented her with a key. His trust in her and his promises had warmed her heart. If she'd own Westfield one day she could stand anything, she'd told herself that night. It was the one thing that had sustained her through life's repeated blows.

"I wish I could run away from my life, even for a little while. Six months would do it," Savannah said, breaking into her thoughts. "If I could clear my mind of everything that has happened in the past few years I know I could make a fresh start."

Riley knew just what she meant. She'd often wished the same thing, but she didn't only want to run away from her life; she wanted to run straight back into her past to a time when her grandparents were still alive. Things had been so simple then.

Until she'd fallen for Boone.

She hadn't seen Uncle Russ since he'd moved away, although she wrote to him a couple of times a year, and received polite, if remote, answers in turn. She had the feeling Russ had found the home of his heart in Munich. She wondered if he'd ever come back to Montana.

In the intervening years she'd visited Westfield whenever she could, more frequently as the sting of Boone's betrayal faded, although in reality that meant a long weekend every three or four months, rather than the expansive summer vacations she'd imagined when she'd received the key. It wasn't quite the same without her grandparents and her old friends, without Boone and the Horsemen, but she still loved the country, and Westfield Manor was the stuff of dreams. Even the name evoked happy memories and she blessed the ancestor whose flight of fancy had bestowed such a distinguished title on a Montana ranch house. She'd always wondered if she'd stumble across Boone someday, home for leave, but their visits had never coincided. Still, whenever she drove into Chance Creek, her heart rate kicked up a notch and she couldn't help scanning the streets for his familiar face.

"I wish I could run away from my dirty dishes and laundry," Avery said. Riley knew she was attempting to lighten the mood. "I spend my weekends taking care of all my possessions. I bet Jane Austen didn't do laundry."

"In those days servants did it," Nora said, swiping her arm over her cheek to wipe away the traces of her tears. "Maybe we should get servants, too, while we're dreaming."

"Maybe we should, if it means we could concentrate on the things we love," Savannah said.

"Like that's possible. Look at us—we're stuck, all of us. There's no way out." The waver in Nora's voice betrayed her fierceness.

"There has to be," Avery exclaimed.

"How?"

Riley wished she had the answer. She hated seeing the pain and disillusionment on her friends' faces. And she was terrified of having to start over herself.

"What if… what if we lived together?" Savannah said slowly. "I mean, wouldn't that be better than how things are now? If we pooled our resources and figured out how to make them stretch? None of us would have to work so hard."

"I thought you had a good job," Nora said, a little bitterly.

"On paper. The cost of living in Silicon Valley is outrageous, though. You'd be surprised how little is left over when I pay my bills. And inside, I feel… like I'm dying."

A silence stretched out between them. Riley knew

just what Savannah meant. At first grown-up life had seemed exciting. Now it felt like she was slipping into a pool of quicksand that she'd never be able to escape. Maybe it would be different if they joined forces. If they pooled their money, they could do all kinds of things.

For the first time in months she felt a hint of possibility.

"We could move where the cost of living is cheaper and get a house together." Savannah warmed to her theme. "With a garden, maybe. We could work part time and share the bills."

"For six months? What good would that do? We'd run through what little money we have and be harder to employ afterward," Nora said.

"How much longer are you willing to wait before you try for the life you actually want, rather than the life that keeps you afloat one more day?" Savannah asked her. "I have to try to be a real pianist. Life isn't worth living if I don't give it a shot. That means practicing for hours every day. I can't do that and work a regular job, too."

"I've had an idea for a screenplay," Avery confessed. "I think it's really good. Six months would be plenty of time for me to write it. Then I could go back to work while I shop it around."

"If I had six months I would paint all day until I had enough canvasses to put on a show. Maybe that would be the start and end of my career as an artist, but at least I'd have done it once," Riley said.

"A house costs money," Nora said.

"Not always," Riley said slowly as an idea took hold

in her head. "What about Westfield?" After all, it hadn't been inhabited in years. "Uncle Russ always said I should bring my friends and stay there."

"Long term?" Avery asked.

"Six months would be fine. Russ hasn't set foot in it in over a decade."

"You want us to move to Montana and freeload for six months?" Nora asked.

"I want us to move to Montana and take six months to jumpstart our lives. We'll practice following our passions. We'll brainstorm ideas together for how to make money from them. Who knows? Maybe together we'll come up with a plan that will work."

"Sounds good to me," Avery said.

"I don't know," Nora said. "Do you really think it's work that's kept you from writing or playing or painting? Because if you can't do it now, chances are you won't be able to do it at Westfield either. You'll busy up your days with errands and visits and sightseeing and all that. Wait and see."

"Not if we swore an oath to work on our projects every day," Savannah said.

"Like the oaths you used to swear to do your homework on time? Or not to drink on Saturday night? Or to stop crank-calling the guy who dumped you junior year?"

Savannah flushed. "I was a child back then—"

"I just feel that if we take six months off, we'll end up worse off than when we started."

Savannah leaned forward. "Come on. Six whole months to write. Aren't you dying to try it?" When Nora hesitated, Savannah pounced on her. "I knew it!

You want to as badly as we do."

"Of course I want to," Nora said. "But it won't work. None of you will stay at home and hone your craft."

A smile tugged at Savannah's lips. "What if we couldn't leave?"

"Are you going to chain us to the house?"

"No. I'm going to take away your clothes. Your modern clothes," she clarified when the others stared at her. "You're right; we could easily be tempted to treat the time like a vacation, especially with us all together. But if we only have Regency clothes to wear, we'll be stuck because we'll be too embarrassed to go into town. We'll take a six-month long Jane Austen vacation from our lives." She sat back and folded her arms over her chest.

"I love it," Riley said. "Keep talking."

"We'll create a Regency life, as if we'd stepped into one of her novels. A beautiful life, with time for music and literature and poetry and walks. Westfield is rural, right? No one will be there to see us. If we pattern our days after the way Jane's characters spent theirs, we'd have plenty of time for creative pursuits."

Nora rolled her eyes. "What about the neighbors? What about groceries and dental appointments?"

"Westfield is set back from the road." Riley thought it through. "Savannah's right; we could go for long stretches without seeing anyone. We could have things delivered, probably."

"I'm in," Avery said. "I'll swear to live a Regency life for six months. I'll swear it on penalty of… death."

"The penalty is embarrassment," Savannah said. "If

we leave early, we have to travel home in our Regency clothes. I know I'm in. I'd gladly live a Jane Austen life for six months."

"If I get to wear Regency dresses and bonnets, I'm in too," Riley said. What was the alternative? Stay here and mourn the child she'd never have?

"Are you serious?" Nora asked. "Where do we even get those things?"

"We have a seamstress make them, or we sew them ourselves," Avery said. "Come on, Nora. Don't pretend you haven't always wanted to."

The others nodded. After all, it was their mutual love of Jane Austen movies that had brought them together in the first place. Two days into their freshman year at Boston College, Savannah had marched through the halls of their dorm announcing a Jane Austen film festival in her room that night. Riley, Nora and Avery had shown up for it, and the rest was history.

"It'll force us to carry out our plan the way we intend to," Savannah told her. "If we can't leave the ranch, there will be no distractions. Every morning when we put on our clothes we'll be recommitting to our vow to devote six months to our creative pursuits. Think about it, Nora. Six whole months to write."

"Besides, we were so good together back in college," Riley said. "We inspired each other. Why couldn't we do that again?"

"But what will we live on?"

"We'll each liquidate our possessions," Savannah said. "Think about how little most people had in Jane Austen's time. It'll be like when Eleanor and Marianne have to move to a cottage in *Sense and Sensibility* with their mother and little sister. We'll make a shoestring budget and stick to it for food and supplies. If we don't go anywhere, we won't spend any money, right?"

"That's right," Avery said. "Remember what Mrs. John Dashwood said in that novel. 'What on earth can four women want for more than that?—They will live so cheap! Their housekeeping will be nothing at all. They will have no carriage, no horses, and hardly any servants; they will keep no company, and can have no expenses of any kind! Only conceive how comfortable they will be!'"

"We certainly won't have any horses or carriages." Savannah laughed.

"But we will be comfortable, and during the time we're together we can brainstorm what to do next," Riley said. "No one leaves Westfield until we all have a working plan."

"With four of us to split the chores of running the house, it'll be easy," Avery said. "We'll have hours and hours to devote to our craft every day."

Nora hesitated. "You know this is crazy, right?"

"But it's exactly the right kind of crazy," Riley said. "You have to join us, Nora."

Nora shook her head, but just when Riley thought she'd refuse, she shrugged. "Oh, okay. What the hell? I'll do it." Riley's heart soared. "But when our six months are up, I'll be broke," Nora went on. "I'll be homeless, too. I don't see how anything will have improved."

"Everything will have improved," Savannah told her. "I promise. Together we can do anything."

Riley smiled at their old rallying-cry from college.

"So, we're going to do it? You'll all come to Westfield with me? And wear funny dresses?"

"And bonnets," Avery said. "Don't forget the bonnets."

"I'm in," Savannah said, sticking out her hand.

"I'm in," Avery said, putting hers down on top of it.

"I guess I'm in," Nora said, and added hers to the pile.

"Well, I'm definitely in." Riley slapped hers down on top of the rest.

Westfield. She was going back to Westfield.

Things were looking up.

End of Excerpt

The Cowboys of Chance Creek Series:

The Cowboy Inherits a Bride (Volume 0)

The Cowboy's E-Mail Order Bride (Volume 1)

The Cowboy Wins a Bride (Volume 2)

The Cowboy Imports a Bride (Volume 3)

The Cowgirl Ropes a Billionaire (Volume 4)

The Sheriff Catches a Bride (Volume 5)

The Cowboy Lassos a Bride (Volume 6)

The Cowboy Rescues a Bride (Volume 7)

The Cowboy Earns a Bride (Volume 8)

The Cowboy's Christmas Bride (Volume 9)

The Heroes of Chance Creek Series:

The Navy SEAL's E-Mail Order Bride (Volume 1)
The Soldier's E-Mail Order Bride (Volume 2)
The Marine's E-Mail Order Bride (Volume 3)
The Navy SEAL's Christmas Bride (Volume 4)
The Airman's E-Mail Order Bride (Volume 5)

The SEALs of Chance Creek Series:

A SEAL's Oath
A SEAL's Vow
A SEAL's Pledge
A SEAL's Consent
A SEAL's Purpose
A SEAL's Resolve
A SEAL's Devotion
A SEAL's Desire
A SEAL's Struggle
A SEAL's Triumph

Brides of Chance Creek Series:

Issued to the Bride One Navy SEAL
Issued to the Bride One Airman
Issued to the Bride One Sniper
Issued to the Bride One Marine
Issued to the Bride One Soldier

About the Author

NYT and USA Today bestselling author Cora Seton loves cowboys, hiking, gardening, bike-riding, and lazing around with a good book. Mother of four, wife to a computer programmer/backyard farmer, she recently moved to Victoria and looks forward to a brand new chapter in her life. Like the characters in her Chance Creek series, Cora enjoys old-fashioned pursuits and modern technology, spending mornings in her garden, and afternoons writing the latest Chance Creek romance novel. Visit **www.coraseton.com** to read about new releases, contests and other cool events!

Blog:

www.coraseton.com

Facebook:

www.facebook.com/coraseton

Twitter:

www.twitter.com/coraseton

Newsletter:

www.coraseton.com/sign-up-for-my-newsletter

Made in the USA
Middletown, DE
10 July 2018